A COMPLICATED GOODBYE

LAURIE CARMICHAEL

 FriesenPress

One Printers Way
Altona, MB R0G0B0
Canada

www.friesenpress.com

Copyright © 2021 Laurie Carmichael
First Edition — 2021

ISBN
978-1-03-912277-2 (Hardcover)
978-1-03-912276-5 (Paperback)
978-1-03-912278-9 (eBook)

Fiction, Contemporary Women

Distributed to the trade by The Ingram Book Company

Dedication:

To the strong woman who supported me as I took 'my leap of faith'- my BFF
Robin, my sister Marion and my Mom, Eileen.

To Daryl, my life, my love, my forever.

To my kids, Dana, Mitchell and Liam. Thanks for believing in all my
crazy schemes.

Lastly, to Charlotte who sat at my elbow every morning as we wrote this book!

We did it!

CHAPTER ONE

"I know you."

"So what ... everyone in this shitty little town knows me! I suppose you believe the stories too."

"I said I knew you, I didn't say I believed the stories."

Rebecca Adams turned to face the intruder who disturbed her peace. She was so seldom able to carve out any solitude, and today she needed it more than ever. It was the third anniversary of her son Indie's death, and she had come alone to visit his grave. She often came to this peaceful place; sometimes she came to hide, sometimes to grieve, and sometimes to dream.

This time she was interrupted.

She sighed, then turned to face the elderly woman seated next to her. She had seen her during other visits to Indie's grave, but she had not been approached by her before.

Why now? Why today? she wondered. Rebecca once again braced herself, expecting to justify her actions or explain her innocence, but the woman remained silent.

Uncomfortable, she turned and eyed her intruder. *What did this woman want?* She really didn't have the energy to deal with this today. The constant intrusion into her privacy had stolen her youth and drained her vitality.

As the two women faced off, Rebecca was taken aback by the calm, nonjudgmental, expression that the other woman wore. It was so unlike the usual condescending sneers that most of the people in Campbell River wore. It seemed everyone wanted a piece of her ... a bite of gossip ... a taste of scandal.

"So what is it that you think you know about me?" Rebecca watched the woman's reaction.

"I know you are Rebecca Adams, and you were accused of killing your child." The woman looked directly at her. "The newspapers call you the Campbell River Baby Killer." She spoke with a thick accent, which made her difficult to understand.

Rebecca felt her anger rise as the woman continued. *Ah, so she was just another cruel person wanting some personal tidbit to share with the other town gossips.*

She fumed and walked away; she didn't want to continue this conversation any further.

"But what do they know?" the old woman called out.

Rebecca halted.

"What I see is a young woman worn down by sadness and grief." The woman reached out and touched Rebecca's hand. Rebecca gasped as the cool hand clutched her own. She wanted to pull away and reject any physical contact or comfort, but instead she savoured it. It had been so long.

"I recognize the despair in your eyes because I've seen it in my own. I only want to help," the woman whispered.

Rebecca was stunned by the offer, she had learned to not trust anyone. *What was this woman's game?* She pulled her hand away.

"I don't need your pity!" she spat.

"I didn't say I pitied you, and I wasn't handing any out either," the woman retorted.

Rebecca turned away and crossed her arms, protecting her fragile heart from further injury. When she turned back, the woman had gotten off the bench, and was moving carefully between the head stones, leaning heavily on her cane, and moving with cautious steps.

"Who are you?" Rebecca called after her. "And how do *you* think *you* can help me?"

The elderly woman turned to face Rebecca. "Magda Bodrug." She nodded. "Read my story, and then we will talk more."

Rebecca watched Magda retreat, and she was curious about her now. *Who is this strange old woman?* she wondered. *And why would she want to help me, the Campbell River Baby Killer? Nobody else wants to help, so why her?* It got Rebecca thinking. *And what's with her story?*

This was the first time in years that Rebecca had felt something stir inside her besides her own crushing grief. For what seemed like an eternity, she had been locked in her own prison cell of misery. *Could this odd woman be the key to my release?* This sparked something in her.

Perhaps I will check out this mystery woman. Give me something to pass the time. Time ... what time is it? She looked at her watch.

Shit I'm late!! I need to get going. She hastened to her vehicle as quickly as her bulk would allow. Her boss Andie Proctor wouldn't mind, but she hated being late. She worked at the prestigious Proctor Automotive and Sales where she kept the ledgers and books.

CHAPTER TWO

Rebecca usually felt exhausted, and today was no exception. The last three years had taken their toll on her mentally, emotionally, and certainly physically. Her weight had ballooned to nearly two hundred and sixty pounds, and even walking to her vehicle was an effort. It anchored her to this sad existence and was forged in the terrible hours of grief, guilt, and community isolation. Rebecca may have been ruled innocent of her son's death, but in the court of public opinion, she had been given a life sentence. She learned to suffer through the daily abuses and insults ground out by the gossip mill in Campbell River's local coffee shops, churches, and businesses.

Campbell River Baby Killer! she scoffed. *I should leave this place and start afresh. If only I could, but I'm such a coward. If I left here would anyone give a damn? It seems no one cares if I live or die.* She admonished herself as she trudged toward her vehicle.

But who would visit you, Indie? She looked back at her son's grave. The headstone read his full name- Indiana James Adams, they had called him Indie for short.

She turned away and opened the car door, squeezing in behind the wheel. She looked up into the rear-view mirror at the dark eyes staring back at her; they looked old, soulless, and used up. It shocked her to realize that they were her eyes! She looked away, but her eyes slowly flicked back to the mirror, and just for a moment, they held their gaze there.

Why are you letting this old woman rattle you? She glowered at her reflection. *Just keep it together, Rebecca, don't start losing it again!*

She gripped the steering wheel, and then forced her thoughts away from the strange old woman and on to the important people in her life; Andie, Olivia, and Jake. Her parents were both gone now and there were so few people loyal to her anymore. Perhaps a new ally would be welcome, but could she be trusted?

Hmmmh? I wonder what Olivia would think about Magda? She would probably tell her to get lost. Perhaps I should too.

* * *

Olivia Baird Proctor was the one person Rebecca turned to for advice and despite Olivia's sharp tongue the two had been friends since sixth grade; the year Olivia and her parents had arrived in town. The Bairds were transplants from Vancouver, and their arrival had sparked a flurry of anticipation. The town socialites had clamoured to be the first to introduce themselves, but much to their dismay, they were firmly rejected by stern rebukes.

The Baird's had clarified—for the nosy and inquisitive—that they had moved there for no other reason than the strict advice of Alex Baird's cardiologist. The specialist had instructed Mr. Baird to cut back on his demanding schedule and excessive lifestyle. He had suffered his second heart attack by the age of thirty-nine, and if he'd wanted to see fifty, he'd have to 'smarten up.' So the Baird's had relocated to the small town of Campbell River, quaint and retiring, but close enough to the corporate world. The townies had quickly learned to leave the adult Bairds alone, but their young daughter willingly embedded herself in the community.

Olivia, their only child, was blessed with an angelic face that masked her cunning nature. She had learned to manipulate any adult with just a bat of her long, sweeping eyelashes and dimpled grin; they adored this fair-haired beauty and fawned over her. At school, the parents loved her, but her schoolmates despised her. Reared by competitive corporate parents, Olivia had learned early to exploit the competition and bend her peers to her advantage.

But the Campbell River girls had seen through her uppity manners, and much to her horror, she had been shunned. Realizing she was alone in this small backwash town she needed an ally, but who could she exploit? Who could she control? She had studied her peers and selected a victim. She set her icy, blue eyes on Rebecca Wright, and recognizing a potential dupe, Olivia had plotted to establish a connection with her. She would use Rebecca to gain the other girls' approval.

Despite obvious differences the two had actually clicked, and from their first meeting they had been inseparable; people had dubbed them 'the odd couple.' And an odd couple they were. Rebecca was the girl next door, a free spirit who was easy to laugh and smile. Peers and teachers alike had found her pleasant and kind. On the other hand, Olivia's was sophisticated and polished; she didn't smile ... she sneered.

In high school, Rebecca was indifferent to social clichés and fitting in with gossipy girls. Her goal was to break free of small town living to explore the big, exciting world. On the other hand, Olivia was driven and cunning; she coveted social contact and loved creating gossip, using social media to spread it. Even now, she wanted to control the town and make it her own, at least until something better came along. Olivia was determined to rise to the top of the social ladder. She would climb over them all, and if needed, she'd use her best friend Rebecca as a stepping stool.

It had just been Rebecca and Olivia for a few years, and then Jake Adams came into the picture. High school bad boy, reckless, fun, and exciting. All the girls swooned over him, but for some reason he had chosen to pursue Rebecca.

Rebecca had met her future husband on the high school track team. The two had participated in cross- country running meets together, enjoying the competition and each other's company. He was boyishly handsome, with an edginess borne from necessity. Jake's early years had been rough; he had been abandoned by his mother at the age of five, and he was abused by an alcoholic father, a brute who used any excuse to tattoo his young son's body with bruises and pepper his mind with vicious insults. Ignored by the social system and rejected by Campbell River society, the boy struggled just to survive until Rebecca's father, Fred Wright, had intervened.

Before Fred stepped in, Jake was headed down a path to ruin. His reckless lifestyle of hard drinking, recreational drugs, and fast cars was eroding his young life. An automotive teacher and cross-country coach at Campbell River High School, Fred had turned Jake's anger and energy toward sports and automotive repair. Fred saw the potential in the young man and had invested his own time and energy in Jakes' budding talents, never dreaming that someday Jake would be his son-in-law. Fred had much bigger dreams for his daughter, Rebecca; she was destined for college and adventure. That was until Indie came along.

In their senior year, Rebecca was the envy of the all the high school girls because Jake had chosen her. His charming smile had been like an intoxicating drug to other girls, but although Rebecca had liked him well enough, she hadn't wanted their young romance to become something permanent. She had future plans, and they didn't include Campbell River and Jake Adams.

Over the years the 'odd couple' had endured as a strong duo, but with the addition of Jake, they had become a tricky trio. Jake added an exciting dimension to the pair, but he also brought along a friend called envy.

Regardless of Jake's commitment to Rebecca, Olivia had always flirted with him. He had firmly denied her advances, and it irked Olivia that she couldn't control him. Even when Rebecca and Jake had announced their intentions to marry and an unexpected baby, Olivia clung to her obsession with Jake. If she couldn't have him now she could wait, she could be patient. In truth though, Olivia coveted Jake and it was an itch that needed to be scratched.

Olivia quietly schemed behind her friend's back. She shamelessly stalked Jake through the good times and the bad, always waiting for the right moment to make him hers. Fate had a funny way of making things happen, even if it was by tragedy.

* * *

Rebecca turned down River Drive, on route to the shop. Jake also worked at Proctor Automotive as part of the talented crew known for reclaiming and rebirthing metal heaps into stunning works of function and beauty. The elite business not only sold and serviced recent car models, but also specialized in the restoration of antique vehicles and muscle cars. Clients from near and far sought out the advice and the skills of Proctor's now famous mechanics. The shop put the little town of Campbell River on the map.

Rebecca was proud of Jake's achievements; he had come a long way since the days of high school shop classes. It had been a long time since she had felt anything toward her spouse; unfortunately, there had been so many challenges over the years.

Jake might be thriving at work, but at home he was an angry, hostile mess. Rebecca had witnessed his back slide into the same habits that her father had once rescued him from. He was drinking to escape his past demons, now rekindled by Indie's sudden death. To survive Jake had pulled into himself, and he brought the bottle with him. He shunned Rebecca, blaming her for their son's death, and rebuffed any attempts from others to console his misery. He drank constantly, and he was frequently absent from their marriage, spending nights away from the house. She didn't know where he went or whom he spent his time with; she was afraid to know. And she wasn't so sure about Jake's loyalty anymore, he had changed. They both had.

Now my husband in name only. Rebecca shook her head. She knew their relationship was failing, but it was too much work and she really didn't have the energy to try to mend it. They were adrift and lost; maybe permanently.

When she and Jake had first started dating, although they had spent time just the two of them, they often hung out with Olivia. The new couple often bounced things off of her and used her as a buffer during difficult times. Over the years she always seemed to be there, ready to listen and lend an ear; especially good at defusing Jake's moods. But Indie's death had devastated the couple, and it also changed the trio; it was fractured. They didn't meet together anymore, and the fun times had evaporated, replaced by accusations and dark looks.

Rebecca had never given it much thought until recently, but something else was different. Now there seemed to be a silent, smoldering jealousy lurking beneath the surface of their friendship. It had started innocently enough with casual flirtations and subtle innuendos, but now she wasn't so sure anymore.

Rebecca shook her head and chided herself. *Shit, Rebecca, you shouldn't be so ungrateful. Olivia's influence with Andie sure saved our bacon.*

It was Olivia who had helped Jake get his job at Proctor Automotive. Shortly after graduating from high school, he had needed to find employment so he could support his new wife and child, and Olivia had facilitated this opportunity. Olivia had just started dating Andie Proctor, the shop owner's son, and she had organized for Jake and the shop owner to meet. The senior Proctor, AJ, was impressed with young Jake Adams' skills, and he had agreed to bring him on as an apprentice ... the rest was history. Jake slipped easily into his new world of cars, mechanics, and fatherhood. Small town life fit him like a favourite worn sweater, and he never wanted to leave the security of his new life. Unfortunately, tragedy and its fallout had shattered his fragile world, leaving his soul wounded and open for deception.

In her darkest hours, Olivia had been there for Rebecca too. Her friend had stood up to the town gossips during the investigation of Indie's accidental death and the bitter trial that followed.

Not long after the trial, the frail AJ Proctor had died, and Andie had taken over the running of Proctor Automotive. Within months, Andie and Olivia had hastily wed, and Olivia had continued to fight for Rebecca, even convincing Andie to hire her as the company bookkeeper.

She recalled that Olivia had taken her to Proctor Automotive and pleaded her case. "She's taken courses in bookkeeping; she knows what she is doing. No one else would dare to hire her. The townies may be our friends and your customers, but they are extremely shallow and narrow minded. Rebecca and Jake are my best friends, and they need our help." Rebecca remembered how humbling the entire scene had been, but she had been grateful for the opportunity when Andie had agreed.

She snapped back to the present. Sitting in her parking spot behind the shop, she noticed Jake was already there, his aging pick-up truck parked in its usual space. He had left home before her this morning, so she had driven in on her own. Rebecca had preferred this option, as it had allowed her to visit Indie; today was her son's day.

She wiped away a lone tear that rolled down her cheek.

As she reached for her keys, her long-sleeved shirt rode up over her wrist, exposing several jagged scars. She tugged the sleeve down, not wanting to recall the memories. The scars were enough of a permanent reminder of her sorrow.

She heaved herself from the car, and then made her way to the shop entrance. It was time to work, and for a few hours she could hide from her life, buried under a mountain of invoices and paperwork.

CHAPTER THREE

For the next three hours Rebecca dove into the intimate workings of Proctor Automotive. The invoices seemed particularly perplexing today, and she needed to address them with Andie, but he was currently in a meeting, so she decided to stretch her mental muscles and take a well-deserved break.

Of all mornings, why did this Magda Bodrug woman pick today to approach me? She'd seen the elderly woman before; Rebecca recalled that she always visited the same two headstones at the cemetery, but she had never approached her before ... why now?

As she ambled to the coffee room she passed the show room area, and behind her back she heard snickering. It came from the two new receptionists Tamara and Ashley, that Olivia had insisted Andie hire to—as she had put it—"glam up the place and draw in the younger male demographic."

"Big boobs and blonde fluff will help increase overall sales, and if nothing else, it will make the mechanics happy," was how Rebecca had heard Olivia pitch the idea to a skeptical Andie. She had persisted, and as usual he had caved.

I don't need this today, Rebecca sighed. *They just add another layer of angst to my daily existence.*

She braced herself and dodged their comments, letting the giggles and sneers bounce off her bulk.

Useless bitches! She smiled at them, then slammed her office door. This single action made her feel brave, if only for a moment. As she sipped her coffee her thoughts floated back to the early morning meeting with Magda Bodrug.

Who cares about some old woman's story? Lord knows I certainly don't need to get involved. I have enough to deal with on my own.

She turned back to the monthly reports, but her mind once again crawled back to the woman.

For God's sake just look her up! She's probably another snoop wanting a bit of trash on me! She felt cranky and ill tempered.

Alright, I'll do it! She hastily typed 'MAGDA BODRUG' in the computer search engine. She waited and sipped her stale coffee as the computer chattered and clicked. After several long moments, the screen filled with multiple search recommendations.

"What the ...!" she exclaimed as she scrolled.

"Everything okay, Rebecca?" Andie had opened her office door, probably because he had heard her cry out.

"Everything's good." She turned off the computer screen and directed her attention to the man in front of her. "Did you need something?"

"Are you having issues with those two?" He thumbed his finger at the front receptionist area. Andie was obviously uncomfortable discussing it, but he had overheard the spiteful comments aimed at Rebecca.

"Heavens Andie, it's nothing I'm not used to. I can handle it." Changing the subject, she handed Andie a folder containing the employee disbursements. "I'm glad you're here because I wanted to give you these."

"Fine. Great. But are you sure you're okay?" Andie's face was furrowed with concern. He was such a kind, gentle man, so different than his dramatic, bossy spouse.

"No worries Andie, and I promise to tell you if they are bothering me. But before you leave, can I book some time to go over the inventory records? There is something that isn't making sense to me."

"Let's plan for nine o'clock tomorrow morning, or as soon as you get into the office?"

Rebecca nodded in agreement, and he slipped quietly from the office, leaving her to her thoughts.

Andie was relieved she was okay; he didn't need any more drama in his little kingdom. Olivia and her endless demands caused him enough turmoil at the office and at home.

He lingered outside Rebecca's office just a moment longer, he worried about her. Then he resumed his journey down the corridor to his own office, flipping through the folder in his hand. As he passed Tamara and Ashley, he wondered why he wasted money on the front receptionists, but Olivia needed to be appeased. Arriving at his office, he sighed and shut the door.

Just as Andie worried about Rebecca, she puzzled about her friend and her boss. *Gosh, Olivia has become so edgy with Andie lately. What do they see in each other? Oh yeah, he has money, and Olivia loves to spend money.*

As the company bookkeeper, Rebecca knew all the intimate details of Proctor Automotive ... well almost all. Although Andie was the owner, everyone knew Olivia wore the pants in the relationship—and according to Olivia's spending habits they were expensive designer pants too!

With Andie gone, Rebecca resumed her search of the internet files.

> **Mother and granddaughter—Bodrug/Lipska Women Murderers — Nature or Nurture?**

Cited one source.

> **Magda Bodrug questioned in unusual circumstances surrounding the death of granddaughter Elena.**

... another entry read.

Rebecca continued to scroll the multiple entries. The citations became more incredulous as the story played out backward on the internet.

The next source cited:

> **Elena Lipska, recently convicted of neglecting to provide the necessaries of life for her 2-year-old daughter, was found dead in her apartment, a possible victim of an accidental overdose.**

She read back further in time:

> **Elena Lipska found guilty after her grandmother provided damning evidence.**

The entries continued in detail about Sylvie Bodrug's short, tragic life:

> **Sylvie Lipska's young body was found today. Evidence suspects long-term neglect and abuse. Elena Lipska further accused of performing indignities to a body. Police will not comment further.**

The oldest source read:

Sylvie Lipska, age 2 years, has been missing for the last 48 hours. The residents of Duncan participate in hunt for missing child.

Rebecca recalled the news story from when she was in high school, and how she and Jake had participated in the search. The town of Duncan was within driving distance of Campbell River, and the two had been eager to assist. She remembered it had turned tragic when the small, fragile body of Sylvie Lipska was found stuffed under the stairs in her own mother's shanty apartment.

Olivia hadn't joined them, saying that she had a date with a mysterious older man. "Told you it wouldn't come to any good!" Olivia had said later, feigning a shudder. "All that rummaging around in the woods ruined your clothes, and they ended up finding her body stuffed in a suitcase in her own mother's house. It will give you nightmares for weeks."

Now years after the event, Rebecca thought about how sad she felt for the poor child and her grandmother. *It was tragic,* she thought, *but what does it have to do with me or with Indie's death?*

Rebecca decided she wanted to talk with the old woman the next time she visited the cemetery. She had questions and needed answers, especially to the big questions that dogged her. *What does this woman want from me? How could she possibly think she could help me?!*

She decided to stay late to look over some inventory discrepancies because Jake had said he was going out after work again. She just couldn't face the empty house with all its sad memories, especially not tonight. Recently Jake's absence seemed to be a common theme in their relationship. They worked in the same shop, and they slept in the same bed, but that's about the only things they did together anymore. This hadn't always been the case. His smile had made her smile ... his laugh had made her laugh.

But now no one smiled anymore, and no one laughed.

She picked up a picture on her desk. It was a family portrait of Jake, Indie, and herself on the front doorstep of the Wright house. Her father had taken the picture after Thanksgiving dinner, the year Indie had died. They had all been stuffed from indulging in turkey, all its fixings, and of course, pie. Indie had loved the pumpkin pie, and the evidence was still displayed on his face and T-shirt.

Her mother, Genie, was sadly absent from the picture having died of cancer three years previously.

I wished Mom had been there to share that day; she would have adored Indie! Dad and I still missed her, but we had so much to be thankful for. She smiled and replaced the photo, then got back to work.

The inventory numbers are not matching the sales invoices, she thought, after she'd been looking at the books for some time. *Something doesn't match here.* She had run the numbers several times and came up with same results. *Does this mean someone is stealing? If they are, it is high end items.*

During her investigation she had also found invoices for a surveillance system that had been charged to the shop. She hadn't ever seen them before, but it made sense with all the expensive equipment and cars on site. *Was this something new or was it meant for the Proctor Estate? I'll mention it to Andie tomorrow.*

She suddenly noticed how quiet the shop had become. She checked her watch and realized it was past eight p.m., so she grabbed her coat and prepared to leave. All the lights were off except in Andie's office, where they still shone, and she could hear male voices coming through the door. She tapped on the closed door and quietly opened it. Andie and Chief Pritchard stood close together, looking at several car magazines that were spilled across the desk. Both men looked up at Rebecca when she entered.

"Oh, sorry, Andie. I just wanted to say good night. Good evening, Chief Pritchard." Feeling awkward, she backed out, then quietly closed the door.

"See you tomorrow!" Andie called after her.

As she walked away, Rebecca heard the door lock engage.

CHAPTER FOUR

Rebecca returned home to find Jake passed out on the living room couch. She was surprised to find Jake at home, lately he had been spending a great deal of time away, usually at Malhouins, the local bar. God only knew what he got up to, most likely drinking and smoking, shooting pool, and complaining about his life. Tonight Jake was splayed out on the couch, the TV blaring, his drunken snores echoing in the room. His breath smelled strongly of liquor and cigarettes. She stared down at the sleeping man and frowned. She realized then that she really didn't care what he had been up to, as long as he wasn't harping at her.

She turned off the TV and shook Jake's shoulder. "Get up and go to bed, Jake. If you sleep here, you'll wake up in the morning stiff and bitchy." He mumbled in his sleep, but didn't stir. She shook harder. His lids fluttered, and he muttered. "Okay Olivia ... okay, I'm going." His words were thick and sticky.

"Olivia? It's Rebecca, now wake up, Jake." Jake bolted upright, rubbing his eyes. He stared around the room, caught sight of Rebecca, and mumbled. "Yeah, I need to go to bed." He stumbled past her, staggering upstairs to the bedroom. She followed him, after stopping in the downstairs bathroom to shake out a couple of Tylenol and fill a glass of water.

She opened the cabinet to replace the Tylenol, and a half full pill bottle fell into the sink. She squinted at the label, *Zoloft 25 mg (antidepressant) take 1 tablet daily*. She placed it back next to other bottles labelled Effexor, Cymbalta, and Zopiclone, the drugs Dr Grainger had been prescribing her to help with her depression. She had stopped taking them all because she experienced headaches, weight gain, and insomnia. She didn't need pills; she just needed the sadness to stop.

I should just pitch them out, perhaps tomorrow. But for now, I should get these Tylenol to Jake. She shut the cabinet on the cache of medications.

Rebecca climbed the stairs and entered the bedroom; she nudged Jake. "Take these." He obediently popped the pills in his mouth and took the offered water. He swallowed them down and drained the liquid, then handed back the empty glass.

"Thanks," he muttered. He was fast asleep before his head hit the pillow.

Later that night, Rebecca lay staring at the ceiling of the bedroom she shared with her husband. Robust snores echoed from his side of the bed as she tried to puzzle out her thoughts. Since reading the internet articles about the old woman and her granddaughter, Rebecca couldn't get the vivid words out of her head. She had been unable to sleep; the sad story had kept her awake. Both women had lost loved ones, and she realized threads of tragedy wove them together.

Why had Magda wanted to talk to me, the town pariah? Well, maybe she just wants to talk with someone and unburden herself? Perhaps she has no one in Campbell River, since most of her life was lived in Duncan. She tossed and turned, fighting with the bedsheets.

As she lay beside Jake, watching him snore, other familiar doubts and questions knotted her stomach and pushed sleep away.

You still blame me for Indie's death. All I see is hate in your eyes. Those eyes so often blood shot and red rimmed from the increasing amount of alcohol he had been consuming down at Malhouins.

She didn't expect a response from the sleeping man. He never said much, but his actions and body language shouted his contempt for her; his veiled anger lived just below the surface of his tightly wound temper.

In the years that they had been a couple Jake had worked to control that temper, but recently it burst free at the mere sight of her. He sounded more and more like his father, Raymond Adams. Life with the Wrights had smoothed out some of Jake's rough edges, but lately he had become so much more argumentative, especially if he had been drinking. Rebecca didn't need another of his verbal attacks in the middle of the night.

She often wondered why they even bothered to sleep in the same room anymore; sex and passion had long since become a thing of the past. Even before Indie's death, lovemaking had dwindled from seldom to never. Soreness and fatigue as the result of his birth, then the all-consuming depression following her father's death had dampened their passion. Finally, the tragic accident that had taken Indie from their lives sealed any chances of future romantic liaisons. Love and passion died with Indie.

She shrugged off the blankets and slipped quietly from the bedroom; she paused in the upstairs hall, feeling saddened and defeated as she caught her reflection in the hallway mirror. Since Indie's birth, and then the loss of him and her father, Rebecca had steadily gained weight. Food had been her quiet friend, providing comfort and reserving judgement.

She knew from the look on Jake's face that he found her repulsive, and she had heard him laugh at her behind her back, making sport of her weight with the guys at the shop. These insults, coupled with the constant fatigue, made it hard to motivate any effort. Forgotten were the long walks and runs in the local woods, a place that had always provided respite and comfort.

Downstairs she picked up a framed photo, recalling memories of hikes and adventures in the deep pine forest that she had shared with her father when he was alive. It was also there, in a flowered forest meadow far from prying eyes, where she and Jake had first made love. She thought of the man snoring in their marital bed, and struggled to revive any of those feelings from that magical and exciting first time. He was a stranger to her now.

She walked through the silent house, pausing to look at pictures of happier times. She picked up a photo of her parents the year before her mother had died; her parents beamed at her. She set it down and looked at another one that showed a happy couple; the groom beaming with pride, his hand resting on his bride's tummy. She recalled their hasty engagement and nuptials after she had agreed to marry Jake. They were so young, just finishing high school, and had been ill-prepared for the demands of such a serious relationship and a new baby.

Jake was so happy then. He couldn't wait to tell everyone about the baby. She sighed.

Things weren't always so hard, she thought as she picked up another picture. Jake was holding Indie, and they were facing each other, both beaming. Rebecca planted a kiss on the baby's face, then carefully put the framed photo back on the shelf. She trembled at the rush of memories that swelled over her. She wiped away a tear that had escaped her eye.

She nocturnal wanderings now found her standing outside the closed door of 'the room' where the accident had happened. Her heart pounded, and her hand shook as she pushed the door open; it moaned in response. The room remained as it had that tragic day. The only difference was that the tall dormer window was closed.

Memories came roaring back.

She was preparing the spare room for a new baby ... Indie was going to have a sibling. Jake didn't know yet, but he would be so excited. She was torn and deep in thought. *I don't want another baby ... not yet ... I have other plans.* She had her back turned, just for a moment. Then she heard a noise coming from across the empty room. Only a moment ago Indie had been playing with his toys on the floor; near the open window. Then ...

Images flooded back ... Indie at the window. A mad dash across the room. A desperate lunge. A whisper of fingers on fabric. A horrified scream ... her own scream. Indie was gone!!

Rebecca snapped back to the present, and a silent whimper caught in her throat. She leaned against the wall to catch her breath and still her pounding heart.

If I'd only I'd been watching him more carefully ... if only I'd run faster ... if ... if, she whimpered. She had run through this scenario over and over again, wishing and begging it to be different.

Rebecca needed to be in Indie's presence, to ask for his forgiveness once again. She drifted into his room, a place of sanctuary, as she often did on other sleepless nights. Everything remained untouched, unchanged, a shrine to their 'lost boy.' Neither of them could bring themselves to change anything, it was too painful. She touched and caressed the items in his room, picking up his favourite blanket and inhaling deeply, trying to catch his scent. Over time, as the smell of him gradually faded, the pain of losing him had only intensified.

"Please forgive me!" Rebecca appealed to the empty space. She wandered the room, pausing to look at treasured items. She smiled at long ago memories, then finally settled into the rocking chair in the corner; it was the chair that she herself had been rocked and soothed in as a baby by her own mother.

She rocked gently back and forth, the motion calming her misery.

Indie, I need to move away from this place and start afresh, but to leave you alone in that cold cemetery would be so hard. Help me be strong Indie. Her mind fumbled with indecision.

She had lost the other baby not long after Indie's fall; the shock and stress causing her to miscarry. She was privately thankful, and she had buried her secret with her lost son. She had vowed that Jake would never find out, he didn't need any more heartache. She owed him that much.

Well, she deliberated, still cradling Indie's blanket. *I will find this Magda Bodrug and talk with her. Maybe, just maybe, this is what I need... a mother figure.*

She closed her eyes and gently rocked herself, easing into a soothing slumber where she dreamed of happier times.

CHAPTER FIVE

Having set her resolve to confront this mysterious woman, Rebecca planned to leave early the next morning and drive to the cemetery, hoping to find her there. To her dismay, the day dawned overcast with rain and saturated streets. It had poured steadily all night, making any rendezvous with the old woman unlikely. None the less Rebecca drove past the cemetery, hoping Magda might be there. The graveyard stood abandoned to the rain and its 'quiet residents.' Rebecca didn't stop, but continued on; perhaps tomorrow would bring a change in the weather and a reappearance of the old woman. Rebecca found herself anxious to learn more.

The rain continued to drizzle down for two full days, drowning the streets and swelling the river, further postponing the meeting Rebecca so desperately needed. In the meantime, she distracted herself with meetings and paperwork during the day and wandering the dark house at night. Today she had spent countless hours in Andie's office running the inventory numbers again, but things still did not add up.

"Let's look more on Monday." Andie sighed, rubbing his aching neck. He rummaged deep in his desk drawer and pulled out a chocolate candy. He kept them hidden in a 'secret compartment' with other important items including his computer password. The secret place was known only to him and one confidant—Rebecca. Although he had been once reluctant to hire her, Rebecca had become a valuable and trusted employee.

"Little pick me up before we leave. Want one?" He offered one to Rebecca, knowing she shared his penchant for sweets. "Don't tell Olivia, she thinks I'm getting fat." He winked as she accepted the treat. Rebecca enjoyed these private moments with Andie, he was a bright spot in her otherwise bleak existence.

"Hardly!" Rebecca scoffed. "Not everyone feels that way!" She knew he spent hours at the gym keeping active; Andie was very conscious of his trim, fit physique. One little treat wasn't going to damage all his hard work, but what about the dozen donut holes she had just eaten? She felt disgusted with her choices.

Perhaps I should follow his lead and start taking better care of myself. She rolled the chocolate over her tongue, enjoying its smooth comfort. *But it tastes so good.*

He looked at his watch, then reached for his coat. "I have an engagement tonight and plans for the weekend. Let's finish our review when we meet on Monday morning," he said, then he paused.

"Rebecca, I know we've been working a lot lately, but I need to ask you a huge favour." Andie hovered around the desk, looking uncomfortable. He seemed to be struggling to find the words.

"Fire away Andie, for you anything." Rebecca peered up at her boss; a bead of sweat glimmered on his upper lip. "What`s up, you seem really nervous?"

"Oh, nothing at all!" he stammered. "I just have to go out of town for a couple of days, and I need someone to watch the shop for me; you know just in case of an emergency or something. And somebody the police could call."

Andie dangled a duplicate set of keys in front of her. "Here are the keys and the password for the alarm system as well." He also handed over a slip of paper.

"Is Olivia going too?" She accepted both items and slipped them into her overcoat.

"No!" Andie almost shouted at her. "Sorry! I'm going away to meet with a friend ... I mean some people Olivia won't want to be with." He looked self-conscious.

"No worries, Andie! You deserve the break, and you can tell me all about it when you get back."

Andie excused himself, saying he needed to make a phone call. He shook his head as Rebecca left. *Sweet Rebecca, I am not going to tell you the details of my private weekend or who I am sharing it with. Not even with you. Not yet,* he thought, smiling to himself.

Meanwhile, Rebecca returned to her office to finish up the weekly reports and expense accounts. She came across the invoices for the installation of surveillance cameras and other equipment; she had set them aside to review with

Andie, but she had overlooked them on her desk. She just needed to know how he wanted them entered in the computerized bookkeeping system.

Shit, I forgot to mention these to Andie. I've got to remember to ask him about this when he gets back. Rebecca glanced at the clock on the wall. *Time to get going home.*

As she tidied the documents, she snorted to herself. *Home! With Indie gone and she and Jake gone in spirit, it was just a building not a home now.*

When Rebecca arrived at the house it was silent ... except for the whisper of old memories. She dropped her bag and keys on the hallway table, then noticed the message light on the answering machine was flashing.

Odd, she thought. *No one calls me anymore, except for telemarketers. Might be Jake, but he would use my cellphone.*

She pressed the play button, and an elderly woman spoke in a shaky voice. "This is Edith Graham, your neighbour across the street. I need to talk to you. Please call. It is urgent." The message ended, leaving Rebecca stunned.

What the heck?! She stared at the now silent machine. *After all this time you're calling to talk! Your false accusation almost sent me to jail!* She played the message again. *Unbelievable!*

Furious, she erased the message and stormed into the kitchen. She pulled open the freezer door and located her favourite ice cream; RockyRoad/Double Fudge. Stunned by the brazen phone call, she soothed herself with bowls of creamy frozen delight and sappy TV dramas—dramas not nearly as exciting or twisted as the one she lived daily.

She did not return the phone message.

CHAPTER SIX

The weekend passed uneventfully; both Rebecca and Jake did their very best to ignore and avoid each other. It was the new normal in the household. As Monday morning broke bright and clear, tensions escalated between the couple. The bright dawn had been clouded by a stormy argument that had left Jake enraged and angry and Rebecca deflated and sullen.

As she pulled away from the house, she focused her thoughts on the meeting she had last week with Magda Bodrug. Driving along in her little Honda, she reflected on the words that had invaded her dreams and left her puzzling. She turned her car in the direction of the cemetery, unsure of what she was hoping to gain. She needed a distraction from her latest fight with Jake; they had fought about their future, again.

Perhaps today? Rebecca thought as she pulled up to the cemetery gate.

Rebecca had a ten o'clock meeting with Andie, but she felt she had enough time to meet with this Magda woman and get to the office on time. Sure enough, a solitary figure sat on the stone bench near Indie's headstone, hunched over with a heavy overcoat drawn tightly around her sagging shoulders. It shielded her against the damp morning.

"Thought you might come." The woman spoke in her thick accent. She faced forward, not turning around as she heard Rebecca approach.

"How's that?" Rebecca asked as she took her seat next to the woman.

"You read the newspaper articles, didn't you?" She spoke slowly, looking straight ahead. "You want to know what other secrets my story might hold." Magda turned toward Rebecca, and she gave her a questioning look.

"Look, what I want to know is why you approached me? What do you want from me?" Rebecca peered at Magda's lined and weathered face. Up close she looked frail, beaten down by life and struggle. She wondered if she would look like this in the years to come.

"I have been watching you for a long time now." The old woman squinted at her. "I see you sitting all alone at your son's grave with no one to support you. You look so sad. Where is the boy's father, I wonder to myself? It seems this town and its people have abandoned you."

Rebecca was taken aback by these comments. The blunt words, however true, rattled her.

"I should just leave." Rebecca started to rise. "This was a mistake," she muttered.

"Please sit, don't go! Let me try and explain," Magda implored. "The first time I saw you I almost fainted because I thought you were a ghost of my granddaughter Elena. The likeness to her is remarkable. This is why I am drawn to you. You make me feel like she isn't gone."

Curious but cautious, Rebecca slowly sat back down.

Magda reached into her handbag, pulled out a well-worn picture, and handed it to Rebecca. The faded photograph revealed a young woman holding a frail looking baby. Rebecca took the picture and studied the faces. To her surprise the girl did indeed look like herself, especially when she was a teenager, before tragedy and weight gain had altered her own image. She handed it back, and the woman carefully slid it back into her pocketbook.

"Is that your granddaughter? And the baby, is it Sylvie?"

The old woman nodded. "You remind me of my Elena." She paused, her voice shaking. "Before the drugs, and the bad men, and before everything went so wrong. I miss them very much. Like you, I am alone."

Magda grasped Rebecca's hand and drew up close beside her. "I know about your tragic story, of course everyone in this small town knows your business. Perhaps if you hear my story and its secrets, you will have the courage to break from the past and create a new life. Don't be trapped in a life of misery. You are too young to be already dead."

Rebecca frowned. "I don't mean to be rude, but is this all about?" Rebecca was worried that this would just open up old wounds, and she couldn't relive the pain once again. The old woman didn't respond, she just sat, staring at her hands. Rebecca was confused, and she needed answers.

"Okay, I read about your granddaughter. She killed her child. My son died by accident. What do you think we have in common? Is there more to your story?"

"Sorrow. We have sorrow in common."

The old woman attempted to stand, but faltered; Rebecca reached to grab her. Together they slumped back onto the bench. They sat engrossed in their own thoughts; the quietness was deafening and raw. Uncomfortable with the silence, Rebecca pulled her hand away and began to speak.

"Okay Magda Bodrug, tell me your story. What could it hurt?" She recognized the elderly woman's energy was failing.

Aware of her time constraints, she added, "But not here. You seem very tired." Had she not offered, Rebecca doubted whether Magda would even be able to make it back under her own steam. She was also intrigued by this woman's sad story and wanted to hear more. She offered her hand to assist the frail woman, and together they walked slowly to Rebecca's car.

CHAPTER SEVEN

During the drive Magda provided directions to the apartment, but otherwise she remained silent. Although she had lived in Campbell River her whole life, Rebecca realized she had never been in this neighbourhood before. The whole area looked run down, shabby ... tired. The lawns were either sun burnt bare or weedy and overgrown with many of the homes looking vacant. Magda lived in a three- storey rundown apartment across from the pawn shop and flea market. As they parked in front of the complex, the elderly woman implored Rebecca to come in for a cup of tea.

"Please!" She clutched at Rebecca's hands.

Rebecca glanced at her watch. "Fine, but just for a few minutes. I do have to get to work."

In the sparse but tidy apartment, the old woman prepared tea and placed a few tiny biscuits on a plate. After serving Rebecca, she settled in her chair and turned to face her. "Now I tell you my story. I am a murderer ... I killed my granddaughter. You are the only person I have ever confessed this to, but I need to start at the beginning so you will understand better."

Rebecca was so shocked that she choked on her tea. She coughed and set her cup down on the table, where it remained untouched and grew cold as Magda continued.

"Please go on!" She sputtered and cleared her throat.

Rebecca sat quietly listening as Magda outlined her tragic past that had led to her great granddaughter Sylvie's death. She sat riveted and was unaware of the passing of time.

It all started after the 1970 Polish Riots, when Magda's husband Miklojac (Mikki), and his brother Vicktor, needed to escape from their home country. The two siblings were involved in the riots against the government; they protested against the exploitation of the markets, when dramatic raises in prices had crippled the consumer. The secret police clamped down on the protestors, killing many innocents, but the brothers escaped capture.

"Mikki and Vicktor were now criminals, and I was also under their watch. We were hunted day and night by the police. Prison was our only future." Magda explained. "With the help of friends, we were able to escape across the Baltic Sea to Sweden, but ..."

Here her voice broke. "We had to sacrifice and leave our daughter Amelia behind with my parents. The plan was to bring her to us as soon as we were settled. Who knew it would take thirteen years? She was only three years old when we left her." She sighed and shook her head.

With the help of the Canadian Red Cross the Bodrug's were able to enter Canada as refugees, settling into the province of British Columbia. Both young men had previously worked in the coal mines in Poland, and they were readily hired by the then booming mines of Duncan. While Miklojac and Vicktor toiled in the dark recesses of the mines, Magda feverishly worked to bring her daughter from the homeland. She called upon the Canadian government; the Red Cross, and Amnesty International to assist her, but Poland viewed the three of them as fugitives and quashed any chances of the family reuniting.

"It was only when Amelia turned sixteen that she was able to make her way to us. Her aging grandparents were no longer able to care for her, and by then the government was softening to the idea of immigration. They allowed her to come to Canada, and when she arrived, we were so happy, but we were also strangers."

She pulled a picture off the mantel and handed it Rebecca. "This is her. She was a beautiful, smart girl."

Magda went on to explain that for a short period the family were happy, rebuilding their lives. They were thrilled to have Amelia back in their embraces, and the young woman worked hard to establish herself in the new town, learning its customs and culture. But she struggled at times to fit in, and most of the time she missed her former life. She missed her grandparents, but mostly she longed for her boyfriend who had been her soulmate since early childhood, when her parents had fled Poland. David Lipska had filled the void they'd left behind, and she continued to correspond with him, desperately hoping they would be together again in the future.

After many years of hard labour, the Bodrug brothers purchased homes, side by side in the miner's district. The homes were small in comparison to the corporate homes, but the home of Magda and Mikki was warm and inviting. Vicktor lived alone as a bachelor, being married to the mine. He loved the physicality of the work, and he loved its dark spaces. Mikki, however, longed to spend his days in the light, away from the cold dark recesses of the earth. The two brothers argued frequently about their work in the mines, and they often clashed about unsafe practices.

When Vicktor was promoted to safety inspector for the new Tunnel 4East being dug by Mikki and his crew, tensions escalated further. Mikki had approached Vicktor with concerns about the safety of the tunnel's ceiling, even refusing to let his men continue until the issues were further explored.

Driven by a yearning to foster his career by impressing management, as well as being pressed by the higher-ups to increase productivity, Vicktor ignored the concerns.

"That fateful night, Mikki was working the area with three other men." She paused, taking a long shuddering breath. "Sure enough, the ceiling collapsed, killing two of the men and seriously injuring Mikki and the other. A cold granite rock fell and broke Mikki's back. He never walked again."

Magda explained that over the next eighteen months an investigation was held. Witnesses were called, mining experts displayed fancy graphs and clever diagrams, and at the very end, Vicktor testified on the company's safety procedures. Magda recalled that upon hearing his testimony she had seethed with outrage and anger, knowing full well it was a fabrication by the company to expunge them of any liability. While his brother lay broken and ruined in a hospital bed, the court found that Vicktor had acted prudently, and he was cleared of all negligence. Like many such incidents, the company attempted to console the survivors and their families by claiming that it was an unfortunate accident that occurred with deep ore mining. Small financial awards were provided to the miners and their families to soothe their pain and loss.

Hush money, they called it, but none the less, the cheques were distributed and cashed by destitute families. The company deemed the case closed, and they sealed the files. But closed case or not, many felt the monies were just a cover up.

The accident file might have been sealed but for the Bodrug family, the relationship between the brothers was irreversibly damaged. Each knew their version of the truth, and whether due to guilt or shame, Vicktor decided to move from Duncan to mainland BC to start a new job with another company.

"He snuck away like a dog with its tail between its legs ... he was a guilty man. Over time we lost contact with him. The last I heard he was living in a nursing home in Nanaimo. After he abandoned us, he climbed the corporate ladder and became a big wig in another coal mine, but he eventually paid the price by sacrificing his soul to the bottle. Now he lives his life as a sad, old alcoholic in the care of others."

She paused and looked at Rebecca. "So many souls lost to the bottle and to pills, eh?" This comment was not lost on her. She waved her hand for Magda to continue.

Left to care for an invalid husband, Magda struggled to make ends meet. She fought endlessly with the insurance companies for further financial assistance. Mikki's medications, therapy, and personal care needs were very expensive, and they drained the family's meager savings. When Magda challenged the accident claim the Human Resources advisor coldly explained. "Your husband didn't complete the documents properly. It is not our problem because he is no longer employed by the company!" The call was ended and the file was closed.

Left with no other choice, the little house on Tuttle Street, the home they had toiled so hard to purchase was sold, and the family move to a subsidized house in the poorer part of town. Unable to finance nursing care for Mikki, Magda was forced to rely on Amelia for assistance; while she herself went to work as a clerk at the local grocery store. Amelia had wanted to start college in the fall, but due to Mikki's illness and the money problems, these dreams were dashed. The tension and stress of caring for a sick loved one took its toll on the small family. All their dreams were destroyed by a large black rock that fell at the wrong time.

One evening, arriving home weary from a long day of work, Magda found Amelia crying in the living room.

"What my dear?" she asked the sobbing young woman. She tried to comfort her, but was pushed away. Although Magda was her mother, Amelia did not feel an emotional connection to her, and she rejected her embrace.

"Oh Mama," she cried. "Papa is becoming so much worse. His temper flares when I try to help him. He yells at me, and today he threw the food I prepared for him on the floor. He said it was slop!" Here Amelia burst into fresh tears, emptying her soul to this stranger.

"I was forced to come to this country because Babcia (Grandma) & Dziadek (Grandfather) were too old to look after me anymore." She wept into her hands, unaware of the wretchedness painted on her mother's face.

Magda had so longed to have her daughter rejoin the family, but never in her worst nightmares had she expected it to turn out so badly. She so wished to soothe her child, taking her into her arms and kissing away the tears, but the time for this was gone.

Amelia raised her head, and then delivered the final blow to Magda's already wounded heart. "I have tried to be a good daughter, looking after a man that I barely know. I cannot take it any longer. I am so sad and so lonely. I have been writing to David, my friend from Gdansk. He has asked me to marry him. I am eighteen now, and I have said yes. I am leaving Mama; I am going home."

Magda turned away so Amelia could not see the ruin of her face.

Amelia continued, "I did not leave my home to come to Canada to live like this, a nurse to an angry old man. I am sorry Mama, but I have dreams too. I will be leaving next week," she whispered to her mother's rigid back.

"How will you pay for the passage? You are too young to marry!" Magda felt faint at the thought of losing her child again. "How will this David support you?"

"David has a good job as an accountant, and he has sent me money to return home. All has been worked out. I am hoping I can help Babcia and Dziadek and then perhaps after David and I are married, they can move in with us. Maybe in time I will return to visit you."

"She left eight days later," Magda explained to Rebecca. Her departing words were … 'In time Mama, we will reunite.'"

Rebecca sat quietly reflecting on Magda's tale. "And in time did she return?"

"No, she did not."

Rebecca suddenly gasped, and she looked at her watch. "Time! What time is it? Oh no! I have to go Magda! I am so sorry! I am late for a very important meeting. Shoot, I don't want to leave you, especially after what you have just told me, but I have to go."

She reached for her purse but looked directly at the old woman and said, "I will return. I promise." She slipped through the door, leaving the old woman alone.

CHAPTER EIGHT

Despite her mad dash across town, Rebecca still arrived fifteen minutes late to work. This morning had been way too complicated. First the fight with Jake, and then the extra time she had spent with Magda, had left her emotionally spent and now very late. She had put the memories of the argument out of her head until now. Jake had been ill tempered again, nursing the boy's night out hangover. He had stormed out leaving her to make her own way to work. They used to drive together, but the deafening silence had been too much to digest.

As she pulled into the back of the Proctor Automotive lot she noticed Olivia's sporty red Porsche was parked there, so she edged in next to it. Like the odd couple, the cars were a stark contrast.

"Seems like the drama continues," she muttered, pulling her bulk out of the compact vehicle. "Olivia is here and early too. That can only mean she is pissed about something! Great!"

As she passed the mechanic bay, she noticed that Olivia was talking with Jake. She decided not to interject. Olivia was great at calming Jake down, and after the 'bust-up' they'd had this morning, he needed to be defused.

They had fought about money again because Jake was pressuring her to sell her parent's home. This was not a new argument; it had been raging since her father had died four years ago. Jake had always wanted to start his own mechanic shop, and the monies from the sale would provide him that opportunity. Campbell River was rapidly becoming a resort hot spot, and the Wright property sat on prime land for development, but they needed to act fast. Olivia kept telling them she knew some real estate tycoon that could make them some big money.

Her father was a widower and after his sudden death, Rebecca had received the Wright's home and the five acres of land it sat on. In his will, Fred Wright clearly stipulated that Rebecca be the solitary recipient and Jake be excluded. This peculiar wish caused yet another rift between the pair; Jake was furious about his father in-law's interference in his life, even after his death. Olivia said the will could be contested, but it would be a costly and lengthy process. It hindered Jake's plans, he wanted the money now.

This morning they had battled fiercely because Rebecca did not want to act on it at all. Selling off her parent's and Indie's memories was too big a sacrifice. She was just not ready for this now, or perhaps ever. The fight had become very heated. Jake had gone red in the face, and she was afraid he was going to physically lash out at her. Scared of his wrath, she had locked herself in the bathroom while he shouted that 'she was selfish and didn't care a bit about what he wanted.' He had pounded on the locked door, and then began to yell.

"Why can't you be more open minded like Olivia instead of being so stubborn? She thinks I could do it!"

He had never hit her before, but he had inherited his father's tendency to use fists to solve problems. Lately he had taken to punching the walls and door frames when he was angry. As he ranted on the other side of the door, she wondered how long it would be before he chose her soft flesh to vent his anger instead of the solid door frame. She shuddered at the thought.

He had finally left the house, slamming the door, and peeling off in his truck.

Rebecca hastened past Tamara and Ashley, doing her best to ignore their snide remarks and titters. As she dashed into the coffee room, she came across Andie, who raised a questioning eyebrow and offered her a cup of dark coffee.

"Sorry Andie. Slept in. I haven't been sleeping well lately." He handed her the cup and she took a swig, grimacing at its bitter taste.

"No need to explain, Rebecca, if anyone would have a reason to have insomnia it would be you."

"I'll meet you in my office in a minute. I quickly need to talk to Jake." She left the coffee room and walked down the connecting hallway to the mechanic bay. There through the window she observed Jake listening intently to Olivia as she inspected the self-inflicted wounds on his knuckles. Rebecca couldn't make out what was being said, but their closeness seemed a bit too intimate for just friends.

She was about to intervene when a voice came from behind her. "Rebecca."

It was Andie. "It's best to leave them to their miseries. Each of them seems to be in a mood this morning! I overheard Jake ranting and raving, and I don't' mean to pry, but are you okay? I mean, can I help with anything ... anything at all?"

Rebecca quietly shook her head and moved away from the mechanic bay door. "No Andie, I'm fine. Jake is just blowing off steam."

"No Rebecca, it is not fine! He shouldn't be allowed to treat you that way; he should be man enough to control himself. I could talk to my friend Kevin Pritchard for you. He could have a little chat with Jake about anger management and self-control."

He placed his hand on her elbow and gently steered her away from the scene. "Come Rebecca, we need to finish that inventory review. I still have a few questions about the final numbers." As she moved away, she looked back and thought she saw them embracing, but it was fleeting.

"Now, Rebecca." Andie pressed. She obediently followed him as he led her to her office and the endless pile of invoices and billings that was her daily grind. He set a fresh bundle of papers on top of the current set, obscuring the note she had written regarding the security invoices.

As they settled into her office, she looked at Andie and tried to be cheerful. "Say, how was your weekend? Looks like you caught a little sun?"

"It was perfect ... just perfect!" He beamed. "Thanks for asking."

Redirecting the conversation, he said. "Now shall we solve this mystery?" He gestured to the invoices piled on the desk. "How was it around here?"

"All quiet! No drama, thankfully!" She shook her head. "At least until this morning, now there's too much." Their eyes met and they nodded, they didn't need to verbalize it further.

Together Andie and Rebecca tallied and reviewed the invoices once again, but there still seemed to be a discrepancy between what was in the computer and what was inventoried in the shop.

"There seems to be a mismatch between the tire inventory and the recorded sales. It appears we are missing at least six pairs of tires and several other pieces of equipment." Andie pondered.

Rebecca looked across the paper littered desk at Andie, who sat gnawing on a pencil. She sat and watched him, thankful that she had the best boss in the world. Throughout the drama of Rebecca's arrest for murder and the police investigation, Andie had been kind and understanding. Proctor Automotive had received a lot of unwanted media attention being the employer of a suspected child murderer, but Andie had ignored the scandal and gossip. He hated being in the limelight, but he despised injustice even more. He became Rebecca's biggest supporter, refusing to believe that she was capable of such a horrible crime, and because of this, Rebecca had devoted herself to the daily checks and balances at the shop. She felt a strong bond with Andie, not just as an employer, but as a true and dependable friend. Rebecca would do anything for Andie, well almost anything; anything except confronting Olivia. No one did that!

* * *

As they paused for a break, Andie thought about the events that had led to him inheriting the flagging automotive sales and repair business from his father six years ago. Arthur James (AJ) had died suddenly of an assumed massive heart attack, and the rumour mill ground out the story that he had been in bed with a younger woman at the time. No one was surprised by this; his marital infidelity and womanizing was well known. Andie's mother had long since exited the marriage and fled to Vancouver, where she had raised Andie under her delicate care.

Andie had remained in close contact with his father and had spent many summers with him in Campbell River, where AJ tried in vain to make him a 'real man.' He had coerced Andie into joining him on hunting and camping trips, but had eventually relented when he realized that these excursions caused more distress than enjoyment for his young son. Although Andie knew his way around a rifle, his father had soon realized that Andie was a scholar not a hunter.

Apparently on that fatal night the 911 call had been placed by a young woman, but no one knew who the femme fatale was. When the paramedics arrived, the only evidence of the woman's presence was the strong smell of flowery perfume.

Andie was astonished when he received the call informing him of his father's death. AJ's doctor had suggested the cause of death was probably a heart attack. Although he had declined an autopsy, Andie still puzzled over his father's death; AJ had recently passed a medical exam, and his only impediment had been mild hypertension treatable by medication. Andie had always wondered if his death was something more sinister. *Who was this woman, and what part did she play in his death?*

Andie was only twenty-six years old when his father passed. He reluctantly relocated to Campbell River to pick up the pieces of the business, quickly learning about the world of car sales, tires, and automotive repairs. He had originally wanted to dismantle the business, but he realized that by doing this he would strip many people of their livelihood, so he put his dreams on hold and dug in. He had always thought it would be temporary, never dreaming he would set down roots in the small burb. Like Rebecca, he had wanted to pursue his dream of attending university to complete his doctorate in art history, but fate had played out differently for both of them. Now they were bound together by tragedy, complex relationships, and paperwork.

Andie had been the most eligible bachelor in Campbell River when he relocated here. His mother had raised him to be a gentleman and provided him an Ivy League education, but the most appealing attribute was his money. Just before his father's death, Andie had started a relationship with Olivia Baird. She was eight years his junior, but this didn't stop her. She had already sought him out, stalking him when he was in town and aggressively pursuing him in Vancouver, where he lived. Everyone thought they seemed an unlikely pair; the quiet bookworm and Campbell River's high school beauty queen.

Following his father's death, Andie had leaned heavily on Olivia for emotional support, and she played her part to perfection. At the funeral she'd clung to him, shedding a few timely tears, but in reality, she was exploiting his vulnerability, sinking her hooks deep into the sensitive young man's soul. It was during this time that Olivia pressed Andie to marry her; feeling overwhelmed and distraught he plunged into the binding relationship. Many thought the marriage was a ruse, including Andie himself. He often felt that it just wasn't a truthful fit for himself or his ambitions.

Advised by his mother and good friends, Andie met with the family lawyer-Clarence Reid to discuss a prenuptial agreement with his future bride. Olivia wasn't thrilled; everyone knew she was marrying for money and social standing; not exactly for love. After multiple temper tantrums and much pouting, she relented when Andie offered to provide a financial bonus at the time of the wedding and also a large yearly allowance. Stubborn but not stupid; Olivia realized if she continued to force her hand, the wedding would most likely not happen. It was already on shaky ground.

Barbara Proctor, Andie's mother, had a private meeting with lawyer Reid prior to the signing. She had made it clear to him that this pre-nup had to be comprehensive and thorough; preventing her daughter-in-law from having any future claims on Andie's estate. She was a seasoned veteran in the world of divorce, and she knew how to play the game.

Over the years the business had demanded a great deal of his attention, leaving Olivia alone much of the time. While Andie toiled at the shop, Olivia created her own reality. She had a huge house built, and she called it Proctor Estate; here she threw lavish parties. Andie rarely participated in these events, choosing instead to quietly entertain small groups of close friends at his lake house cabin. Olivia also fled the cold winters, going on expensive cruises, and leaving Andie at home. The rumour was that she took a different young man with her on each trip. Andie enjoyed her time away, relishing the peace in his life. Her lavish trips and her boys were the least of his concerns.

Andie certainly was not the power-driven car mogul that AJ Proctor had been. He struggled to exude the same confidence, feeling more comfortable hiding behind the office desk or poring over art history books then out flogging the latest sports models. He did however have a strong business savvy, and he was able to drive the bottom line far into the black. He dedicated himself to keeping up with the latest trends in automotive repairs, and he insisted his mechanics attend courses to advance their skills. Jake had been one of these eager students in Andie's mechanic shop, advancing from changing tires to tinkering on antique and rare cars. Andie also invested in innovative equipment to service the needs of his customers. The shop had become known as the place to go if you needed your car fixed, and antique car restorations were also a thriving branch of the business. The only flaw in the business plan was Olivia's overzealous shopping sprees. She often exceeded her allowance, spending lavishly, especially on herself. Andie earned it, and Olivia spent it. It was how the Proctor relationship existed.

* * *

"Could it just be an inventory mistake?" Rebecca asked Andie again. She had been shifting through the reams of paper on her desk. "Things just seem to be walking out the door, completely unnoticed."

Perhaps not so unnoticed, Andie thought. "Excuse me for a minute; I just need to check something out in my office. Why don't you take a break? I'll be right back." Andie scooped up the paperwork and went across the hallway to his office. Once there, he firmly closed the door behind him.

She shrugged, stretched her stiff neck, and headed to the staff room. When she passed the mechanic bay, she spied Jake hard at work on the engine of an older muscle car; he was becoming quite the expert. Jake looked up from his work and their eyes met for a brief moment. He frowned, and then looked away. She stood for another moment, hopeful that he might look up again. It didn't happen.

As Rebecca poured herself a stale cup of coffee, the overhead speaker blared. It was Ashley's high-pitched, squeaky voice. *"Darren Burke, please go to Andie's office immediately. Darren Burke to Andie's office."*

Rebecca jumped at the noise, slopping coffee on her hand and sweater. "Shit!" she cursed aloud.

She set the cup down and wiped at the mark, but the stain was already setting in. As she swiped at her sweater, she heard the mechanic bay door slam and saw Darren Burke stomp down the hallway, muttering under his breath.

"Now what? What does the little fag boss want?"

Rebecca watched as Darren knocked on Andie's door, and then entered the office. She saw Andie sitting in front of his computer screen patiently waiting for his mechanic, but then the door closed, obscuring her view. Moments later, she heard loud voices coming from behind the closed door.

"Well fuck you, asshole! There is no way you can prove this!" It sounded like Darren's voice.

The mechanic flung open the door and started to leave the office, then hesitated. He turned and stood riveted in place; the veins of his neck bulged, and his face was flushed a deep burgundy. Behind the glowering stare, Rebecca could see that he was weighing his options.

"There you are wrong, Mr. Burke." Andie calmly responded. "I have proof, and you know it; you've seen the evidence. Now please leave before I call the police. You are terminated as an employee. Leave now!" Andie pointed toward the door.

"What about my last paycheque? You owe me money!" Darren lurched toward his employer and towered over him, entertaining a menacing glower.

Rebecca stood in the door of her office, watching the confrontation occur. "Andie, do you need help?"

"Yes, Mrs. Adams, I could use your assistance with Mr. Burke." Andie's voice was calm and collected, but Rebecca could see his hands were shaking.

"What do you want me to do?" Her voice quivered. She was afraid the incident was going to turn ugly, perhaps violent. It made her think of Jake's outburst this morning.

Do all men act this way? she wondered.

"Mr. Burke just needs his final cheque, and then he will exit the building. Can you take of care of that, Mrs. Adams?"

Rebecca nodded, unable to speak.

Andie turned back to the enraged man. "Do we need a security escort, Mr. Burke? Shall I call Chief Prichard so his officers can help you find your way off my property?"

"No! Just give me what is owed," Darren spat. As the hulk of a man passed Andie's desk, he sent papers and other items crashing to the floor. "Evidence my ass!"

"No problem," Rebecca said. "I can write you a cheque. How much is owed?"

"I think five hundred dollars should suffice, shouldn't it, Mr. Burke?" Andie ignored the big man's insults and tilted his head questioningly. "That should square us up! After all, six pairs of tires are worth more than your outstanding wages."

The bigger man glared down at Andie. "Fine, so let's do it." He followed Rebecca into her office where she prepared the cheque. Darren paced back and forth across the room, muttering under his breath.

"That little fag is going to pay, and his little papers are no evidence. There is no way he can use it against me, it's not like he has cameras on us!" He looked up to realize that Rebecca was watching him.

"Has this little creep been watching us? Is he videoing us?" Darren snarled.

Rebecca looked away and quickly wrote the cheque as Burke peered into the corners looking for possible hidden video cameras. His temper was starting to boil over as he prowled her office, and Rebecca wanted him out of there fast!

Suddenly he turned on her; she was part of the establishment that had accused him of theft.

Perhaps it was this fat bitch who ratted me out! He suddenly lashed out and pushed over her desk; everything crashing to the floor. Satisfied with his purposeful destruction, he snatched his cheque and left the office. Rebecca stood stalk still, paralyzed by Burke's actions.

A dark squall of anger followed him down the hallway, and people cleared a path, allowing this raging bull to exit the shop. Rebecca looked around at the debris of her office; the place looked like a war zone. She plopped down in her chair; her knees felt weak, and she wasn't sure if her legs would support her.

As her pounding heart calmed, she started to slowly pick through the papers on the floor, but she would need assistance to put the desk upright. Mixed in the debris were the surveillance invoices she had forgotten to give Andie, but now it was starting to make sense.

Maybe this is how he knew Burke was stealing. She picked up the creased paper. *If Andie secretly installed cameras, then these invoices make sense now. I wonder how long this has been going on.*

She was distracted by a shout in the hallway. Burke had shoved past Olivia as she entered the building, jostling her coffee mug and spilling her favourite fat free caramel macchiato on the floor and her designer shoes. The sticky mess slopped on the multiple shopping bags that adorned her arm. She shrieked in anger and protest, concerned that the liquid might have ruined the items she had just purchased.

"What the hell!" Olivia yelled after Darren. "Idiot!"

She flung her bags onto the receptionist's desk and glowered at the mechanics that had come into the reception area. They stood with heads close together, whispering and gossiping about the unfolding drama. The building had been stunned into silence, a rare thing for a noisy mechanic shop. That was until Olivia bellowed

"Get back to work ... the show is over!"

The workers scattered to escape Olivia's attention, even Jake!

She wiped the coffee mess off her shoes and hands then turned her attention toward her husband. She stalked him to his office. "What was that all about?"

"Theft." Andie exhaled, collapsing into his chair. "Burke has been stealing tires from the inventory."

"Really? How did you find that out? Did he just walk in and confess?" She was surprised Andie had the spine to confront anyone, especially someone the size and stature of Darren Burke.

"Give me some credit, Olivia ... of course he didn't. I was suspicious, so I confronted him with the evidence, and then I fired him, but he didn't go quietly!" Andie shook his head and stared at his wife. "It's been a trying day, so what do you want? I'm busy, so make it quick."

Olivia was taken aback by her husband's abrupt attitude. Normally he was very quiet and soft spoken; he never talked back to her. She crossed her arms and studied the man she had been married to for the last six years; she thought she knew him, but maybe not so well after all.

"Well, aren't you being the tough guy today!" she scoffed. "This place might make a man out of you after all! Just like your dad, but I doubt it."

She smiled to herself as she thought about Andie's father; they had been secret lovers until that terrible night when he suddenly died during their lovemaking. They often made love on the same desk where Andie now sat. *I wonder if he knows about that little fact.*

When Andie continued to keep his head down and ignore her, she snorted and turned on her expensive heels, in search of Rebecca. If Olivia couldn't get a rise out of him, she certainly could enjoy tormenting Rebecca.

"Goodbye Olivia, and shut the door behind you!" Andie dismissed his wife.

"Fine!" she snapped, slamming the door behind her. She walked into Rebecca's office only to find it turned upside down, but her intended victim was missing. Knowing Olivia was in the building and would scold her for the coffee stain on her sweater, Rebecca had gone to the ladies room to wash it out. She narrowly missing Olivia's intrusive visit.

"Well shit," Olivia sulked. She knew Jake and the other mechanics would be busy avoiding her after this morning's events, so she decided to go home and get ready for her night out. She had done some extra special shopping, and she was excited to try on her new items. She sashayed out of the building, smiling to herself.

"Someone is going to get lucky tonight!" she giggled. As she got into the car, she sent a text from her cellphone to her lover. She started the car and peeled out of the parking lot.

As Rebecca returned to her office, she was confronted by Jake, who was coming in from the mechanic bay. He was agitated, but he appeared to be in control. "I need to talk with you," he demanded. "What the hell happened to your office?"

"Darren Burke happened." She pointed to the desk. "Can you lend a hand?"

After Jake helped her upright the desk, she stopped and waited. "What did you want, Jake? Hasn't there been enough drama for one day?" She sighed. This day was turning into one big headache.

"Crazy, eh? What was that all about? Sal said that Andie accused Darren of stealing tires. No shit, that asshole has been stealing for years!" He laughed. "I thought Andie was cleverer than that. I never thought Burke could slip that past him."

"He didn't." Rebecca stared at her spouse. "He got caught! Eventually all sneaky liars get caught."

Jake stopped laughing; he didn't like Rebecca's tone. "I just wanted to let you know I won't be home tonight. Some of the guys and I are going out ... you know to defuse after what happened earlier. Just thought I'd let you know."

He turned to walk out of the office, and then stopped. "About this morning; I was a jerk ... sorry."

"Whatever!" Rebecca blew him off, wishing he would just leave. She was tired from the events of this rather dramatic morning. First the fight with Jake followed by her meeting with Magda, and now the shocking events at the shop. She felt drained and exhausted, and she did not want to engage in another verbal duel with her spouse. She was still outraged by Jake's demands to sell the Wright family property. She wasn't ready to forgive or forget his vicious outburst this morning. Feeling rebuffed, Jake marched out of the office, leaving her to regret her comment.

Shit! He tried, and I was just a bitch. Rebecca was just getting up to follow him when Andie entered her office.

"Thanks for taking care of Burke." He appeared shaken and pale from the confrontation.

"Sit Andie, you look like you're going to fall down." Rebecca offered him a chair, and he slumped into it.

"Wow some morning, eh?" His voice was strained, and he uttered a long, shaky sigh. "Surprised myself!" He looked up, and their eyes met. The unspoken message was clear.

"Well done, boss!" Rebecca reached across the messy desk and squeezed his hand. He squeezed back, and then awkwardly withdrew his hand. They sat for a couple of moments with the desk clock quietly ticking away; each absorbed in their own thoughts.

Andie spoke first.

"I've got another problem. The Armstrong National Car Show is next week, and Burke was part of the team. I'm going to need to take another mechanic. Do you think Jake would be up to something this big? His skills are exceptional, but is he ready for the demands of something this intense? He seems a bit stressed lately, but you know him best."

Do I? she wondered, but instead she exclaimed, "Wow Andie, he would be thrilled!! Have you asked him yet?" Despite their marital strain, Rebecca wanted to see Jake succeed. Perhaps this would boost his mood and ease the tensions at home. If this was the case, she was all in.

"Not yet. I wanted to talk to you first."

"Go for it, Andie. He's in the mechanic bay now if you want to ask him. It would certainly give him a confidence boost. God only knows he could use something exciting like this!"

Andie rose from his chair and turned to leave. "You're okay with this idea? It means we will be gone for eight days? You're alright with being alone at home and managing the shop's day to day operations? I know you can handle the place, and I have asked the receptionists to keep the bookings slow, as most of the mechanics will be going to the show."

Eight days on my own? she thought to herself. *Sounds like a vacation to me! It will give me the chance to talk more with Magda and have some alone time. God knows I could use it.* She eagerly nodded and said, "No problem, Andie. Go talk with Jake. He'll be thrilled."

"Then it's set."

Andie started to leave the office, but he turned back. "While I'm away, I'm going to need you to be here to open up in the morning, and then lock up at night. Because of the recent shop theft, I've asked Randi Everett, the shop foreman, to have the staff return their keys. I may reissue them, but for now only you, myself, and Everett will have keys. I don't trust Ashley and Tamara to do the lock up ... I'm afraid they'd forget to set the alarms. Then I'd really get robbed!" he chuckled.

"No problem, Andie. I still have the extra keys." She patted her sweater pocket. "Is the security code still the same as it was last week?"

"No changes right now. Then I guess we're set to go, except you should also have the key to my office and my desk." He handed her the additional keys, and she slipped them on the ring with the others.

"Please make sure you lock both. I don't want Olivia digging through things while I'm gone. Now, let me go tell Jake the exciting news."

A couple of minutes later, Rebecca heard a whoop coming from the mechanic bay.

I guess Jake got the good news. Rebecca smiled, not only because it would make Jake happy, but because it bought her eight days of peace and quiet. She let go a deep, satisfied sigh.

CHAPTER NINE

"I cannot stay too long; she's starting to get suspicious." Jake rolled over and kissed the curve of Olivia's pink, firm bottom. They had rendezvoused at the secluded guest house on the Proctor Estate; Andie was out tonight, so they weren't afraid of getting caught.

She smiled at him and laughed. "It's about damn time considering we've been doing it since ..." She grinned mischievously. "Do you recall our first time?"

"Must we always do this, Olivia; it certainly does not cast me in a great light?" He flipped the sheets aside and started to pull on his trousers. She lunged forward and wrapped her arms around his neck, then plastered his face and neck with kisses, and nibbled on his left ear.

"Go on now, Jake. I know you remember," she whispered. She bit harder, making him wince.

"Yes of course I do, it was on *my* wedding night!" He brushed her away like an annoying fly.

"Yes, on *your* wedding night. Too bad it wasn't *our* wedding night!" She flopped back on the bed, pulling him backward. He rolled over on top of her and gazed into her icy blue eyes.

"Why are you such a bitch?"

"Because I can be!" Olivia purred.

She pushed him off and plucked her discarded robe off the floor; she had purchased the satin robe especially for tonight. She tied the sash around her thin waist and then sashayed over to the dresser. She opened her purse and turned back to him.

"Now we have something more important to talk about before you leave." She pulled a slim cigarette from her purse and inhaled deeply.

"Oh, how I love these things, just about as much as I love having you inside me." She giggled.

He scowled, and his face reddened.

She loved to watch him blush; it made her feel in control.

The sexual relationship between Olivia and Jake had run hot and cold throughout the years, but this kind of talk always made Jake uncomfortable; it reminded him of his infidelity. He never thought he would be the kind of man that cheated on his wife, but cheat he did. After the wedding night incident he had tried to be a faithful husband, but things changed after Indie's birth. He justified his behaviour by using the age-old excuse that Rebecca was too tired and sore after childbirth to satisfy his needs. When Olivia had made herself readily available, he'd eagerly participated. But with each momentary lapse, he further indentured himself to Olivia, and Olivia kept solid records.

Following Indie's death, Olivia had nursed his wounded soul and eased his tensions. He exorcized his demons with sex and booze, further forging the chains that bound him to Olivia. By the time The Armstrong National Car Show came around Olivia owned him heart and soul, and now she was calling in the debts owed.

"We've been through this before, Olivia." He turned away so she couldn't see him clenching his fists. "This real estate friend of yours, Dave Simpson ..."

"Blair Simpson," she corrected.

"This Blair Simpson says he can get over five million for the Wright's house and property?"

He finished dressing, pulled his boots on, and then checked his watch. It was getting late, and although he didn't care if he was, he didn't fancy another argument with Rebecca.

"Rebecca and I had another row about it this morning; you know how she feels about the family home. I'm getting nowhere with her! What do you want me to do?"

He rubbed his face with his hands; he was tired from a long day's work at the shop preparing for the upcoming show. He was so excited for this opportunity, but Olivia's demands were sucking the energy from his body and soul.

"You can divorce her for God's sake! Get on with it!" she snarled at him. She was fed up with his stalling. "You tell me you don't love her, so why don't you just do it?" Her beautiful face was distorted with indignation.

He felt his anger rise in response. Lately he was having an increasingly difficult time controlling his temper. Just that morning when he and Rebecca had argued, he had battered the bathroom door with his knuckles. He took a deep, cleansing breath, then replied to her accusations.

"I'll talk to her when I return from the show, but for now I have to go."

Sensing she had pushed him too far, she crooned. "You are right, Jake; you can do it after your return." Then she unknotted the sash, letting the robe slide to the floor, and pressing her naked body against him.

"Now let me send you on your way with a smile." He feebly resisted her advances, but she was his kryptonite, and he had never been able to resist her. Leaving was lost in his lust and desire.

* * *

On the drive home, Jake thought about the women in his life; of course, there was his wife, Rebecca, whom he had married as a teenager just out of school. The relationship had never been perfect, but when he'd found out he was going to be a dad; he'd vowed he would try to be better than his own lousy father. Things had limped along until Indie's tragic death, and then they imploded. He was destroyed. His world had collapsed when Indie died; his marriage died that day too. He just hadn't had the balls to pull the plug, but now he was ready because he had Olivia and they had plans.

"Olivia," he muttered to himself. She was a like a forbidden drug to him; his own personal heroin. He had resisted Olivia when he first started dating Rebecca, and when she had gotten pregnant, he had doted on her, vowing to be a great spouse and father.

But on his wedding night he had succumbed to alcohol and lust, and it wasn't with his new wife.

He shuddered when he recalled his failure. The day had been a whirlwind with the wedding ceremony and the celebration that followed. Everyone wanted to share a drink with him and congratulate him on the marriage and the baby. One led to two, which led to a steady blur of whiskey shots and handshakes. It wasn't long before his eyes were blurred along with his judgement.

He had put his new wife to bed early; all the wedding events and the demands of the pregnancy had left her exhausted. As she lay on the bed in their honeymoon suite, he remembered he had kissed her on the forehead and smiled at her. His head was swimming, but he felt happy and content.

"I love you, Rebecca Anne Adams, my wife, and I promise that we will never go to bed angry. Now sleep while I shut down this party."

He had staggered back to the party with the intentions of having a final drink with his buddies. Fred Wright, his new father-in-law, was nowhere to be seen, and most of the older crowd had left leaving just the young rowdy adults. Jake was summoned by his school buddies.

"Hey old married man, come over here and have another drink!"

"Old man," he retorted. "Let's see about that."

Many whiskey shots later led him to Olivia's willing arms.

"Hey Mr. Adams; future daddy," she crooned in his ear.

He was having trouble standing up, and he leaned on her for support. Olivia pulled him to the dance floor and began rubbing herself against him. Her firm body mixed with her perfume was intoxicating. He was having trouble resisting her advances, but he was married and off limits.

"Whoa ... stop," he slurred, attempting to remove her hands from his body. "Say, where is your date, Andie?"

"Gone home because he's no fun, but you are!" She pressed against him, feeling him respond. She clung tighter not wanting to release him from her clutches. He tried to push her away, but the sudden movement made his head spin. He suddenly felt very ill and started to make for the door.

"Need fresh air," he gulped. Together the pair wobbled out the door to the back lawn of the Campbell River Resort. Olivia steered him toward a secluded place under the shadows of a large oak tree. There they collapsed into a tangled heap.

Jake rolled onto his back and took several deep breathes. The cool night air and the refreshing smell of recently cut grass eased his nausea and spinning head. After a couple of long minutes, he leaned up on his elbow and turned to the young woman sitting next to him.

"Thanks, Livie," he murmured. "This feels great! I just needed some fresh air."

She smiled down on him. She had been watching his every move, waiting for the right moment. Her full lips were curled into a seductive pout. "What you need Jake Adams is me."

"What!" Jake sputtered. "No!"

His protest was cut short by her lips eagerly pressing down on his. She devoured him, taking his tongue into her mouth. She stroked his body, finding his manhood and caressing him until he responded. His overheated body and alcohol dampened conscience reacted to her advances. His hands found her hair, pulling her closer, and then he roughly rolled on top of her. His hands bruised her soft flesh as he grabbed and kneaded her willing body.

Olivia pushed him up and reached behind her neck, unhooking her halter dress. Her firm breasts spilled out, and she offered them to his lust.

Suddenly he pulled away.

"This isn't right, Livie." Jake pushed himself up; the action setting off the nausea again. He flopped back down on the grass, moving away from her.

"Don't call me Livie; you know I hate that name. And don't get a conscience now; we've been dancing around this issue for years. I know you want me; it is obvious to me, and to everyone else. The only reason that you married Rebecca is because of the baby!"

Her face was contorted with anger; she was seething at being rejected. Nobody refused her. Nobody! She had waited long enough, and tonight she would own him.

Spurned by shame and alcohol, he lunged forward and slapped her face. She gasped in surprise.

"Jerk!" Olivia spat, and she began striking him about the head and face. Jake grabbed her hands and pushed her onto her back. He looked down at her. Her dress lay in ruins. She was flushed, and her breasts heaved in anger; her lips were pulled back in a knowing smirk.

"Like it rough, big guy?" She pulled him to her, smothering his face and neck with kisses and bites.

Fueled by lust and alcohol, he forced himself on her. He pulled away her remaining clothes and entered her with frustration, with lust, and pent-up need. Although their coupling was brief, it sealed Jake's fate for all eternity. She climaxed, calling out his name.

"Jake Adams, you are mine. I own you!" Little did he know at the time just how true those few words would turn out to be.

Afterwards they gathered themselves together, and they attempted to put straight their disarray. Her clothes and makeup were ruined and her hair a mess, so he certainly wasn't going to let her go back to the party. Olivia was an advertisement of their actions and his betrayal. He bundled her into her car and sent her on her way, promising to call her as soon as he was back from his honeymoon. He would have said anything to get her to leave ... he didn't want anyone to see them, especially in this state.

He recalled his acute embarrassment when he had returned to the party and ran directly into Fred Wright. The older man took one look at is son-in-law's dishevelled appearance and read the shame in his eyes. He knew immediately what had happened.

"Best to take a shower before you get into bed, you smell like a cheap perfume store."

Fred started to walk away but turned back and looked directly into the young man's blood shot eyes. He shook his head in disappointment. "This will be our little secret, Jake. Rebecca will never know from me as long as I live. I don't want to see my daughter hurt."

Now, sitting in front of the house, his thoughts returned to Fred's promise. The old man had been true to his word; he never gave up his secret. Fred had been a great mentor and a father figure to him when he was younger, but later he had become an obstacle and a source of frustration; an impediment to his future.

Too bad you had to die to keep your secret. He winced at the thought of his father-in-law's untimely death, and then shook away the memories. Jake looked up and saw the house was dark and empty; Rebecca must be working late again.

Good. I need to take a shower, he thought as he sniffed his shirt. *Good advice, old man. I do smell like a cheap perfume shop.*

CHAPTER TEN

Proctor Automotive was a hub of phrenic activity over the next week. The mechanics participating in the automotive show were scrambling to finish the work on the 1967 Shelby GT500 Mustang that Andie had entered into the competition. As well as completing the finishing touches on the showpiece, the crew needed to bring Jake up to speed on the expectations of the show. Jake was an excellent apprentice mechanic, but now that he was playing in the big leagues, the senior mechanics needed to educate him on the nuances of the show.

"You're in the big leagues now, sonny!" The older mechanics clapped him on the back, and Jake beamed. All his dreams were coming true. Well almost all, the problem with Rebecca remained, but he wasn't going to let that spoil things for him anymore. He was ready and willing to move on; he just needed to keep Olivia under control until the right time.

Andie had splurged for new uniforms for the team, and Jake now needed to be fitted. As well as the team uniforms, Andie wanted his mechanics to be well dressed in the sharpest attire for the after-show parties. The Armstrong National Show was the highlight of the car show circuit, and Andie wanted to make a big splash this year. The team had been working very hard to make a name for themselves, and Andie was determined to put Proctor Automotive on the map.

With the excitement of the upcoming show, Olivia had let Andie know that she expected to be involved in the event, and that she especially wanted to assist with dressing the team.

Normally Olivia avoided the shop, only coming by to occasionally visit the receptionists or torment Rebecca, but suddenly she was a constant presence. Her interference wasn't welcomed.

Much to everyone's surprise, Andie put his foot down and blatantly refused her involvement. Since his recent weekend away, people had noticed that Andie Proctor seemed to have grown a spine. So when Andie said his wife's meddling in the shop was a hindrance; everyone was shocked—and frankly relieved that their boss was finally taking some control.

"Olivia, this is a technical trade show, not a fashion show. Everything has been taken care of, and you would be bored." He had been very calm and patient, but with the deadline drawing close, Andie was feeling beleaguered.

"Rebecca, tell him that I won't get in the way. I just want to go for the shopping and to attend the posh after-show parties!" She whined and stomped.

"You would be in the way!" Andie tried again to ignore his demanding wife. "If you want to go shopping, why don't you take Rebecca and go for an early dinner?" He walked away then, leaving Rebecca to deal with Olivia. "This is my final word on the issue!"

Rebecca shuddered at the thought of eating dinner with a testy Olivia, and shopping would be a form of torture. Rebecca had no desire to shop for clothes that wouldn't fit, nor did she have the funds to afford these items. She shrugged. "Sorry Olivia got to help everyone get ready." She quickly slipped out of the office before Olivia could respond.

Abandoned by her audience Olivia fumed, and then on her spiked heels she bolted from the shop. "We'll see about that!" she hissed.

With the coast clear Andie slipped back into his office; he had so much to do before the show, and Olivia had set him behind. He felt like a coward, but he couldn't deal with her right now. As he laboured over the details, Rebecca brought in a handful of keys and placed them on his desk. They were the remaining ones that Randi Everett had gathered from the shop mechanics. It had been her job to round them up.

"Last of the keys." She gestured toward the pile.

Andie nodded, not looking up from the work on his desk. "Good job. Do you still have yours?"

"Yup."

He swept the keys into a drawer, then locked it. He looked up momentarily from his paperwork and smiled. "Enjoy your evening. See you tomorrow."

CHAPTER ELEVEN

As she left the shop, Rebecca decided to pay a visit to Magda. She drove past the cemetery to ensure that Magda was not visiting at the grave sites, but finding it deserted, she kept on driving to her apartment. She stopped at Charlotte's Confectionaries (CC's) to pick up something to treat the old woman.

When she arrived, she plucked the box from the front seat, and walked towards the main entry of the building and buzzed the intercom. Once inside she approached Magda's apartment door, but her route was blocked by a tall, dark haired man.

"Excuse me!" She tried to side step around him, but the intruder continued to block her way.

Rebecca was startled by this stranger's aggressive behaviour. *Should I run, should I scream? Who is this menacing person?*

Suddenly Magda's front door swung open. "Let her be, you brute, or I will call the police! Shoo!"

Magda gestured to Rebecca, who carefully stepped around the man and escaped into the apartment. Magda slammed the door in the interloper's face.

"Who the hell is that? Should we call the police?" Rebecca gasped.

"No, he is the landlord of the building, and he thinks he can intimidate us. He is nothing but a bully." She waved her hand in the direction of the door.

"Come sit down, my dear. You are shaking." The elderly woman guided her into the small living room. "Sit ... sit. So nice to have you visit me. I see you brought treats." She took the box from Rebecca's shaking hands and went to the kitchen.

"Magda, aren't you afraid of him?"

"Him?" the old woman scoffed. "He's just a big wind bag. I have my own protection, so don't worry." She patted a wooden table, next to her chair. "It's right here. Now, tea or brandy?"

Rebecca marveled at the old woman's resilience. "Brandy!" She laughed.

"Good choice! We have a drink; it will calm your nerves, and I assume you want to hear the rest of my story."

With nothing pressing at the shop to draw her back, Rebecca settled into the settee and sipped at the strong spirits. The whiskey warmed her and settled her shocked nerves.

"When I was last here you had just told me that Amelia had decided to leave and go back to Gdansk. Are you okay to tell me the rest of the story? You said that Amelia never come back to you."

Magda took a heavy sip of her drink, then stared off into space. Rebecca was starting to believe that the woman hadn't heard her, but finally she started to talk.

"No. She never came back. She died."

Rebecca's heart sank. This poor woman's story only got worse and worse. "What? I'm so sorry."

Magda waved her off. "Let me tell you the rest." She began.

True to her word, Amelia returned back to Poland. Her new fiancé had provided the money for the ticket.

"I am sorry, Momma," Amelia sobbed at the airport. "I promise I will try to come back. But for now, I must go!" She hugged her biological mother and fled.

"That was the last time I saw her."

Rebecca learned that Amelia had returned to Gdansk, where she wed David Lipska, and had a little girl they named Elena. As promised, the young couple had helped her elderly grandparents until their deaths. At times monies arrived from the old country, as Amelia tried to soothe some of her parent's distress, but the meager amount was not enough to cover the mounting medical bills. Once Amelia left, life steadily slid down hill for Magda and Mikki. Magda was unable to manage the deteriorating health of her husband, and she reluctantly had to have him admitted to a government institution. Over the following two years he developed multiple bedsores, and he died as a result of infection.

"He was so very unhappy. At one time he was a vibrant man, with a brilliant sense of humour; he loved to make me laugh. After the accident, he was reduced to a withered shell, angry and bitter. He only made me cry, we never laughed anymore. Sadly, his death was a release for me!"

Magda sipped her drink, and then poured herself another finger. She offered the bottle to Rebecca, who replenished her own glass. Each sat quietly sipping until Magda spoke again. The alcohol opened the vault to her memories, and she poured her heart out to the young woman sitting across from her.

"My daughter Amelia and her family were very happy in their home in Gdansk. They would send me many letters and pictures of themselves and their life. I was glad for them, but I missed Amelia, especially after Mikki died. We talked about my returning to Poland to come live with them. I was so excited about this, but it never happened.

The room remained silent as she reflected on her memories.

"What happened next? How did Amelia die?" Rebecca was reluctant to ask, but she wanted to know how the story ended.

Magda rose unsteadily and shuffled across the room to the shelf lined with picture frames. She plucked one up and handed it to Rebecca.

"This picture is of Amelia, David, and Elena a week before the accident."

Rebecca looked at the picture of Magda's family. They looked so happy. It tugged at her heart, and it reminded her of happier days of her own, with Jake and Indie.

"Accident?"

Rebecca handed the photo back to Magda, who gently caressed it with her gnarled fingers, and then placed a kiss on each of the faces. She placed it on the table beside her, then turned her attention back to Rebecca.

"On the way back from the cinema, a drunk driver ran a red light; Amelia and David were killed. Little Elena was sleeping in the back, and by God's miracle she was saved. I remember the night the Polish police called. My heart was broken; I thought I would die from the pain. First my poor Mikki, now my beautiful daughter was gone too. But Elena was still alive, and she needed me." She wiped away a tear and took a sip of her whisky to give her courage to continue.

"The will named me as Elena's next of kin and legal guardian in the event of her parent's death. I don't think they ever believed that something as tragic as that would ever happen or perhaps they would have given her to someone in Poland. I had to hire a lawyer to help me get my granddaughter. At first the

Polish government wouldn't let me bring her here, they thought I was too old and wanted her to stay in Gdansk. She was a Polish citizen, and I was a political refugee. Eventually the Polish government relented, and Elena came to live with me in Canada. But it all cost so much. I lost my job because of all the time I had taken off travelling to Poland, and then the lawyer bills ate up my remaining monies, and also Amelia and David's. The tragedy left me heartbroken and penniless, and now I had a stranger to raise."

"Elena was ten years old when her parents died, and it took me nearly two years of struggle and red tape to get her home to me. She had spent two years with multiple foster parents, and they said she was a difficult child! Bah! She wasn't difficult, she was broken. Her parents were dead, and she was being shuffled back and forth between strangers. No one was there to hold her and let her grieve. She was alone and had to be tough to survive, so they called her difficult. It took so long, and then when she finally came to me, she was an angry little girl who didn't trust anyone. It wasn't easy."

"She never really settled well into the community of Duncan. I had no job and we struggled for money, so I needed to go on social assistance. I didn't have money to buy her nice clothes, and with her strange accent and poor English, she struggled to fit in at school." She sighed.

"Things got really bad when she entered high school and started running with bad people. She withdrew from me even more. I knew she was drinking, and then the drugs started." She trailed off.

Rebecca looked up at the old woman across from her. It seemed that Magda had shrunk since she started her story; as if releasing her sorrow had deflated her person. Rebecca was concerned about her; she looked pale and was rubbing her chest.

"Are you okay Magda?" She reached forward and lightly grazed her hand. The old woman startled at Rebecca's touch.

"My dear, I'm sorry, but my heart hurts sometimes. I am tired now, and I need to rest before I tell the last part of my story." She attempted to rise on shaky legs, but Rebecca encouraged her to sit.

"Sit please. I will let myself out. Can I visit soon?"

"Please do, but call me first." She pulled a pencil and paper from the side table drawer and wrote down her phone number. As Magda replaced the items, Rebecca noticed something metallic glinting in the back of the drawer.

She took the paper and slipped from the apartment, looking around for the creepy landlord. As she exited, she spied him skulking around the corner, watching her movements.

"What a creep!" she shuddered. Realizing that he could hurt Magda, she thought, *Jake will be away for the next week, so I think I will visit more frequently to make sure she is okay.*

She entered Magda's phone number into her cellphone for safe keeping. She also wanted to hear the remainder of the Bodrug story; she felt like she had found a kindred spirit.

CHAPTER TWELVE

Rebecca cringed as the front door slammed shut. Jake had stormed out, annoyed that Rebecca was brooding and ignoring him. He was so excited about the upcoming car show that it was all he talked about during the brief conversations he had with Rebecca.

"It is so cool ... all the new clothes and the classy uniforms. Just look at me, I'm coming up in the world!" Jake was modelling his new duds for Rebecca.

"Andie said that I can take the next level of apprenticeship courses after we return from the show." He turned, seeking Rebecca's approval, but she sat staring out the window.

"Are you listening to me? Nice!" he snapped. "Here I am trying to tell you how excited I am about the show and all the wonderful things that are happening to me and you ..." He waved his hand at her. "You're ignoring me!"

He gathered up his clothes and left the room.

"Jake!" she called after him.

Infuriated with herself, Rebecca pulled up off the couch and headed upstairs to the bedroom in an attempt to soothe his anger. She didn't mean to ignore his excitement, but she was distracted by her own thoughts. She had been thinking a lot about Magda and her tragic family events. She had found comfort in the older woman's presence and had decided to seek her out again tomorrow after the team had left for the show.

"Sorry, Jake. I am excited about you going to the show." She said to his back. She reached out to touch him, but he pulled away. "You really deserve this; you have been putting in so many extra hours."

"Whatever!" he snorted. He pulled on his new uniform jacket and turned toward her. Rebecca looked at his face and only saw disgust. Jake brushed past her, heading for the door.

"Going out," he mumbled, leaving her standing her the bedroom. A moment later she heard the front door slam.

"Well, shit!" Rebecca muttered. She looked at the new clothes and uniform gear strewn on the bed. Jake had left in such a rush he had deserted his new treasures, leaving them in a haphazard wrinkled mess. She slowly gathered the items into her arms and headed to the laundry with the bundle. Over the next hour, she carefully pressed and sorted the clothes into his suitcases. *It's the least I can do. I do want him to be happy.*

As she pulled the suitcases from the closet, her old running shoes fell from the top shelf, striking her in the head. She rubbed her head and laughed out loud.

"Well, that wasn't so subtle! I guess the universe just gave me a tap on the head. Is it trying to tell me something?" She placed the shoes on the bed beside the freshly pressed clothes.

So, what is it? Should I start running again? She shook her head. *Not with all this extra weight, I can't!*

Rebecca turned back to the suitcase and started to carefully pack Jake's items. As she shut the lids and zippered the case closed, the well-worn sneakers came back into view. She set the cases aside and noticed dried dirt was still wedged in the treads, and as she plucked at the smudges, she recognized the distinct red colour; it was from the Lachlan Pathway.

When was the last time I wore these? she thought to herself. *It must have been before Indie was born because I sure didn't have time after that.* She set them on the floor. *I can't run, not yet, but I can walk.*

She leaned down and tugged on the shoes. Her belly fat caught across her middle and made it difficult to lace up the shoes. She puffed and pulled, and at last she was able to complete lacing them. She leaned back on the bed to catch her breath.

Wow, that was harder than I thought it would be. Rebecca turned her feet from side to side, studying the shoes. *I think I'm going to keep you on. No sense in wasting energy taking you off again.* She pushed up from the bed and tested the sneakers out. They felt a bid odd but comfortingly familiar.

She glanced at her watch; she had a plan. *If I hurry I can get to the store before it closes. I think I will make a nice send-off dinner for Jake before he leaves. It's the least I can do.* Downstairs she pulled her purse and coat out of the closet and padded toward her old Honda, her old shoes giving her a new spring to her step.

She prowled up and down the grocery market aisles, selecting a marbled steak and fresh vegetables. She had been distracted this morning and felt awful that she hadn't been a bit more attentive to Jake's excitement. Rebecca wanted to mend some fences before he left, and she was hoping to talk with him in more depth when he returned from the car show. She was no fool to think that the marriage wasn't in trouble, but perhaps with some counselling ... well, who knew. She also decided to make Jake's favourite dessert, chocolate cake. As she strolled, she could hear snickering from behind her. Two young women she recognized as part of Olivia's 'social posse' were standing with their heads together; whispering and giggling. Snippets of their conversation carried down the aisle.

"Take a look at her; I swear she is getting bigger every day. I remember her from school, she was so fit then, and now she is as big as a whale." Rebecca looked directly at the pair as she neared them. She mustered her courage and nodded at them. "Susan, Cara," she mumbled and passed by.

Both women stared at her, and she caught one last cutting comment before she turned into the next aisle. "Did you see those shabby sneakers? She can't be thinking about taking up running again, what a lark." Their voices trailed off.

Rebecca felt colour seep into her cheeks. *Bitches!* She pushed the cart toward the cashiers, where she read a poster for the upcoming community race, Dash for Cash, sponsored by Proctor Automotive. The race was scheduled for September 4th; it gave her an idea.

I can run if I want, you just wait and see. While Jake is way, I can start training again, and by the end of August I will enter Dash for Cash. So there!

Rebecca admired her newfound determination; she felt empowered. She paid for her groceries and hastened to her car; she wanted to get started on Jake's dinner.

By six o'clock Rebecca had the cake baked and frosted, the vegetables chopped, and the coals heating in the barbeque. She had taken the time to bathe, curl her hair, and make the extra effort to look nice. Now all she needed was Jake. She looked at the clock.

Maybe he got caught up with further preparations for the show? I'll text him.

She was hoping he would be surprised by her efforts and it would make up for the last few days of tension. She messaged him that dinner was ready, and asked when she could expect him. Her phone chimed, and she eagerly read the text.

The message read: '*Won't be home until much later. Going out with the boys.*'

Her heart sank. She set the phone down and looked at all her hard work.

I shouldn't be surprised. A chocolate cake cannot cure anything. She felt disappointed and looked at the food on the counter. *Or can it?*

Her eyes had latched onto the frosted cake; she pulled open the utensil drawer and brought out a fork.

She had befriended food on many occasions, and the cake would ease her wounded heart. Just as she set to devour it, she spotted her old runners sitting by the back door. Slowly she set the fork down, recalling the taunts she endured at the grocery store.

She caught her reflection in the front hall mirror.

I am so tired of people's negative opinion of me, but I am my own worst critic! The fat shaming has to stop ... now!

Looking away from her image, her attention was drawn to a framed picture of her parents that was sitting on the hall table. Her father had always been her biggest cheerleader and supporter until his tragic death in a car accident.

What would Dad say if he saw me now? she thought. *He'd kick my butt, is what he would do! He would tell me to get on with it.* She paused for a moment, and then shouted aloud. "Enough!"

Rebecca bundled the whole cake in the rubbish bin, then went up to the bedroom. She shoved aside the suitcases and dug through the closet. She located a pair of Jake's old sweat pants and a loose T-shirt, knowing none of her old exercise garments would fit. She donned the garments and at the back door laced up her old reliable sneaks.

"Well, here we go!" she said to the pictures on the hall table. "Now where should I start?" She caught site of the dried red clay on her shoes and said, "Lachlan Pathway it is!"

Twilight was just creeping over the mountains when Rebecca arrived at the mountain pathway. It was still early summer and it had rained the previous day, leaving the area cloaked in a misty blanket; the fresh new grass was covered in fat droplets. As she took a cleansing breathe, the cool air tingled her nose and made her feel refreshed and reborn. She couldn't recall the last time she had felt this way, and she welcomed the sensation.

She surveyed her surroundings; running in the dark wasn't the safest, but she was familiar with the terrain, having run and walked it many times before with both her father and Jake. She enjoyed the mountain's rugged beauty and its solitude. It was perfect for restarting her exercise program far from prying judgmental eyes. She locked her little Honda and entered the pathway area, where she stretched and prepared her unfamiliar muscles. She started at a brisk walk, and then picked up her pace to a slow jog. She had to stop on multiple occasions to catch her breath. As she rounded the sharp corner at Skye Pointe Bend, her feet slipped on the damp, rocky pathway. Nearly careening over the steep edge, she flailed for a moment and grasped a tree branch to regain her balance.

"Holy shit!" she gasped, teetering on the cliff edge. She peered cautiously over the embankment to the raging waters below. In the dim light, she looked into the turbulent waters of Campbell River.

If I'd fallen over, I could've been swept away, and no one would be able to find me. Would they even care? She sighed recalling her recent disappointment.

She picked herself up and brushed the dirt from her clothes. This time taking more care, she eased her way down the remainder of the sharp slope to the parking lot below. Despite her nearly fatal fall, she had enjoyed her first run. Her limbs felt heavy and her muscles ached, but she felt invigorated.

As her little car puttered home, she caught sight of a fancy vehicle hidden in the shadows of the parking lot. *Could that be Olivia's car? What would she be doing out here?* Olivia's sporty red Porsche was a distinct feature here in Campbell River, but the light was poor now so she couldn't be sure.

Was there someone it in? She was sure she could see two shadows with their heads close together. Suddenly a deer darted out in front of her car, narrowly missing her.

I'd better get home before I do myself in! She drove home without further incidence, vowing to return every evening to practice and re-familiarize herself with the race course.

CHAPTER THIRTEEN

"Slow down, Olivia!" Jake shifted her off his lap. His legs were going to sleep with her sitting on top of him in the confines of her tiny red sports car. "Why couldn't we get a hotel room? This isn't exactly comfortable!"

Normally they snuck into the Proctor Estate guest house located in a secluded area of the property, but today Olivia insisted they must go someplace else.

"We can't go to Proctor Estate because Andie and his creepy friend Chief Kevin are there. I find that man is always watching me; it's like he can see into my soul. He's so weird." She shuddered. "Anyway, we need a private place to discuss our plans."

"You're being paranoid, Olivia." Jake rubbed his face. "And these so-called plans of yours are going nowhere."

He was tired and didn't want to fight with her. He needed to be fresh for tomorrow when the Proctor team was leaving for the car show. This was an opportunity of a lifetime, and he didn't want to mess it up. He hoped this would further launch his career, and right now Olivia's crazy plans were on the back burner.

"What? Going nowhere?" she hissed. "Don't get me started, Jake Adams. You need to stop stalling. I told you to speak with the lawyer again, there must be something we can do about Fred Wright's will."

"I did go see him, and he told me all I could do is divorce her. He said I could battle her to get half the property, but it could be a lengthy process because the will stipulates that Rebecca is the sole heir. I bet old man Wright added that clause to the will, because he knew about our affair." he frowned. "Shit!

We need money now. And you burn through money; you've already spent your annual allowance!"

"I know! You don't have to rub it in my face. It's expensive to keep up my image!" Olivia scowled, then turned the blame back on him.

"Shit Jake, why didn't you let Rebecca die when she slashed her wrists? She gave us two chances to get rid of her, and instead you, the big hero, jumped in to help out. She's so pathetic, she couldn't even kill herself."

She paused, and an evil smile played across her face. "What did the lawyer say would happen if she died?"

"Jeez, I would get it all, but I'm not going to kill my wife, Olivia! I've done enough of your dirty work!" He turned away from her. He didn't want her to see the disgust on his face.

"No, but she can kill herself! We just need to give her the final push."

"How? Throw her off the cliff into the river!?" He gestured toward Lachlan Pathway. The couple had chosen this secluded park because it was usually deserted at this time of night. They had only seen one lone car in the parking lot.

"No idiot, she can kill herself. Perhaps pills; she certainly has enough of them. I've seen your medicine cabinet, and she has a total pharmacy. The quack of a doctor she sees keeps prescribing her all sorts of things: antidepressants, mood elevators, diet pills. Old Doc Grainger probably just wants her to go away too." She grinned.

"And we can help her do that." She giggled and lunged at Jake.

"How?" He sighed.

She climbed back onto his lap. "Leave it to me, lover. I've got ideas." She nuzzled his neck and nibbled his ears. He inhaled her perfume; it was a new scent called 'Devilish,' and it overwhelmed his resistance.

As the couple kissed and fondled, the glare of headlights played across the car, lighting it up. The lone car in the lot was leaving the area now; Jake squinted at the bright headlights as it passed by.

Was that Rebecca's car? Is she spying on us? He didn't think she was that clever. He tried to see more clearly, but Olivia pulled his attention back; the car's ownership soon forgotten.

CHAPTER FOURTEEN

Sometime during the night, Jake came home and once again crashed on the couch. That is where Rebecca found him, snoring soundly, so she shook him awake. "Jake! You need to get up. Andie wants you at the shop early this morning, and it's already seven o'clock."

He awoke with a start, then staggered upstairs for a shower. A waft of spicy, exotic perfume trailed after him.

"Gee, you stink of bad perfume. I thought you were out with the boys last night; it smells like you were drinking at the perfume counter. Toss me out your clothes, and I'll throw them in the washing machine for you."

"I said I was out with the boys, so are you doubting me?" He glowered. "And never mind, I'll throw them in the wash myself."

He abruptly closed the bathroom door in her face. She blinked in surprise and went downstairs to the kitchen to fetch him a cup of coffee.

Hung over again, she thought. *This is happening too often. When he returns, we definitely need to talk. Things cannot go on this way.*

Several minutes later he exited the bathroom, freshly scrubbed and more alert. Rebecca met him with the strong black cup of coffee, just the way he liked it. "Thanks." he muttered.

As he tossed his clothes in the washing machine, he jostled the cup, slopping the inky liquid onto his clean T-shirt. "Shit! Now I'm going to be even later!"

Jake thrust the cup back at her, spilling coffee on the floor and down the front of Rebecca's housecoat. He dashed back upstairs where she could hear him rummaging through the dresser drawers. He had struggled into a clean shirt and now clambered downstairs pulling his suitcases behind him.

"Thanks for packing my bags," he muttered, then after slamming the front door, he was gone. She heard him rev his truck engine and roar off down the street.

"Have a good time at the show and good luck," she called to the empty space. She shook her head. *So much for attempting to reconcile.* She thought as she stripped off her soiled housecoat. In his haste to leave, Jake had forgotten to start the wash cycle.

Might as well add it to his load. Opening the lid, the strong smell of perfume washed over her. *Holy crow Jake, did you bathe in it?* Rebecca didn't usually wear perfume, and the only person she knew who regularly doused themselves was Olivia, and this was not her usual scent. She puzzled about it, then poured soap in the machine and turned it on hot.

Need to wash that stink away.

Rebecca went about tidying up and getting ready for work; she planned to arrive late, not wanting to be pulled into the day's drama, especially if Olivia was going to be in attendance. Olivia still continued to quietly sulk, but she seemed to be scheming about something. When she did appear at the shop, she was all whispers with someone on her phone.

I bet she'll crash the event. Rebecca surmised. *Nobody would be surprised!*

When Rebecca eventually arrived at the shop, the mechanics had just finished loading the show car in the cargo van, and were lashing it down to prevent any damage to the vehicle during transport. Andie had rented two other passenger vans, and the crew was loading their suitcases and personal items. The area was a flurry of activity; everyone was preparing for the departure, but Jake was nowhere to be seen. And thankfully, Olivia was absent.

"Morning Andie, all set to go?"

Andie was standing with the senior mechanic, Randi Everett, reviewing a checklist of necessary equipment for the show. Rebecca could see he had everything well in hand; Andie was a very capable organizer. His organizational skills had been tested on many occasions, both at work and in the community; he was the sponsor for the annual Dash for Cash event she was contemplating entering.

"All set Rebecca, you sure you will be okay? I will have my cellphone on at all times if you need anything. Chief Pritchard is doing to be joining me as a guest at the show. He will be flying down in two days' time, so Deputy Janice Sinclair will be available if you need any help; feel free to call her."

Rebecca nodded. She had often seen Kevin Pritchard, the Campbell River Police Chief, at the shop talking with the mechanics and visiting with Andie. He was an avid car collector, and he and Andie seemed to have a developed an automotive bond.

She recalled that Chief Pritchard had been one of the few on the police force that felt she was innocent of Indie's death. He never believed the testimony of the principal witness—her neighbour, Edith Graham—that claimed Rebecca had pushed Indie from the upstairs window.

She remembered that his comments at the trial had helped soothe her worries. "That old gal is as blind as a bat. Even with her glasses on she can barely see past the tip of her nose! How can the Crown Prosecutor believe such lies? You did not push your son, he tragically fell." Thank God for the man's diligence on the case; if it wasn't for him, Edith Graham's testimony may have sent her to jail.

Edith Graham. She called again last night. There was another message on the phone. I wonder why she suddenly wants to talk to me so badly.

She was startled from her musing by the blaring of a horn.

"Best get this show on the road. We have many hours of driving before us!" Andie had leaned into the van and was laying on the horn. "Let's get going folks. Say where is Jake?" Andie looked around, and moments later Jake came running from behind the shop area.

"Sorry boss! I was just finishing up on ... a car I was working on."

Jake hastily tucked in his shirt and smoothed his hair.

"Oh hi, Rebecca, I gotta go."

For appearances sake, he planted a chaste kiss on Rebecca's cheek and bundled into the van with the rest of the crew. As he pulled the sliding door shut, his glaze carried over Rebecca's head toward the shop. She followed the direction of his glance and spotted Olivia peering out from the mechanic bay door; she blew lusty air kisses at the crew.

"See you soon guys." she called out.

Rebecca waved goodbye to the crew. "Good luck!" she said to the passing vans. She waited until the vehicles had vanished before entering the shop. She was curious as to what Olivia was up to in the mechanic bay.

She skirted the front receptionists and headed toward the mechanic bay in search of Olivia. She pushed the heavy doors open and found the area deserted. "Olivia?" she called. Her voice echoed in the empty space. She walked through the bay to the back doors. Standing on tiptoes, she peeked out the back windows and saw Olivia get into her car. She sighed in relief as the red Porsche zipped off the lot.

Although she was still curious about what Olivia had been doing, it was probably best she hadn't found her because she wanted to update some of the inventory files while Andie was gone. Since the recent incident with Darren Burke, she wanted to ensure nothing else was amiss.

Now let's see what I can do to freshen up Andie's files. I wonder if the up-to-date password is in his desk because he does change the password on a regular basis.

Determined to get started on the task, she let herself into Andie's office. She sat down in his chair and unlocked the desk; it didn't take long for Rebecca to find the new password. It was in the secret compartment where Andie stored his treats. When she pulled a little harder she was surprised to find that the drawer extended out another eight inches, and in the back portion of this compartment there was a box containing multiple computer disks, each labelled with a different date.

What's this all about? She plucked one of the disks from the box dated three days ago, and then inserted it into the computer. She saw a surveillance video of Proctor Automotive come up on the screen, divided into four separate views: the mechanic bay, the store room, the front reception area, and the hallway leading from the front reception to the bay.

"You crafty fellow!" Rebecca laughed. "You have been watching us! That explains the invoices that I came across." She watched the video some more and chuckled to herself. Having viewed enough, she pulled it from the machine, then slipped it back into its case. She selected another disk.

I guess this is how you found out that Burke was stealing. I wonder what other mischief you have seen? She scanned the next disk. *Doesn't look too interesting; just Proctor business as usual.*

She replaced the disks, not realizing that she misfiled them. She pushed the drawer closed and typed the password into the computer.

Now down to business.

Rebecca spent the remainder of the morning sorting and updating the inventory files. Pushing back from the desk she looked at her watch, it was only noon. She got up from the boss' desk and prowled the empty shop; the receptionists were working on updating the brochures and displays, and the two remaining mechanics were working on an old truck. She was torn about leaving early, but Andie had said to take some time off. She would need to return to lock up at six o'clock, but she did want to check on Magda. It had been a couple of days since she had visited her, and the creepy landlord made Rebecca feel uncomfortable.

Stopping at the receptionist desk, she called to Tamara and Ashley. They were busy tidying the front reception area and seemed engrossed in conversation.

"Ladies." They looked up.

"Yes Rebecca?" They responded in unison.

"I'm going to take some time off this afternoon, but I will be back at six to lock up. I have my cellphone with me if you need anything. Here is my number." She handed them the slip of paper, then turned to leave.

"See you at six." She returned to Andie's office to secure the desk drawer and the office door before she left.

CHAPTER FIFTEEN

On the way to her car, Rebecca placed a call to Magda from her cellphone. She had decided she was going to cook a late lunch and bring it to Magda's to share with her. The steak and vegetables she had planned to serve Jake sat uncooked in her refrigerator. She thought it would be nice to share a meal with someone, and she was eager to hear the remainder of Magda's sad tale. She felt comfort in this woman's presence.

"Hello, who is this?" croaked a shaky voice.

"Magda, it is Rebecca ... Rebecca Adams?"

"So nice to hear from you! Are you coming to see me? I so enjoy our visits. You are becoming like family."

Rebecca suddenly felt teary. She hadn't had a real family since Indie's accident. It felt so splendid to be part of something again, for so long she had been isolated.

"You bet. I'm going to make lunch to bring for us, and I will be there within the hour."

"How wonderful, and I will be waiting. Come soon. We have much to talk about!"

Rebecca quickly drove home, then prepared the steak and vegetables for their meal. Just as she was wrapping up the food and placing it in a cooler bag, the phone rang. She let the phone go to message because her hands were covered with food matter.

"Rebecca, I am calling you once again. It is Edith Graham, your neighbour. Can we please talk ... soon?"

The message ended, and the machine beeped. Rebecca stood with her mouth hanging open. *Really! Again? As if I don't know who you are!*

Rebecca washed her hands, then erased the message. *She sure is insistent. Perhaps I'll give her a call sometime, but for now I have a delicious luncheon to share with my new family.* She bundled the food items into an insulated carry bag, then headed for the door.

Across the street opposite the Wright house, the curtains parted as Ethel Graham replaced the phone in the cradle and peered out the window. Here at her perch in the living room window, she spent much of her time watching the comings and goings in the neighbourhood. She considered herself the neighbourhood watch, but the neighbours just thought she was a busy body. It was from here that she claimed she saw Rebecca Adams push her young son from the bedroom window. She reached for her thick lensed glasses and peeped out the window. As Rebecca drove past in her car, Ethel strained to see.

Is that Rebecca Adams? I wish she would call me back. I need to tell her something. I want to right a very bad wrong. She sighed and continued her ongoing surveillance.

CHAPTER SIXTEEN

Rebecca pulled into Magda's parking lot, on the lookout for the strange landlord. *Coast is clear!*

She eased from the car and moved swiftly across the lot, bundling the bag of food with her. She pressed the intercom buzzer and patiently awaited entry. When it didn't open she tried again and then Magda's voice came over the speaker. "The door lock is broken; it doesn't work. I will come to let you in!" When Magda finally opened the front door Rebecca was met with a broad smile and an exuberant greeting.

"Pozdrawiam moją córkę. Proszę wejdź!!"

"Pardon?" Rebecca was taken aback by the greeting.

"Come in. Come in. I just said you were my daughter." She waved the young woman into the building and gave her a big huge. Rebecca returned the embrace in kind.

Rebecca pulled away and as they walked towards Magda's apartment she showed Magda the cooler bag. "I brought food; steak and vegetables."

As Magda's pushed open her apartment door she exclaimed. "Beautiful, let me set it out for us. Now sit and relax!"

Magda took the food to the small kitchenette and dished out the meal on plates. She returned to the living room, the aroma wafting in with her. "It looks delicious, and you are so kind!" She handed a plate to Rebecca.

"Shall we say a prayer? To remind us how blessed we truly are?" They bowed their heads and Magda said a few words blessing the food and their new friendship.

They ate in silence savouring the fare. Satiated, Rebeca insisted on clearing away the dishes and packaging up the remainder. She placed the leftovers in

Magda's sparse refrigerator, insisting Magda keep it for her tomorrow's meal. Magda graciously accepted as her budget was very tight. As Rebecca cleaned, Magda made tea. She had offered her guest another sip of brandy, but Rebecca declined as she needed to return to the shop to complete the lock-up, and she also she wanted to get in another run tonight. She was just starting to regain some balance and agility during her nightly runs, but with the trail hazards, adding alcohol to the mixture could spell disaster and mishap.

With mugs of sweet steeped tea and full bellies, the women sat enjoying the quiet companionship that had developed between them. Eventually Magda interrupted the tranquillity.

"Shall I continue?"

Rebecca sat back deeper into the worn armchair. "Please do."

"I think I told you Elena had a difficult time adjusting to her new life here ...

Rebecca sat listening to the story of Elena's steady decline into a life of drugs, bad men, and depravity. She became more and more reclusive, spending little time at home. They argued constantly; Magda sought to curb Elena's behaviour, and Elena rebelled by spiralling out of control. Magda worried constantly about her, especially when Elena didn't come home for days and nights at a time.

The police brought her home on many occasions, sometimes due to wild intoxicated behaviour and sometimes for soliciting money for sexual favours. Besides stealing money from Magda's purse, Elena was using sex to earn money to feed her drug fueled demons. The police were reluctant to arrest her; it would have meant too much paperwork. Magda had begged the officers to take her in and get her help, but nothing seemed to change the downhill course Elena's life had taken.

During this time, Magda found out Elena was pregnant; the father unknown. It could have been a fellow junkie or a man who paid to use her for sex. She arrived ill and battered, begging to crash at Magda's; she promised she would reform her ways. She said she wanted to be a good mother.

"I want to be a good momma like mine was to me. Before she and papa died, they both loved me so. I will be better. I promise. Just let me stay."

At times Elena tried hard to change her behaviour, eating better, and trying to stop smoking, but her addictions drew her back to her old habits. Her promises didn't last long, and eventually Elena gave birth to a frail baby girl she named Sylvie. The babe was dependent on the street drugs her mother had used throughout her entire pregnancy.

"She was addicted, just like her junkie mother. The poor baby spent months in hospital, withdrawing from the drugs that sickened her as she grew in her mother's womb. Sylvie was frail, and in the first few months it didn't look like she would live to see her first birthday. Elena told me she hoped the baby would just die in her sleep because it would be easier for her. I knew she didn't mean easier for the baby but for herself."

The old woman shook her head and locked onto Rebecca's eyes. "Each time Sylvie came home from the hospital it wasn't long before she was readmitted for another reason. Malnutrition, pneumonia, skin infections; the poor babe suffered it all. Elena cared nothing for the child, just her next fix. I wanted to adopt Sylvie, but the social workers insisted a child is better off with their own parent, even if they are a worthless drug addict," she spat.

The social system had set Elena and Sylvie up in their own little apartment, but it was no place to raise a baby; more a flop house and drug den then a home. To keep her apartment and continue receiving welfare monies, Elena grew clever. Before the social worker came by for 'well baby checks', Elena would hurriedly tidy up the place and temporarily toss out her fellow druggies. She knew how to play the game.

Despite Magda's involvement baby Sylvie did not thrive, and Elena complained to the social workers that the monies she received were not enough. The truth was her mother barely provided for Sylvie, using the milk money to feed her own addictions. Magda attempted to intervene but her pleas fell on deaf ears. As soon as the social worker left, the drug users would return like rats to a rotting feast. They often brought others and some even worse than themselves.

"I did what I could and Sylvie often stayed with me, especially when Elena wanted to party. I provided her good food and medicine when she needed it. She was a sickly baby but a merry soul. She always had a happy disposition, despite Elena's neglect. She was my joy ... my happiness ... my reason to live."

"I was sick the night Sylvie went missing. I was laid up in bed suffering from the flu, and I still regret I didn't take her. I was worried I would make her sick, but all I did was make her dead."

A silence hung between them, until Magda continued.

"Her own mother supplied the drugs that killed her! The police believed it happened during a party that Elena hosted. They think someone put something in the baby's milk, probably as some sick joke! Sylvie's autopsy showed fentanyl, a strong pain killer, in her system. It stopped her breathing." She sighed.

"Elena told the police that Sylvie had been abducted. She told the police that someone at the party had stolen my precious girl. She played the part of the distraught mother, weeping and begging them to find Sylvie. Foolishly we believed her. And well, the rest is history. She was only twenty months when she left me."

Rebecca could feel Magda's anger; it was palpable in the room.

"I remember the search for your granddaughter; my husband and I volunteered. Jake and I were still in high school, but I remember how sad I felt when she was found. Oh Magda, I'm ..."

The old woman interjected.

"Yes, she was dead all along, stuffed in a suitcase under the stairs in her mother's shabby apartment. Damn her ... damn her all the way to hell. Someone stuffed my poor baby in a suitcase. Elena denied doing it, but she was so drugged up she couldn't remember anything. I know she lied, she was an expert at it!"

The woman had slumped in her chair; deflated and exhausted, her head hanging low. Then she unexpectedly rose and asked Rebecca to leave.

"Forgive my rudeness, but all this talking about such bad memories has made me so very tired, you must go. Please, we will talk later."

Magda pulled up from her chair, leaning heavily on her cane and shuffled unsteadily on her feet. Rebecca leapt forward to assist the elderly woman.

"No!" The old woman shook off the help. "No help! Thank you for coming, but please leave."

As they reached the apartment door, Magda turned to apologize; trying to explain. "I am sorry I cannot tell any more for now. There is more to Sylvie's story that you must hear, but this hurts my heart so."

Magda closed the door in Rebecca's face. It clicked shut leaving Rebecca on the other side, staring at peeling paint. Rebecca was stunned by Magda's bizarre statement, but mostly she was worried about Magda. The old woman's health seemed to be failing since she started to tell Rebecca her story. She turned to leave but paused. She thought about going back to check on Magda, but she knew she needed to respect the woman's space. Walking to her car, Rebecca vowed to make visiting Magda a priority.

CHAPTER SEVENTEEN

I cy blue eyes closely observed Rebecca as she entered Magda's apartment building. Olivia had borrowed Andie's BMW and waited until she saw Rebecca leave the shop, and then she had followed her. She hadn't driven her red Porsche because she wanted to be incognito, better to stalk Rebecca. If Rebecca was going to be manipulated into taking her own life, Olivia needed to know more about her recent habits. The friendship had become strained over the past year, and Olivia had no idea where Rebecca spent her time.

For years Rebecca had been chased and harassed, especially by Gretchen Berg, the Gazette reporter who had coined the label, 'Campbell River Baby Killer.' Now that the trial had ended and the story had gone stale, no one sought her out or followed her; even the reporter had stopped hounding her. Rebecca had fallen of the radar, with only the label tagging along, so she would have been very surprised to know that Olivia was stalking her.

I feel like a spy! Olivia chuckled to herself. *Too bad it wasn't for something more exciting.* She had followed two cars behind Rebecca, turning when she turned, and was surprised when she stopped outside a shabby apartment building.

What the hell? Who lives here? She had parked across the street and waited. She watched as Rebecca pressed the intercom and several moments later an elderly woman greeted her. They seemed to know each other.

Curious? Best wait and see what this is all about. She sat patiently for about sixty minutes, and then she got restless.

"This is boring," she snorted. She had been checking out her Facebook and Instagram pages on her phone but had lost interest. She had tossed her phone on the seat when she had noticed a scruffy man who seemed to be checking her out. *There are so many weirdos in this neighbourhood!*

Olivia didn't want a confrontation with this man so decided to leave, but she fully intended to return. As she drove away, she watched the man from the rear-view mirror; he used a key to enter the same front door that Rebecca had recently entered.

"The creep must live here; nice place." she scoffed.

Olivia had pulled a U-turn and passed the building again, but she decided not to park this time, choosing instead to drive to Charlotte's Confectionaries to tank up on her favourite coffee beverage.

I need to know who Rebecca is visiting. Who does she know in this neighbourhood? What is she up to? Finishing her drink, she got back into Andie's car and returned to the apartment block.

Good, Rebecca's car is still here.

Olivia circled the block and found a parking spot under a large tree. Slipping from the vehicle and ensuring it was securely locked—she didn't trust this shanty neighbourhood—she walked toward the apartment building. She wanted to check out the woman's name on the tenant list, but was unnerved by the strange man. She dug in her bag for her can of pepper spray; if the creep returned, he was going to get a healthy dose. She quickly scanned the list, and under apartment 106, found the name, "***Bodrug, M.***"

Who's M. Bodrug?

Olivia heard the front door open, so she ducked behind a hedge and spied Rebecca leaving the complex. She seemed to be upset.

"What are you up to, girlie!?" A gruff voice came from behind her. Olivia jumped in fright, emptying her entire can of pepper spray into the man's face.

As he screaked and rubbed his burning eyes, Oliva beat a hasty retreat. She didn't want to stick around when it wore off; she couldn't imagine the hulk of a man would be too happy. Besides she had some homework to do, and she also had to get ready for her trip to Las Vegas. She was planning on surprising both the men in her life.

CHAPTER EIGHTEEN

O livia snickered as she drove herself back to Proctor Estate. She was laughing at the man's expense; amused by his frantic reaction to the chemical sprayed in his face. She enjoyed thinking about his pain.

Serves you right asshole, sneaking up on me like that! She punched in the security gate code and drove up the gravelled drive to the lavish mansion.

She was pleased with herself; the surveillance had been productive so far, but she needed more to guarantee success. She had learned that Rebecca only spent time grocery shopping, walking at Lachlan Pathway, and visiting the cemetery, but other than that her life was pretty dull and insignificant; no one would even miss her if she was gone. Rebecca had no secrets, except for this 'new friend,' and Olivia would have to check out this 'M.Bodrug'.

Time to ruin your life, Rebecca. One by one your supports are disappearing, and soon it will be your turn.

She grinned as she tossed her keys on the front hall table. At the well-stocked bar, she poured herself a glass of red wine, then ambled into her office where she settled in front of her computer. She booted up the device and waited for the internet to come on line. While she waited, she sipped the wine, its heady bouquet relaxing her. She was still wired from her day of spying, and the angry confrontation with that 'weirdo' had left her unsettled.

This spying shit is tiring! She stretched and leaned back in her chair. *I need to know more about this woman that Rebecca is visiting, she might play to my advantage.*

She thought she knew everything about Rebecca but apparently, she didn't. As far as Olivia was aware Rebecca had no other family; both her parents were gone, and she had no siblings. During all the tragic events in Rebecca's life, she,

Jake, and Andie had been the only people to stand by her. No other relatives had ever come forward to provide support. Thinking back, Olivia couldn't remember Rebecca ever mentioning an elderly relative, so who was M. Bodrug?

"Relatives!" She snorted and took a big gulp of wine. "I certainly could live without some of mine!"

Olivia had an elderly aunt that was a financial and emotional burden; a real mill stone. During a rare sentimental moment, Olivia's mother had taken on the care of her spinster aunt. The old crone was her mother's only remaining relative, and Gloria Baird had felt obligated to support her; nobody else wanted her. So, when the Bairds relocated to Campbell River, Auntie Edith had come too.

However, obligation didn't necessarily mean they wanted her too close; she was an odd woman with bizarre outbursts and tendencies to fabricate elaborate stories. Gloria Baird wanted her physical needs met—but at a very long arm's length!

Olivia's mother had settled Auntie in a little house, complete with a housekeeper and gardener, on the opposite side of town from the Bairds. The first employees lasted only two weeks before they fled the house, unable to cope with the eccentric old lady. Unable to maintain long term help, Olivia was assigned the chore. Every week Olivia would bear the humiliating burden of visiting the old woman, and even assisting with her care.

One time the old bitch made me clean out the spiders in the attic! She shuddered as she remembered the dark, musty attic and the horrid hairy spiders that threatened to drop into her hair.

I should lock her in the attic and see how she likes it.

In high school, Olivia was worried that people would find out that the old woman was a relative and paint her in the same light; a nasty shade of crazy.

As she waited on the computer, Olivia recalled the frantic phone call from her mother *'to come home immediately'* because her father was ill. Alex Baird had been taking multiple medications to control his heart condition, including a blood thinner for an irregular heartbeat. Olivia had arrived to chaos and a hysterical mother; Gloria was never known for coping well with illness. Her father had been complaining of severe stomach pain all day and just as Olivia arrived, he vomited copious amounts of blood; splattering himself and his daughter. Olivia reeled away in horror. How dare her father do this to her!

She was initially paralyzed by the ghastly scene, but she managed to call 911 and dispatched her parents to the hospital. After the ambulance pulled away, lights flashing and sirens blaring, she was left to deal with the bloody chaotic aftermath. There was so much blood; it had sprayed her clothes and hands. She scrubbed the offensive 'stuff' off her person ... it took forever to feel clean again!

After Olivia's father death, a devastated Gloria Baird moved back to Vancouver, offloading the care of her aging aunt onto Olivia.

As she poured another glass of red wine, the dark burgundy colour sparked more memories. Olivia shuddered. *It was a real tragedy; my best pair of expensive shoes was ruined, and worse, I inherited my 'crazy' auntie!* She swirled the dark liquid, downed the glass, and poured another.

She rubbed her hands together unconsciously, attempting to wash away the memory of the blood. From that day forward even the thought of blood made her feel weak and vulnerable; something she hated about herself.

Years later, she was still paying for her aunt's lodging, food, and medical bills, secretly using some of the yearly allowance she received from Andie. She felt it was an enormous waste of her monies; the woman was a burden. Olivia had had little contact with her Auntie Ethel until she realized she could manipulate the old crone to do her bidding.

Ethel's property was kitty-corner to the Wright's; her front windows faced their side yard. Although the woman was unstable and a threat to Olivia's image, the set-up couldn't be more perfect; she now had her own personal spy. From that day on, she had continuing surveillance of Rebecca, and of course, Jake. She made Auntie report all comings and goings at the Wright house.

Initially Auntie Ethel refused to spy, that was until Olivia played her trump card. It turned out that the old woman was afraid that Olivia was going to put her in a nursing home.

"Nursing homes are for loopy, broken-down old people! The staff will lock me in my room, and no one will come to visit me. And they will starve me." She begged Olivia for mercy. "Please don't send me away. I will do whatever you want."

"Don't worry dear Auntie, I won't send you away," she had crooned." But I do need you to do something for me, and then everything can go on the same. You can continue to live here in your little house and I will provide for you, but remember this is only if you do as I say."

Realizing she was locked in a no-win situation, the elderly woman silently nodded in agreement; she would do her niece's bidding. The old woman was afraid of her young niece, but worse than fear was the knowledge she needed Olivia's reluctant generosity to survive. Like many people in her life, Olivia now owned the old woman. She was another of Olivia's puppets with strings to manipulate and pull anytime Olivia desired.

I need to do something about Auntie. Olivia sipped her wine. She *knows too much about me, and she has secrets she could use against me. Perhaps it's time to put her away for good! But for now, let's find out what Rebecca has been up to.*

She entered the name she had found at the apartment into the computer search engine, then waited. Several minutes later the computer rewarded her patience with the same information that Rebecca had previously uncovered.

Oh my, what have we here? Interesting! She pondered her next steps. She clicked 'white pages' on the computer, then typed in 'Magda Bodrug.' She was rewarded with a phone number.

Time to place a call. She grinned.

CHAPTER NINETEEN

Unaware that Olivia was watching her from Andie's car, Rebecca hastened across the parking lot. She checked her watch. *Damn it, late again!* She sped all the way to Proctor Automotive, arriving just as Tamara and Ashley were about to leave.

"We thought you had forgotten about us?" Ashley huffed.

"Sorry ladies. See you tomorrow!"

Rebecca locked the doors behind them, and then checked the remainder of the shop, ensuring all the doors and windows were secure. As she walked through the empty building, she found herself scanning the roof lines for hidden cameras. She recalled the locations from the video tapes and with careful observation was able to spot two of them; one in the mechanic bay and one in the office corridor.

Whoever installed them certainly knew their stuff. If Andie wanted them to be a secret, they certainly are well hidden. Clever Andie, I guess I will have to mind my manners!

She glanced at her watch and noticed the light was starting to fade. *I must get going if I want to fit in my evening run.* Her muscles were stiff and achy from her previous run, but she found she actually welcomed this sensation.

She set the alarm, then drove off toward Lachlan Pathway, her thoughts returning to the earlier events at Magda's home. The woman's story gave her lots to ponder while she ran.

* * *

It had been two days since the team had left for the car show. All had been uneventful at the shop, and Rebecca was cherishing the peace and quiet. After she locked up the offices and started her drive home, she felt a sense of calm. It was a fair evening; a light breeze stirred the leaves along the tree lined boulevards. She remembered other evenings like this; ones spent strolling with Indie in his buggy, Jake at her side. She passed the cemetery and spied Magda seating on the bench near her family's gravestones. She had been planning on visiting her friend tonight, so she turned into the parking lot to offer a ride. She wanted Magda to continue her story.

Rebecca walked quietly through the headstones, respecting the serenity. She quietly whispered Magda's name and touched her shoulder. The woman startled, grabbing at her chest.

"Oh, it's you, Rebecca! I need to catch my breath! I was dreaming of Elena, then suddenly you were here, staring down at me. I thought she had come back to haunt me! In this light you look so much like her."

"I am so sorry!" Rebecca grabbed the older woman's hand. "I didn't mean to frighten you; I just wanted to offer you a ride home. It is getting late, and I didn't want you walking alone."

"Many thanks," Magda sighed. "Let's sit for just a minute. I apologize for my bad behaviour the other day. I am not the little old lady you think I am. After I finish my story you might think differently of me, and I have grown so fond of you."

Rebecca looked at Magda, and she wondered what this gentle old woman could have done that was so shocking. Magda had loved her family and only wanted the best for them.

Magda patted the bench, indicating Rebecca to join her. Quietly she slipped her withered hand into Rebecca's. The two women sat side by side, each engrossed in their own thoughts; their new bond was a soothing balm.

The evening blush had faded into indigo when Rebecca finally spoke.

"I should get you home, Magda. It's starting to get late, and I also should get home as well." She was going to an empty house, but that suited her just fine. The peacefulness was soothing after the last months of turmoil. She stood and offered her hand to the other woman.

Magda rejected the assistance, and she slowly rose from the bench. She turned and looked directly into Rebecca's face, her face suddenly flushed with emotion.

"Why are you rushing away to an empty house that you share with that wicked man? You've told me how he treats you, and yet you continue to waste your life with him." She stabbed a finger at Rebecca. "You need to change it, and soon!! Be brave, Rebecca Adams. Leave him! Do it before . . . "

Rebecca pulled back in surprise. "What?"

Magda only shook her head and shuffled toward Rebecca's car. Rebecca stood riveted in place, her mouth agape; she was stunned by the woman's sudden outburst. Magda was clutching the car door handle and breathing deeply when Rebecca finally caught up with her; her face was ashy and damp. The older woman suddenly dug in her purse and pulled out an inhaler. She rapidly fired two doses of medication into her mouth and inhaled deeply.

"For my heart, it is nitroglycerin." She gasped. Within a few minutes her breathing eased, and the colour returned to her ashen cheeks. "I need to sit." Rebecca opened the car door and eased Magda into the passenger seat, then moved around to the driver side and climbed in. Magda sat silently, offering no conversation or explanation.

Rebecca started the vehicle and headed toward the cemetery gate. "I need to know ..." she started to say, but Magda interrupted.

"You want to know why I spoke that way to you. I'm sorry; I am a silly old woman. I speak without thinking." Magda sat rigid in her seat, and the twosome drove in silence.

Rebecca didn't know that Magda was still shaken by a threatening phone call she had received last night. Magda was unsure how to approach the subject, so instead she remained silent. *How can I tell Rebecca I was threatened by her best friend, Olivia Proctor? The betrayal would be so painful!*

Not long after Rebecca had left last evening, the phone had rung. Magda was tired and thought twice about answering, but she assumed it was Rebecca, so she picked up. *She's probably calling to ensure that I'm okay.*

"Hello, is that you, Rebecca?"

"No Magda Bodrug, it is not Rebecca, but you'd better listen! I know all about your little dirty secret; it was interesting reading on the Internet. It may have been a few years ago, but I'm sure a little call to the local newspaper would refresh the story. Yeah, the newspaper would love a story about the Duncan baby murder and how you were implicated in your granddaughter's death! This boring old town could use a thrilling news story since the Campbell River Baby Killer story has gone stale. Just think how they would react when they discover that the Duncan murderer has moved her and is pals with our local villain? Does your dear sweet Rebecca know about your dark past?" The woman on the phone had laughed; her voice was cold and cunning.

"Listen old woman," she had continued. "Do not contact her again!"

After the woman had hung up, Magda had replaced her phone in the cradle and sat trembling. She had read the caller display, and it had flashed 'Proctor Estate.' She didn't fear for her own safety or reputation; let the bitch print the story, but what would it do to Rebecca?

Magda had spent the night fretting over this conversation; she needed to convince Rebecca of Olivia's deception before it was too late. She feared Rebecca could not survive another attack on her fragile person.

She had decided to visit the cemetery today; being near her loved ones gave her strength. She needed to warn Rebecca; she must help her flee the evil woman's grips. She was exhausted from the worrisome night and was grateful for the ride home. She just didn't have the energy to talk.

The awkwardness was palpable.

"No, I actually need to know how to get to your house from here. I can't recall the route. But now that you mention it, what did you mean?"

"I am an old woman who should keep her mouth shut." She gave brief directions, and several uncomfortable minutes later, they reached her apartment. Rebecca offered her arm to assist Magda, and this time she accepted. She maintained her stony silence as the pair lurched slowly up the walk. Hurt and confused by her friend's behaviour, Rebecca turned to depart. It was then that the old woman finally spoke.

"Please come see me tomorrow evening, and I will prepare dinner. We will talk then." With this she turned and shuffled inside, leaving a baffled Rebecca standing outside on the walkway.

CHAPTER TWENTY

The following evening Rebecca arrived as planned and was met by Magda at the front door; apparently the 'lazy landlord' had yet to fix the locking mechanism. As she followed Magda into the dimly lit apartment she wondered. *How will I be received after Magda's outburst last night?*

Although not extravagant by any means, Magda took pride in her home, keeping it neat and tidy, and Rebecca enjoyed its hominess. She peered at the many pictures placed throughout the room. The air smelled of cooking, and to break the awkwardness, Rebecca spoke first.

"Smells great!"

"Please sit for a moment before we enjoy our dinner. I saw you admiring my photos; do you have pictures of your own boy?"

Rebecca pulled out her cellphone. "Yes, on my phone. Let's see, I just need to type in my password, it's *'INDIE.'* It's kind of obvious being my son's name, but it's my way of keeping him close."

Rebecca scrolled through the device's memory and located Indie's pictures in the gallery App. She handed the phone to Magda, who flipped through the album's images. Rebecca was surprised by her friend's skill and comfort in using her cellphone; her own father had felt cellphones were a nuisance and preferred to use a 'good old fashioned' phone instead. Not for Magda, she was a skilled operator!

Noting Rebecca's surprised look, Magda smiled. "Elena had a phone like this; she showed me how to use it so I could look at the pictures she took of Sylvie. She even showed me how to take pictures and videos too."

She tapped on the camera App, pointed the phone at Rebecca and took her picture. "Surprised an old woman can use this?' She laughed. "Such clever things these little phones."

Magda finished looking at the pictures and handed the phone back to Rebecca. "Such a wonderful looking boy, such a loss!" Rebecca quietly nodded in agreement.

Magda returned from her tiny kitchen with two hearty bowls of vegetable soup and thick slabs of bread. "Not a fancy feast, but it's filling." She handed a bowl to Rebecca, who willingly accepted it.

"Delicious!" Rebecca slurped the soup with gusto. She hadn't eaten much all day, trying to lose some unwanted weight. After they finished the simple meal, Magda cleaned up the dishes and returned with two steaming mugs.

"Now we talk." Magda said as she placed the cup of tea on the table next to Rebecca.

Rebecca picked up the cup and blew on the hot liquid. "Tell me the rest of your story, Magda."

"No," the older woman replied. "Time to tell me your tale. How did you come to be this?" She waved a hand over Rebecca's person.

"What?" Rebecca choked on the hot liquid. "Me? Where would I start?" She stared at Magda, who coyly peered over the top of her chipped mug.

"At the beginning of, course!" Magda settled into her chair and crossed her arms.

* * *

"My story actually started after my mother passed away. I don't often talk about it; she had died the year before after a battle with cancer, and I was pretty lost without her. Olivia and Dad really tried to fill the gap, but I was still very sad and lonely. That was when I started running as a distraction, and I met Jake.

"I think we were both running away from something, but we ended up running into each other!" Rebecca laughed out loud.

"You know Magda, we both just loved spending time in the woods; the pathways and trails around Campbell River are so gorgeous. We found the running and hiking allowed us time to de-stress, when school and family got to be too much. There was one particular spot we loved to go to; it was a pretty meadow filled with flowers. It was far from the constant chatter of Campbell River; it was so peaceful. Here we could talk about our dreams, and as our relationship changed, we needed some alone time. It was here where we made love for the first time." She blushed enjoying a happy memory.

She looked up to find Magda studying her; quietly listening. "Go on."

So over mugs of hot tea, Rebecca relived her life story.

The night before graduation she and Jake met once again in their meadow; Rebecca needed to talk with Jake privately. The craziness of the past two months with exam preps, the pressures of post-secondary applications, and the increasing arguments with Jake had left Rebecca tired and worn. She found herself craving sleep and often lacked any appetite. Worried about her health, she made an appointment with her family physician, Dr Dwight Grainger.

She was horrified when he laughed and explained. "The only thing wrong with you, young lady, is that you are pregnant. Approximately six weeks."

She didn't laugh, she didn't cry. She didn't want a baby; she wanted it out of her. She wanted this done And mostly she needed her mother's advice, but cancer had stolen her mother away.

With the discovery of her pending motherhood, Rebecca found herself desperately missing her own mother. Agnes Eugenia Wright (Genie) had died of breast cancer ten months prior after a three-year fight filled with hospitalization, debilitating drugs, and a hopeless prognosis.

Genie Wright died as she had lived, quietly and dignified, slipping from their lives in the silence of the night. Rebecca missed her sage advice and subtle sense of humour. At times Rebecca wondered what had drawn her parents together; her father so outwardly physical and robust in contrast to his demure, socialite wife. He had stolen her from city society to the quiet world of small-town living. Together they had thrived, and they produced a daughter that they had loved and doted upon.

Genie's leaving had stolen Rebecca's spark; it punched a big hole in her life, and Jake had come along at the exact moment to fill the void in her broken heart. She had to admit the physicality of Jake was a pleasant distraction, but sometimes his rocky past and his ongoing insecurities were too challenging for her. She wondered how she was going to cope with this problem growing in her belly.

What am I going to do now? This cannot be happening. I don't want this baby, but I need to at least let Jake know before I end it. I can't image he'll want it either.

"Oh Mom!" she wept aloud." I sure could use your advice now."

She knew her gentle mother would have taken her hands, and then with her calm words she would have soothed Rebecca's angst. *Breathe. Just breathe, and be truthful to yourself, darling.* Then her mother would have firmly hugged her. Rebecca longed to absorb her strength.

Be truthful? The truth is I don't want this baby, and I want to leave Campbell River. I want my own life! Jake must know the truth! She felt empowered by her mother's memory.

The next day, things didn't go as she had hoped.

When they arrived at their hideaway Jake had wanted to make love, but she had turned away, explaining she needed to discuss something very important. He had sulked, mistaking her need to talk as just another argument about her upcoming departure for university in the fall. She had planned to leave, to pursue her studies in business, and Jake wasn't pleased.

"Don't be like that, Jake," she pleaded, clutching at his hand. She needed him to understand, but he roughly pulled his hand away. Her sense of empowerment was evaporating, so she just blurted it out!

"I'm pregnant, Jake! We're going to have a baby."

"What!?" Jake had whooped. "I'm going to be a dad!?" He beamed and grabbed Rebecca into his arms, then picked her up and spun her around. His face said it all; he was thrilled with her news.

"Put me down, you're making me sick," she had gasped. He had set her gently down, treating her like she was going to break.

"I am so sorry. Are you okay?" Jake asked. She waved him away, then sat down on the wool blanket spread out on the grass. He plunked down next to her, his face flushed with excitement.

Rebecca had spent a sleepless night trying to find the words to tell Jake she wanted to terminate the pregnancy. She decided that this was the only option, and she had already organized it with Dr Grainger. *We are kids ourselves. What do we know about raising a baby? The only solution is to get rid of it.*

"Jake ..." she began after her stomach settled. "We need to talk, because I've made a decision." She had set her resolve, but he kept interrupting her. She had misjudged him about the baby!

"Sure Rebecca. This changes everything!" He grabbed her hands between his. "This means you won't be going away to school after all. I'm going to be a daddy!" He rambled on. "We need to tell everyone! Does Olivia know? We need to call her?!" He reached for his phone.

"No wait, Jake!" She lunged at him, trying to grab the phone away. "Please let's wait for now. We need to keep this to ourselves."

Mistaking her despair for enthusiasm, he hugged her tightly and said, "You're right, it's our secret, but let's announce it at the graduation party tomorrow night. Won't they all be surprised, shocked would be more like it. Bad boy Jake and sweet, studious Rebecca are going to have a baby!"

Suddenly his facial expression changed. "We cannot have a baby."

Finally! she thought. *He understands!* She breathed a sigh of relief.

"Jake," she started again. "We can't have a baby because ..."

"Because, we're not married!" he whooped.

"WHAT!" She gasped in horror. "No, that's not what I meant!" She tried in vain to make her point, but Jake suddenly got on his knees, grabbed her hands, and stared directly into her eyes.

"Rebecca Anne Wright, will you marry me?" His faced beamed with excitement and anticipation.

"No!" she hastily replied.

Coming back to the present, she turned to Magda. "You can imagine how that went over!"

CHAPTER TWENTY-ONE

Jake lay stretched out on the bed in his hotel room, relaxing after a demanding day at the show. Andie had splurged and allowed each of the mechanics to have their own modest room. Some of the guys had brought their girlfriends or wives along; Andie wanted to let them have some alone time to celebrate their successes. Andie had invited Jake to bring Rebecca, but he declined.

"Someone needs to stay behind to run the shop, and Rebecca is the only candidate," Jake explained. He didn't want her to come; he needed the space and time alone to evaluate his future. It was all very confusing with so many thoughts pulling at him. He felt he was in the middle of an emotional hurricane and just wanted the winds to die down and give him some peace.

A sharp rap on the door interrupted his reflections. He pulled himself from the bed, it was probably one of the other mechanics wanting to go drinking again, but all he wanted was a night alone. He pulled the door open and was met with a squeal of delight.

"Baby!" Olivia leapt into his arms, driving him backward into the room.

"Olivia?" he gasped.

"Yes baby! Surprised?" She slammed the door behind her, hastily securing the lock and chain.

"That ain't the half of it," he sputtered as she pulled him to the bed and pushed him down. She ripped open her coat, revealing only smooth tanned skin.

"Oh my!" he sputtered.

Later, satiated and content, Jake pushed up on his elbow and caressed her cheek. The sex was great; it was the pressure release he needed, but he realized he was in danger. "Olivia, you can't be here," he whispered in her ear.

"No Jake, you are wrong. I can be anywhere I want to be." She giggled and kissed him hard.

Jake pushed her away, and gave her a firm shake.

"You're not listening. You can't be *here* ... *here* in this room. If Andie finds out, he'll fire my ass. It will ruin everything I have been working so hard on. Now pull yourself together!"

He tossed her coat at her to cover her nakedness.

"What *you* have been working on! What happened to us?" She tugged on her coat and sat sulking on the bed.

"Olivia, if we want this to work you can't be found in my room," he interrupted her whining. "You need to clean yourself up and go to Andie's room or go home. Andie will be shocked that you barged into the show, but at least I can keep my job."

She ignored his pleading instead pursuing him into the corner of the room where she pressed against his body. He gasped at her caressing touch; she certainly knew how to get his attention. She smothered him with kisses, and he tried to push her away. She was wearing that intoxicating spicy scent again, and he was losing the battle.

"Nope, it ain't gonna happen! Nope." He groaned, then finally gave in to his desire. He lustfully pushed her down on the bed, ravaging her skin with hungry kisses.

"You're mine, lover. I own you, body and soul." Olivia smirked as she bit his ear.

Later in the shower, as they soaped up each other's body, Jake made it clear that if they were going to succeed in their plan she would have to play her part. "When I get home, I will tell Rebecca I want a divorce, but let me handle it. I can probably get half the monies in a divorce settlement. Do you understand?"

She nodded and wrapped a towel around her lean body, then turned to dry his back. Olivia had no desire to be the wife of a mechanic shop owner any longer; she had bigger plans, and she had been working on them while Jake was at the car show.

She chuckled, remembering the phone call she had placed to Magda Bodrug last night. She had scared the wits out of the old gal and couldn't imagine that she would be contacting Rebecca anytime soon. It meant one more support was pulled away from Rebecca.

"You're right, I can't be seen coming out of your room. Now I need to go and torment my poor husband." She brushed past him on the way to the bathroom. "I've got to make myself presentable. I don't want to look like I've been with another man."

She shut the door in his face, leaving him wondering what he had gotten himself into.

CHAPTER TWENTY-TWO

Rebecca and Magda had spent another enjoyable evening together, but now she left Magda dozing in her chair and headed out for her evening run. On the drive to Lachlan Pathway, Rebecca had time to think on that pivotal day so many years ago.

"What do you mean, no?" Jake shouted at her. Rebecca was sitting on the blanket, and he was standing, towering over her. "You're having my baby! I made that baby ... me!"

He paced back and forth in front her.

"I believe that I was there too, and I have some say in the matter!" She stood up to face him, but he still loomed down over her. His face was distorted with emotion. Jake momentarily walked away, but then circled back. "Well, what's your answer? You agreed to have sex with me and told me you loved me, so what's the deal now?"

Rebecca plucked up her courage, but she needed to make sure he was listening, really listening.

"Jake, please hear me out. I don't want to have a baby ... not now. I want to go to school, and then possibly have children."

She had hardly gotten the words out, when he erupted! His faced flushed deep maroon and the vein on his forehead pulsed. He clenched his fists at her and roared.

"What? You can't mean that you want to get rid of it? Is my baby not good enough? Am I not good enough?" He marched away from her this time, his body rigid with rage. "You will not get rid of this baby like it is some kind of garbage. It is my child too, Rebecca Wright!" His voice shook with emotion as he broke into a frantic run.

Rebecca caught up to Jake at the parking lot. He was leaning against the rear panel of his aging pick-up truck, drawing heavily on a cigarette. He was calmer now, but he would not make eye contact. He threw the spent cigarette butt at her feet, not wanting her to draw closer. She was surprised he hadn't abandoned her to walk home on her own.

"Jake," she started, but he abruptly cut her off.

"Get in the truck!"

They drove along in silence, Jake's anger oozing from his pores. People had warned her about his temper, and for the first time, Rebecca actually felt afraid of him.

Fred Wright had been mentoring Jake during shop classes, and he was aware of the young man's hair-trigger temper. "Jake is a good kid and has come a long way, considering his family situation, but Rebecca, is he the one for you? Don't forget your dreams."

Fred worried about his daughter and had provided sage advice when he realized the young couple was getting closer. He guessed they were probably intimate and hoped, actually prayed, that they were being safe. Rebecca remembered her father had looked her in the eye during that 'uncomfortable conversation' and had pleaded. "Be safe! Be wise, my darling girl. Your life may depend on it!"

"Too late now," she sighed, looking out the truck's window. She couldn't face looking at the angry young man sitting next to her, and wondered how she was going to tell her dad.

He screeched to a stop in front of the Wright house, and as Rebecca started to open the door, Jake reached across and pulled the door shut.

"Before you get out, I need to say something."

His demeanor was calmer now, so she paused to listen.

"Rebecca, when you told me I was going to be a dad, I couldn't believe it. I was thrilled because my old man told me I would never amount to anything, and I probably didn't even have the balls to make a kid. Now here you're pregnant, and I'm thinking... wow, this is unreal! I'm going to be a dad, something I had always dreamed of." He paused to take a breath, and Rebecca could see his face was flushed with raw emotion.

She tried to interject, but he waved her off.

"Let me finish what I have to say. When we were, you know, doing it, you said you loved me. Were you just saying it, or do you really mean it? I mean I love you, and I think you love me too, so we can make it work. Come on Rebecca, we're going to be parents; isn't that the most important thing now? Not fast cars, partying, not moving away and going to school. You can always do that later, when the kid is bigger. The kid ... our kid!" He was feverish with excitement.

He clutched her hands and pulled her close, planting kisses on her hands, face, and lips. "I'm scared too Rebecca, but we can do it. With your brains and my good looks, we're going to have a pretty fantastic kid! Say yes, Rebecca. Be my wife, and have my baby!" He placed his hand on her stomach.

Rebecca felt absolutely overwhelmed. Her head swam, and she felt nauseated. She needed to get out of this truck, away from this riptide of emotion.

"Please Jake, I just need to think," she stuttered.

"Just say yes. Please Rebecca?" He implored. He looked so earnest and sincere. She truly believed he loved her, but she felt torn, could they actually make it work?

Suddenly she found herself saying, "Yes Jake. I will marry you."

"What? Did you say yes?" Jake whooped. "You did say yes, didn't you? You won't regret it!" He hugged her so tight it smothered her, and she had an uneasy feeling she was going to regret this decision. Regret it for a long time.

CHAPTER TWENTY-THREE

Olivia planted a final kiss on Jake before leaving his room. She had just finished freshening herself up after an afternoon of passion, and she wanted to tattoo his lips with her infamous 'pouting pink' shade.

"There you go, lover. One last kiss so you won't forget me." She whirled around on her stiletto heels and opened the door. She carefully checked the hallway before leaving the room. "See you later."

She giggled at the pretty pink sheen on Jake's lips.

"Get going." He roughly pushed her into the hallway, then wiped her mark from his mouth.

Olivia sashayed to the elevators, pulling her suitcases behind her. She approached the front desk and flashed her most beguiling smile, then began the game of coercing the clerk into breaking the hotel rules. She had pouted, she had sulked, and finally he slipped her a card key to 'Mr. Proctor's suite' when she slid a two-hundred-dollar bribe across the counter. She planned to use the key to slip into the suite and surprise Andie. He wasn't going to be happy, but her unannounced arrival was going to confirm who wore the pants in their relationship.

The suite was on the twenty-fourth floor, high up the north tower, far away from the remainder of the crew. *Curious?* She reflected as she waited for the elevator.

Reaching the room, Olivia slipped the key in the lock and pushed open the door. She assumed Andie would be down at the car show, so she would have time to prepare her surprise. She could hardly contain herself; she was having such fun so far! Sex with Jake had made her toes tingle, and now the delight of trashing Andie's careful plans was exhilarating!

"Think you can leave me at home, I don't think so," she gloated as pushed the door closed, not noticing the Do Not Disturb sign.

Very nice Andie. She scouted out the room.

The suite had a separate living room and bedroom area divided by a closed door. *Very fancy! I could stand hanging out here for the week.* Olivia admired the fine décor, and she ran her fingers over the well-stocked bar. Two glasses and a bottle of champagne bottle sat unopened on the bar.

Perhaps he was expecting me after all.

She pushed the bedroom door opened and gasped in surprise. Lying on the king-sized bed, entwined in a lover's embrace, was her husband and Kevin Pritchard. Both men were deep asleep in a post coital slumber, oblivious to their unexpected visitor.

Clasping her hand over her mouth, she quietly backed out of the room, leaving the door ajar.

"Holy fuck!" she whispered to herself. She couldn't believe what she had just witnessed.

Shit ... Andie and Kevin Pritchard? I had always wondered about my husband's sexual preference, but never in my wildest dreams did I imagine this scenario! She stifled a giggle with her hand.

Olivia clutched her handbag and plunked down on the couch. *What the hell am I going to do?*

Suddenly she smiled; an evil cunning smile. Rummaging in her handbag she located her cellphone; then she slipped off her heels and stealthily crept back into the bedroom. She carefully approached the bed and took several photos of the couple; ensuring she captured both men's faces in the images. Lucky for her neither man stirred.

Slipping quickly back into the living room area she gathered her shoes, handbag, and suitcases and exited the suite; the door clicking shut behind her.

Andie stirred. Something had awoken him from his slumber.

Was someone in the suite? Perhaps the maid or cleaning staff? Hadn't he put out the sign requesting privacy? He slid carefully off the bed, not wanting to disturb his lover. He donned a plush terry hotel robe and paused at the doorway.

Hadn't we closed the door? He recalled that the air-conditioning was blasting so hard they were both freezing. They had closed the bedroom door to make it cozier and also to provide more privacy, but now it stood open.

"How strange?" he said quietly.

As he tugged the robe tighter against the room's chill, he caught the strong scent of perfume.

Smells like Olivia's overpowering new fragrance. He sniffed the air.

Andie hated that scent because it tended to invade and spoil any place she entered. It must have come with him from home, permeating his luggage and clothes.

Can I never escape her? He was suddenly startled by a sound behind him.

"What's strange?"

He turned to find Kevin standing in the doorway, wearing an identical robe. His ruggedly handsome partner leaned against the bedroom door frame; his steel grey eyes studying Andie. Many people found that steely stare intimidating, but Andie was intoxicated by his lover's gaze and found he was flustered by his closeness. Kevin Pritchard close or far always made his heart rate quicken.

"You scared the heck out of me!" Andie laughed nervously, clutching his robe closed.

Kevin pulled him into a tender embrace. "What's up? Are you nervous about us being together? We're safe here; no one will know our secret. Now come back to bed. We have time before you have to be on the show floor."

Kevin gently directed Andie back to the bedroom. "Pull the door shut, it stinks of perfume in there. It must be one of the maids." As Andie pulled the door shut, he was haunted with the sensation that someone had been in the suite invading their private sanctum.

CHAPTER TWENTY-FOUR

Olivia had barely gotten out of the room and down the hallway before she burst out laughing. As she groped for the elevator button, she brayed out loud. Her pretty face was contorted with mirth; tears running down her face smearing her carefully applied makeup. She was a red-faced mess as she waited for the elevator doors to open. She couldn't wait to tell Jake, to tell everyone, to tell the world.

"Unbelievable! Andie Proctor and Kevin Pritchard are gay lovers!" She squealed aloud.

The elevator door slid open, and she staggered into the lift overcome with glee.

"Wow!" Olivia wiped the tears from her face. She captured her reflection in the polished finish of the elevator panel. She laughed at the image that reflected back her likeness. For once in her life, she didn't care how she looked because she felt jubilant. She pulled a Kleenex out of her purse and dabbed the spoiled makeup from her face, reconstructing her image before the doors slid open.

Her time in Las Vegas had come to an end; she had some unexpected evidence, and she intended to use it against Andie. With the pictures secured on her phone, she had some serious work to do before Andie and the team arrived back home. She had five days to hatch her new plan; not only was she going to release Jake from his burdensome marriage, but she was also going to destroy Andie's life as well.

"Oh, such fun!" She gleefully handed the room key back to the front desk clerk. "I don't need this anymore; I have other plans. Call me a cab, honey. I'm going home!" She reached over the desk and gave the surprised clerk a sloppy kiss.

Later that night at the airport while waiting for her flight, Olivia purchased a burner phone and transferred the pictures from her cellphone on to it. Next, she typed in Andie's cellphone number, attached the phones, and pressed send. "Let the games begin." She laughed out loud.

CHAPTER TWENTY-FIVE

The Proctor Automotive team arrived back at the shop on Wednesday morning. Everyone was in high spirits except Jake, he was pissed. He had arrived home the night before on a heady cloud, jabbering up a storm about the events of the past eight days. He had even hugged Rebecca and given her a big kiss, but then awkwardly withdrew, and pulled a beer from the refrigerator. He had even acknowledged that Rebecca had bought his favourite beer.

"Thanks, good suds," he had taken a long gulp, then continued. "You should have seen us. We dazzled the competition. The car outshone everyone else by a mile. Andie let the team do all the demos, and I even got to be part of the 'big show.' People were actually asking me about my work and how I improved the fuel performance on the vehicle. People wanted to talk with me ... little old nobody Jake Adams from Campbell River!"

He had paced back and forth; the room electric with his enthusiasm.

Rebecca had sat quietly, taking it all in. She hadn't seen Jake this fired up in a long time. She was really happy for him and wanted to hear more about the show.

"This brings me to something I want to discuss with you." He whirled around, pulled a chair up to Rebecca, and took her hand. He took another gulp of beer and locked her attention with his eyes. From the look in his eyes, she was hopeful he wanted to reconcile. She felt a glimmer of hope for their future, until he broke the bubble.

"I want to start my own shop. It would be great for me to have my own business. I know it would be loads of work, but I could do it." His voice was high and strained with passion.

"I know what you are thinking, how could I afford it?" He continued on staring directly into her eyes and holding her hands.

"We could sell this place."

Rebecca pulled her hands loose. "We've talked about this before. I'm not going to sell the house, no matter what Olivia's business tycoon says. You know how I feel about this."

He stood up so suddenly that his chair fell over with a bang, his face a mask of anger and disappointment. Rebecca jumped back and retreated out of his reach. She'd recently seen that same look and was afraid he would lash out at her again; this time she didn't have the protection of the bathroom door.

"Olivia was right, she said you'd never go for it." He threw his beer bottle against the wall behind her head. "If you won't do it the easy way, I guess I'll have to force you ..."

Before he could finish his statement, Rebecca fled the kitchen to the safety of the locked bathroom. She was afraid of what by 'force you' meant.

"It's over Rebecca Wright! We are over." She cringed behind the locked door as he slammed his fists against the wood. "I'm leaving you, and I will have what's mine! You took my son from me, but you are not going to take this away too!"

Long after he roared away in his truck, she lay curled in a ball on the bathroom floor, the words echoing in her head. "It's over ... you took my son from me." Such hateful, hurtful words.

She fell asleep on the tile floor and awoke the next morning cold and stiff. She listened for sounds, but it seemed that Jake had not returned during the night. She slowly pulled herself off the bathroom floor and dressed for the day's events. She looked at herself in the mirror and was shocked at her image. She had dark circles under her tear swollen eyes, and her hair was lank and tangled. She had been doing so well; she felt some of the old Rebecca coming back, but now her hard work was destroyed by his cruel words.

She struggled into clean clothes and headed to the car, at least Andie needed her. Thank God for that, it gave her an anchor in this stormy sea. She dreaded facing Jake at work today.

* * *

At Proctor Automotive, the team celebrated over dark black coffee laced with whiskey. Their heads were feeling a bit thick; they had been celebrating with their spouses and families late into the night and the whiskey helped clear the fog. Each member of the team had dragged in a little late, everyone except Jake. He had been in early, actually very early, as he had slept in his truck at the shop. His anger was raw and palpable. The other members mistook his sullen behaviour for being seriously hungover. Randi Everett, the crew boss, clapped him on the back.

"Little hungover, bud?" Jake turned and glared at him.

Jake spotted Rebecca as she slipped into the mechanic bay behind Andie Proctor. She looked like shit; he was so embarrassed by her appearance. Their eyes briefly met, until Jake broke the contact and stared at the floor. His thoughts festered with rage. He thought about Olivia and their conversation at the hotel in Las Vegas; he had plenty of time to mull it over during the long night, tossing and turning on the hard seat in his truck cab. It was becoming clearer to him what he needed to do. He hadn't talked to Olivia since the afternoon in the hotel; she had just disappeared, not turning up at the show as she had planned. Jake assumed that Andie had forced her to return home and she was holed up somewhere, sulking. He decided to send her another text; they needed to plan for their future together.

He searched his pocket for his phone, only to realize he had left it in his jacket pocket. He had hung his jacket on the back of his chair last night when he had returned from the show, but in his rush to leave the house, he had forgotten it.

Damn, I will need to call her instead. I need to find a land line. He sighed and crossed his arms. His head was throbbing, and he could really use a drink.

Andie entered the mechanic bay and thanked the team for their brilliant work, congratulating everyone for their exceptional work and dedication to the project. He also praised their newest addition to the team, Jake, for his input to the show. Jake smiled and nodded, acting like he cared, but he was actually thinking about having sex with the boss's wife.

"Now, one more piece of exciting news." Andie smiled at his team. He paused to study the excited people in front of him, but his enthusiasm was temporarily dampened by the memory of the strange text that he had received while at the show.

Will their attitude change when they find out who I truly am? He fretted.

Andie's thoughts returned to the moment when 'the anonymous text' had appeared on his phone. He had been on the show floor when his phone buzzed; he had opened the attachments to find pictures of Kevin and himself in their hotel suite. He had nearly collapsed as he scrolled through the intimate images; he quietly excused himself and went in search of Kevin. They met up in their suite, where Kevin took the phone from his partner's shaking hands.

After scrolling through the pictures, Kevin gathered Andie into his arms. "It could only have been Olivia. I thought I recognized the stink of her perfume in our room. She obviously flew here with the intention of surprising you ..." But here Kevin laughed. "Instead, she got the shock of her life!"

The two men looked at each other and despite the obvious invasion of their privacy and future consequences, they burst out laughing. "I guess our secret is out of the bag!" Andie sighed.

"It'll be okay." Kevin interjected.

"What do you mean? This is going to ruin us!" Andie was shocked by how calm Kevin was taking this devastating news.

"We're not ruined; we're just two gay guys coming out. It happens every day, well perhaps not in Campbell River. Won't everyone be surprised?" He burst out laughing until tears ran down his face; Andie couldn't resist and soon joined him.

"I'm actually relieved," Kevin said as he stifled his laughter. "Now we can get on with our lives. We don't have to hide from anyone, and that includes Olivia."

He hugged his partner and looked him the face. "Now, Mr. Proctor, it's time to go back to the show and wow them! We have lots of time to plan. Olivia will not win, not now, not ever. We own our lives." The couple embraced, and then returned to the show floor, their spirits flying high.

Andie had tried to connect with Olivia since then, but she had blatantly ignored him. He knew she would be at scheming at home, plotting her revenge. They would need to brace themselves for her tactics. So this morning in front of his staff, he shook off the cloak of worry, and continued. "Proctor Automotive has been approached to feature in an upcoming episode of *Fancy Rides*. The producers say the work we have been doing is remarkable, and they were very impressed."

"Really boss!?" Sal Michaels, one of the mechanics, blurted out. A roar of excitement echoed through the room. Even Jake was pulled out his funk. The grown men chattered like excited school boys.

Andie waited until the men had settled down. "The show is scheduled to air in one month's time, so all that hard work you've done ..." He paused. "Well, we need to put in more."

"No worries, boss!" someone called out.

"Fine by me!" shouted another.

"Can't wait!" They all agreed.

The team was buzzing with excitement, the fatigue from earlier was now replaced by electrified energy. Andie was pleased to see the team's engagement; he knew he couldn't do it without them. He took a deep breath and called them back to order.

"I also wanted to let you know that I will be working from my private cabin for the next couple of weeks. I need to take some personal time, but I will be in constant contact. Randi will be working with the mechanics, and the filming crew and I will be in the background making recommendations."

Andie ended the meeting with more thanks and congratulations, and then as the group disbanded, he summoned Rebecca and Randi into his office. "Please shut the door behind you."

"Thanks for everything you two have done for both me and Proctor Automotive. All of this would not have been possible without your tireless commitment. I will be leaving the office shortly, but I will be in contact with both of you." He reached over the desk and grasped both of their hands.

"I will also be making a personal announcement on social media within the hour. It will state that I will be divorcing my wife and moving on with another relationship. I won't get into details now, but I will discuss it with you later."

Both Randi and Rebecca quietly applauded their boss, they couldn't be happier for him. Rebecca only wished she could feel the same about her own life.

"It's about time," Randi said, shaking Andie's hand.

"Thanks so much. Shall we get down to business, then?"

Ass the trio sat with their heads together, planning for the upcoming events at Proctor Automotive, Jake was in the mechanic bay, whispering into the land line. He had reached Olivia's phone, but she didn't pick up, so he left a message.

"Olivia, it's Jake. Let's plan to get together tonight. I haven't seen you for so long, and I *need* to see you." He knew it was risky to leave a message on her phone, but things needed to change, and soon.

I need to be done with my wife, one way or another, he thought.

He had spent most of the night thinking about Olivia's plans; divorcing Rebecca would be a long dirty event, so he mulled over the alternative—and the alternative was deadly. They definitely needed to talk, but for now Sal was bellowing at him to join the group.

CHAPTER TWENTY-SIX

J ake was right about Olivia, she had returned from Las Vegas in a hurry, but it wasn't because Andie had sent her packing. Andie had never even seen Oliva, but she had seen him and much, much more. Olivia had returned home armed with damning evidence and a smug sense of self-assuredness. She had holed up at Proctor Estate, scheming and planning, and purposely ignoring Andie's calls. She had spent her days reviewing the prenuptial agreement that she had been forced to sign. She was looking for loop holes, and anything to make it void and null.

Could lying about your sexuality be a reason to make this document void? she wondered as she reviewed the papers.

For now, she had booked an appointment at Clarence Reid's office; she needed to discuss this stupid piece of paper with him. It needed to go away! She didn't think the lawyer would do anything to help; he had worked for the Proctor family for many years and was very loyal to them.

"Loyalty my ass!" she scoffed. She despised him, and the family he represented.

Before she entered the office, she readjusted her cleavage in her low-cut blouse, reapplied her lipstick, fluffed her blonde hair, and smiled at her image in the rear-view mirror. She was ready for battle, and Clarence Reid was such an easy target.

She sashayed into the offices of Clarence, Duncan, and Pratt at ten o'clock, four days before the Proctor Automotive Team was scheduled to arrive home. She had work to do, and the law office was her first stop. Armed with the photos on her cellphone and the prenuptial agreement, she approached the receptionist, Lyla Henderson, who was also the office busybody. Lyla gushed and fawned over Olivia, and then escorted her to the conference room, where she waited for Clarence to arrive. Lyla had left the door ajar; hoping some juicy bits of gossip would float down the hallway.

Olivia was impatient to get this matter settled; she glowered as the lawyer entered the room. She found him repulsive, but she was willing to play the game. She flashed her sweetest smile and settled her cleavage on the table, allowing him a better view.

The old pervert took the bait. She studied him as he studied her chest. Clarence Reid resembled an old ugly toad; a fat tub of jiggling, sweaty maleness, and he sat leering at her. She winced in revulsion.

"Good morning, Mrs. Proctor." He smiled. She leaned forward to give him an even better view of her chest.

"Mr. Raymond Duncan is your usual lawyer, so what is it I can do for you today?" He knew it could be a potential conflict of interest, but he was transfixed by the blonde across the table. He fantasized what those breasts would look like naked.

"For one thing, you can stop looking at my tits and look me in the eyes." She sneered at the man.

Her voiced was loud and carried down the hallway where she heard Lyla giggling. Reid got up and slammed the conference room door; he didn't need Lyla spreading gossip amongst the other staff. He certainly didn't need any hassles. He was planning to retire in the next six months; his personal physician advised it, and his wife Lorraine harped about it. His exit strategy had been coming together as planned, until this morning when Olivia Proctor barged back into his life.

"Now, Mrs. Proctor. I am sorry if you think I have been inappropriate, I apologize. I am here to serve you with professionalism and sincerity. Shall I invite Mr. Duncan to attend this meeting?" He grovelled and sweat ran down his puffy face, his eyes bulged further from his head.

"Cut the shit, Clarence!" Her eyes gleamed with intensity. "I know all about your 'handsie' ways. Two of your employees, Margie and Adyson, are close friends of mine. They told me about certain inappropriate advances and the hush money they received. They were afraid to lose their jobs if they blew the whistle and reported you to the law association, I however, am not."

She paused. "I can however be discreet, but that is only if you decide to do something for me. We don't need Duncan for now, do we?"

He could only nod.

As she leaned forward this time, the lawyer's eyes stayed glued on Olivia's icy blue eyes. She pushed a folder containing the prenuptial agreement across the table.

"You need to make this pile of crap to go away. I was coerced into signing this, and now I want it amended."

He gulped and wiped his brow, worried he was crossing the line, but perhaps he could appease her with a quick peek at the documents, and then send her back to his associate Duncan. Reid pulled open the folder and studied the papers. They contained the prenuptial agreement that he had drawn up between Andie Proctor and Olivia Baird, prior to their wedding. Both had been consenting adults and as he reviewed the documents, it was pretty much iron clad. His associate lawyer, Raymond Duncan, had counselled Oliva separately to prevent a conflict of interest, the very thing he was now facing.

Clarence set the documents onto the table and spread them out. He used his tie to wipe away the sweat that threatened to drip onto the paper.

This isn't going to go well. He worried to himself. *Olivia isn't going to like it; I wonder what she'll do if I can't make this go away?*

"Well..." he stammered. "The prenuptial is pretty solid, and I recall that prior to signing it you were provided separate counsel on the document by Raymond Duncan. I don't recall Mr. Duncan bringing forward any issues, correct?" He swallowed and looked up, expecting her to lash out.

When she didn't respond, he continued. "I don't know what I can do to help you. The only way it can be rescinded is if both you and Andie decide to make it null and void."

Olivia sat quietly studying him, so he went on. "Has Mr. Proctor decided to change the agreement?"

"No," she hissed.

"So what is it I can do for you then?" He eyed her warily; he really wanted her to leave. She spelled trouble with a capital 'T'.

"What if the marriage was entered into under false premises? In other words, if he lied about whom he really was?" She was thumbing through her phone.

"I'm not sure what you mean? Andie Proctor is a credible person. It's not like he has a false identity." The lawyer was confused.

"No, but he is gay!" Olivia pushed the phone across the table to the lawyer.

Clarence Reid's jaw fell open as he scrolled through the images. "Oh, my!" Was all he was capable of stuttering. "Andie Proctor and Kevin Pritchard? Wow!"

He took a long, deep, cleansing breath; the images lingered in his brain. He needed Duncan in here, especially now because things had gotten very complicated, but instead he blundered on.

"The document is still valid. Jake's sexuality and infidelity can be used in a divorce, but if you pursue that route because of the prenuptial, you will end up with nothing. You could sue him for damages, mental distress, but my advice is to go and seek counsel with your husband. Perhaps he will reconsider altering the document. Has he seen these pictures?"

"Of course he has you idiot!" she spat. "So you're telling me there isn't much you can do for me?"

Reid cringed away from her and decided this meeting needed to end. "Sorry no, and I can't discuss this any further. I suggest you book an appointment with your usual attorney, Mr. Duncan, who could advise you on divorce proceedings, if you'd like?"

Attempting to dig himself out of this mess, he continued. "I should have made this clear earlier, but since I represent Andie as a client, it would be a conflict if I counselled you any further. I can have Lyla organize a meeting with your lawyer."

He flushed and sweated through his shirt. He was afraid of her fury and wondering what she could do to him, when suddenly his chest felt heavy.

Olivia snatched the documents off the table and stomped toward the door.

"Don't bother; I have other options to explore." She paused and sized up the pale, sweaty man. "Best mind your manners old man because I would hate to report your bad behaviour to the authorities or your dear wife Lorraine."

She spun on her heels and exited the offices, passing Lyla in the hallway. "You best check on your boss." She smiled smugly. "Old Clarence isn't looking too good."

Lyla hustled down to the conference room, where she found her boss pale and sweaty.

"Please call 911, Lyla!" He gasped." I think I'm having a heart attack."

CHAPTER TWENTY-SEVEN

At the end of the business meeting, Andie took Rebecca aside. "My social media announcement is going to have some negative fallout for you. Olivia will be furious, and she'll likely turn her anger on you. Please tell me you will be careful."

She nodded in response, unable to make eye contact. She was still shaken from Jake's verbal tirade last night. She had been working so hard on getting stronger, but now she felt she was looking up from the bottom of a dark well.

It's over ...

You took my son from me ...

The words echoed and re-echoed in her mind. She struggled to put on a brave smile for Andie.

"I'm going to be okay, Andie, really. I'm so happy for you." She wasn't sure who she was trying to convince more, Andie or herself.

Rebecca slipped from his office before he could say anything more; she didn't want to lose it in front of him. She was so confused about everything; she just needed to take a few minutes to get it together. She slunk into her office and closed the door behind her. She thumped into her chair and put her head down. She felt completely numb and exhausted.

She slowly focused on the task at hand. Andie had entrusted her with the media announcement; it was her job to connect with the local newspaper regarding the success at The Armstrong National Car Show and the upcoming TV debut on *Fancy Rides*. She hoped that Gretchen Berg would not receive this assignment; the reporter had tormented Rebecca during the trial and made her life intolerable.

Her words were slow to come to the page, as Jake's words kept invading her thoughts.

Divorce ...

You took my son from me ...

Now I'll take everything from you ...

Suddenly, her cellphone chimed in her purse. She had received a text message. She pulled it out and read the message.

'Got your message. Let's meet tonight.'

It must be a wrong number. Rebecca set the phone back down on her desk and returned to her computer. She was just struggling through the final draft of the media announcement and wanted to review it before sending it to Andie for his approval.

More words bubbled up.

If you won't do it the easy way, I guess I'll have to force you.

She shivered.

Her phone chimed again; it was another message. It read:

'Hey lover, can't wait for tonight. It's been far too long, and we have things to plan. Love you Big J.

It was signed L'

Big J, I used to call Jake this? And who is L? She looked at the phone number. It seemed familiar, but her clogged brain struggled to recognize it. She set it down and rubbed her weary eyes.

I really need to finish this. She did a final review and hit the print button.

The phone chimed again.

'Time to take care of business. Time to take care of your wife.'

What? She was stunned by this final message. The writer had obviously meant it for someone else, but it certainly rang true to her situation. *Are these messages for Jake, and they were sent to me by mistake?*

She gasped. "It sounds very sinister!" She was worried. *I need to talk with someone.*

She knew it would be Olivia she turned to for help, but she cringed, especially after Andie's warning. It seemed she knew Jake better than anyone, and lately he seemed to have her ear. What had he confided to Olivia? Rebecca needed to know the truth.

She sent a hasty text to Olivia.

'Can we meet for a quick coffee? I need your advice. Please!'

Moments later, a response chimed on her phone.

'Fine, but you're buying!'

Rebecca pulled her purse out of the drawer and dashed down the hallway, stopping at Andie's' closed office door. She gently tapped, then poked her head into his office. "Sorry Andie, I've just got to pop out for a minute."

She set the media announcement on his desk and fled his questioning look. As she drove away, she shuddered at what she might be walking in to. *What am I going to find out?*

CHAPTER TWENTY-EIGHT:

By the time Rebecca reached the café and had ordered her tea and Olivia's specialty coffee, she was a bundle of raw nerves and sweaty stress. She didn't want to face the inevitable, that her marriage was ending and she didn't know what to do next. She had a sneaking suspicion that her best friend knew and was helping to facilitate its demise.

She placed the hot beverages on the table and sat anxiously fidgeting with her cup, waiting on Olivia's attention. She wrung her hands in anticipation.

"Olivia," she began. "Could you please take a look at these text messages that popped up on my phone? I'm confused, and I really need your advice on this, and well, on something else, it's kinda important."

Rebecca nudged her cellphone across the table toward Olivia. Olivia looked up from her own phone, a glint of annoyance playing across her icy blue eyes. "Sure give me a minute; I just have to finish something."

Rebecca toyed with her own phone and watched the reflections of people sitting behind their table. She knew too well their stares and furtive glances. Rebecca looked away and rubbed the scars on her wrist. She felt the same dangerous feelings welling up and needed to distract herself. Despite her best efforts she could feel her anxiety rising; she couldn't just sit and wait for Olivia any longer.

I gotta do something or I'll explode. She fidgeted with her phone. A thought suddenly came to her. She typed a reply to the messages.

'Who is this?'

Across the table Olivia's phone chimed once again; she chuckled to herself as she read the latest message. Was her lover playing games, right under his wife's nose? Olivia smirked and typed her reply.

Rebecca's phone responded. *Is this the mystery person at last?* She fully expected the message to say 'wrong number.'

What? She suddenly recognized the number ... it had come from Olivia's phone.

'Hey love, real cute. Are we playing games? You know it's me, your sexy Livie. Meet you tonight at seven o'clock. Don't be late; we have to finalize our plans about your wife.'

The text messages all made sense now. Had she been so blind to her friend's deceit that she had missed the other clues too!?

The flowery perfume ...

The late nights ...

The long glances ...

The whispers in dark corners ...

She now understood that "L" meant Livie; it was Jake's pet name for her best friend, and the pair was planning to meet. A meeting with deadly undertones.

Her head reeled, and her memories flashed back to all the times Olivia had been there as part of their lives; at the wedding as her maid of honour, the night Indie had been born, at her father's funeral, and through the devastating trial.

Had she been beside them or between them?

"What is this all about?" Olivia finally asked.

Rebecca opened her mouth, but nothing came out. She started to shake violently, her mouth felt dry, and she thought she was going to be sick. She reached for her cup of tea to take a sip to hydrate her parched lips, but she misjudged her reach. She knocked it over, spraying hot liquid across the table onto both her and Olivia's laps.

"You clumsy oaf, look what you did!" Olivia stood up, wiping away at the stain on her leather jacket. "It'll probably be ruined!"

Rebecca stood up and feebly attempted to dab away the liquid. "Why Olivia? Why?" she whispered.

"Why what, Rebecca?" Olivia snapped. She noticed the patrons of the café were staring at them.

"Haven't you people gotten enough to gossip about yet?" she yelled at the curiosity seekers. They quickly looked away. She turned back to Rebecca. "What the hell is your problem, and what is this text message nonsense?"

Olivia snatched Rebecca's phone. She read the text message on the screen and couldn't help but laugh.

"Oh my! Well that certainly changes everything, doesn't it? I must have gotten your phone number mixed up with Jake's. No wonder he wasn't answering." She thrust the phone back at Rebecca. "Here, take your phone," she snapped.

"Olivia, how could you? You were my best friend." Rebecca recoiled from Olivia's touch.

"You act surprised! We have been in love with each other for years; right under your nose. He turned to me when you selfishly forgot him; like when you killed his son! You don't' deserve him!" she spat. "He's mine now, and we will be taking everything from you. And I mean everything!" The level of her voice intensified; her voice becoming shrill.

Olivia pushed passed Rebecca toward the coffee shop exit. Before she left, she suddenly turned and hissed. "No more hiding it from the world, Rebecca." She waved at the café patrons who sat riveted to their seats, eyes agog, and mouths hanging open. "Now you know, and so does everyone else!"

Rebecca grabbed Olivia's hand, preventing her from leaving. As she did her sweater sleeve rose upward to expose the ugly scars on her wrist.

"Let go!" Olivia tried to shake off Rebecca's grasp. As she pried at the fingers binding her wrist, she felt the scars on Rebecca's arms. Olivia fixed her steely blue eyes on her and hissed under her breath.

"Why don't you just kill yourself? It's not like anyone would care!" She needed to advance her plans, and she had the perfect audience to witness the beginning of Rebecca's downhill spiral. No one would be surprised if in the near future, Rebecca ended up dead!

"And do it right this time!" she hissed.

With Olivia gone, Rebecca turned and fled the café to the safety of her little Honda. She shuddered as she recalled that she had shared all her darkest secrets with this woman. Olivia had been so important to her at one time, and now she discovered that for years she had been betraying her.

Now what? I have to hear what you have to say, Jake. I need to hear it from your lips; your lying deceitful lips. She dialed his number. It rang and rang.

Why won't you answer? I bet you forgot your phone at home in your jacket. She had seen it hanging on a kitchen chair.

She was starting to feel frightened; the familiar dark thoughts were returning, and they made her scars itch. She shook her head. *No. I can't think about that now.* She rubbed her forehead to push the thoughts away, but she knew the doubts remained not far from the surface. Jake and Olivia's betrayal had done a good job of stirring up the demons.

CHAPTER TWENTY-NINE

When Rebecca arrived home, it was empty. Nothing had changed since she had left this morning, and it was obvious that Jake had not been there since leaving last night; his jacket was still hanging on the back of his chair. He had stormed out in such anger that he had forgotten it. His cell phone was in the pocket of his jacket, and it was chiming with incoming text messages.

She dropped her keys and purse on the living room floor, then dug the phone out of his coat. She held it in her hand and decided she needed to read his text messages.

I need to know! Evidence of the affair would certainly be stored on his phone.

Jake still had an old phone, he didn't believe in buying new ones that required passwords, so accessing his information should be easy. She pressed the 'on' button and the device opened, making it free for her to review. *Good thing you like old technology, Jake.*

She took a deep breath and started to read his private texts, then paused. *What more will I find out if I keep looking?* She braced herself for the worst and read the texts anyways. It was better to know, but as she scrolled through the multiple messages, her heart sunk. There in clear text was evidence of the affair, it was all true!

She thumped down onto the floor, her legs and world collapsing; the betrayal was all consuming. So many emotions swam in her head ... fear, disgust, and hopelessness. As the tears coursed down her face, she wondered. *How long has this has been going on? What else is on his phone?* She probed further, selecting the photos App labeled: *'My Girl.'*

Do I really want to see more? Some sad desperate part of her did, and the pictures left no doubt of their involvement; also the timing of the images proved it had gone on for some time. She sat on the floor, holding the offending device.

"How could I be so naive? How could I be so stupid!?" she yelled to the silent house.

As she continued to scroll, she found other images that made her skin crawl. Intimate pictures of Jake and Olivia clearly displayed how they had evolved from friends to lovers. She gagged in revulsion and dropped the phone in her lap.

"What? Oh my God, you were sleeping with her at the time of our son's death and following the funeral. And during the trial too! I thought you said you were there for me ... you bastard!" she cried.

She did not need any more proof. She threw the phone on the ground in disgust, hoping it would smash. She wouldn't allow him to have his memories. She moaned. "I just cannot face any more loss and humiliation!"

Rebecca shivered as despair crept over her like a cold mist, enveloping her into its shroud. Fear seeped up her cold limbs, settling deeply in her heart. She looked down at her hands where the evidence of her desperation was tattooed on her skin. She sat rubbing the scars on her wrists, and she wept. She cried for her father and for her lost son, but mostly for her lost dreams. The dark thoughts that had plagued her on other sad days and nights whispered in her ear.

Murderer ...

Victim ...

Pathetic loser!

Rebecca clamped her hands over her ears and shook her head back and forth, trying in vain to block out the noise in her head. *Stop! Stop, it's too much. I just need this to end.* Her old scars itched. *I want the pain to stop.* As she leaned against the wall, her eyes settled on the downstairs bathroom, where the abandoned pills called to her.

I could just take all those damn pills that Dr. Grainger has foisted on me over the past years? Taking a handful of those would do the trick.

She slowly made her mind up; now it was time to act. She pulled herself up on the wall and made her way to the bathroom. There in the medicine cabinet shelves were the antidepressants, sleeping pills, and mood elevators all prescribed to 'make her life better.' Now they would help end her life.

With one swipe of her hand, she tumbled the containers into the sink, their contents spilling out in a kaleidoscope of colours. Grabbing a handful, she made her way back to the living room. There she grabbed a bottle of Jake's vodka from the liquor cabinet, plunked down on the floor and rolled the pills around in her hand, the dye staining her hands green, red and blue. She sat on the floor and swirled the clear liquid in the bottle; its downward spiraling reminding her of her life and its hopelessness.

"Well then!" She spoke aloud. "Let's do it!!"

She slammed the bottle down on the floor and stuffed the pills in her mouth, then took a long draw on the bottle. With a shuddering gulp, she swallowed the mass down; she gagged and almost vomited but she managed to keep it down.

No one will mourn my loss. She was resolved; now she just needed to wait.

She leaned her head against the wall to settle the spinning feeling. Her eyes were feeling heavy, and she was beginning to feel drowsy. She spied a picture of Indie on the mantel; he was wearing a large cowboy hat and riding a miniature rocking horse. His toothy grin lit up his face. It was a happy memory; his second birthday.

My son, I am so sorry I didn't stop you from falling. It was my fault; I should have been a better mother.

As she waited for death, she gazed at other family pictures on the mantel. Clustered together were various pictures marking joyous occasions; pictures of her wedding, her father holding a newborn Indie, and Jake sitting with his son on his lap. She smiled at the images and tried to keep her eyes open; they felt so heavy. As she started to doze off, an image of Indie full of life and vigor suddenly appeared to her. In her drugged haze, it seemed he was trying to tell her something.

His sweet boy's voice pleaded, *"I love you, Mommy! Stay and remember me!"*

She shook her head. *I must be totally crazy!* She rubbed her eyes. *The pills must be making me hallucinate.*

Other images of her family, including her loving mother and father, floated in front of her eyes. She saw her father, shaking his head and saying, *"No Rebecca; not this way, my brave girl!"*

She looked again at the pictures on the mantel, the images blurring as the drug cocktail took effect. Suddenly a horrible sensation of dread made her regret her actions.

"Shit, if I die, then they win. No ... No ..." she moaned out loud. "I need to get help!"

Struggling to get up, Rebecca fell down on the living room floor; her legs felt spongy, and her head was dizzy. She felt her heart clench with fear. *What have I done? I need help ...but who do I call? I don't trust the ambulance service ... I remember how they treated me when Indie fell.* Her head swam and her eyes blurred, but a single thought came into her head.

Call Magda.

She pulled her purse over and clumsily dug for her own phone. Blurry eyed, she located the stored number and was able to dial it.

Across town in Magda's small apartment, the phone rang. She shuffled over and grabbed it, but she worried it might be the horrible woman who had called yesterday and threatened her. She paused with her hand over the receiver, but something tweaked her to answer this call.

"Yes, who is it?" she asked. No answer came and she was going to hang up, when suddenly a slurred female voice whispered, "Magda ... help ... help me. I've made a mistake, please help!"

"Who is this? Speak up, or I will hang up!" the elderly woman demanded.

A very soft, frail voice continued. "Magda, don't go. It's me, Rebecca. I made a stupid mistake ... I took some pills, and I need help." Then the line went dead.

"REBECCA!" Magda yelled into the phone. "REBECCA!"

What should I do? I need to call the ambulance. Panicking, she fumbled with the phone, but she was eventually successful in calling 911.

"911. What is your emergency?" the operator asked.

"I need help! I mean my friend needs help. She has tried to hurt herself," Magda blurted out.

"Calm down, ma'am. What is your friend's name, and what has she done to hurt herself?" The operator was having trouble understanding the ramblings of the frantic woman.

"Her name is Rebecca, and she says she took a bunch of pills. Oh, please help her!" Magda was desperate.

"What is Rebecca's address? I need to know so I can dispatch an ambulance out to help her," the operator calmly probed.

"I don't know her address," she gasped. "But I know her last name. Adams ... her name is Rebecca Adams."

"Rebecca Adams." The operator typed the information into the computer. The address came up as 19 Riverside Drive. "I will dispatch an ambulance immediately to your friend's residence."

"Can they get there in time?" Magda asked.

"We will do our best, ma'am."

The ambulance arrived at the Riverside address within ten minutes; there the paramedics found an unconscious woman lying on the floor. A variety of pills and a partially empty bottle of alcohol were found lying next to her. As the female paramedic attempt to rouse the woman, her male partner made an observation.

"Did you know this Rebecca Adams is the same woman who was accused of killing her son three years ago? I remember this house. I attended the scene when that poor little boy was killed. It was terrible; they say she pushed the boy from his bedroom window."

He pointed toward the upper level. "It's disturbing, being back here!"

"Didn't they find her innocent?" the female paramedic replied as she started an intravenous in the woman's arm and applied oxygen.

"Inconclusive evidence," the man responded. "Personally, I think she is guilty!" He shook his head in disgust.

"Keep your opinions to yourself, and act like a professional!" his partner snapped." We have a job to do. Now notify the emergency department that we are on route".

CHAPTER THIRTY:

As the paramedics bundled Rebecca into the ambulance to transport her to the hospital, Magda paced in her apartment; the EMS dispatch had told her they were taking Rebecca to the Campbell River Hospital. Should she go there ... she needed to know that Rebecca was going to be okay? Although the friendship was relatively new, the old woman had forged a bond with this vulnerable young woman. The problem was Magda didn't drive and had no money for a cab; the hospital was two miles away from her home.

"I guess I can walk if I go slowly, it won't make my heart hurt too much." Magda pulled on her overcoat, grabbed her pocketbook and keys, and then gathered up her walking cane. She exited her apartment, determined to check on Rebecca. As she locked the door, she heard footsteps behind her in the hallway; she realized it was her landlord.

"Ms. Bodrug!" he bellowed at her. His voice boomed and echoed in the narrow hallway. "Your rent is due today! Late rent means eviction!" he said with a sneer.

Magda stared the man down. "I'm going to the bank to get your stinking rent." She shook her cane at him, brushed passed, and made her way down the hall.

"I better get it," the man yelled after her. "Or you may need to find a new place to live!"

The landlord slunk along and followed her from the apartment building; all the while keeping a look out for the blonde bitch who had peppered sprayed him last week. His eyes and skin had burned for hours, and he didn't want a repeat performance.

Drudging along, it took Magda hours to make her way to the Campbell River Hospital. She had donned her overcoat, thinking the day was cool and overcast, but as she made her way along, she realized she was overheating. She needed to stop often and rest. At one bench she removed her heavy coat and carried it over her arm; it had become a burden. Her face was flushed, and her breath came in short, heaving bursts by the time she reached the hospital. As she approached the Emergency Department nursing station, she paused to calm her beating heart.

The nurse looked up from her computer as Magda spoke. "Can you help me, please?"

The nurse rushed to assist the elderly woman; she looked terrible. "Please sit down, ma'am. What can we do to help you?" She ushered the woman into a seat, concerned about her flush appearance and rapid respiration rate.

"Can you tell me if Rebecca Adams was brought to the hospital? The 911 operator told me she would be coming here for help. I need to know she is okay." Magda accepted the offered chair.

"Yes, she has been admitted, are you family? But more importantly, ma'am, are you okay, you seem very flushed?" The nurse leaned over Magda and checked her pulse; it was rapid and irregular.

"No, but I am a close friend, like a mother to her. And as for myself, I just need a sip of cold water." She puffed and clutched the nurse's hand.

The nurse gently pulled her hand away and said, "Let me get that glass of water and check on your friend. Now stay right here, and I will be right back." She left Magda and went into the main area for some water, and also to check on the status of Rebecca Adams. She approached the monitoring station.

"Hey Bev, do we still have Rebecca Adams here? The overdose patient? Someone is here asking about her; an elderly woman who seems unwell herself."

"Nope." Bev responded. "She was admitted to the medical observation on F7 about ten minutes ago. Psychiatry is planning to see her later, when she is more awake and medically stable. Say Mr. Adams doesn't happen to be with this older woman, does he? We have been trying to get through to him? He's not been answering his cellphone."

"Only her, but thanks, Bev. I best get back." The nurse returned to the triage area and found Magda sitting where she had left her. Offering the glass of water, she noted that the woman appeared less flushed. Magda sipped the cool water and thanked her.

"You are kind, very kind. I feel much better."

"I found out about your friend. She has been admitted to the hospital in Unit F7 for observation. If you want, I can have someone take you." The nurse started to explain, when suddenly a man came rushing in with a large cut to his forearm.

"I need some help!" he yelled. "Cut myself pretty good!"

The nurse turned away from Magda to assess the injured man. "You stay here, while I take this man to the suture room. I will be right back."

As the nurse hustled the man off to the treatment area, Magda scanned the hospital map on the wall. *Unit F7, I can find this on my own. Don't want to be a bother*, she thought and rose slowly; she leaned heavily on her cane and made her way to the elevator. She located Unit F7 by following the signage on the walls. Once outside the unit, she discovered she needed to 'buzz in' to gain entrance. The unit was a locked one, meaning entrance and exit were controlled to prevent patients from slipping away. She depressed the intercom/door camera button outside the unit, and waited.

"Yes?" The intercom crackled.

"I'm here to visit Rebecca Adams."

"She's just been admitted. No visitors yet," the voice said. "You will have to wait."

"Excuse me, but how long?" Magda asked. The voice on the intercom did not respond. She buzzed again.

"You will have to wait." It snapped and cut off.

Magda looked around and found a small alcove off to the left; several chairs with worn and cracked vinyl were lined up against the wall. She made her way over and struggled to sit. Her legs and feet were aching and sore from her long walk. She noticed that the dull throb in her chest that usually relaxed with rest was continuing to gnaw at her. She pawed through her coat pockets for the medication she usually sprayed under her tongue to relieve the pain.

Drat, I must have left it on the bathroom counter. She leaned her head back on the wall and massaged her breast bone. She started to doze off when she was startled awake by voices; it was two staff members standing outside the locked door.

"Buzz us in, Meghan." A man's voice spoke to the intercom.

"Come on in." It responded.

The door swung open and momentarily paused. Magda recognized the opportunity and slipped over to the opening. She peered around to see if anyone was watching, and when she saw that the coast was clear, she entered the unit. She read the names on the patient room doors as she walked down the hallway, and she had success with the third door on the left. She pushed the door open, then crept in.

CHAPTER THIRTY-ONE

In the bed attached to an intravenous drip and oxygen tubing, lay her friend. Rebecca's face looked pale, except for a smear of black across her chin and neck. It was from the medication they had forced down into her stomach to absorb the pills she had ingested. Magda felt her heart break when she looked at the young face resting on the pillow. She pulled up a chair and clutched her hand. Rebecca stirred slightly, but then she resumed her deep, drug induced slumber. Suddenly the door opened, and a nurse stepped into the room.

"Oh, I didn't know Ms. Adams had a visitor." Magda started to rise to leave.

"No worries. Doesn't matter to me, now just sit and relax. My name is Agnes, and I will be her nurse for this evening. Here, please have a seat in this chair, and then you won't be in the way as I check her vital signs." She gestured to the chair.

Magda tossed her overcoat and cane over the back of the chair, and she watched as the nurse took Rebecca's pulse, respirations, and blood pressure, and then shone a small flashlight in Rebecca's eyes. "Everything is good. Are you family of Ms. Adams?"

"No, but she is a very good friend. Like a daughter to me."

"Nice," the nurse responded. "Everyone needs friends. Say, has her husband been in touch with you? We haven't been able to reach him on his cellphone. Does he have another contact number?"

"Try Proctor Automotive, he works there."

"Fantastic, I'll try him there." The nurse set a bag on the table. "Here are Ms. Adams' belongings. The clothes were ruined and were thrown out, but here is what else she came in with." Suddenly, a cellphone chimed from inside the bag.

"There it goes again! It's been doing that a lot. Someone sure wants to get a hold of her." The nurse pointed at the bag. "Perhaps you should answer it." She turned and left the room, leaving Magda to hold vigil over the patient.

Magda pulled up next to Rebecca's bed and whispered, "You must leave before it is too late, and I can help you. I have ideas to help you, Rebecca, but sleep for now. We will talk more when you awaken." She squeezed the sleeping woman's hand.

Leaving Rebecca to rest she stood up to use the washroom; it had been a long walk from her apartment. She needed to splash water on her face and freshen up. She knocked into the overbed table, causing the items in the bag to spill onto the floor. A cellphone skidded across the floor, landing in front of Magda. She leaned over and picked up the device; the fall to the floor had activated the screen.

"Clumsy fool!" she reprimanded herself.

She turned the phone over in her hand, and gasped. Displayed on the screen was a picture of Jake Adams and a blonde woman she assumed was Olivia Proctor; the image graphically showed the couple in an intimate moment. She sat down, stunned by the blatant betrayal.

"Oh no!" She looked at the woman in the bed. "Is this the reason you tried to hurt yourself?' She was shaken by the picture and rocked in her chair. She leaned forward and whispered in Rebecca's ear.

"They can only win if they make you feel alone, and you are not alone. You have me!" She sat and quietly prayed for guidance. Beside her, Rebecca slept peacefully.

CHAPTER THIRTY-TWO

Across town, Jake Adams heard his name being paged on the overhead intercom.

"What now?" he muttered under his breath. "This can't be good!" Today was turning out to be one of those kinds of days.

As the message repeated, Randi Everett gave him a questioning look. Jake shrugged, set his tools down, and cleaned his hands. He'd only been back in town less than a full day, and his life was already a shit show. He'd had a fight with his wife, then had to sneak out of the shop to defuse Olivia, and now he had just returned from this meeting to be summoned to Andie's office. He feared the worse.

Did Andie know about them? He thought about this morning's events.

Olivia had arrived at the shop ranting that Rebecca had caused another scene. Not wanting everyone at the shop to witness this drama he'd pulled her aside, but once Olivia got rolling it was hard to control her. Today she was a freight train of emotion, and it was careening out of control. He requested to take his lunch break early and ushered her to his truck.

"This has to stop, Olivia. You have to stop bothering me at work because it's going to get me fired!" he said through gritted teeth.

They went to Lachlan Pathway to talk, as it was more private than the shop. As Jake drove, Olivia raved on that 'she wanted to mess Rebecca up', and that she wanted to 'hurt the bitch!' She had sworn, and yelled, and cried, then he finally figured out that a private message meant for him had been sent to Rebecca's phone by mistake. A very revealing private message! Once Olivia had calmed down enough, he asked to see her phone.

He read the text message string.

"Well shit!" He threw the phone at her. "It's out there now, and it's pretty clear we're lovers. Now it makes sense why Rebecca was freaking out. I already told her that I wanted a divorce, and I was going to talk with her *privately* tonight. But now ..." He stopped when he was interrupted by Olivia.

"Yes, she sure was acting like a freak, and it was horrific!" Olivia ranted. "Rebecca was making such a fool of herself, and me too! People were even videotaping us on their phones!"

"What? How could you be so stupid? They taped this!?" His head hurt thinking about the damage one misdirected text message had done.

Olivia didn't answer, she just sat and pouted.

CHAPTER THIRTY-THREE

As he walked to Andie's office, Jake worried about his future and regretted his past. Olivia had rescued him after Indie's tragic death, but he was beginning to realize Olivia's affections had become his torment. Some of her ideas were criminal; she was actually beginning to scare him, and now he feared for Rebecca's safety too. He knew what Olivia was capable of, and it made him shudder! His thoughts brought him back to almost four years ago when Fred Wright had died.

His death was no accident. He swallowed back the guilt that washed over him. But he could not afford any more time on the past because it was done; he had to move forward, he had to focus. He took a deep breath and knocked on Andie's door.

As he waited, he wondered. *Did Andie know about the 'assumed' affair? A dirty piece of gossip like this would spread like wildfire in this town!* He groaned to himself. *Would he care? He would probably be happy to get rid of Olivia and make her someone else's problem!*

"Come in!" Andie called from behind the closed door. He had been preparing to leave and work from home when he had received a phone call from the Campbell River Emergency Department.

"I heard the intercom, what's up?" Jake stood in the doorway waiting for Andie to invite him in; nothing about the man's demeanor indicated he knew about the affair.

"I'm sorry, but the Campbell River Emergency Department just called, and Rebecca has been admitted. They have been trying to reach you, but apparently you haven't been answering your cellphone." Andie looked concerned; they both knew he had a soft spot for Rebecca.

Jake patted his pocket. "Shit! I left it in my jacket pocket, and it's hanging on the chair at home. I guess I forgot it there. May I use your phone?"

"Sure, no problem." Andie gestured toward the phone. "Let me step out so you can have some privacy." Andie slipped from the office and closed the door.

Jake stood quietly for a moment; he had mixed feelings about coming to Rebecca's rescue again. Not so long ago he had loved her. Loved her like no other. That was before everything went to shit. He had never truly believed she had pushed Indie from the window, but none the less she was responsible for his death. She hadn't been watching him; she had been inattentive. A good mother wouldn't have let her child fall from an upstairs window. He could never forgive her. Ever!

"I don't want to help her again," he confessed aloud, but he dutifully placed the call because he knew he would be painted as the bad guy if he didn't.

I'm so done with all of this. Maybe it would be better if both Olivia and I just left. Put this place behind us before something bad happens again. We just need money, he thought as he dialed.

The emergency room staff informed him that Rebecca had been rushed to the hospital because of an apparent overdose. "She is stable, and currently in Observation Unit F7. I will transfer you to them," the nurse said.

As he waited for the line to connect, he thought. *She should have just died.*

"Mr. Adams?" the voice on the phoned asked. "Are you Rebecca Adam's husband?"

"Yes I am. Can you tell me what is going on with her?" He rubbed his head; he could feel a headache coming on. He felt so much older than his twenty-five years; he ached with fatigue.

Boy I could so use a drink! He found himself craving alcohol more and more often. He worried that he was turning into his old man; in more ways than one.

"Sir?" the voice asked. "Are you still there?" Jake's hadn't heard what had been said on the phone.

"Sorry, I missed that."

"The psychiatrist, Dr. Amaran, wants to meet with you to discuss your wife's treatment. We need you to come to the hospital this afternoon."

"Fine," he muttered. No sense in fighting it. Maybe they would commit Rebecca permanently, so he could be free of her and all this madness.

"Good, then we will see you shortly." The call ended.

Jake decided to go home and collect his cellphone, then let Olivia know about Rebecca. He didn't want to face this situation alone, but he'd just have to suck it up. Olivia was too volatile and unpredictable to go with him to the hospital, but for now he needed to tell Andie that he was leaving. He also needed to size up his boss; he was worried that Andie had learned about the 'coffee shop calamity.'

I need this job! I've worked too hard to let it be taken away! I've lost too much already! He left the office in search of Andie. He found him in the reception area, talking to Kevin Pritchard. His boss and the chief were obviously good friends, and he had often seen them talking about cars here at the shop. Just recently Pritchard had joined Andie as a guest at the car show.

Jake cringed when he noticed Pritchard observing him from across the room. He despised the man, and no doubt the feeling was mutual. Pritchard and his deputies had probed every part of Jake and Rebecca's private lives when Indie died. Rebecca was eventually found innocent, but the damage had been done, and Jake didn't trust him.

"Good morning Chief Pritchard." Jake muttered. His disdain was barely hidden behind his gritted teeth.

"Mr. Adams." Pritchard locked him with his steely grey eyes. "Sorry about your wife." He knew about the drama that had occurred between Rebecca and Olivia this morning, as an off-duty officer had been in Charlotte's Confectionaries when it broke out. She had called to let her boss know that the incident had been captured on various cellphones, and it was undoubtedly loaded up to the internet by now.

"I just thought you'd like to know that the Adams woman is the centre of attention again. She and Olivia Proctor are mixing it up down here at CCs." Deputy Janice Sinclair had explained to the chief.

When Pritchard had checked the internet, he'd shuddered. It appalled him how insensitive people could be; they had taped and uploaded this humiliating moment. He felt sorry for the Adams woman, but he was more worried about Andie. He had driven quickly to the shop to talk to him before some careless asshole let him know that his wife was having an affair with Jake Adams. In the past Olivia had been involved with several men, and each time Andie had turned a blind eye, but this time it was all a bit too close to home. During the investigation of Indiana Adams' death, Pritchard had learned of Jake's infidelity, but was unsure with whom; now the mystery woman was revealed.

Hasn't Rebecca been through enough? And now she is in the hospital again. Pritchard ground his teeth and glowered at Jake. He was disgusted with how the man treated his wife.

To break the tension, Andie interrupted. "Jake hadn't you better be getting along to the hospital. Give my best wishes to Rebecca." Andie ushered him toward the door.

"Tell her we are thinking about her." Chief Pritchard added. Jake shot him an angry look and stomped out of the building. Moments later, they heard the tires of his old beat-up Chevy truck peel from the parking lot.

"Chief Pritchard, I believe you had wanted to discuss something in private." Andie gestured toward his office, away from the reception area. As soon as the door closed, Kevin turned to Andie. He locked eyes with his partner. "Did you see it?"

"I saw it." Andie nodded "I just received a phone call from my mother. I have no doubt that it had barely hit the internet when she called. She was horrified! We all know social standing is a big thing for her! She's already called the family lawyer, Clarence Reid."

"What did he say?"

"Well, it seems poor old Reid is in the ICU at Vancouver General Hospital. According to my mother, Lyla Henderson, his office manager, spilled the beans and detailed what happened. So, get this ... my dear wife paid him a visit right before he collapsed. Olivia came in trying to void the pre-nup we signed, and when he either wouldn't or couldn't, she threatened him. I guess he collapsed shortly after that."

"Wow!" Kevin was shocked. "Threatened him about what?"

Andie shrugged. "I don't know, but I can only imagine!"

"So, what's next?" Kevin asked

"Well, I've been busy. I need to get out of that monstrosity of a house and move to the lake house. I have already talked with the housekeeper, Agatha. She is packing all my clothes and personal items and sending them over. We can stay there, it's private and secluded."

The phone rang.

"Sorry I have to take this, I am organizing for a moving company to transport my paintings, art collection, and books to the lake house. I don't want to leave them behind; as I'm sure Olivia would have a bonfire. She has no appreciation for the finer things in life." He smiled at his partner "The finer things like you!"

After Andie completed his call, Kevin addressed the other looming issue.

"What are we going to do about the pictures? You know she'll use them against us?"

Andie shook his head and smiled.

"I'm already working on that too. I have drafted a social media release and with your approval, I intend to upload it to the Internet. It announces that I am divorcing Oliva, and also it states that I am in a relationship with a new love interest." He grabbed Kevin's hand. "I feel so grateful to have you in my life!"

"Do it, let the world know about us. I'm ready!" Kevin stared into Andie's eyes. He admired his partner's new found strength, and they would need it to face the potential backlash that might come with the announcement. They embraced until finally Andie pulled away

"I just need to finish going through some security surveillance tapes before I leave. When I caught Burke stealing, I started reviewing the tapes, and they contained some pretty damning evidence. The cameras also revealed some interesting details on my wife's infidelity; it has certainly been an education. There are only a few really old ones to review now, and then I'm planning to send them to my lawyer. It shouldn't take more than an hour, then I'll meet you at the lake house."

They embraced once more, then Pritchard left, leaving Andie to post the announcement and kick start their new life together. The announcement read:

"Automotive mogul, Andie Proctor, and police chief, Kevin Pritchard, are pleased to announce their ongoing relationship to the world. After recently separating from his wife, Olivia Baird Proctor, Andie Proctor is thrilled to proclaim that after years of bitter unhappiness and abuse at the hands of his estranged spouse, he is able to freely enter this new and exciting time with his life partner. The couple has retreated to a private location to start their new lives. The couple would like to extend many thanks to friends and family for their ongoing support and love. The Proctor divorce is pending. Olivia Proctor could not be reached for comment."

Andie decided he would send this personal statement, along with the one that Rebecca had completed announcing Proctor Automotives' recent success at The Armstrong National Car Show to the Campbell River Gazette reporter, Gretchen Berg. She was known as the 'the paper's gossip monger' and he knew from experience that Gretchen despised Olivia; his soon-to-be ex-spouse had treated her poorly at many social events. Oliva had snubbed the reporter, and Andie knew that Gretchen would love sticking it to her.

CHAPTER THIRTY-FOUR

Jake rushed home and screeched to a stop in front of the house. He flung the door open and was confronted by the remains of the EMS visit. Scattered on the floor was discarded medical equipment and wrappers. Next to this was an empty bottle of vodka and a variety of pills. In the bathroom he found the remainder of the pills; bottles were spilled across the floor and emptied in the sink.

"What a mess!" he exclaimed, re-entering the living room. He kicked the empty bottle. "Bitch drank my vodka!" He needed to find his cellphone.

I left it in my coat pocket, he thought as he retraced his steps from last night. *Then I hung my coat on the kitchen chair.* He went into the kitchen and found his jacket thrown on the floor, but when he dug through his pockets, he came up empty handed.

"Where the hell is my phone?" Jake muttered aloud. He looked around and found parts of the case lying smashed on the living room floor. He stirred the garbage with his foot, but his cellphone was not amongst the rubble.

Shit! She must have taken it. His thoughts spun, as he realized that if that was the truth, then there was a good chance she had gone into his private files and found some pretty revealing pictures.

What did you see, Rebecca? Did you get the shock of your life, and is this why you did this? He pondered as he looked at the mess on the floor. He didn't feel proud of himself. He went to the kitchen and used the land line to call Olivia. She laughed hysterically at the news.

"She tried to kill herself with pills and booze, eh?" she brayed. "I told you she might do that! Too bad she didn't succeed. Shit, the woman has nine lives!" She was annoyed that this attempt had been unsuccessful, yet again.

"I want to come with you to the hospital, and together we can enlighten the doctor on what a lunatic your wife is. Everyone knows she's unstable, especially if they saw us on the internet. It was a great fight!"

As Jake listened to her, he made a decision, and Olivia wasn't going to like it.

"You can't come to the hospital for now because I know you, and you'll probably blab something inappropriate. Let me scope things out first, then I'll talk with you later." He hung up quickly; he didn't want to discuss it any further, but he could feel her seething from afar.

When Jake arrived at the hospital entrance, he was shocked to find Olivia standing in the lobby already waiting for him. She had showed up unannounced; she wasn't going to let him off the hook so easily.

"Damn it, Olivia! Didn't I tell you not to come?" he sighed and pulled her over to a private area in the lobby where they wouldn't be overheard. "Well, since you're already here and are determined to stay, we'd best make a plan before meeting with the doctor. Now don't cause a scene!"

Jake turned to her. "I think she has my cellphone, and we both know what is stored on that. Damn! I should have gotten a new one with password protection. How much do you think she knows about us?"

"Well, she knows we're lovers, and if she's seen our photos and videos, then she's been very well educated." Olivia couldn't help but laugh aloud, but when she saw Jake's brooding scowl, she stifled it.

"Keep your voice down!" Jake hissed. He didn't like institutions, including hospitals and police. Since Indie's death he had learned not to trust anyone in a uniform. "You don't know who might be listening. We need to get our story straight, and we need to be smart about it."

Olivia pouted and sulked. She didn't like to be told what to say.

Watching her reaction, Jake decided he'd had enough. "The way you're acting right now maybe it's a bad idea for you to be here." He stood up and pulled at her arm. "Leave now, and I'll call you later."

"Hell no, I'm not going anywhere!" She shook him off. "I'm not missing this drama. I am tired of skulking around and hiding!" Her voice was getting louder and shriller; people were starting to stop and look at the duo.

"Sssh ... fine!" He grabbed her arm. "But if you come to the unit with me, you need to shut up!"

"But, of course." She leaned in and daringly planted a kiss on his lips.

"Stop!" he hissed, but couldn't help smiling at her recklessness.

"Later." she whispered in his ear. He silently prayed that this wouldn't backfire in his face.

CHAPTER THIRTY-FIVE

Magda sat holding vigil over the sleeping Rebecca. She heard people talking outside of Rebecca's room; pieces of the conversation drifting in.

"Why didn't she just die? Shit, she can't even get this right!" This was a woman's voice.

Magda leaned forward to peer through the crack in the door. She recoiled; it was Jake Adams and Olivia Proctor, the people from the camera. She was horrified by the comment she'd just overheard.

"Please wake up!" she whispered, gently shaking Rebecca, but she slept on.

Outside the door, Jake hissed. "Be quiet, Olivia! You can't talk like that, someone might hear. We also need to ensure Rebecca is asleep and not listening."

Magda heard them push open the door. "I hope she isn't covered in blood and nastiness! Yuck!" It was Olivia's voice again. The couple paused momentarily outside the door, and Magda overheard Jake once again warn his companion to behave. His voice was tense.

Magda panicked. She needed to hide; she couldn't be seen here, but where? *The bathroom!* she thought.

As she pulled the cane from the back of the chair her overcoat slid to the floor, but she couldn't worry about that for now, she had to hide. She hobbled over to the bathroom just before the couple entered the room. The hospital door latched behind them; now they were in the room all alone with Rebecca. Magda wanted to overhear their plans, so she pushed the bathroom door open a crack.

What are they up to? she worried to herself. *How can I let others know about their plotting?*

Then it struck her that she was still holding the cellphone. "I can!" she whispered. "I have this fancy phone. Elena taught me how to record Sylvie's playtimes. I did it many times before. Now let me see."

Magda located the appropriate camera app and pushed the video record button. She edged the door open slightly wider, then eased the phone into the space. She started recording the interaction.

Jake peered down at his sleeping wife. "Looks like she's out cold. Rebecca?" He gave her shoulder a rough shake. She murmured, but didn't rouse.

"Well, she isn't dead yet, but perhaps we should help her along. Wouldn't a little air in her intravenous line stop her heart? On TV it always works, so why couldn't we give it a try?" Olivia was already looking through the bedside drawers. "Hmm, I need to find a needle and syringe."

"Do you really think that they're going to leave sharps items and needles in a psychiatric unit around suicidal people?"

"Shut up!" Olivia hissed. "What do you suggest then; we smother her with a pillow?"

"Now that would be a bit obvious, wouldn't it? Just be quiet for now, and let me think. Do you actually have any smart ideas not this stupid shit you've been suggesting? We can't get caught; we have already dodged the bullet once when old man Wright died. We can't press our luck if we want to successfully get out of Campbell River!"

Knowing Rebecca was passed out and with the door firmly shut, Olivia continued to scheme out loud.

"Give me a break, lover." She stuck her tongue out at him. "Do I have to remind you that your wife has already tried to kill herself twice before and now this time?" She pointed at Rebecca. "It wouldn't surprise anyone if she finally did it; we just have to help her be successful. She just needs that extra little push."

She continued. "I've been thinking a lot about this. If we take away everything and everyone that she loves it should be enough to force her to end her life." She ticked off the items on her fingers.

"Her old man is out of the picture." Tick.

"She has lost her best friend!" Tick.

She paused and then grasped his hand. "And Indie is dead. She caused it Jake; your boy is gone!" Jake momentarily looked away and blinked away tears. She squeezed his hand, but continued.

"Now you are going to divorce her." Olivia ticked off the final item on her fingers and looked down at her former friend. "So our dear, sweet Rebecca has nothing to live for anymore. We just have to force her to face the fact that she is nothing to anybody."

Jake had questions about her plans. "I agree it is not a bad idea, but will it be enough to push her to the brink? She still has her work at Proctor Automotive, and Andie will always be on her side."

"Don't worry, I can solve that problem; I will just give Andie an ultimatum. Either he fires Rebecca or I will expose his secrets. Then boom, Rebecca's shaky house of cards will come toppling down."

"Expose what?"

"Just hang on a moment, I'll get to that." She pulled out her cellphone and scrolled through the images.

"While you were gone, I took a little trip to old Clarence Reid, you know that sleazy lawyer of Andie's? It turns out that the pre-nup is solid, and if I divorce the little creep, I get nothing, however ..." She paused and held her phone out for him. "We do have some other leverage."

Jake took the phone Olivia had thrust at him. He was confused until he scrolled through the pictures, then he was shocked. He just about dropped the phone in disbelief.

"What? Andie and Chief Pritchard are lovers?" He couldn't believe what he was seeing. His mouth hung open as his brain tried to process the information. *Andie maybe, but surely not Pritchard? There was no way; the man was all bluster and manliness.*

"Where did you get these pictures?" He handed back the phone.

"In Las Vegas, at the hotel." She laughed at her handiwork. "After I left you I went to Andie's suite, and I let myself in. You wouldn't believe my surprise when I opened the bedroom door and found them together."

"They didn't see you?"

"Nope, they were both sound asleep, so I got lots of pictures. Great shots, eh? It leaves no doubt who they are and what they had been doing!" She was proud of her accomplishment.

"Then just before I left Las Vegas, I sent him the pics from a burner phone. He must have shit himself when he got them." She tapped the phone. "He's probably figured out by now they're from me. Who else? I've been ignoring him to let him steep in his own distress. I intend on using them to our benefit." Olivia smirked at her own cunningness.

"What if it doesn't work? What if he doesn't buy into your blackmail scheme? Surely Pritchard will see through your tactics."

Jake was skeptical that Olivia could pull off her blackmail plan. He knew Andie's reputation was important to him, but he had many people who loved and supported him, and now this included a very influential Chief Pritchard. "I can't see 'the chief' letting you get away with this; blackmail is illegal you know."

Olivia snorted at him. "Jeez Jake, give me some credit! If this plan doesn't work, then I have other things up my sleeve. You know we've talked about this before, and we do have a back-up plan."

"What do you mean?"

"Oh, for God's sake! Haven't we talked about this many times before?" She pointed at Rebecca. "Perhaps we can just drug her and push her off a cliff or something. I've been following her, and she does like hanging around Lachlan Pathway. It has some very treacherous spots you know; maybe she could have a bad fall. A strategically planned fall."

"Sssh, someone is coming," Jake said. They moved apart.

The door opened, and the nurse from earlier entered. "Oh, I see Mrs. Adams has some more visitors. Are you Mr. Adams?"

"Yes, I am, but you must be mistaken about other visitors because Mrs. Proctor and I are the only two people she is close to."

"Oh," the nurse responded. "I'm sure some older woman was in visiting earlier." She peered around the room, then shrugged, and directed the duo toward the door. "But now, Dr. Amaran is waiting for you."

Magda waited until she was sure the three had left the room before she came out of hiding. No one had noticed the old woman peering through the crack in the bathroom door or the overcoat lying on the floor. They had no idea that Magda had been secretly taping their conversations.

She eased the door open, stumbling back into the room. Her legs were shaking from the long walk to the hospital, but it was now shock that made her tremble. She had just overheard the planning of an innocent woman's murder! She made her way to the chair and plopped down; her chest was aching and she felt sick with worry for her friend. As she placed the cellphone on the overbed table, her hands tremored.

I must let someone know and I need to leave a note for Rebecca; she has to listen to this terrible confession.

Looking around the room she found a pencil, and then on a paper towel from the bathroom, she wrote: "LISTEN."

Magda set the phone and the note on the overbed table, then stood up to go in search of a nurse or doctor. She wanted to find someone to whom she could tell her story. As she pulled the door open, she felt a crushing pain in her chest. Her breath caught in her throat, and her vision swam. She felt herself falling, and she could do nothing to stop it.

My heart! she thought as her vision darkened.

Nurse Annie Simpson was doing the fifteen-minute 'safety checks' on Unit F7, when she came across a woman lying on the floor outside Room 3A. "What the hell!" she gasped. She knelt down and gently shook the woman, then checked her pulse. She wasn't any patient of theirs, and she didn't recognize her as a family member either. "Ma'am? Are you okay? Ma'am!"

The woman only responded with a groan. Her pulse was weak and thready; her skin was cool and clammy. "This is not good. I need help."

She leaned back and yelled down the hallway. "I need help! Call the resuscitation team STAT!!" Turning back to the woman, she reassured her. "Help is on the way!"

CHAPTER THIRTY-SIX

R ebecca's eyes fluttered open. Unfamiliar lighting, grey blue walls, and blue striped curtains surrounding the bed she was lying on came into focus as she rubbed her blurry eyes.

Where am I? She leaned up on her elbow.

She noticed that an intravenous had been inserted into her right arm, and clear liquid dripped from a bag suspended from a pole. The room swam in front of her eyes, so she flopped back to let the vertigo pass. Suddenly her senses came rushing back, including her some of her memory.

Oh yeah, the hospital. But how did I get here? All I remember is taking the pills and booze? She thought hard, her memories slowly coming back. Her mouth tasted like a dirty, old boot and when she wiped her lips, her hand came away black.

They must have given me something to clean up the pills I took. I sure could use a glass of water. She dangled her legs over the edge of the bed and willed the swoon to go away. *Breathe.* She inhaled deeply.

As the spinning stopped, Rebecca became aware of a commotion outside her door. Multiple voices spoke over each other, alarms were going off, and running footsteps could be heard. Easing herself to a standing position, she clutched the IV pole for support, then tried to peer around the partially open door.

Curiosity drove her towards the sounds and on shaky legs she carefully approached the door. She cracked the door open further and witnessed an ongoing emergency. Someone had collapsed and the resuscitation team was working to revive them. As Rebecca watched the activity, one member moved aside, revealing the identity of the person on the floor.

"Magda?" she gasped aloud. The attending physician looked up. "Do you know this woman?" she asked. "Does she have any medical conditions?"

"Yes I know her; I think she has heart problems, and she takes a spray for it … nitroglycerin." Rebecca moved forward to see her friend.

"Thanks, now please stand back and let the team do their job. Anything more you can add?"

"Not that I can recall." Rebecca suddenly felt weak; she needed to lie down.

"Can someone please take the patient back to her room?" the doctor directed. "Thank you for your help."

"Is she going to be okay?" Rebecca was frightened for her friend.

"We are doing what we can, but now please go back to your room." A staff member took Rebecca by her arm, redirected her back to her room, then closed the door.

Rebecca sat on her bed and plucked at the tape that held her intravenous tube. She could hear the voices of the medical staff who were working on her friend. She was anxious to learn more about her condition, but she dared not interrupt again. As she sat waiting, Rebecca saw a cellphone sitting on the table, and she reached over to pick it up. As she did, a piece of paper fluttered to the floor. She stooped to pick it up, setting off another head rush.

On the paper, in scratchy printing was a single word, 'LISTEN.'

"Listen?" she puzzled aloud. She turned over the paper and found nothing else. She turned her attention back to the phone. She recognized it; it was Jake's, and it was the same one that contained the explicit pictures of the affair. *I'm not going to allow you your dirty little pictures! Let's take care of these.* She activated the phone to delete the vile images, but as she flipped through the photos, she came across a video date stamped ten minutes ago.

What the hell? Is this what 'LISTEN' is all about? She wondered as she pushed the button. On the miniature screen Rebecca was able to recognize both Olivia and Jake standing over her hospital bed. The clip appeared to have been taken by someone hiding behind a partially closed door. She could make out the outline of the bathroom door across from her; it now stood open, but no one was there.

Who took this video? The clip played, and she watched in shock as Jake and Olivia planned her death.

"Oh my God!" she gasped. "What am I going to do?" She sat rocking back and forth on the bed, attempting to calm her racing heart and clear her befuddled mind. Slowly her thoughts were becoming clear. *How dare they?! The people I thought loved me are actually talking about killing me!* Suddenly she felt a deep burning anger starting to well up in her gut.

She remembered lying on her living room floor waiting for either death or salvation when Indie had appeared to her. It was his manifestation that had sparked her to call for help, and now it was his memory that ignited a burning flame deep in her soul. She felt Indie's love and her parent's strength flowing through her veins. Her dismay was turning to rage!

"So you're going to try and kill me, you assholes?! No way! It ain't gonna happen." She spat out the words and clenched her fists in anger. Her body trembled with fury!

First, I've got to get out of here, and then I have to leave Campbell River. The problem was that she was locked in a psychiatric unit and was at the mercy of her husband and the doctors! Jake could have her committed; she had certainly given them enough reasons.

Her thoughts boiled. *Being here is placing me in a very vulnerable position. If they convince Jake that I am not mentally competent, they can detain me and ply me with all sorts of medications and treatments. Their 'psych drugs' will just turn me into the same mumbling zombie like last time, and then I won't be able to defend myself. What would stop Jake from returning and carrying out his plans to kill me? I'm sure he and Olivia could make it look like some kind of accident.*

Rebecca looked at the phone in her hand and considered her options. *It certainly contains some shocking evidence, but how can I use this to my advantage? One thing I do know is that I need to get out of here ... soon.*

"But, how?" she spoke aloud. She was so deep in thought she hadn't noticed that a nurse had entered the room. She quickly tucked the phone under the pillow.

"Oh Mrs. Adams, I see you are awake. My name is Agnes, and I will be your nurse this evening. Now how are you doing?" She smiled at Rebecca.

She thought of the other times she had been admitted to the hospital following the previous two failed suicide attempts. *They'll probe me with questions and analyze my answers, looking for reasons to question my sanity. I know I'm going to have to play along to improve my chances of being discharged.* She pondered. *Or is escaping this place another option? Play the game Rebecca, if you want to find a way out of here.*

So as the nurse asked her questions, Rebecca stared blankly back in return. "What did you say?" She slurred her words and acted drugged.

"I asked how you were feeling, Mrs. Adams." The nurse waited patiently for a response.

Rebecca smiled sheepishly. "Fine, no actually I feel kinda woozy, and rather silly too. I made a foolish mistake; I didn't really mean to take the pills. I was overreacting to a stupid fight I had with my husband." She chattered on, hoping the nurse was buying her story. She ended her speech by saying, "So I think I need some help and would like to talk with the doctor. Is there a chance that I can speak to her tonight? And could I get something to eat?"

Pleased with her patient's response, the nurse said, "Good idea, Mrs. Adams. I will get Dr. Amaran to see you tonight. She has already spoken to your husband and your friend, and we are all in agreement that you should stay for a little while. Just until we are sure you are not a risk to harm yourself again. I'll go and let the doctor know you would like to see her. Now what can I get you to eat?"

Agnes wasn't completely certain Rebecca wasn't trying to con her, but it was a busy evening, especially since the recent emergency crisis that had occurred just outside this very room. The tension and anxiety of the other patients was palpable tonight. This patient was the least of her concerns; she was still dopey from the drugs she had taken.

"Sure that's a good idea. A sandwich would be great, but don't fuss too much. I know you are busy."

The nurse nodded and turned to leave.

"By the way, your friend, the old woman who visited you earlier, was the one who collapsed in the hallway. She is now in intensive care, I thought you would like to know. I just hope this won't upset you too much."

Rebecca slowly shook her head. "What old woman? I don't know who you are talking about or why she was in my room?"

The nurse was puzzled, maybe she was mistaken. Perhaps the old woman was in another room after all, but she didn't have time to dive into it more. "I'll be back, now just rest." She left the room, pulling the door closed behind her.

CHAPTER THIRTY-SEVEN

R ebecca waited for the door to click shut and then sprang into action. According to the nurse, the plan was to keep her indefinitely, so she was going to have to try to escape. So she carefully detached the IV from her arm, placing pressure to prevent bleeding. She searched the room next, checking for her clothes and personal items; she came up empty handed. The personal belongings bag only contained her purse and her own cellphone. No clothes, but at least there were her shoes.

"Shit! Jake and Olivia have already met with the doctor, and I can just imagine what tale they have told the psychiatry team." She cursed aloud in the room. "I can't exactly slip out of this place in this hospital gown or in the nude. I need something to wear."

It was at that moment she saw the overcoat that Magda had placed over the chair; it had slipped to the floor and was partially hidden. Rebecca pushed the chair aside and pulled the coat out. She recognized it; it was the coat Magda often wore when she visited the cemetery.

If this is Magda's she was probably the one who took the video clip. What a shock for her to see and hear all of this! She thought of the cellphone. *But why was she here in the first place? I can't remember anything.* She silently rubbed her head.

Rebecca picked up the coat and as she searched the pockets, lost memories slowly seeped back. *I called her, and I asked her for help. She must have called the paramedics, and then she came to check on me. Wow! I am so blessed to have her in my life. But Magda what have I done? My selfish actions may have killed you, so I can't waste the opportunity you have given me.*

She found Magda's keys, pocketbook, and a head scarf in the pockets. *I can use these items to disguise myself. No one will pay much attention to an old woman coming to visit someone in the hospital, and when they do find out I am missing, they will be looking for a younger person anyway.*

She put Magda's keys and pocketbook back in the pockets, pulled on the heavy coat, and tied the head scarf on her head. She checked her appearance in the bathroom mirror, then adjusted the scarf to cover more of her face.

Looks convincing! She smiled at her reflection.

She ripped of her patient identification bracelet and threw it on the floor. Rebecca was determined to reclaim her life. She pulled her own purse from the garment bag, grabbed Jake's cellphone, cracked open the door, and checked to see if there was anyone in the hallway. The area was empty, but she could hear loud voices coming from the common room, and the intercom blared overhead.

"Assistance required in the common room ... assistance in the common room."

Rebecca heard footsteps running down the hallway, so she pulled the door closed and waited until they passed.

Peeking out again the hallway was empty, so she quietly slipped out of her room, hoping to remain unnoticed. Sneaking down the corridor, Rebecca reached a locked door; beside it was the intercom/door camera that Magda had encountered; Rebecca depressed the button and held her breath.

"Yes?" the intercom responded. The anonymous voice could see the same old woman from before standing in front of the door camera.

"I'm leaving now. I need you to let me out please."

"Fine," the disinterested voice responded.

The door lock released, and then it swung opened. Rebecca quickly slipped through the space and into the corridor. *So far, so good!* She gripped the hand-rail and eased her way along the hallway, her legs still feeling leaden from the medication in her system. As she made her way along no one seemed to notice an old lady; everyone seemed to rushing about doing their duties.

Perfect, it's better to stay hidden in plain sight! Now where is the exit? She saw direction signs hanging from the ceiling. *Exit to the left. ICU to the right.* She considered her options.

She was conflicted; she needed to leave before the staff realized she was missing, but she owed Magda her life. So she turned right and crept cautiously down the corridor to the ICU, keeping her head low and avoiding eye contact. When she reached the intensive care entrance it was also locked, and admittance was required via a similar intercom as the psychiatric unit.

"Shit!" she cursed under her breath. "Now what?"

Rebecca didn't want to draw attention to herself; she was afraid of getting caught and dragged back to her own locked unit. She had just made up her mind to leave when the doors suddenly swung open from the inside. The members of the resuscitation team were talking amongst themselves as they left the ICU, so no one noticed as an old woman slipped through the open door.

Rebecca crept past rooms checking for Magda, and finally located her three doors down from the nursing station. Cautiously peeking in, she was relieved to find the room was empty except for Magda. The ICU staff was busy attending to another medical crisis next door providing Rebecca the opportunity to slip unnoticed into Magda's room. The elderly woman was attached to a heart monitor, oxygen, and various intravenous drips, and she looked very ill. Rebecca sat down next to her bed and picked up her hand.

"I'm so sorry, Magda. I never meant for this to happen." She held the woman's hand against her cheek and whispered. "Thank you! Thank you so much for everything! I cannot begin to tell you how much you mean to me." It was her turn to pray. "Please God don't let me lose my last support! Don't let this good woman die!" It was her turn to hold vigil by Magda's bedside, but exhaustion and the drugs floating in her system waved over her, and she nodded off. As Rebecca dozed, she dreamed wolves were hunting her; they wanted to tear her heart out. These terrifying creatures wore Olivia and Jake's faces.

"No." She moaned in her sleep. In her dream, the wolves chased her through the forest and forced her to the cliff edge; they stepped closer and closer.

Suddenly she startled awake. She heard voices coming from down the hall and knew she must flee, but she didn't want to leave Magda alone. The old woman looked so vulnerable.

"I need to go now and get to safety, but I promise I will come back and help you." She leaned down and kissed the old woman on the cheek. "I love you, Magda."

The voices were coming closer.

She checked the corridor, and the staff was still outside the neighbouring room. She knew they would be coming to Magda's room next, so while they were distracted, Rebecca slipped out and went the opposite direction, making her way to the hospital EXIT. She darted out the door into the cool night, scurrying along in the shadows, fearful that at any moment someone would grab her and drag her back to the hospital. Two blocks away she stumbled and fell to her knees, skinning them on the rough pavement.

Rebecca stood up and limped into a side alleyway, away from the busy main street. She slumped down against a fence to catch her breathe. As she gasped for air and clutched the 'stitch' in her side, she realized that she was in terrible physical shape. She had once taken great pride in being on the track team in high school, but the years had made her soft and spongy. Her recent running along Lachlan Pathway had helped, but not enough. As her breathing eased, she took stock of her situation. Both of her knees were scrapped and oozed fresh blood, Magda's coat was soiled and dirty, and the scarf had fallen off her head.

"What a mess!" She cursed aloud. "I'm out, but what the hell am I going to do now? I certainly cannot go home because I'm sure Jake and Olivia are waiting to finish me off. I cannot go to the police because they will just pack me back to the loonie bin! Think Rebecca think!" She rested her head against the rough boards of the fence and considered her situation. She leaned forward and assessed the wounds on her knees. *I wonder if you have a tissue in your pockets, Magda.* She turned out the overcoat pockets. *Pocketbook and keys, but no tissue.*

Having to make due, Rebecca compressed the wounds with the edge of the hospital gown. Under the heavy coat, no one would notice the bloody stain. With the wounds addressed, she turned her attention back to the items in her lap, then suddenly thought, *Magda's keys! I can hide at her place. No one knows about the connection between us. I should be safe there for the time being.*

She dumped everything back into her purse and struggled to her feet, steadying herself on the fence. Peering down the empty street, she was still surprised that no one was looking for her. *No police ... no hospital security.*

She found the errant scarf lying on the ground near the road. She plucked it up, secured it snuggly on her head, and started her journey to Magda's apartment.

CHAPTER THIRTY-EIGHT

A cross town, Jake and Olivia had arrived at the Wright house to remove some of his personal items. It was hard to return; it was a place of happy memories, but it also housed great angst, and pain, and loss. They opened the front door, then stepped through the debris left by the paramedics.

"Nice mess, Jake!" Olivia scoffed. "Why don't we really mess this place up!"

"Leave it, Olivia. I just gotta get some clothes." He left her alone in the living room, and she couldn't resist wreaking some havoc. She swept a collection of family photos from the mantel and as the glass shattered on the floor, she giggled with joy, grinding her heels into the smiling face. All the parts of her plan were falling into place; Jake was finally leaving Rebecca and moving in with her. Olivia's heart was bursting with joy.

She turned to find Jake looking solemnly at a photo of Indie and Rebecca, a photo of happier times.

"What's with you!?" she snapped. She ripped the photo from his hands and threw it on the floor with the other pile of destruction.

"Stop it Olivia, there is no need to be so nasty. This was once my life too; there's no need to be so cruel!" He plucked a picture of Indie from the debris and placed it back on the mantel.

"What does it matter if we trash this place, it will just look like she did it herself!" Olivia crossed her arms and pouted. Jake glowered at her, but he didn't say anything. She kicked the rubble at him.

"Go sit in the truck. I'll be right out!" He shoved her toward the door. "Go ... now!"

"Hurry up!" she huffed, stomping off to his truck. She sat sulking in Jake's rundown truck; she didn't like being spoken to like that. Egging for a fight, she placed a phone call to Andie.

"What do you want, Olivia?"

"I want you out of my house. Right now!" she spat.

"Already done. I never liked that monstrosity anyway; I am moving to the lake house. I much prefer my gardens and the privacy it offers. And yes, Olivia, Kevin and I both know about the photos, and if you think you can blackmail us, then you're very wrong."

"Don't you threaten me, little man," she yelled.

He hung up, leaving her holding a silent phone. She tried calling him back, but only reached his voice mail. She sent a text message instead.

> **'What kind of game are you playing?'**

She waited, but there was still no response. Furious with him, she sent him another scathing text.

> **'You might not be interested in the pictures, but I bet everyone else would. Won't everyone be surprised to find out what your relationship with our chief of police is all about, especially if the media gets hold of this story?'**

Her phone chimed, and the message read.

> **'Too late, Olivia! Read the internet!**

"What?" She went online and read the social media announcement.

> *Andie Proctor, automotive mogul, announces divorce from his wife of 6 years.*
>
> *Today Andie Proctor announces he is divorcing his wife Olivia Baird Proctor. The couple is separating citing irreconcilable differences. Proctor states he is moving on with his life announcing a new relationship with Kevin Pritchard. The new couple will be retreating to their lake home for privacy. Neither Proctor could be reached for comment. Reported by Gretchen Berg.*

Olivia went ballistic. She leaned on the truck horn and screaked out the window. "Jake, get your ass out here!"

CHAPTER THIRTY-NINE

Jake was just finishing the last of his packing when he heard a horn blaring and Olivia yelling from the truck window.

"What now?" He cursed under his breath. He left the house, leaving the door unlocked. There was nothing there worth stealing; when Indie died everything of value to him had been taken. He slammed the door shut on this chapter of his life and dragged his suitcase to the truck.

"It's about time!" Olivia yowled. "I need you to read this."

Jake flung the case in the back of the truck, then yanked the cab door open. Hoisting himself into the truck, he turned to her. "What was with the trashing of the house?" he growled.

"Who cares about the house; look at this! Andie has a sent out a media announcement. He's ruining my plans. He's making a fool out of me!" She shoved the phone in his face. Fed up with her tantrums, he snatched the phone from her. He read the statement and was shocked by Andie's bravado. "So what are we going to do now?" He pushed the phone back at Olivia and started to drive away; she was beet red and fuming.

"What are we going to do? We're going to post those pictures online and make him regret crossing me! Then we're going to turn up the heat on your wife."

She fussed and fumed, and then returned to re-read the media clip. "How dare he? I will not let any more people mess with my life!" She wheeled on Jake; he could see the fury in eyes.

"You do recall what happened when old man Wright decided to interfere in our lives? He ended up dead!" she hissed. "He was going to spill the beans on us; he was going to tell Rebecca about our affair."

Jake screeched the truck to a stop and grabbed her arm.

"Enough Olivia, I don't want to talk about my father-in-law's death. Most of the time he treated me pretty well, and I'll never forgive myself for what *you* made me do to him. When I loosened the lug nuts on his car, I just thought it would shake him up and scare him; not kill him. I had no idea it would cause the car to flip over and he would die!" Jake swallowed the lump of guilt caught in his throat.

Olivia sprang on his words. "Now wait a minute, I didn't make you *do* anything. It was just a suggestion. I was just thinking out loud. Don't pin his death on me Jake, you were the one who tampered with the tires. Now let me go!"

"How dare you? You are just as much to blame for his death as me!" he shouted at her. "It was your idea!" His eyes were popping out and his face was flushed, but he released her arm.

She started to interject, but he cut her off.

"Stop it, Olivia! Just stop it!" Jake was so angry he could have easily pushed her out of his truck. He had never struck her before, but it was getting harder with each of her rash outbursts to control his anger. Sometimes his hand itched to give her a good hard smack.

"Perhaps we shouldn't talk anymore, not until we both cool off. Now where are we going?" he said through gritted teeth. He started to drive again; his hands clenching the steering wheel.

"My house. Andie is at his lake house." She sat quietly on the far side of the truck, rubbing her arm. For the first time, she was concerned she couldn't control his behaviour.

They drove on in silence, each wanting the other to apologize. Jake brooded … Olivia schemed.

As Jake turned into the driveway, Olivia received a text message from Andie. Olivia read the message out loud.

> I have been assessing my options Olivia, and I want a divorce. According to my lawyer the pre-nup is still valid, so you lose! I have also come across some evidence that would put you and Jake away for a long time. Seen any good videos lately? I saw one, and you are pure evil. Now leave me alone or I will send this surveillance video to the media!'

"What the fuck does this mean?" Olivia was dumbfounded.

"Could this have anything to do with Darren Burke getting fired? Some of the guys said that Andie might have a surveillance system at the shop?" Jake worried aloud.

For a brief moment Olivia was actually shaken, but she was certain Andie was bluffing. "How would I know? He surely doesn't have any such evidence, and if he did, wouldn't he have shown Pritchard?" They both stared at each other. "Does he think this gives him the upper hand?" Olivia wanted revenge. "Oh, you will pay Andie, and so will Rebecca!"

* * *

When they arrived at Proctor Estate there was no sign of Andie or Kevin, or anyone. The housekeeper, Agatha, was also gone, and the house was eerily quiet. Olivia dragged Jake from room to room looking to trash Andie's personal possessions, but it was obvious that he had removed the most important ones prior to her arrival. She was very disappointed; she had planned to destroy his precious collections.

Jake just followed her as she stormed through the house, his steps heavy, his body weighed down with fatigue. He avoided offering any opinions, not wanting to get into another fight with her. He was worried about the 'video evidence' that Andie had mentioned, and there was so much going on that he just wanted to have a drink. He wanted to forget this day, and then to go to bed and sleep forever.

As they passed the liquor cabinet, Jake grabbed a bottle of Andie's expensive eighteen-year-old single malt Scotch. The amber liquid promised to numb his swirling brain; he took a long pull on the oaky liquor.

As Olivia ranted on, he tipped the bottle back again. The alcohol burned a hot path down to his stomach. It was the first time he had felt any warmth in a long time; his soul was in a cold, dark place. He took yet another long sip, it was starting to relax him, the stress of the day was loosening, and he felt lighter.

Olivia dragged Jake into her bedroom—Andie and Olivia had not shared a bedroom for years—and he collapsed down on the bed. He kicked off his boots and settled back; he felt weary. He set the bottle on the bedside table; his eyes were getting heavy, and he didn't want to spill the Scotch. While he lay in a boozy haze, Olivia sat beside him on the bed and fretted over her cellphone.

She had been reading the responses to Andie's' social media announcement.

'Good for you, Andie! All the best!'

'Hurrah, you've final left her!'

'To Andie and Kevin. So happy for you! Take care of yourselves!'

Nobody seemed disgusted by his announcement; it made her seethe. She needed a tension release and knew that the best way to purge the anger from her system was sex. She turned to Jake; he lay on his back ... snoring.

"Jake!" She shoved his shoulder. He murmured and rolled over. Snores echoed from his side of the bed.

"Well, damn it!" She pouted. "Go ahead and sleep, asshole. Get some rest; you're going to need all your energy. We have work to do. Rebecca needs to die!"

CHAPTER FORTY

While Jake snored and Olivia plotted, Rebecca slowly made her way across town to Magda's apartment. She crept down alleys and lurked in the dark, fearful of discovery and incarceration back at the psychiatric unit.

"I feel like some kind of spy in a cheap mystery novel." She yawned. "But all I really want is to lie down and sleep." Like Jake, she wanted to sleep forever and not remember.

As she rounded the final corner, she spied the lights of the landlord's place two doors down from Magda's were out and no one seemed to be moving about. Rebecca breathed a sigh of relief; she needed a private, secure refuge to hide for now. She had to reflect and plan her future.

Taking another look around, she limped across the road to the dark apartment; her gait was impaired by the crusted wounds on her knees. They had started to ooze and blood was trickling below the hemline of the overcoat.

"I must get inside before someone sees me and is suspicious of a stranger lurking around the building." She easily slipped through the main entrance, but now in the poorly lit hallway she fumbled with Magda's key fob; there were so many keys, and Rebecca struggled to locate the correct one in the dim light. Unfortunately, she dropped the bundle, and they jangled onto the floor. The noise echoed in the silent corridor; suddenly a light flicked on under the landlord's door. Rebecca lunged for the keys and slunk back into the dark. She held her breath as the landlord poked his head out of the door and scanned the hallway.

Must be that old biddy across the hall trying to avoid me. "Rent was due today! Pay by tomorrow or I throw your sorry old bones out on the street." He muttered.

Finding nothing of obvious interest, he pulled his head back in and turned out the light.

Rebecca waited in the darkness until she was certain the landlord had returned to his apartment. She tested each key in the lock, muffling the jangling noise with Magda's scarf. On the third attempt the key slid into the lock, and the lock clicked open. With a sigh of relief, she pushed open the door, hoping the aged hinges didn't decide to chirp. Once inside she pushed the door shut, then carefully clicked the bolt in place. She stood silently in the shadows listening and waiting, but the night slept on.

Once she was convinced that no one was coming to break the door down and drag her away, she let out a shuddering breath. She looked around Magda's small tidy home; it appeared that she had left the place in a rush. On the small table beside her favourite chair sat a cold cup of tea and a half-eaten sandwich; dried up and curling at the edges. Eyeing the remnants, her stomach growled in response. With shame and humility, Rebecca snatched up the dry sandwich and stuffed it down, satiating her hunger.

She shuffled into the sparse bedroom and collapsed on the small bed. The gravity of her situation came flooding back, and she surrendered to the waves of exhaustion. Thoughts, feelings, ideas, and memories flooded her head. Her whole world had been turned upside down, but now she needed to sleep.

Rebecca lay back on Magda's pillows; surprisingly she felt nothing but weariness, bone aching fatigue. She was all out of tears.

Staying here in Campbell River is a living death; I need to leave, but how? These were her last thoughts before she faded into a dreamless sleep.

The next morning Rebecca woke disoriented and confused, the light in the room seemed different. It was filtering in from the wrong angle. Her body ached from her adventures from the night before. She was still clad in Magda's heavy overcoat and soiled hospital gown. She felt dirty and wanted to wash away not only the grime, but the betrayal of the last twenty-four hours. Struggling to her feet, she made her way to Magda's cramped bathroom. There she shed her disguise, found a bar of soap in the cabinet, and stepped into the small shower, where she scoured away the blood and dirt. Her tense muscles relaxed in the hot steam, and her fatigue washed down the drain, along with the dirt.

Rebecca toweled herself dry and secured the damp towel around her body. Sitting on the edge of the tub, she examined her knees. The edges of the scrapes were red and inflamed. *I wonder if she has anything to dress these wounds.*

She opened the medicine cabinet, and inside were multiple pill bottles. Rebecca turned them over in her hand. *Lanoxin, furosemide, nitroglycerin, and enteric coated aspirin.* Magda did suffer from heart disease, after all. Other pill bottles with names she struggled to pronounce also lined the shelves. She set the bottles back inside the cabinet, suddenly feeling like a trespasser. She found some rubbing alcohol and dressing pads, and then began to attend to her wounds.

"Not half bad," she said. "Now I need something to wear."

Opening the closet, Rebecca found a loose sweater and skirt to cover her nakedness. She brushed out her long dark hair and braided it into a loose plait. Looking in the mirror she saw dark circles under her eyes and lines around her mouth, she recognized the same sorrow in Magda's face. The old woman had borne her soul to Rebecca and she had often studied the sadness etched on Magda's face. Now the same letters of distress and sadness were reflected on her own face.

"So now what Rebecca?" She asked her reflection. "First I need to go back and see Magda, to make sure she is going to be okay. Then I need to plan on getting on with my life."

Looking around Rebecca, realized the old woman could not return to this shabby place.

She needs nursing assistance or help from family. But from whom? I know most of her immediate family is dead, but could she have any other relatives? She considered her options.

Walking into the living room she recognized the pictures of her daughter, granddaughter, and great granddaughter, and there was a wedding picture of Magda and her husband, but she didn't see anyone else; she knew she was going to have to search for answers.

"Sorry Magda, I'm going to have to snoop, but I need more information, and hopefully there are papers or perhaps letters that will tell more of your story."

Rebecca peered in closets and searched Magda's dresser drawers for anything to give her clues. The house seemed devoid of any other personal items, except for the pictures on the mantel and bedroom dresser. When she reached forward to pick up a frame, she accidentally knocked another picture onto the floor, shattering the glass. As she picked up the broken frame, the picture escaped and floated under the bed.

Clumsy me! She berated herself. *Now I need to clean up this mess. I wonder if Magda has a broom?* She lifted her bulk from the floor and went in search of one. She located a broom in the small pantry closet and started the process of cleaning up the glass; some had gone under the bed. She pulled back the coverlet and knelt down; here she located a wooden box.

What's this? Rebecca pulled out the box and sat on the floor, taking the pressure off her battered knees.

Darn it's locked, but wait, I have keys. She struggled to pick it off the floor; the box was far heavier than she expected. She set it on the small table beside Magda's chair. Once again, she was faced with a mass of keys, but this time she could take her time, and it was light out too. She flipped over the keys one by one until she turned one and heard the lock release.

"Ah ... at last!" she exclaimed. She slowly opened the lid, revealing a surprising treasure inside. Here amongst the pictures, papers, and letters sat an envelope filled with money! A lot of money!

"What the heck?" Rebecca gasped aloud.

Rebecca counted the money in the envelope; there was over four thousand dollars in small bills. *Why isn't this in the bank? I better make sure this is secured away, I don't want that horrid landlord coming in and finding it.* She tucked it inside a bible at the bottom of the box.

As she continued to search the box, she came across three bullets, rolling around the bottom. *Do you perhaps have a gun to go with these?* she pondered, and then remembered. *Magda had said she wasn't afraid of her evil landlord, and then she had tapped the table beside her.* Rebecca opened the table drawer and inside laid a handgun!

"Why Magda, you do continue to surprise me!" Rebecca laughed. "Why do you have a gun?"

She checked the gun to find it empty. She cradled it in her lap and felt less vulnerable, even if it was unloaded.

Rebecca spent the next hour removing each item for the old wooden box, studying its relevance to the owner's life. Besides the money, the box contained a fragile old photo album of people from the old country; their names were now lost to history. Inside were pictures of Magda as a young woman, Amelia her daughter and more recently, pictures of Elena and Sylvie. As she dug deeper, Rebecca found articles about Magda's missing great granddaughter Sylvie, and then the horrific discovery of her body.

Other items included the details of Elena's pending murder trial, and then the final article about Elena being found dead of an overdose. The caption read:

'CASE CLOSED! Child murderer found dead of self-inflicted drug overdose. Is Hell good enough for this child murderer?!'

Rebecca shuddered at the callousness of the words. It reminded her of her own trial and the exploitation, especially on social media. She set the articles down on the floor, then contemplated the similarities between the old woman and herself. Both had tragically lost loved ones and carried a similar burden.

As she sat on the living room floor, she thought about the last time that she had come to visit Magda; it had been the night before Jake came home from the car show. She had mixed feelings about his return; part of her would be happy to see him, but a larger part was sad that the short hiatus from arguments and stony silence was coming to an end.

When Magda had confronted her, the conversation had turned heated. "You're a silly girl! Why do you want to continue to live such an unhappy life? Don't be like me, I carry such sadness in my heart. You should be allowed to live a life of happiness and freedom from this place. Now please sit down, I need to finish my story, and then we can start to plan how to get you started on your new path!"

Rebecca had been surprised by another of Magda's outburst; most times the elderly woman was restrained and calm, but that day she was very agitated. She had pulled up close to Rebecca, looked her directly in the eyes, and said, "I will tell you something I have never told another person."

"After the trial Elena was released on bail, pending sentencing. The courts gave her over to my care and she was living with me. One day I had gone out grocery shopping, and when I came home, I found her passed out on the bed, a needle sticking out of her arm; the syringe still contained some rotting poison. Her drug dealer had apparently come by while I was out. She had adamantly denied she had been using when I let her stay at my home, but it was obvious she had once again lied. She was a master at lying! When I walked into the room and saw her, my anger raged. I knew she had to pay for what she had done to Sylvie ... so I killed her! I simply pushed the needle plunger deeper, and I watched her die. I just stay and watched her take her last breath."

Rebecca had just sat there, her mouth hanging open. Magda had looked at Rebecca's surprised expression and shrugged. "No one questioned Elena's death; she was just another druggie overdosing."

"Now you see how life can drive you to desperate actions." The old woman had gripped Rebecca's hand and turned her wrist over, exposing the scars. "Desperate times make people do desperate things!"

Rebecca had pulled her hand away, uncomfortable with the way the conversation was going, and embarrassed about her past weakness. She didn't respond, just continued to sit quietly as Magda had gone on.

"Please understand I want to help you to leave, before something bad happens to you. I feel you are in danger! Be smart, Rebecca ... follow your heart!" She had grabbed Rebecca's hand back and held it tightly. She had never told Rebecca about the threatening phone call from Olivia. It had chilled her to the bone, and she feared the betrayal would crush Rebecca.

"I would do anything to have Elena and Sylvie back, but it is too late for them but not for you! Please let me help you plan your escape! Please!"

Rebecca hadn't known how to respond to these words, so she had only nodded. She had no idea how Magda could help her, and now she regretted her silence. She thought she would have more time to talk it over with Magda, but now it might be too late. That evening was only two days ago, but it seemed so much longer. Now she sat in the same place; thinking everything was happening too fast. Looking around the bleak room, lined with sad memories, she understood one thing for sure.

You were absolutely right, Magda; I have to find my way out of this mess ... somehow.

Finding no other helpful information for relatives or contacts, she started placing the photos and memorabilia back in the box, settling the bible deep at the bottom. As she repacked everything, she found an envelope containing Elena's old passport, expired driver's license, and her Polish birth certificate. She looked once more at Elena's images, studying the young woman's likeness.

Hmm, you know I do look remarkably like her. She sat looking at the items in her hand, then paused as she began to put them back in the box. *I think I'll keep these, who knows if they might come in handy.*

Rebecca placed the documents on the floor, relocked the case, and then returned it to its hiding spot. She proceeded to put the gun, bullets, and Elena's ID in her purse; she wanted to keep them close at hand, they made her feel safer.

"Magda," she said out loud. "We need to talk more. I need to ease my conscience and I also to let you know everything will be okay with me. Somehow I will get back to see you in the hospital."

She sat and thought for a moment, considering the next steps.

For now, I need to go back to work and my house, making it look like I don't know anything about Jake and Olivia's plans. I need to keep the upper hand on these two monsters, she thought as she prepared to leave Magda's apartment.

CHAPTER FOURTY-ONE

It was the end of the day, and Andie had one more surveillance disk to review before heading to the lake house to be with Kevin. He had completed the media announcement, so now he turned his attention to this final disk. He doubted it contained any evidence of Olivia's infidelity because it was over four years old, and he wasn't sure why he hadn't deleted it already.

Surely the affair hasn't been going on that long. But why does this date seem familiar? The disk was date stamped January 11th.

He stretched and yawned, then inserted the disk into the computer. The first few minutes of images were pretty ordinary; just the staff moving about the shop conducting business. That was until he noticed that one camera had captured Olivia entering the mechanic bay after the rest of the staff had gone home. Now he was curious because Olivia never went into the bay; she didn't want to get 'oily and stinky.'

As he watched, a conversation between Olivia and Jake became very heated. Jake was changing the tires on an older model sedan, and Olivia seemed to be ranting at him. He turned the volume up and was shocked when the discussion turned deadly. Then Andie witnessed Jake loosen the lug nuts on the car's right front tire, and when he was finished, the two embraced, and then left the service bay.

"Oh my God!" he gasped, shaking. Andie was horrified by what he had just witnessed ... a plan for murder.

"Now the date makes sense," he murmured. "It was the very next day, January twelfth that Fred Wright died in that dreadful accident." He had been sitting in this very same spot when Randi Everett had come in the office and told him.

He had turned on the news and learned more about the details. The police had said that the roads were icy and Fred's car, a late model sedan, had slid and repeatedly flipped. The man had been thrown from the vehicle and died instantly. No one suggested that a loose tire could have been the cause; it was probably 'driver error' the news stated. Andie recalled that he had breathed a sigh of relief when the police had cleared Proctor Automotive of any negligence.

Now he felt no relief. He felt physically ill sickened by his wife's malicious behaviour. But now he had evidence in grainy Technicolor, and he needed to right this terrible wrong.

Rebecca had been destroyed by her father's death. She was so close to him. He recalled that she had been unable to cope with this devastating loss and had attempted to take her own life.

Now she is back in the hospital again because of my wife's treachery. His guilt overwhelmed him. *If only I had known earlier about the evidence on this disk, I could have prevented her anguish.*

"If you could do this to an innocent man Olivia, what would you do if you found out about this evidence? I have lived in fear that you would expose my private life, but now I fear for Rebecca's safety. I've got to find her and let her know. Then I will tell Kevin everything." He spoke aloud in the empty shop.

Andie copied the evidence to his computer under a desk top file he labelled 'Tire Inventory,' and then onto a USB stick. He locked the disk in the secret compartment of his desk, and slipped the stick into his jacket pocket. Then he fled the building, first securing his office door, and then ensuring the building doors were locked and the alarm was set.

He sat in his car, thinking about his next moves. *I cannot go the hospital to see Rebecca because I am not family, and they won't let me in to see her.*

Andie put the keys in the ignition, and they jingled together as he started the car. He recognized the house key that he had insisted Rebecca give him. It was just after the end of trial, and he had been worried about her mental state. Knowing that she had already attempted suicide in the past and that she was in a very dark place, he had been worried that she might do something again.

"Please let me have a key ... just in case." He recalled that she had just silently nodded, and then handed it over. They didn't need to talk about his worries; they both understood the unspoken concerns.

He could try to text her, but he assumed she didn't have access to her phone. He decided he would go to the Adams' house and if it was empty he would use the key to let himself in and leave a message for Rebecca.

As he drove slowly up to the house, he recognized Jake's truck sitting in the driveway. He could see shadows moving around the downstairs rooms. It must mean that Jake and Olivia were inside.

Andie parked in front of the neighbour's house, turned off his lights so he wouldn't be seen, then waited and watched. Not too long after, Olivia stormed to Jake's truck, and that was when Andie's phone rang. He picked it up, and immediately recognized Olivia's shrill voice saying that she 'wanted him out of her house now.' He cut her off before she could get really going. His phone chimed again; a text message had arrived to his inbox. He quietly read the message that threatened to expose himself and Kevin. He shrugged; two could play that game.

He carefully drafted a response to her message; he wanted her to know he was aware of her treachery and would certainly use it against her. He pressed send, and then watched as she reacted to the words. Suddenly the truck horn started blaring, and Olivia started yelling out the window.

He chuckled.

Next Jake stomped out, dragging a suitcase with him. The truck roared away from the curb, its tires squealing in protest.

After Andie was certain that they had left and were not returning, he approached the house. All the lights remained on and the door was unlocked; he wouldn't need to use the key after all. Andie carefully pushed the door open and was assaulted by the mess created by the medics, and the rest that he assumed was Olivia's handiwork.

Sure enough, in the living room he recognized Olivia's rage; the smashed and ruined pictures and personal items thrown on the floor were all evidence of her tirade. He stepped over the debris. *I can't leave Rebecca to find this mess. I wonder where she keeps the broom.*

Andie made his way through the broken glass shards, discarded medical wrappers, and other wreckage to the kitchen where he found the broom closet. Pulling out the broom and dust pan, he went about the business of restoring order to the house. He dumped the discard pills from the bathroom, and the broken glass and medical wrappers from the living room in the kitchen bin;

then smoothed out the damaged photos. He looked around for a piece of paper on which to write a note.

He wrote:

"REBECCA CALL ME ASAP.
ANDIE-555-376-0954. IMPORTANT!"

Now where to leave this note so Jake and Olivia won't come back and destroy it? Hmm ... perhaps in her toiletry drawer along with her toothbrush and other personal items. That is one place I am sure her cheating husband won't be digging through! He mused to himself.

He tucked the note on top of her toothbrush and facial cream and pushed the drawer shut. Before leaving the house, Andie turned out the lights and latched the door closed, this time using the extra key to secure the house.

As he drove off to hide out at his private cabin, he whispered to the air, "Be careful, Rebecca ... I pray that you are safe."

* * *

A police car sat across the street, where Officer Derek Hoffman watched the goings on at the Adams' house. He had been notified of Rebecca's AAMA (absence against medical advice) and had driven by to see if she had returned home. As he observed the premises, he was entertained by the curious activities at the household. The missing patient wasn't there, but everyone else seemed to be.

Hoffman had observed Jake Adams, the patient's husband, arrive with a blonde woman. *Probably Olivia Proctor*, he assumed. He had seen the internet clip too.

He had heard smashing sounds and shouting, and Hoffman had thought about intervening until 'blondie' stormed from the house, followed several minutes later by Adams, pulling a suitcase. No sooner had the couple left, when he observed Andie Proctor enter the house. The officer could see Proctor moving around, appearing to be cleaning things up. Then he watched as he turned out the lights and locked the door.

Curious? he thought.

Officer Hoffman placed a called to the hospital, reporting that he was unable to locate the AAMA patient. The hospital clinical clerk explained that the mental health form signed by the police department to detain the patient for twenty-four hours had now expired. There was no further need to try and locate her.

"Unless the patient tries to harm herself again, she is free to go," the clerk explained.

Hoffman closed the file, figuring it wasn't worth bothering the 'Chief' with such petty issues. He pulled away from the house; it was time for a well-deserved coffee and donut break so decided to head to Charlotte's Confectionaries.

As the officer drove away, the curtains across the street in Ethel Graham's bedroom window twitched. The old woman squinted out her window.

I must talk with you, Rebecca, why won't you call? I have something I urgently need to tell you. She fretted and decided to keep vigil. She desperately needed to speak with the young woman when she came home; if she did.

CHAPTER FOURTY-TWO

That evening as Rebecca hid in the darkness at Magda's apartment, she reflected on the recent events of the last twenty-four hours. She was seething with rage; in her whole life she had never felt this level of anger. She was well acquainted with grief and despair, but betrayal and anger were new nemesis.

She had decided to sleep one more night at Magda's, and as dawn introduced the sun to the new day, she felt invigorated. For the first time in months, Rebecca felt something besides soul withering despair and aching apathy. Her path was now set, she just needed a plan.

I need to go home, she decided. *I cannot stay here forever, and since I haven't been able to find a next of kin for Magda, I will help her out. Perhaps she can come live with me, but she's definitely not coming back here.* She pulled herself to her feet, stretched her stiff muscles, and then eased out of Magda's apartment, into the quiet of the new day. *Time to go home, and this time I have security.* She patted her left hip where she had tucked Magda's gun.

Twenty minutes later, Rebecca stood hidden in the hedge rows across the street from her home. She had been staking it out, observing anything that suggested Jake and Olivia were lying in wait. She felt ridiculous with this cloak and dagger activity, so she crept out, then cautiously approached the house. Rebecca pulled the keys from her purse and unlocked the front door. She touched the weapon secured in the waistband of the skirt she had borrowed; its cool metal eased her anxiety and made her feel protected.

Walking back into the house she expected to find the mess left from the paramedic visit, and was surprised to find it in good repair. She noticed that Jake's jacket was missing so it was obvious that he had been there, but if Olivia had been on the scene, she thought the place would have been absolutely trashed. When she entered the living room there was no evidence of the EMS visit, but she did find signs of Olivia's handiwork. All the family photo frames were missing and the walls were marred and bruised by flying objects. The floor, however, was clear of any debris, and the rumbled photos had been straightened out and were stacked on the mantel.

Someone started to wreck the place, but then they stopped and cleaned it up? Odd? Did Jake have a change of heart? These emotions quickly evaporated when she walked into the bathroom and found a note stuck to the mirror.

I'M IN LOVE WITH OLIVIA AND HAVE NEVER BEEN HAPPIER IN MY LIFE.

DON'T TRY TO CONTACT ME. JAKE

Rebecca pulled the note from the mirror, and then reread it. She didn't realize it until just now, but she was actually relieved, because this ragged piece of paper was her ticket to freedom. Tracing her fingers across the hastily written words, she reflected.

I don't feel that sad. In fact, not at all! What I really feel is release. I don't have to play this stupid game anymore. Hope you're happy, Jake ... good luck with Olivia! We'll see how long it lasts.

She looked up at the mirror and caught her reflection. She paused to study herself. *Well girl, what next? Are you going to let them win? I can play this game too. Let the love birds have each other, because all I want is to get on with my life. And if those two idiots think that they can drive me to kill myself, they are sadly mistaken.* Smiling at herself, she ran her hands over the baggy clothes she was wearing. *Now, I need to morph back into the real Rebecca. The girl who used to be strong, adventurous and well ... happy.*

She pulled off the borrowed clothes and flung them on the floor, carefully placing the gun on the edge of the sink. She inspected her body in the mirror, and for the first time in months, she didn't wince at her appearance. Rebecca noticed that she had lost some weight over the past few weeks, and she liked what she saw.

Yup got some work to do, but that's okay.

She crumpled up the note, tossed it into the garbage, and then opened the medicine cabinet to empty out the remains of Jake's toiletries. Next, she purged the remainder of the pills and their empty containers; that period of her life was over.

"Bye, Jake!" She chuckled as she lobbed the objects into the bin; she then opened the next drawer containing her own toiletries items and was astonished that someone had left a note there. She unfolded paper and read it out loud.

REBECCA CALL ME ASAP. ANDIE-555-376-0954. IMPORTANT!

"Why the hell was Andie rummaging in here?" She said as reread the note. "Were you the one who cleaned up the house?"

Suddenly feeling vulnerable, she donned a towel; she needed to get dressed to face the day. She decided she didn't want to discuss anything over the phone, certainly not while alone in this house; she needed to talk to Andie in person.

What is so important that you needed to leave me a note in amongst my personal times? Rebecca puzzled. She took the gun and secured it in her purse, then drove to Proctor Automotive; her newly found bravado ebbed as she neared the building. She feared the place now.

CHAPTER FOURTY-THREE

Andie had returned to the shop the following morning; he had intended on staying at the lake house but things had changed since he had discovered the evidence on the video tapes. He sat wringing his hands in his private office.

I wonder if Rebecca is okay. I haven't heard from her since I left that note in her bathroom drawer. Did Jake and Olivia go back and destroy it? What should I do? He fretted.

He had spent a sleepless night wondering and worrying. He got up and paced; turning the USB stick over and over in his hand. Kevin had been very worried about his agitation, but Andie had remained closed mouthed. He felt he needed to give the evidence to Rebecca first and let her decide what do with it, but his resolve was fading the longer he didn't hear from her.

I should have given this to Kevin; he would have known what to do with it. He was just reaching for the phone when the door to his office flung open. Standing in the doorway was Olivia.

"What do you want?" he gasped in surprise.

"Everything!" she smirked. "Well almost everything, just not you!"

"You think you are so funny, don't you, Olivia?" He tried to regain his composure.

The whole situation with Olivia and Jake had rattled him deeply. Murder, attempted murder, and deceitful plotting were not anything he was prepared to handle. This was Kevin's world, and he needed him more than ever now. He gripped the edge of his desk to prevent his hands from shaking. He hated how this horrid woman had such control over him. He wanted her out of his life, and he would do anything to get rid of her.

"Again Olivia, what do you want!? Your little fight with Rebecca has been broadcast all over Campbell River, so everyone in town knows about your affair with Jake. And as far as my new relationship, social media has taken care that, so feel free to post your nasty pictures to the world. You have no further control over me! Now leave." As he pointed toward the door, the USB stick fell from his hand. He scrambled to grab it, but Olivia intercepted it first.

"What's this?" She picked it up, turning it over in her hand. "Something important?" She relished toying with Andie, and she loved to watch him squirm.

"Give it here!' Andie demanded.

"It must be really important for you to react like this. Maybe I should just destroy it." Olivia dropped it on the carpet, then placed her spiked heel on top of it.

"You have to do something for me first Andie, and then I'll let you have it back. Decide quickly." She stood with poised her heel just above the plastic.

"Stop it! What do you want? It contains all my business accounting information. I can't lose that." He gritted his teeth, but he knew he had to play it cool.

"I want you to fire Rebecca! Today! You shouldn't have that irrational bitch working in our establishment."

"Our establishment?" he taunted.

"You're testing me, Andie? Do you want me to destroy your precious files? Do you?" She scoffed at him.

"Fine, it's done. I will tell her today. Now give me the stick!" He reached his hand out to her.

Perhaps it would be safer for Rebecca to be far away from this place. He paused, then stared his wife down.

"Good boy Andie, and now one more thing. Jake won't be coming to work for the next couple of weeks, so make sure he gets his pay. And give him a raise ... a big one." She turned to leave. "And give him Randi Everett's job too!" She walked toward Andie, holding out the device. When he reached out to take it, Olivia dropped it into the coffee cup that Andie had left unattended on his desk; it was now saturated with the dark liquid.

"Oops, clumsy me!" Olivia laughed, and then turned to leave. "Do it Andie, or else!"

"You bitch!" Andie rescued the stick from the cup and shook the liquid off. He dabbed at it with his silk tie.

"Tamara!" He bellowed. "I need rice!"

Olivia's laughter could be heard as she strolled across the parking lot to her red Porsche.

CHAPTER FOURTY-FOUR

Rebecca pulled open the door to Proctor Automotive and was surprised when Ashley came dashing up behind. "Hold the door" the blonde called out. As she pushed past Rebecca the bag she carried dropped to the floor and grains of rice spilled out.

"Andie, I have the rice! I'm coming!" She bellowed then turned to Rebecca. "Andie is looking for you. If you're going to see him, take that!" She pointed at the bag on the floor. "What a mess."

Rebecca carefully picked up the torn bag, pinched off the hole, and then pushed opened the office door. Andie sat at his desk, typing vigorously on his computer; several computer disks were scattered on his desk.

"What the heck is going on, Andie? What's with the rice?"

"Oh Rebecca, I'm glad you're here. I'm not crazy, the rice is to help dry out a damp USB stick. I need to protect this." He was flushed and flustered.

"Okay, so what can I do to help? I got your note." She placed the torn bag on the desk and picked up a disk.

"You can sit down, Rebecca. Let me catch my breath. I need to tell you something." He paused and took the disk from her. "First, are you okay? The hospital was looking for you but, I told them I hadn't seen you."

"I foolishly tried to hurt myself, but I'm okay now. Thanks for your concern Andie, but I'm not going back to the hospital. I'm done with pills and treatment. And if you're going to tell me about the affair between Rebecca and Jake, I already know all about it." She shook her head, remembering the cellphone videos and the pictures.

"I'm so glad you are okay, but Rebecca there is something else..." He closed his eyes.

Rebecca sat, quietly studying her employer. *What next?* she pondered.

Andie took a moment, and then slowly divulged Olivia's latest treachery. Rebecca's mouth hung open as she listened.

"She actually took pictures of you and Kevin in Las Vegas? This keeps getting more horrible! She will stop at nothing until she destroys us all."

Andie quietly nodded. "We were not ready to announce it to the world, but Olivia forced our hand. So yesterday I uploaded a message to social media, announcing my divorce and my new relationship with Kevin. I think this may have stymied her blackmail plans, but unfortunately she has made other threats as well."

"Like what?"

Here he stopped, struggling to go on. "She wants me to fire you or she'll leak the pictures to the Campbell River Gazette. Can you imagine the scandal if those explicit pictures get published, especially for Kevin? I can't have that, so ..."

"Are you firing me?"

Suddenly Andie's demeanor changed. He abruptly pushed back from his desk and walked across the room. He flung open the door to his office. "Yes, Rebecca," he stated very loudly, his voice carrying into the front reception area. "I am firing you!"

Rebecca was surprised by this sudden outburst. *Why are you acting this way? Are you afraid of what Olivia will do if you don't fire me?*

She didn't have time to think, because Andie pulled her from her chair and roughly marched her to the shop's front door. "You are being fired for business reasons; it is nothing personal. Now please give me your keys and go!"

Rebecca slowly pulled the shop keys off her key ring, then handed them to Andie. He accepted them and walked back to his office. She was suspicious of what he was doing. *So if it's just an act, how do I play my part in this horrible game?* She thought.

"What?" she sputtered and stumbled after him. He blocked her, then grabbed her arm. This time he paraded her past the reception desk where Tamara and Ashley stood with their mouths gapping open.

"You heard me, Rebecca! I cannot have someone working for me who has your ongoing problems. You are an embarrassment to me and the team, especially now that we are going to be featured on *Fancy Rides*. I have a reputation to keep! Now leave before I have to call the police."

He turned to a bug-eyed Tamara and Ashley. "Ladies, can you call my wife for me? I need to let her know that I have purged the problem!"

He took a deep breath and looked directly in Rebecca's tear-filled eyes. He hated to treat her so poorly, but she had to leave the shop in disgrace if he was going to turn the tide on Olivia's game. He needed Rebecca to look genuinely shocked for the audience in the reception area. For years the two 'blonde bookends' had been feeding Olivia a steady stream of shop gossip, and today Rebecca's pleas must convince Olivia that he had truly fired her. Andie knew his wife would want to know every detail, down to the very last tear shed.

Taking Rebecca by the elbow, he escorted her to her car, and she winced as he forced her into her vehicle. He leaned into the car; tucking the USB stick into Rebecca's shaking hand. They were far enough away from prying eyes and listening ears, but he still whispered. "Please take this and review it. Trust me!"

She looked at the item in her hand. "What's so important on here?"

"Listen Rebecca, there is something you have to ..." He started to explain, but he was suddenly interrupted by Ashley's voice blaring over the intercom.

"It's your wife on line two, Andie. She insists that she talk to you now. I'll put her on hold for you."

"I must go, but please watch what is on the USB, Rebecca; it will explain things! Trust me." He repeated his urgent message, then retreated back to the shop. He hoped that Rebecca would understand his subtle meaning, and then possibly forgive his behaviour.

Once inside the building Andie slammed his office door, but before he picked up the phone, he fired a rapid text to Rebecca.

'I needed you to play along with my plan. Review the evidence on the USB stick. We will talk further.'

Andie took a cleansing breath, and then picked up line two; Olivia's acidic voice came over the phone.

"Well Andie baby, did you fire her? Remember I can only hold my tongue for so long, and I certainly wouldn't want to slip your secret pictures to the press. What a scandal it would be!"

Before Andie could respond, Rebecca stormed into his office. "Andie how could you? I have worked loyally for you all these years, and this is how you treat me." she yelled. She had read the text message and now clearly understood her role in the game. Her voice was loud and clear, and it carried out to the front reception desk. Then for Olivia's benefit, Rebecca sobbed loudly. "Why Andie?"

She bawled loudly, then flung herself out the office door, stumbling past the stunned receptionists. The duo immediately sprang to their phones, thumbs rapidly texting out the latest drama.

"Are you satisfied?" he asked his wife. He could hardly contain his wrath.

"Well done, Andie. Your little secret is safe ... for now." Olivia hung up, leaving Andie shaken and rattled. He sat clasping his head. *Oh, poor Rebecca, what have I done? God help you when you see that video!*

Outside the shop, Rebecca shuffled to her car wiping away the 'crocodile tears.' She hoped the scene she'd created was convincing enough for the blonde audience, and for Olivia. She had understood Andie's text message and hoped she was able to foster the drama. As she turned back to look at the shop, she spotted Andie in his office window. She cried out, "You betrayed me! Damn you Proctor! Damn you!"

She shoved her bulk into her car, then peeled out of the parking lot. She hoped her histrionic departure would ease the strain on poor Andie.

CHAPTER FOURTY-FIVE

R ebecca parked in the driveway of the house she had grown up in and had recently shared with her husband. Walking up the stairs, she reflected on the last few years.

If walls could talk, what tales this place could tell.

Rebecca set her keys down and checked the answering machine; thankfully there were no further messages from Ethel Graham. She knew she was stalling, hesitant to know the contents on the stick.

Do I really want to know? Can I handle anything else? she wondered as she turned it over in her hands. *Well, I might as well get it over with.*

She plugged it into the computer, and multiple thumbnails came up, each one with a date stamp. She clicked on the top one, and it opened a video of the mechanic bays; it showed the mechanics at work, busily going about their daily routines. The images were a bit blurry, damaged by the stick's swim in Andie's coffee cup.

So, what's so important about this? she puzzled. *Is this how you found out Darren Burke was stealing from the shop? Hmm ... what else did you see?*

She clicked back to the list of thumbnails and noticed that some had a small red flag next to them. *Curious ... what does this mean?*

Rebecca clicked on a video marked with the date that Darren Burke had been fired—and the same day she had foolishly attempted to kill herself, and suddenly she was witnessing the drama that had happened that morning. She heard Tamara on the overhead paging system, summoning Burke to Andie's office. Time elapsed, and then Burke moved from Andie's office into her own. She saw the other mechanics rush into the reception area and watch as Burke stormed from the shop. She knew the rest of the story, so she fast forwarded until she saw Ashley page Jake to Andie's office. She knew Andie had informed him of her admission to the hospital. She witnessed the disgust on Jake's face, then heard him mutter and curse. She clicked off the video and stared out the window. His comments still dug a furrow through her heart.

Across the street, she spied her neighbour Ethel Graham toiling with a pull cart. She was attempting to maneuver it up the steep stairs to her front door, but she nearly fell as the cart slipped. This was the same woman who had accused her of pushing her son from the upstairs window. As she watched the woman struggle, Rebecca felt her anger rise. The trial was devastating enough, but for over three years now, Rebecca had been forced to watch Ethel Graham conduct her daily business; oblivious to the ruin her lies had caused. She actually hoped the old woman would fall so she could witness it.

As she watched, Rebecca recalled that the old woman had left two phone messages claiming she needed to talk with her. *Well ... since I am opening up secrets, this time is as good as any to talk with you. So old woman, it better be worth my while.* She removed the USB stick, pocketing it for safe keeping. She crossed the road, and then offered her assistance.

"Here Miss Graham, let me help you with that." Rebecca took the cart and guided her up the steep steps. Ethel willingly accepted Rebecca's arm, but without her glasses, she was having trouble identifying her rescuer.

"Thank you dear, but who are you!?" She blinked at Rebecca.

"It's Rebecca Adams from across the street. Do you remember you called and said you needed to talk to me? You said you had something important to tell me."

Ethel squinted at her, an awkward pause spanned between the twosome. "Oh bother!" She stumbled on her words. "My memory isn't as good as it could be, but I do recall that I telephoned you . . . I have to explain something to you."

She rubbed her eyes and studied Rebecca. "Now what was it again ... oh yes!" She gasped and peered from side to side, scanning to ensure no one was lurking nearby. "But it isn't safe for us to be seen on the street together. She might be watching."

"Who are you afraid of Miss Graham? Who are you looking for?" Rebecca was taken aback by the woman's peculiar behaviour.

"My niece!" She suddenly dashed into the house. "You must come later!" She firmly shut the door in Rebecca's face.

"And they call me crazy!" Rebecca laughed out loud. "That was a waste of time." Rebecca didn't realize at the time that a return visit would have a dramatic impact on her life, but now back in her own home, she sat at the computer and opened up the flash drive once again. It was time to explore the remaining videos. She scrolled through the list and came upon one dated nearly four years ago; beside it was the same little red flag.

What do you want me to see, Andie?

She clicked on the file and watched a video of Jake and Olivia in the mechanic bay. The image was very grainy and the audio did not work; it seemed the USB stick was permanently damaged from its coffee dip. However, as the poor quality video continued, she was able to glean that Jake and Olivia were arguing about a certain car that Jake was installing winter tires on. The car seemed familiar, and as Jake moved around to the other side of the car, she recognized the license plate. It was her father's vehicle, and Jake seemed to be loosening the lug nuts on the right front tire!

What are you up to Jake? Are you purposefully tampering with dad's car? She frowned and attempted to adjust the audio, but with little success. She could only catch every second or third word. But what she did hear left her cold.

She clasped her hand over her mouth. She was horrified at the words ... loosen ... nuts ... tires ... fall off ... an accident that would kill him ... tamper with the vehicle ... kill him.

Were Jake and Olivia responsible for her fathers' death? She recalled the police reports had suggested driver error and poor road conditions as the cause of his death.

Rebecca clicked off the video and sat still; still as death. Suddenly her family home felt cold, scary, and unsafe; she didn't want to be here anymore. She touched her purse where Magda's gun was stored, and the feel of the hard metal comforted her. She had never fired a handgun, but she could learn. She may need to protect herself.

"Who knows what they have in store for me?" she whispered. "But it isn't going to be good, especially after what I heard on Jake's phone." Her thoughts were a tangled mess.

Why didn't Andie ever clue me in? How long has he known about this, and why hasn't he given the evidence to Chief Pritchard? She rolled the thoughts on the tip of her tongue. *This is one big horrible mess ... I need to know more!*

CHAPTER FOURTY-SIX

Rebecca climbed up into the attic; she hadn't been up there for a few years, and the place was dust covered. She was looking for the police reports of her father's accident. She tugged open the filing cabinet drawer where she kept important papers, including the deed to the house, her marriage certificate, and Indie's birth certificate. As she sifted through the documents, she located both the official accident and coroner's reports. This was the first time she had looked at either report; in the past she couldn't face the reality of his death. This tragedy had driven her to despair, so much so that she had tried to take her own life.

Her father had been taking a trip to Vancouver on the day of the accident. He never gave her a reason for why he was going there; he had simply hugged her goodbye and told her he would see her in a couple of days. He gave his grandson a tickle under the chin, and waved. She never thought that would be the last time she would see her father alive.

Later that week, a real estate agent named Blair Simpson had left a message on the answering machine saying that Fred had missed his appointment. Rebecca thought back to the day Olivia had talked to her father about selling the house.

"You know, Mr. Wright, you could get some serious coin for this place. It would certainly go for a lot of money, especially with this aggressive real-estate market. You are getting older and this place is a lot of work. If you sold it, you could get a smaller, more manageable place, and perhaps have enough left over to help Jake and Rebecca get their own place. I know a really good real estate agent." Olivia had pulled a business card from her Gucci purse and handed it to Fred. "His name is Blair Simpson."

Is this why they want me dead, so they can sell the property and take the money? I hope dad's death and possibly mine are worth it!

As Rebecca turned the unsealed envelopes over in her hands, she could feel her anger turn up another notch. She dusted off a chair and sat down. She needed to know the truth ... her very life depended on it. She ripped the envelopes open, and then began to read.

Date: January 12th, 2016 1013 hours

Location: Mile maker 203- 30 miles southwest of Campbell River.

The accident involved a single car, late model dark blue Buick. Skid marks and road conditions indicate the driver Frederick James Wright lost control of the vehicle and hit the guardrail. Speed of impact to be estimated at 50 miles/hour. The impact on the rail caused the vehicle to flip over three times. The deceased was located approximately 10 feet from the vehicle. It appears the victim had not been wearing a seatbelt and had been thrown free. EMS pronounced the victim deceased at the scene. Family was notified by Officer Kevin Pritchard.

Rebecca stopped reading. She distinctly remembered the police notification like it was yesterday. She had collapsed in a heap on the floor, unable to comprehend the words she was hearing. When she answered the door, she had been holding Indie, and he had been shrieking in response to his mother's odd behaviour. Jake had scooped up his distraught child, trying to soothe him as the officer continued his explanation.

Chief Pritchard, new to Campbell River, had been very compassionate and offered to call Victim Assistance, but Jake had said 'they would be okay.' After he left, they were far from okay. Jake had thrust Indie into her arms, then crumpled into a pile on the floor where he bitterly wept.

He kept saying. "I'm so sorry. I'm sorry! This shouldn't have happened!"

Rebecca remembered that he had eventually pulled himself together, standing up and wiping his eyes, and then instead of consoling her—his grieving wife—he had gone to call Olivia. "She needs to know," he'd whispered.

She thought it very insensitive then, but it all made sense now.

She read further:

On examination the vehicle was located upside down in the ditch next to Mile Maker203. The vehicle sustained damage to the right front passenger panel caused by the impact with the guard rail. The roof was caved in and the windshield was smashed. No other occupants were located in the vehicle.

Right front tire was located ~ 12 feet further down the ditch. The lug nuts appear to be sheared off.

A small note suggested:

The lug nuts may have been sheared off as a result of the impact with guard rail or the loose lug nuts could have caused the loss of control. However, it is the opinion of the accident investigation, that road conditions and driver error were the cause of this deadly incident.

Further follow-up:

Receipts for automotive repairs and maintenance were found in the vehicle. Repairs were completed at Proctor Automotive. Officers interviewed mechanics Jake Adams and Randi Everett; both were cleared of any negligence.

Report closed.

Rebecca set the report down, realizing it was urgent that she review the surveillance videos at Andie's shop. She had to obtain a clean copy; it was pretty clear now that Jake's tampering had caused the deadly accident. She never would have dreamed Jake was capable of such horrible actions, but he hadn't acted alone. His partner in crime was Olivia, and it was obvious her influence was the catalyst that had put the event in motion. Jake had always been influenced by Olivia's opinions; during the early months of their marriage, she remembered a huge fight they had over money because of Olivia's meddling. The tense moment eventually passed, but she had never forgiven Jake for his disrespectful behaviour and the influence that Olivia had over him.

As she closed the door on the attic, she knew it was imperative she talk with Andie right away. She was afraid her boss would go into hiding and she would never get the evidence she needed. She pulled her cellphone out of her purse and sent him a text.

'Andie, the USB stick was damaged. Do you have a copy?'

A response came a minute later.

'Yes. I have posted it on my desktop in a folder named: Tire Inventory. Please be careful.'

She responded.

'We have a problem, Andie! You took away my keys. Can you meet me there? I want to copy the video for myself.'

Andie read the text, then sighed. He didn't want to go back to the shop, but neither did he have a copy of the videos. Everything was stored on his work computer; perhaps that was a stupid move on his part.

He typed another message.

'I'll meet you at eleven o'clock. Kevin has just gone to bed, and I want to make sure he is asleep before I leave. Meet me at the back of the shop.'

Rebecca sent a response.

'See you then. You be careful too!'

She returned her cellphone to her purse, and as she dug for her car keys, her hand bumped against the cold steel of Magda's gun. Pulling it out, she turned it over in her hand. *I can't carry this around with me, but where can I store it and these documents so that Jake won't find them and destroy them?*

Rebecca thought for a minute, and then it came to her; her secret 'hidey hole' adjoining Indie's room. When she was little Indie's room was her bedroom, and Fred had built her a special play area where she could stash away her secret treasures. It was built under the rafters, and the secret door blended perfectly with the wainscoting. She recalled how she had spent many hours of happy play in this special hide away. As she grew into adolescence and adulthood she had put away childish things, and now a dresser blocked the entrance. She wasn't even sure Jake knew about this place; she herself hadn't thought about it for years.

Perfect, I'll stash them in Indie's room. Jake wouldn't look in there; he can hardly even go into our son's room anymore.

She dashed up the stairs, moved the dresser aside, then secured the items inside an old cardboard box. Along with the reports and the damaged USB stick, she also tucked Jake's cellphone into the space, after turning it off and removing the battery and SIM card. She placed the gun on the bottom of the pile.

Don't want him calling his phone; if it rings in here, he could find it and destroy all the damning evidence. She reassured herself that the evidence would be safe, returned the dresser to its usual place, and pulled the bedroom door shut.

Keep my secret baby boy ... Mama has to go put Daddy in jail.

CHAPTER FOURTY-SEVEN

Rebecca parked behind Proctor Automotive, in the shadowy corner of the lot between two cars waiting for servicing. The lot was empty and the building was dark; Andie hadn't arrived yet. She slipped down in her seat, watched, and waited.

Several moments later, the headlights of Andie's BMW swung across the front of Rebecca's little Honda. She stuck her head up and watched Andie exit the car. He seemed to be looking around, searching for anything suspicious. Rebecca quickly exited her vehicle and whispered loudly. "Andie! Over here!"

He hadn't seen her and jumped back in alarm; this whole situation made him nervous. He waved her over to the back door of the shop, concealed in darkness far away from the glaring lights of the front lot.

"We'll go in this way." He unlocked the door, and then turned off the alarm system. They made their way through the mechanic bay to the front offices; their footsteps echoing in the empty building. Rebecca had spent many late nights here before and had never felt uneasy, but tonight the building held many dark corners and frightening obscurities. As she passed the work benches, she grabbed a large screwdriver and stuffed it in her coat pocket; this simple tool gave her comfort and security.

Andie unlocked his office door and ushered Rebecca inside. He only turned on the desk lamp, wanting to minimize the lights that could be seen from outside, especially if Olivia and Jake were watching them. He now regretted texting Olivia about the surveillance videos, and he hoped she hadn't figured they were stored on his office computer.

He turned to face Rebecca.

"I am so sorry! I was so worried you didn't understand the drama this morning, but I had to make Olivia believe that I had truly fired you. You do know I would never do that to you?"

Rebecca took his hands, squeezing them. "Of course, Andie, but these videos ... why didn't you take them to Kevin?"

"I felt you needed to see them first. You had to witness what they had done to your father! They killed him, Rebecca!" Andie was visibly shaken, but he continued. "I was so stunned, perhaps I wasn't thinking straight. This whole thing is so incredible; the people we're married to are cold bloodied murderers! I was looking for evidence of my wife's infidelity, and happened to come across that ... that video." He paced in the office.

"I was worried for your safety, and I just knew I had to get you away from here, so I copied the videos on the USB stick so you could review them in private. Unfortunately, its swim in my coffee cup ruined it. Now we're right back here anyway ... I should have made other copies, but I panicked."

He typed his password on the computer, then manoeuvred the mouse over the desktop files. "This might not be the safest place for us to meet, but now we don't have a choice. Please be quick."

Rebecca sat down in his office chair and clicked on the video dated January 11th. As she watched the pair plot and scheme, Andie nervously looked at his watch. He had been gone for thirty-five minutes already, and he was worried Kevin would awaken and wonder where he was.

Rebecca had been so engrossed in viewing the files that she hadn't noticed his distress. "Andie, why don't you leave, and I'll make a copy of these files, and then get the hell out of here."

He nodded in agreement. "Go out through the back door, it will lock behind you. For your protection I'll set the alarm; then you will need to deactivate it and reset it when you leave. I'm planning to change the locks tomorrow, and I'll reset the security code as well, but for tonight, it's still the same."

Andie turned to leave. "Rebecca, will you be okay?" Distracted, she only nodded, then went back to studying the videos.

"Stay in touch," he said as he pulled the office door shut.

Now alone, Rebecca clicked on the red flagged file. Everything was there; Jake and Olivia arguing, the plotting, the coercion, and finally the tampering.

The same words she'd heard on the corrupted USB stick were clearly articulated on the video clip. Their cold-blooded confession echoed in the empty office.

These two monsters have to pay, but there is no punishment severe enough to fit the crime. She shook her head in disgust. *I have to make a copy to add to my evidence, and the pile just keeps getting bigger!*

Rebecca searched for a computer disk and pulled on the desk drawers, but they were locked. She then found one on the bookshelf behind her. She plugged it into the computer and started copying only the red flagged files.

It didn't take long to download the files; now she just had to get to a safe place. As she completed the data transfer, she heard voices coming from the reception area. She stopped and eased the office door open. She stretched her ears to listen; she recognized the voices. *It's Jake and Olivia, and they are heading for Andie's office. Why are they here? Do they know about these videos?*

The voices were coming closer.

She slipped across the corridor into the staff room, staying hidden in the shadows. Unfortunately, she hadn't enough time to shut the computer down; it sat open and vulnerable to prying eyes. As she hid, she ensured the copied disk was safely stored in her coat pocket. Her fingers also touched the screwdriver she'd brought from the mechanic bay. Squirreled away in the dark, her heart was banging so loud she was sure they could hear it. Despite her fear she wanted to listen to what they were saying, so she took a deep breath and crept closer.

As she eavesdropped the words that drifted down the corridor were hard to distinguish. *I have to know what they are saying. I need to get closer, and then perhaps I can capture it on my phone just like Magda did.*

She crept quietly out of the staff room into the reception area, then ducked behind the desk, attempting to get closer to the conversation. She pulled out her cellphone and started to record. She clutched the screwdriver to her chest ... it was her only protection.

CHAPTER FOURTY-EIGHT

"Hurry up, Jake. I don't want to be seen hanging around outside the shop; someone might see us and notify Andie. The last thing I want to be charged with is breaking and entering." She prodded Jake. "I have this bunch of keys I found at the house. Will any one of them work?" She fumbled with a key ring loaded with multiple keys. "Don't you have a key to the mechanics door?"

Jake took the key ring and flipped through the bundle. "Not anymore. Everett took all the extra keys away from us before we went to the car show. After Burke was caught stealing, Andie didn't want everyone having access to the shop." He tried several keys with no success.

"This is going to take forever! I wish I had some of my tools, they would make short order of this bastard." He banged his fist on the door in frustration. She took the bundle and tried key after key until she suddenly shouted. "Holy shit, I found it!"

"Sssh ... we've got to be quiet," Jake whispered as he pulled Olivia through the door. In their haste they neglected to deactivate the security system; the silent alarm rang at the police station. Seeing an alert at Proctor Automotive, the duty officer dispatched rookie Officer Alex Hoffman and Deputy Edward Manning to check out the scene.

Ignorant of the alarm, Olivia and Jake headed into Andie's office that Rebecca had just vacated. Olivia turned on the overhead light and went to the computer on the desk. They were unaware of Rebecca hiding behind the receptionist desk, listening to their conversation.

"The only thing I can think of is that he must have installed some kind of surveillance cameras in the shop, and if he has videos they'll most likely be on his computer." Both she and Jake had been thinking about the text message

Andie had sent earlier threatening to expose them on 'some video'; they had no idea what it was about. They knew that Burke had been caught stealing at work and assumed that Andie must have used some kind of video surveillance to capture him committing this crime.

If he's been taping us, we could be in big trouble. I wonder where the cameras are located, and if can we turn them off? Olivia looked around the room. *He's probably watching us right now!*

She sat down at Andie's desk and was surprised that he'd left the computer open; he was usually so compulsive about locking the device. She scrolled through his documents and files, nothing obvious leaping out at her. She also searched for anything about the surveillance system.

"Why don't you look on the desktop?" Jake suggested. They both studied the folders ... *2016 Show items ... General Inventory ... Tire Inventory...*

"I don't see anything obvious here, Olivia. Perhaps he has something in his desk."

He tugged on the drawers, but they were locked. Andie's letter opener was on the top of the desk, so he jammed it into the lock and forced it open. He rifled through the drawers and came up emptied handed. He jerked the right-hand drawer in frustration, and it pulled out further, revealing the hidden compartment. Multiple disks scattered across the carpet.

"Jackpot!" Jake shouted. "Look at all of these! It seems Jake has been spying for a long time!" He randomly picked up one disk and inserted it into the computer, then scrolled through the images. It revealed day-to-day shop routines, but it also showed scenes of Olivia and Jake whispering and kissing in the coffee room. He pulled it out and inserted another; once again it revealed them embracing in the reception area. Jake looked at the collection of disks; the labels read 2016, 2017, etc.

Fear crept up his spine. "Holy shit, they go back years! Could he have evidence of us tampering with Fred's car? I need to find any video from January 2016. Help me look, Olivia?" They dropped to the floor and searched through the disks, desperate to find anything marked January 11. As he tossed them aside, he finally came across one labelled: *Save for Rebecca.*

He loaded the disk into the computer drive, and they both watched as the video showed images of them in the mechanic bay, plotting Fred Wright's death. Both sat in stunned silence until Olivia finally spoke.

"Oh my God!! If this gets out, we're fucked!"

She pulled the disk out and wagged it at Jake. "I wonder how many copies he has of this and if he's shown it to his boyfriend?" Olivia was gnawing on her well-manicured thumbnail.

"If he'd shown Pritchard we wouldn't be standing here, we'd be studying the inside of the jailhouse walls." Jake rubbed his hands over his face.

He paced back and forth. He felt like a caged animal; his fear was rising, and he needed to act. He suddenly swept the computer off the desk, then Andie's personal items went flying onto the floor. He crashed his foot through the computer screen; it sparked and crackled.

"Holy shit Jake, what are you doing?" Olivia dodged the flying objects.

"Destroying evidence! We need to get rid of the stuff on his computer." He ripped the hard drive off the desk and dashed it to the floor; then battered it with the desk lamp. "It has to look like a break and enter!" Jake hoped the damage he had inflicted on Andie's computer would interrupt any current video surveillance as well, otherwise everything that had happened this evening would be captured on tape. Things were getting more complicated.

He started picking the disks up off the floor. "Olivia, put these in your bag! We need to take them with us, and then get out of here. We've been here far too long." When they had collected all the disks off the floor, they scoured the desk for any others. Then Jake broke open a file cabinet and rummaged through the papers, littering the floor. He pushed pictures and awards off the shelves, glass and trophies smashing amongst the papers. As Jake ravaged the office, Olivia sat motionless.

"Babe," she gasped. "I think Andie may have given Rebecca a copy. Earlier today when I came to confront him, he was fussing over a USB stick, and now I don't see it here in his office. If she has it ...?"

Jake interrupted. "Then we need to find it and destroy it. If Rebecca has seen it, we need to silence her. She needs to disappear and soon, before all of this gets out! But for now ..." He stopped. "Is that a siren I hear?"

Jake looked out the window and spied the police car's red strobe lights off in the distance; the wailing sirens growing closer. He snapped off the office lights.

"Shit, we're so stupid. I think we must have tripped the alarm. Quick, let's go out the back way!" They snuck out of the office, passing the reception desk where Rebecca remained hidden. They fled out the mechanic bay door just as the police pulled around the front. He aimed the truck in the direction of his former home, desperate to search for this damning evidence.

"We need to check for that USB stick. If Rebecca has it, she may have it stashed at home."

CHAPTER FOURTY-NINE

As Olivia and Jake fled out the back of the building, Rebecca slipped from her hiding spot, and looked around in panic. She had also heard the police sirens, and she, too, was afraid to get caught. If the police found her, they could easily take her back to the psychiatrist unit, or worse, to jail.

I need to hide, but where? She could see the police officers outside the building, checking for any signs of entry. *It won't be long before they discover that Jake and Olivia left both the front and back doors open. The mechanic bay is my only option.*

She scurried down the hallway, passing Andie's office. The desk drawers were ransacked, and the secret compartment containing the disks was empty; the office was in complete disarray. Olivia and Jake had done a grand job of destroying evidence, and now Rebecca was left holding the bag. Leaving the chaos behind, she ran down the hall to the mechanic bay. She heard the door open in the reception area, and then voices calling out.

"Is there anyone in here?" Flashlights illuminated the dark.

She desperately looked around for a place to hide. One of the show cars was parked over a mechanic pit where the staff had been completing some maintenance. Rebecca slid underneath the car into the dark oily abyss. She lay there, hoping the dark space would hide her presence. The smells in the unventilated area was overwhelming, and she gagged aloud. She clapped her hand and over mouth, hoping they hadn't heard.

Andie stood outside in the main reception area, talking with Officer Eddie Manning. He had been notified by the police of a 'silent alarm' that had been activated at his commercial property. His cellphone had rung when he was halfway home, so he had pulled the car safely over on the side of the road, and answered it.

"Mr. Proctor, this is Officer Manning from the Campbell River Police Department. It appears that there has been a break in at your automotive shop. Would you be able to meet us there?"

Damn! Andie had thought. *Had Rebecca accidentally set off the alarm?*

He had told the officer he could meet him at the shop, and now as he inspected the mess in his office, he knew the surveillance disks had gone missing, and the hard drive was smashed beyond repair. All the evidence was gone! He now regretted leaving Rebecca alone and hoped that she had found what she needed before the hurricane Olivia had blown through.

"Do you know who might have done this, sir?" Deputy Manning shone a light around the mess lying on the office floor. "Anything missing?"

"I think it was probably a disgruntled employee looking to cause problems. I recently fired someone for theft. His name is Darren Burke, so perhaps you could talk with him."

Andie wanted to deflect the police so they would leave as soon as possible. "I will need to check the office for missing items, but for now let's just leave the mess. I'll have my staff help me clean it up in the morning."

Meanwhile, Officer Alex Hiscox was in the mechanic bay area searching for evidence of the intruder. He discovered the back door was ajar, so he stopped to secure it. He shone his flashlight around the bays, including underneath the car where Rebecca was hunkered down. He would have searched further, but he was interrupted by Andie entering the area and flipping on the overhead lights. The glare temporarily blinded them all.

"Don't bother checking in here," Andie instructed. "If Burke was anywhere, it would have been in the office's looking for money. Just secure the door please, and we will return to the reception area. Gentlemen ..."

Andie escorted them back to his office. "It has been a long night for me, so if I could come back in the morning to finish this it would be greatly appreciated. I will do a thorough check for missing items, and then come by the station to file a report."

The officers agreed, and they left Andie to lock up the shop. He circled back to his office, re-locked the door, and turned off the lights, plunging the area—and Rebecca—into complete darkness.

As Andie drove home, he called Kevin, waking him up. "We have to talk," was all he said.

CHAPTER FIFTY

While Officer Hiscox checked the mechanic bay for any evidence of a break in, Rebecca huddled down deeper into the pit; she slunk to the darkest corner, hoping that this would be enough to keep her hidden. Just as the officer was starting to knee down to shine his light under the vehicle; the bright overhead lights were flipped on. Rebecca shrank away from the glare.

"What the heck? Who turned on the lights?" the officer snapped, shielding his eyes. "Oh sorry, Mr. Proctor, I didn't realize it was you." Rebecca could hear Andie's voice, but the conversation itself was not clear. Suddenly the lights in the bay went out, and the officer pulled the connecting door shut, leaving Rebecca alone in the dark.

"Holy shit, that was close!" Rebecca whispered, peeking over the rim of the pit. She could hear voices coming from the office areas, then the building lights turned off, and everything went quiet. The alarm indicator on the back door turned from green to red; it glowed like a single eye in the dark.

She pulled herself from the pit, and then stole toward the door connecting to the office area. She peered through the glass window and found the office and reception areas deserted.

Seems like everyone has left the building. Looks like the coast is clear, but I think I'll wait a bit longer until I make my getaway; just in case the police are watching the building. She looked down at her clothes, she was dirty and grease covered. *I'll wait here in the bay, I'm pretty grimy!*

She slumped down on the beat up couch the mechanics used while taking their breaks. "Can't make it any dirtier," she laughed, leaning her head back. She pulled out her cellphone and checked that she had saved the recording. Slipping the device back in her pocket, she found her lids getting heavy.

Light filtered into the mechanic bay windows, dancing across Rebecca's closed eyes. She squinted as she looked around the room. For a moment she was disoriented; then she sat bolt upright.

"Shit, I fell asleep ... what time is it?" she gasped aloud. She looked up at the clock; it said it was eight-fifteen a.m.

Oh my God, the staff will be here any minute, if some aren't already. She turned her ears toward the office and reception area, straining to hear. *All is quiet! I need to leave quickly!*

Rebecca checked her pockets and found the disk still safely secure. She dashed toward the back door, dumping the screwdriver she'd been clutching back on the work bench. She didn't need its protection now, the computer disk was all she needed. She punched the password into the alarm system, then exited the building. She hoped to never have to return here again.

CHAPTER FIFTY-ONE

Magda lay in the hospital bed waiting for death. The last three days had been filled with poking and prodding by well-meaning medical staff, but the reality was that her time was limited, and she was glad. She hoped to soon leave this earth to reunite with her family, especially her beloved Sylvie. She looked forward to embracing them and returning to a time long before struggle, strife, loss, and pain.

She had hoped that Rebecca would have come and visited. The young woman reminded her so much of her granddaughter Elena, before she slid into a drug induced oblivion. Elena was lost to her, but she believed that something good could come from Elena's death, perhaps even a new life for Rebecca.

Why didn't she visit? she wondered; recently her thoughts were jumbled. *I want to talk to her. There are things I need to give to her.*

Her mind slowly cleared.

Rebecca called me and said she needed my help. She struggled to grab hold of the fleeting memories. *I called the ambulance for her, and then I came to see her here!* Thoughts and images whirled in her head.

Magda suddenly gasped. "The video! I took pictures of that man and his whore! I must let Rebecca know." She urgently needed to talk with Rebecca.

The ache in her chest worsened. *I must do this now before it is too late. I will write Rebecca a note, and I also need to send that nice police Chief Pritchard one as well. He needs to know what I know!* She pushed the call button to summon the nurse.

Phyllis Arthurs, Magda's nurse, heard the call bell ringing at the nursing station. "Yes, Mrs. Bodrug, what can I do for you?" She spoke into the intercom.

"I need to talk with you. Can you come please ... now?" The old woman's voice was no louder than a croak, making it difficult to hear.

"I will be there in a few minutes. Is it urgent?" Phyllis had just finished some patient rounds, and she was hoping to catch her breath before she had to head out for more.

"Please ... now," came the response.

"Okay, I'm coming," Phyllis rose and made her way to Magda's room.

Magda pulled forward in the bed as the nurse entered the room. She rasped. "I need paper and a pen to write a letter. You must help me!" She clutched her chest, groaning.

"Calm yourself Mrs. Bodrug, please try and relax. You're making yourself worse. Now lie back, dear." Phyllis attempted to get Magda to lie back, but she resisted.

"I am dying, and I need you to help me write a note to my friend, Rebecca; I feel she is in grave danger. Please, I need paper." She released the nurse and collapsed back, lying still as death on the bed. Phyllis reached forward to assess her pulse; Magda batted her hand away. "I am fine, but please get me paper and a pen."

Phyllis returned with the items, hoping this would settle her patient. She was worried; the elderly woman had severe heart failure, and her prognosis was very poor. It was unlikely she would survive this hospital stay. Magda thanked her, then waved her way.

Magda pushed the assist button to ease the bed into an upright position; even this minimal exertion made her breathless, and it took a moment to calm her drumming heart. Magda slowly scribbled the two notes. Her shaky hand made the task difficult, and she had to rest between lines of text. She reviewed the words, folded the letters, then addressed them with the appropriate recipient's name. Satisfied with the content of each, she set the pen down and eased her bed down to a recumbent position. She pressed the call button once again; she needed the nurse to deliver these notes. For Rebecca, it was a matter of life or death.

At the nursing station, the call bell chimed again.

"In a minute, Mrs. Bodrug." Phyllis sighed. She needed to ignore the woman's demand for a moment.

Magda lay fretting. The nurse had not come yet, and she desperately needed to talk with her. She needed to ensure that she would deliver the letters; it was of utmost importance. She pressed the call bell button again. This time the unit clerk at the desk answered her summons, and when she had reassured her that the letters would be given to Nurse Arthurs, Magda reluctantly handed over the items." I'll make sure she gets them ma'am, but now I need to get back to my desk. I hear the phone ringing."

Once at the desk, the clerk plopped the letters down next to Phyllis. "I knew you were busy so I answered the call bell this time. These are Mrs. Bodrug's letters. She wants you to deliver them." Then she turned away to answer the ringing phone.

Phyllis turned the letters over in her hands. Both had a name scribed in shaky hand writing, but neither had an address. Chief Pritchard's was easy enough to deliver, but the other one to an *Elena Lipska* would be more difficult. *Who was this woman, was she family?* She got up, went to her locker and placed them in the pocket of her scrub jacket; then returned to finish some charting on her patient's files.

The evening settled into late night calm as patients retired for the night, and Magda lay listening to the sounds of the hospital ward. The staff had moved to the nursing station where their voices drifted to her room. The soft murmur of their voices soothed her anxieties and stress, but she still needed to confirm the nurse would follow through with her needs. It was so important to her, so she once again rang the call bell and waited. Phyllis reached to turn it off ... just for a moment.

In the dark, Magda waited. Suddenly the room became bright, and she felt warm and light. She felt a familiar touch on her hands and brow, and she was certain she saw Amelia and Mikki standing beside her, and in the background, Elena stood holding Sylvie. She longed to join them. Pushing her blankets aside, she rose on unsteady feet and reached for them. A sudden bolt of pain struck her in the chest, and she collapsed to the floor. She closed her eyes and smiled as death took her home. "Goodbye Rebecca, but now I am going home to Mikki."

The cardiac monitors rang at the nursing station. The staff sprang to attention; the monitor in Room 14—Mrs. Bodrug's room—had 'flat-lined.' The staff dashed to the room to find the patient lying on the floor. She was pale and unconscious; obviously her heart had stopped. Phyllis started CPR, then called out, "Call the Code Team."

As she worked to revive her patient, her conscience plagued her. "I should have answered the call bell sooner. I am sorry, Mrs. Bodrug." Phyllis worked harder, fueled by guilt.

The Code Team arrived and took over the patient's care, but after several long minutes, the lead physician determined the actions were fruitless, and the team stopped treatment. "We're done here. Our patient has succumbed to her heart failure." The doctor turned to Phyllis. "We need to notify the family, who should I call?"

Phyllis shook her head. "I've never seen anyone come visit her." In the chaos she had forgotten about the letters in the locker.

"So sad," the doctor said. "No one should die alone."

CHAPTER FIFTY-TWO

Rebecca needed to get home; the conversation she overheard between Jake and Olivia had spurred on the urgency. She needed to know if the items that she had hidden in Indie's room remained undiscovered. She didn't think Jake would trash that space; it was sacred to him, and he rarely entered it, but she wouldn't put it past Olivia.

Would they find the 'hidey hole?' She struggled with her thoughts and fear. *Could they have found the evidence?*

She knew they would destroy anything implicating them and once this was done, she knew she was next; her life was definitely in danger. Rebecca needed to retrieve the evidence and find a place to hide out until she could hatch a plan. She was completely on her own now.

She drove up to the house, looking for signs of their presence. The kitchen door stood open. They had obviously been there, but were they still inside?

Neither of their vehicles could be seen, so she crept up to the house and pushed the door open. As she entered the space she wished she had Magda's gun, it provided her comfort, and she was determined to use it if necessary. The house was eerily still, but the place had been turned upside down. Drawers had been pulled open and carelessly emptied, closets were ransacked, and items were strewn about. There wasn't one nook or cranny that had not been violated. *They had been thorough, but how thorough?* She worried as she dashed upstairs to Indie's room. Once there, she discovered that even it had been plundered.

"Bastards!" she spat. "You couldn't even leave his stuff untouched!"

She sucked in her breath; luckily the dresser covering the 'hidey hole' entrance was still in place. The drawers were pulled open, and the items emptied on the floor, but the dresser still stood guard over the hidden doorway. She pushed the dresser aside, then yanked the secret door open; the box storing the evidence was still intact.

"Whew!" Rebecca sighed with relief. "Now I've got you two!" she said, hugging the box to her chest.

She suddenly noticed her clothes and hands were covered with grim and oil from the bottom of the mechanic bay. *I need to take a shower, and then get out of here.* She moved into the bathroom taking the box with her. She looked in the mirror, and rubbed at a smudge of grease.

"Rebecca Wright, you are either very brave or nuts!" She laughed as she recalled last night's adventures; she had been reckless, but it had paid off. She now had the evidence she needed.

She reached into the tub and turned the shower to hot. The room filled with steam, and as she started to remove her soiled clothing, the computer disk fell on the floor. She picked it up and placed it safely on the counter; this small, flat disk was her lifeline, she had to protect it. She felt a wave of emotion pass over her, and her face burned with heat!

It must be from the shower. She touched her face. *No ... it's an internal flame.* She felt a passion burning in her heart, a place that up until recently had been a cold dead wasteland. She stripped off the remainder of her soiled clothes, letting them fall on the bathroom floor. As she kicked them aside, she stepped on another pile she had left earlier.

Magda's clothes. I must launder and return them to her. She paused. *I know ... I can hide out at her place while she is the hospital!*

She rubbed the mist off the mirror and looked directly into her eyes. She studied the reflection; her eyes no longer looked sad and old, there was a glow to them. *To begin anew the old must die,* she thought. *These were Magda's words and they hadn't made sense then, but now they do. Clever Magda ... the old me must die!*

Rebecca stepped in the shower; the water pelted her skin, flushing away not only the night's grime, but also the pain and worry of her past. Going under the water was like a baptism to a new life. As the dirt washed away down the drain, so did her attachment to this life of sadness and betrayal. She emerged from the water clean and born anew.

She scrubbed herself dry, donned fresh clothing, and hastily packed a bag of personal items. She didn't want to tarry in case 'they' returned. The last thing

Rebecca wanted was a confrontation, not now at least. She had things to plan. Before leaving she entered Indie's room and put it back in order, but she left the hidden door open. She knew Jake and Olivia would return to search again; she wanted them to sweat about what might have been secured in this secret spot.

Rebecca wanted to take a piece of her son with her, a physical memory, so she selected his favourite blanket and toy, placing them in her bag alongside Magda's gun. Next, she went to the living room and picked up the wrinkled photos, selecting one of her parents and Indie. Then she took a moment to fling the images of her and Jake into the fireplace.

"You're going to burn, Jake ... in more ways than one," she scoffed. "Now I need to check on Magda."

CHAPTER FIFTY-THREE

Rebecca spied Ethel Graham peeking out from her lace curtained window. She braked, then pulled the car over. She flung the door open, thinking. *There is something I need to do before I check on Magda; I need to talk with the old hag who accused me of killing my son. I need to know why she accused me. I've always wondered why she lied. Did someone coerce her?*

She climbed up Ethel's shabby overgrown sidewalk. The yard had once been very well manicured, but lately it had slipped into decline. The front door was blocked by an overgrown hedge, hiding the porch from the road. Rebecca rang the bell and heard the chime echo in the house, but no answer came. She patiently rang again. She peered in the window, trying to catch a glimpse of the interior, but the dusty window obscured her view. She was turning to leave when she heard the scratchy sound of a chain lock being pulled, and then the lock turned. An aged face peered through the crack in the door.

Ethel blinked at Rebecca. "Can I help you? You look familiar? I'm not wearing my darned glasses; I keep losing them!" Suddenly the old woman stepped back and opened the door; she had recognized Rebecca.

"You came back," she croaked. "But is it safe?"

"Safe from whom?"

"From her," her neighbour whispered. "She is evil." Ethel's eyes darted back and forth; then she abruptly hauled Rebecca into the house. She slammed the door behind them, then reset the locks. Peering through the dirty window, she surveyed the area for intruders. Rebecca followed Ethel into the cluttered living room; it was very unkept and neglected. Every space was piled with newspapers, magazines, and old papers and books; there was very little room to move or to sit.

Ethel collapsed into an overstuffed chair placed strategically by the window; the same spot where she claimed she had witnessed Indie's accident. On the table, next to the chair, sat her lost spectacles.

Rebecca felt very uncomfortable sitting across from the woman who had made the false accusation. Her emotions were running raw after three years of pent-up anger; hurtful words brewed behind her lips. She selected a chair, removed a pile of old photos, and prepared to confront her accuser.

"Miss Graham, you have been calling me and leaving messages. You said you wanted to confess something, what is it you need to tell me?"

The old woman put on her glasses and stared at Rebecca; then her gaze was drawn to the house across the street; Rebecca's house. Long moments dragged on, and the woman remained quiet. She seemed to be struggling with her thoughts; then she started to slowly speak. She pulled off her thick lensed glasses, turning them over in her arthritic hands.

"I'm not sure what it is." She shook her head. "Sometimes I have trouble remembering."

Rebecca was frustrated; she would have to coax the old woman's memory.

"Miss Graham, do you remember me. I am Rebecca Wright, and three years ago you accused me of killing my son. You told the police that I pushed Indie from his bedroom window." It sounded cold and blunt even to her own ears, but this was her only chance to confront this woman.

Rebecca turned and motioned to the window. "How could you see anything when your eyesight is so bad? And from this window it is difficult to see anything anyway, even with good eyes. Why? Why did you tell the police this story?" Her voice was demanding and shrill.

The old woman braced herself. "I lied," she whispered, barely loud enough for Rebecca to hear.

"You lied!" Rebecca shouted. Her vison had gone dark. "Why on earth would you lie about something like this? Do you realize the hell I have lived through these past three years?" Rebecca was enraged; she stormed toward the old woman. She placed her hands on Ethel's chair armrests, then leaned down. She shouted in her face. "Why?"

The old woman shrunk back, thinking Rebecca was going to strike her. She had been hit before and was afraid of another assault. "She said she would hurt me if I didn't tell the police you killed your boy. She made up a story and forced me to tell them. I'm so sorry!" She reached to grab Rebecca's hand.

Rebecca pulled away from the old woman, accidentally sweeping a pile of clutter off the table next to Ethel. Things came crashing down; papers and photos floated to the floor and pooled at her feet. A particular image caught Rebecca's eye. She picked it up; it was an old graduation picture of Olivia!

"Why do you have a picture of Olivia Proctor?"

"Olivia Proctor is my great niece," Ethel blurted out.

"What?" Rebecca interrupted. "No way! Olivia told me she had a crazy aunt that the entire family avoided, but I never dreamed it was you! The crazy aunt is you!" She was stunned. For years Olivia had kept the secret from her; all this time it was right under her nose, right across the street.

Ethel shrank back in her chair, looking smaller and aged. Looking down at her hands, she took a long, deep breath.

"I heard the screaming that day; it was awful. I was sitting by the window, watching the world go by. It was a lovely fall day, and I was enjoying the colour of the leaves. I couldn't find my glasses, but I could still see the leaves." Her voice was shaking as she recalled the events.

"I looked out the window when I heard screams; I wanted to know who was making that ungodly noise, but I couldn't see very well because of my poor eyesight. I found my glasses, and then I went to the front doorstep, to see what was going on. I saw the young woman holding her child and screaming; the man was standing over her. The boy wasn't moving; he must have been badly hurt or dead."

Ethel shook her head, remembering the tragic event. Tears seeped from her old eyes. "The police and ambulance came, but the woman wouldn't let him go. She kept rocking him and wailing, saying over and over, *It's my fault ... it's my fault.*'

She paused. "Later I learned that the boy had fallen from the upstairs window. Do you remember this sad day?" The emotional output had drained the old woman; she slumped back in her chair, closing her eyes.

"Who made you lie to the police?" Rebecca demanded.

"My niece," she blurted out.

"Olivia told you to lie?" The confession hit like a lightning bolt. "She made you do this?"

The old woman slowly stood and shuffled across the room; she unbolted the lock, and then pulled the door open. "Miss, you need to leave. I cannot help you any more, please leave! It's not safe." She stood trembling as Rebecca approached.

Rebecca pulled out a piece of paper from her purse, and she quickly wrote on it. She grabbed Ethel's arm, and stuffed the paper in her hand. "Here is my cellphone number. I won't be staying at my house for now, so if you need to talk more, call me at this number."

Ethel peered at the paper, then whispered. "Please leave."

She pushed Rebecca through the door. It closed abruptly, and Rebecca heard the old woman secure herself inside. She stood on her neighbour's doorstep, holding the picture of the Baird family; it was another piece of the puzzle.

CHAPTER FIFTY-FOUR

Rebecca drove away, keeping her eyes glued to the road in front of her. She resisted looking in the rear-view mirror. *Don't look back Rebecca ... don't look back. Look forward to the future ... there is nothing back there for you!* She needed to safely leave the neighbourhood before placing a call to the hospital. Jake and Olivia would eventually circle back and attempt to catch Rebecca at home because they would be desperate to steal any evidence. She had driven several miles now, so she pulled her car over and pulled out her cellphone.

As she waited for the operator to answer, she reflected on what she had learned about Ethel Graham and her relationship with Olivia. *I would never have guessed. Olivia had gone out of her way to avoid her elderly aunt. Who knew that for all these years she's lived right across the street from me?*

"You are so deceitful Olivia, curse my stupid naivety!" She blurted out.

"I beg your pardon!" a voice said in her ear. "This is the Campbell River Hospital, may I help you?"

"Yes. I was hoping you could tell me how Mrs. Magda Bodrug is doing?"

"One moment please, and I will transfer you to the head nurse on Unit 5A; she can explain what has happened." The operator transferred the call, leaving Rebecca hanging.

"What do you mean ... has happened? Is Magda okay?" She was answered by silence.

Rebecca feared the worst, and then a voice came on the line. "This is Andrea Banks, Unit 5A head nurse. Are you family?"

"Yes, I am Elena, Elena Lipska, her granddaughter." It was a small lie, but it wouldn't do any damage.

"I am very sorry to inform you that your grandmother passed away last night. We didn't know of anyone to contact. Again, we are very sorry for your loss. Is there anything I can do for you?"

Rebecca could barely speak. Her throat had closed up, and she was struggling to form words. "No, there is nothing you can do. Thank you for caring for her."

"I'm sorry," The head nurse said. Giving this kind of news to family never got any easier. She then realized that she was talking to an empty phone; the caller, this Elena Lipska, had hung up.

On the other end of the line, Rebecca wept, letting her sobs purge her soul. When her tears had subsided, she wiped her tear-stained face on her sleeve, then turned the key in the ignition. *I need to get to Magda's apartment before that beast of a landlord gets wind of her passing. I need to retrieve some personal items, including the box hidden under the bed.*

She felt guilty thinking it, but she could use the money in the box. With limited funds, it meant survival for her, and she thought Magda would actually want her to have it. She pressed her foot on the gas pedal, straining the little car's old engine. She wished she could fly; time was of utmost importance. As she pulled into the apartment parking lot, the tires of her little Honda squealed, and the engine chugged with exertion.

She had made excellent time in getting there, but when she got inside the building it appeared she might be too late. *He's already lurking around the hallway to Magda's apartment.*

"Excuse me, what are you doing?" Rebecca boldly faced the landlord. He turned to face her, his eyes shifting from side to side.

"The old woman has not paid her rent. She knows the rules. No rent, and I throw her out!" He stopped when Rebecca brazenly stepped into his personal space. The man towered over her; she was repulsed by his body odour, and he reeked of alcohol. He might be dangerous, but she *was not* going to back down. She faced the man, and shouted. "She's been in the hospital, you idiot! How could she pay her rent?!"

"How I know this?" he muttered. "And who are you anyway? You that woman who attacked me? You the one that pepper sprayed me?" He took one hesitant step back from Rebecca.

Rebecca had no idea what he was talking about, but she decided to play along. "Yup, I sure was. Do you want more?" She put her hand in her handbag. There was not spray there, but the cold touch of the gun gave her strength.

"I call the police on you ... you crazy bitch!" He stormed off to his apartment, a verbal tirade following him. He turned back, shaking his fist at her. "I throw the old woman out, you wait and see!"

Rebecca took a deep breath to steady her nerves, then tried to put Magda's key into the lock, but her hands betrayed her. She shook like a leaf. *Calm yourself girl. Just get yourself inside, away from this menace.* On the next attempt she turned the key, then quickly hustled into the small, dark space. She felt safe here, at least temporarily. She had work to do and only had a short period of time before the landlord would return with the police.

CHAPTER FIFTY-FIVE

"Phyllis?" Jamie Arthurs called from the laundry room. "Do you want me to wash your uniforms?"

Phyllis Arthurs rolled over and looked at the clock. The time read eleven-thirty. *Wow, I certainly slept in.* She stretched and yawned. The memories of last evening's shift came drifting back as she looked up at the ceiling. She cringed as she recalled the old woman's death.

"Oh, you are awake. I thought you were still sleeping. Rough shift last night?" Jamie sat down on the bed next to his wife. Phyllis nodded but remained silent. She did not want to discuss it with her spouse; she didn't think he would understand.

"Say, I found these in your scrub jacket pocket, and I wasn't sure if you wanted me to throw them out." He handed her the makeshift letters. Phyllis swung herself to a sitting position; taking them from him.

"I forgot about these; an elderly patient wrote them last night. I was so busy that I didn't give her much attention. Then her heart stopped, and we couldn't do anything." She looked at the crumpled paper in her hands. "I wish there was something I could do to make it better." She sighed.

Jamie drew his wife to him, and he gave her a hug. "There is something you can do. Deliver her letters for her." He gave her another hug, then left her to her thoughts.

Phyllis turned the letters over, studying the names. Delivering the letter to Chief Pritchard wouldn't be difficult, but the other one to Elena Lipska might be. Pulling the phone book from the bedside drawer, she flipped through the pages but came up empty.

Perhaps I can phone the unit and get the old woman's address. Maybe if I go there someone will know this Lipska person. She placed a call to the unit, and the clerk provided Phyllis with the address. She quickly showered and decided to take her dog Bella for a walk. Being new to Campbell River she checked Google maps for directions; Magda's apartment building was only a few blocks from her own house.

"Going for a walk Jamie; taking Bella." She laced up her shoes and snapped the leash on the excited pup.

The mid- summer day was warm, and the sky was clear. She donned her sunglasses and swept the letters into her pocket. It took Phyllis about twenty minutes to reach Magda Bodrug's address. As she drew closer she saw a group standing outside the apartment building; it included a police officer in a heated discussion with two other people. As she approached the group, she heard the patient's name being spoken.

Reining in the eager pup, she watched the drama unfolding. She could hear the man's voice rising in anger and frustration. She decided to approach with caution; parts of the conversation were very tense.

"Ma'am do you have the right to enter this apartment building? Mr. Invonitz, the landlord, says you aren't the renter?" The officer was separating a large foul-mouthed man and an impatient young woman. She overheard the woman explain. "Mrs. Bodrug died last night in the hospital. I am Elena Lipska, her granddaughter. My grandmother would want me to remove some personal items from her apartment."

The woman was showing her identification to the officer; being a rookie on the force, he didn't recognize Rebecca.

"Are you the executor?" the officer quizzed her. "I think it would be best if you leave and come back with further papers indicating you have the right to enter the premises."

Phyllis had been quietly watching the situation; now she decided to interrupt. "Excuse me officer, I might be able to help." She had the letter for this Elena Lipska; perhaps the contents might help settle this battle.

Officer Hiscox was feeling overwhelmed by the situation and certainly didn't need onlookers. "Ma'am, please step back. I have everything under control here."

Phyllis insisted. "Please listen to me! I need to talk with Elena Lipska. I have a letter for her from the woman who lives in this building. My name is Phyllis Arthurs, and I looked after Mrs. Bodrug last night in the hospital, I was her nurse. Mrs. Bodrug wrote this letter just before she died, and she begged me to deliver it." She reached out to hand it to Rebecca, but the officer intercepted it.

Officer Hiscox took the paper and turned it over in his hand. It was indeed addressed in shaky handwriting to 'Elena Lipska.' He unfolded the paper and read the contents aloud.

> *To My Dear Elena,*
>
> *I am dying and hope to see our family soon.*
>
> *This is my last will and testament.*
> *Before I die, I want to leave my meager possessions to you, my granddaughter Elena Lipska.*
> *They are located in my apartment-106 1369 Green Hills Way, Campbell River.*
>
> *Please use them to start a new life.*
>
> *Your loving grandmother,*
> *Magda Bodrug.*

"This was written by Mrs. Bodrug?" the officer questioned Phyllis. "Did you witness her signing it?"

Phyllis nodded at the officer. She knew she was stretching the truth but it was close enough; she wanted to atone for her neglect last night.

"This means nothing!" The irate Invonitz spat. "Stupid bitches!"

The officer had had enough of this drama. "Sir, you need to quit with the language, and Ms. Lipska, do you have keys?"

Rebecca dangled the keys in front of the group. "Yes, I do and I also know the code for the front door."

"Okay Mr. Invonitz, we have enough evidence to prove that this woman indeed has the right to enter the apartment. Now, I need all of you to disperse."

Invonitz refused to move. "The old woman owes me money for this month's rent." The officer shook his head and grimaced in frustration.

"I will pay it," Rebecca interjected. "I will keep the apartment for the next month while I sort out my grandmother's affairs." She left to collect the cash to pay the landlord, and when the transaction was completed and the others had dispersed, Phyllis approached the officer.

"Excuse me sir, I have one more letter. Mrs. Bodrug wanted me to give this to Chief Pritchard. Would you mind delivering this to him?" The officer took the offered letter from Phyllis.

"What's this all about?"

"I have no idea, I never read it, but listen I've got to go, my pup is getting kind of antsy."

Officer Hiscox glanced again at the letter, and then placed it on top of his clipboard. "This is going to take me forever to write up." At the car, he tossed the clipboard on the empty passenger seat; the letter floated down between the seat and the console. It remained unseen and forgotten.

CHAPTER FIFTY-SIX

O livia was sitting in her car, hidden in the alley across from the Wright home. She had started her surveillance again when they had found the videotapes in Andie's office. She was certain that Andie had given Rebecca a USB stick, and the last search had come up empty handed. She pondered and waited. *It must be on her person or she has it stashed somewhere else, but I need to get it from her.*

Olivia had wanted to bring Jake along to provide the 'muscle', but presently he lay snoring in their bed; hung over once again. She had been watching the house all day, and she was surprised when she saw Rebecca walk up the front sidewalk toward her Aunt Ethel's house.

Why would she be going there? Olivia wondered as she chewed on her thumbnail, turning it ragged.

The visit had only lasted twenty minutes, and then Rebecca had driven away in her dilapidated little car.

Should I confront Auntie Ethel or follow Rebecca? She decided to confront the old woman first; Rebecca's junkie car would be easy enough to locate. After all Campbell River wasn't that big. *Now, it's time to check on Auntie, and see what she is up to. She'll probably be nagging me for some money again. Not like she deserves it.*

She counted out some cash, and then put the wallet into her coat pocket. She didn't want to bring her new Louis Vuitton purse into Auntie's nasty old shack; she didn't want to get any dirt marks on it.

Yeah, I have a few bucks, enough to keep her eyes open and her mouth shut. She had parked up the street and cut through the overgrown bushes to the back door.

This place is such a dump; I should just burn it down, with her in it. It would only take one match. She chuckled to herself. *No one would miss her, especially me.*

She unlocked the back door, then silently entered the house. Auntie Edith was prone to forgetfulness, especially when it came to keys and eye glasses, so Olivia had kept a copy of the keys, *'for emergencies of course'*. She found Ethel holding the receiver of an old phone, and she was trying to leave a message; a piece of paper sat on the table next to her. Olivia stood in the doorway listening.

"Miss, it's me, Ethel Graham. We talked just a few minutes ago. Please call me back. I must tell you more. Be careful of Olivia, she wants to hurt you and is out to get you."

Ethel turned around and was shocked to see her niece hanging over her shoulder. "How long have you been standing there?" She hadn't heard Olivia come into the room. She snatched the paper off the table.

"Long enough!" Olivia slapped the phone out of the old woman's hand. The phone and the receiver clattered to the floor, but the call did not disconnect. The message continued to record on the other end.

"What have you been up to? Didn't I just tell you to keep an eye on the house across the street and nothing more? It was a simple request, just put your damn glasses on and watch." She picked up Ethel's glasses and crammed them onto her face, bruising the bridge of her nose. The elderly woman cried out in pain. Olivia was sick to death of this whiny old woman.

"Please don't hurt me!" Ethel cried out. Olivia grabbed the old woman's arms and gave her a shake. To steady herself Ethel clutched at her niece's coat, but she accidentally ripped the pocket, causing the contents to spill out. Several items clattered to the floor, including Olivia's wallet that bounced under the armchair and lay unnoticed amongst the other debris.

Outraged by the ruin of her coat, she pushed the old woman away. Ethel staggered and fell backward, striking her head on the bricked hearth. She lay motionless. Olivia looked on in surprise. *Was she dead?*

Olivia poked Ethel with her foot, the woman didn't move. She nudged her leg next, and when Ethel didn't respond, she knelt down to check her pulse. It was then that she noticed the pool of dark blood seeping from under her aunt's head.

"Oops! I think I just killed her!" She continued to stare at the dead woman, and then shrugged. "Well, that takes care of that problem." She dusted her hands clean.

She pulled herself up, and it was then that she realized the phone was still off the hook. She hastened over and listened; there wasn't anyone on the other end. She thought about re-dialing, but it was an old rotary phone, so she placed the receiver back in the cradle.

I wondered who she was calling. Olivia decided she better get out of there before someone saw her exit Auntie Ethel's house and wondered what was up. She saw the keys that had fallen from her pocket, stooped to pick them up and turned to leave, but then paused.

I could make it look like a break in gone bad and that poor old Auntie got caught in the crossfire; the police won't question her injuries that way. She pushed things over and emptied drawers, adding to the clutter and rubbish already on the floor. Olivia stood back to admire her handiwork, then she stepped over the dead woman.

"Say hi to dad for me!" she laughed. "The two of you can have a drink in Hell!" She flung the backdoor open, leaving it hanging ajar.

CHAPTER FIFTY-SEVEN

Later that day Rebecca sat on the floor in Magda's apartment nursing the last few drops of Magda's brandy. She raised her glass and toasted her old friend. "To you Magda, with love," she spoke aloud, sipping the alcohol.

She shifted through the items she had placed on the living room rug. They were separated into three piles. On the right were the personal times she had brought from home: Indie's favourite toy and blanket, a few pictures, and her parent's wedding rings. This small pile represented her past life. On the left sat the evidence she'd collected: Jake's cellphone, her phone, the USB stick, the police reports ... it represented the present. In the middle lay Elena's ID, Magda's money, and the gun. Was this the future?

She took a drink and welcomed the calming sensation it brought. The last few weeks had been anything but calm; a whirlwind of activity and emotion, but she knew there was more to come ... much more. Rebecca sipped and pondered her situation. *Why do people kill?* She swirled the amber liquid.

Money. She decided, then took a sip.

Jealousy. She deliberated, then crunched the ice in the glass.

Revenge. She determined, picking up the bottle and emptying the remainder into her glass.

She watched the ice spin around and around. It reminded her of her life, a constant spiral of madness.

"*Well Rebecca, how are you going to get out of this situation?* She looked around the cramped apartment. *I definitely have to leave Campbell River.* She picked up Elena's ID and pondered.

Her cellphone disturbed her thoughts; it was Ethel Graham again. *No more today Ethel, I cannot do anymore craziness for now.* She set the phone down and drained the last drops from the glass. She felt very sleepy; her eyes were heavy, and she yawned. She wobbled to the couch, curled up, and nodded off; the drink having its desired effects.

As she drifted into sleep her final thought was: *Is killing me the only option?*

The early morning sun peeked into the apartment windows and danced across Rebecca's face. She raised her hand to block the light and squinted at the clock on the wall, it was just past five o'clock. Her head thumped in time to her pulse and her mouth felt sticky; the alcohol taste was tattooed on her dry tongue.

She searched Magda's medicine cabinet for a bottle of aspirin, shook out two tablets and dry swallowed them, then returned to the living room to search for her phone. She wanted to know if Andie had called; she was worried about him, especially after the recent media announcement. She flipped through the messages and saw one from last night. It was two minutes in duration!

Holy crow, who is this from? She wondered as she scrolled through the call display. *It's from Ethel Graham's number.* The effects of last night's brandy was gone all accept for the residual headache; she rubbed her thumping temples.

She pressed the play button and listened as Ethel stammered on, then she a heard a crash, followed by a loud bang. It sounded like the phone had been knocked to the floor, but the call had not disconnected. She could hear a woman's voice threatening Ethel; she gasped as she recognized it—Olivia! The phone recorded sounds of arguing, then a shrill scream, and then the call ended abruptly.

Rebecca stared in horror at the phone in her hand. *Did Olivia hurt the old woman? Oh my God, I have to go check on her.*

She grabbed her purse and keys, then hurried to her car. In her mad dash, she didn't think about calling the police, or about the danger she was placing herself in. She just raced thought the quiet streets; she was in a panic to reach Ethel. *I hope it isn't too late to help her.*

She braked to a halt down the street from Ethel's home, the tires screaking in protest. Rebecca could see Ethel's front door from this vantage point. The house seemed very quiet; eerily quiet. She didn't see the old woman peeking down from her usual perch. Not a good sign, but it was still early in the morning.

She suddenly felt afraid. *Could Ethel be hurt or worse dead? Could Olivia know about the phone message Ethel left me?* Her heart pounded; she could feel it in her temples. *Is Olivia hiding out, waiting for me?*

Rebecca decided she needed something to protect herself. *Shit! I forgot Magda's gun at her place. I need to arm myself.* She entered her own home through the back door; it remained unlocked like she had left it. She stepped into a cyclone of destruction; Jake and Olivia had created quite a mess the last time they searched. The broom closet door hung open; a wooden bat was propped against the wall.

She reached for it and turned it over. It was Jake's; years ago his baseball team had engraved his name on it and given it to him as an early baby gift. It was for future ball games between father and son. He had once treasured this item, now it sat forgotten in the closet. She slung it over her shoulder, the weight made her feel more secure.

Hang on Ethel, I'm coming! She marched across the street, climbed the steps, pushed past the overgrown bush, and peered in the dirty front door window. She couldn't see much, so she banged loudly on the door. No one responded, so she waded through the dry burnt grass and weeds, moving around to the back door. The door swung ajar, banging against the frame.

She paused. *Hmm? Kind of unusual, Ethel usually keeps the place locked up pretty tight.* Shouldering the bat, she stepped into the doorway and called out. "Miss Graham ... Ethel, are you okay?"

No response.

She stepped deeper into the house. Creeping slowly forward, bat in hand; she reeled in shock when she entered the living room. Ethel Graham lay on the floor, and it was obvious that she was very dead!

"Holy shit!" Rebecca gasped, dropping the bat on the floor. She pushed the arm chair aside and knelt beside the old woman. She was cold to the touch, her eyes stared upward. Blood had wept from a wound on the back of the head; it was a sticky drying mess on the floor beside her body.

Rebecca crawled backward in revulsion. As she clawed away from the corpse, her hand landed on something on the floor. She flinched back. It was an expensive red leather wallet with Gucci tooled on the outside. Its clasp had fallen open exposing a driver's license; the owner was Olivia Proctor.

She grabbed the wallet and scurried away from Ethel's battered body. She stood looking back and forth between the wallet and the dead woman. Olivia had obviously been here recently; she didn't go anywhere without this wallet, and especially her credit cards.

"I know Olivia did this to you because I overheard it on the phone!" She spoke softly to the dead woman. "I want to call the police, but I have to play this right. I need them to understand that Olivia killed you."

Rebecca started to dial from her cellphone, but then she paused. *Wait a minute, how am I going to explain my presence here in Ethel's house? Everyone knows about our history, and will assume I did it! I certainly have a good reason to kill her ... revenge!* Her thoughts returned to last evening; she had just been thinking about this very reason, but her revenge wasn't aimed at Ethel; there were others on her radar.

"No way is anyone going to pin this on me!" She was horrified at the scene in front of her, but she realized it may have changed the game for her. She looked down at the item in her hands. *Shit, my fingerprints are on everything.*

She pulled her sweater over her hands and scrubbed the wallet, removing her fingerprints. She looked down at the dead woman on the floor and the debris she lay in. Right next to her body, amongst the clutter, laid Jake's bat. Rebecca picked it up, and rubbed her sweater down its length.

"Well Jake, your bat can protect me after all. My prints might have been on it, but hopefully so are yours. It seems Olivia staged the scene to look like a robbery to divert the suspicion from her, but I know better." She tapped her cellphone. "I have the recorded message."

She looked down at Ethel's' body and felt very sad for the woman. *No one deserves to be treated so poorly, and then discarded. I know just how that feels, so Olivia has to pay.*

She carefully stepped over her neighbour's body, being careful not to tread in the drying blood. She needed to find Ethel's phone; it was an old rotary dial. She found it on the floor, the handset returned to its cradle. Someone had hung it up, after Ethel had left her message on Rebecca's cellphone; probably Olivia. Pulling her sweater over her hand, she carefully picked up the receiver and dial 911.

"911. How may I help you?"

"I think my neighbour might be hurt, she isn't answering her phone or the doorbell."

"What is the address?"

"Number 532 Riverview Place."

"What is your name, ma'am?" the operator asked, but the line had gone dead. Rebecca carefully replaced the handset and stepped over Ethel. "I've got to get out of here quickly, but let's add some suspicious pieces of evidence. Let's make them really pay Ethel."

Before she planted the wallet, Rebecca turned it over in her hand, careful not to leave any new prints. She opened the wallet and riffled through its contents. It was stuffed with plastic ... Olivia loved her credit cards. The bill holder also contained six hundred and seventy-five dollars in various bills.

"Nice little stash, Olivia." She removed the large bills but left the rest. "Don't want to be too greedy!" She plucked out a Platinum Visa Card, thought for a moment, and then pocketed it.

This could come in handy. Now where to put the wallet? she thought. She stepped forward and then gently tucked it under Ethel's body, careful not to disturb any other evidence. She gagged as she moved the body, then quickly jumped away before she vomited. Next, she carefully lifted the wooden bat, holding it with her sweater sleeve and rolling it across the pool of blood. She wanted some of it to adhere to the bat. *I hope you can explain this, Jake.*

Rebecca turned back to the dead woman. "I have to go Ethel, but I will make sure Olivia pays for what she did to you!" In the background, she heard the wail of an ambulance approaching. She slipped from Ethel's house leaving the back door ajar and then quickly retreated to her own house. It was still very early in Campbell River, just after six o'clock, and the street remained quiet and still.

She locked and barricaded herself inside. Rebecca thought about fleeing and returning to the safe haven of Magda's apartment, but she decided to wait to ensure that the EMS team and police did a proper job of caring for Ethel. She shook her head in disbelief that she even cared; at the beginning of this week she had loathed and hated this old woman. Years ago, her words had ruined her life, but now Ethel's confession and tragic death had saved her. *Thank you, Ethel Graham ... thank you!*

CHAPTER FIFTY-EIGHT

J ake was nursing another hangover this morning, and he didn't have the patience to deal with Olivia's ranting. She was marching around the kitchen, frantically looking for her wallet. Her banging and crashing made his head pulsate. It felt like he had cut glass between his temples, and the loud noises she was creating aggravated his headache and poked at his temper.

"Explain to me again, what happened last night?" Jake asked, rubbing his bleary eyes, and longing for a drink.

He had been sampling an expensive bottle of Andie's Scotch when Olivia had arrived home last night. She had been gloating about 'taking out the last piece of trash.' He hadn't truly understood what she was yapping on about, but it had been a good enough reason to tie one on. They had polished off the Scotch, and then retired to the bedroom for a round of lusty sex

As he made his way to the liquor cabinet, he felt unsteady and wobbly; a drink would solve this, but the cabinet was nearly empty. *If only she'd stop talking.*

"Aren't you listening?" Olivia harped. "Do you have cotton wool in your ears?" She picked up a glass and flung it at him. He batted away the item, just barely dodging the flying glass as it hit the wall behind him.

"What the hell Olivia, you could have cut me with that. Seriously?" He shouted at her. "Now who is going to clean that up and the rest of the mess in here? We live like pigs." His blurry eyes moved around the room. Dishes were stacked on the counters; leftover food dried on them, and the smelly garbage was overflowing. Since they had moved into Proctor Estate, it had been steadily going downhill. Agatha, the housekeeper, had recently quit.

"I'll find someone!" she hissed. Olivia looked haggard this morning, not her usually put together self. This whole 'Rebecca thing' seemed to be wearing on her. She had been gnawing on her manicured thumbnail, turning the edge raw and ragged.

"I told you last night when I came home that I think I killed Auntie Ethel. I didn't mean to, but she was being so annoying, and well, I pushed her. She fell and hit her head, and then she was bleeding everywhere. But that isn't the worst of it; I think I dropped my wallet in her house!" She paced back and forth across the kitchen, obviously very agitated.

"So what are you going to do about this?" Jake sighed.

"Me? Don't you mean us?" she hissed, flinging a dish at him. He dodged it and marched over to her, menace in his eyes. "What is wrong with you!?"

Jake's right hand twitched; he was really having trouble controlling his anger. He slammed his fist down on the counter. Olivia cringed and pulled away. Her mascara had streaked, and her nose was running. She looked a right regular mess!

"I'm really sorry, just kind of feeling rough this morning, too much booze." He pulled her into his arms. Olivia stood stiff and ridged, but she finally melted against him. They were each other's kryptonite.

"You go get cleaned up, while I tidy this mess." He waved at the kitchen. "Then we'll go pay Auntie Ethel a visit. I'm sure everything is okay. The old bird is pretty tough ... now you go." He watched her tight bottom sashay away.

"Shit, there is nothing about this that is okay. If she did kill the old girl and her wallet is there then we have some fast talking to do." He muttered, but there was nothing he could do for the moment, so he picked up the apron that Olivia had dropped on the way to the bedroom and surveyed the disaster surrounding him.

Jake donned the apron and attacked the kitchen clutter. He put on a pot of strong coffee and as he cleaned and scrubbed, he sipped the dark brew and pondered their next move. *I wonder where Rebecca is hiding out. We need to deal with her.*

CHAPTER FIFTY-NINE

Rebecca sat watching Ethel Graham's house. The EMS team had arrived, lights and sirens blaring. From her vantage point at the kitchen window, she watched as the team approached the front door and knocked repeatedly without answer.

Sorry fellas. She silently shook her head. *Poor Ethel cannot answer the door. Go to the back, go around the back.*

As if they had read her mind, they moved through the weedy yard to the back door, hanging ajar. She watched as the team entered the house. She heard someone cry out, but she couldn't make out the words. Suddenly one of the medics exited the house and threw up on the sun burnt lawn. The remaining medic followed close behind, radio in hand. She overheard his words.

> "Dispatch this is EMS Team #2. You'd better dispatch the police to this location. It appears the patient is now a victim of foul play."

The medics remained outside, unwilling to re-enter the home. Several minutes passed before the police screeched to a halt in front of the Graham residence. An interchange occurred, and then one officer drew his weapon, leaving the other to secure the area with yellow police tape. Neighbours started to gather outside on the street, drawn to the scene by the sound of sirens. Everyone was jockeying and pushing for the best view, and the street was buzzing with gossip and speculation. The local news team had also arrived and were setting up, having heard the dispatch on the police scanner. They lived for this type of big news scoop, and even loud mouth Gretchen Berg was in attendance.

Rebecca shook her head in disgust. *Didn't take long for the vultures to descend!* She turned away from the window; it brought back too many unpleasant memories. But now she was stuck here, she didn't dare leave the house, she had to stay hidden, especially from the police. She looked around the shambles of her house, and then decided that since she was 'locked down,' she would change clothes and pack a few more personal items. She had left in such a rush last time that she hadn't taken much with her.

She made her way to the bedroom and pulled open the closet. She pulled out a pair of jeans and a sweater, discarding her dirty clothes on the floor. She donned the jeans and was very surprised when they didn't fit; they were actually a little loose. She dropped them to the floor and tried on several other items. She modelled the items in the mirror. *Not exactly falling off me, but they are definitely looser. And wow, are they outdated!*

Rebecca dug through her remaining wardrobe. *What am I going to do now for clothes?* Looking down at the pile on the floor, she spied Olivia's Platinum VISA card sticking out of the discarded pants pocket. Grinning, she reached down to pick it up. She shrugged into her housecoat, pulling the sash tight.

Time to go shopping! Gee thanks, Olivia. She gave the card a quick little kiss, then skipped out of the bedroom. The living room was a wreck; the computer had been tipped over on its side, the keyboard lying on the floor. She righted the terminal and reattached the mouse and keyboard.

Hope this still works. She booted up the machine and crossed her fingers. The device chattered and sputtered in its electronic language. As she waited, she planned. The evidence in Ethel's home would certainly shine a negative spot light on Jake and Olivia, but Rebecca decided to create further problems for the pair.

I already have enough evidence on my father's death. She thought about the documents at Magda's apartment, as well as the video. *I'm sure Chief Pritchard would love to see it, so I'll send it to him.* As the computer continued to chirp and chatter, she reflected on last night.

I have another idea too. She grinned to herself. *If Olivia and Jake want me dead, I guess I am going to have to help them along.*

So while the police investigated the scene at the Graham residence, Rebecca shopped. First, she visited the local hardware shop. *If you're going to kill me, you'll need some tools.* She clicked on the selections, then ordered a heavy hammer, two tarps, gloves, rope, and duct tape to be sent to the Proctor Estate. She selected the 'RUSH ORDER 'option and labelled it 'ATTENTION OLIVIA PROCTOR.'

If you're going to bury me, you're going to need a shovel. She clicked again and chuckled to herself. *Actually, I think this shovel is going to bury both of you in the long run.*

Next, you'll need some new clothes, if I you're going to leave town. She scrolled through the network and found a ladies' shop in the nearby town that delivered. *Now let's see, what does 'Olivia Proctor' need?*

Rebecca spent the next hour ordering new clothing in her own size. *I'm no size two, but I am going to look classy!* The extensive list included pants, tops, two pairs of runners, two track suits, jackets, and blazers, and of course several expensive accessories: scarves, purses, and shoes, lots of shoes. The final bill totalled over five thousand dollars! For a moment she felt guilty knowing Andie would be footing the bill, but she considered it severance pay.

She completed the order and directed the items to be delivered to Magda's apartment; she couldn't have them delivered to her own house. The last thing she did was book two, one-way tickets to the Mayan Riviera in Jake and Olivia's names. She booked the departure for two days after the Dash for Cash race.

After you kill me, you have to run away and hide … might as well do it in luxury. Does Mexico have extradition rules? She booked the couple a one month vacation at an expensive resort. Tasks completed, she smiled with satisfaction. Her plan was starting to take form; it just needed a bit more fleshing out.

Oops, forgot about luggage. They'll need that too! Click, it was done.

After finishing her online shopping excursion, Rebecca peeked out the window. The coroner was just loading Ethel's body into the 'death wagon.' It made her shudder at the memory of her young son being taken away in a similar vehicle many years ago. She closed her eyes and turned away, steadying herself on the window sill. *Don't think about it, Rebecca. Just look away.*

She willed her eyes open and looked at the wreck of her family home. She started picking up items and righting the furniture that had been toppled. Rebecca moved from room to room, cleaning and tidying, going faster and faster, hoping her busy activity would outrun her memories. She finally slid down the living room wall, collapsing on the floor; she was totally spent. She closed her eyes and recalled happier times spent in this room: Christmas mornings, birthdays and …

A knock on the door interrupted her memories.

Her eyes started open. *Who could it be?* She feared the worst. *What if it was Olivia and Jake?* She had nowhere to go or hide. She was only wearing a housecoat, and she had bare feet. *What am I going to do?*

Rebecca peeked out the door's peephole and instead of Jake and Olivia; it was Chief Pritchard standing on her doorstep.

CHAPTER SIXTY

D r Angela Wilson, the medical examiner (ME) assigned to the case, stood outside the victim's home doing an initial survey of the scene. The house and the grounds were unkept. The lawn was burnt and overgrown, the paint on the house was carelessly peeling, and the windows were grime covered. At one time it might have been a quaint cottage, but now it was a dump.

"It's been a while since someone has done any work out here in the yard," she commented to the two ME technicians who were donning their personal protective equipment (PPE) and preparing their cameras and kits for the job ahead. Angela was already dressed for the investigation.

"I want pictures of both the outside and inside of the home. I think this might be a case of elder neglect and abuse as well. The police have briefed me on the victim and the state of the house inside."

She pulled out her notepad and reviewed the briefing notes with the techs. "The owner of the home is an Ethel Graham; age seventy-eight. Single, no known family in the area. Tread lightly folks, and take lots of pics."

Dr Wilson led the team into the victim's residence. Wilson was known for her 'eagle eyes' and never missed a clue. She was very thorough, her victims deserved diligence. She entered the house via the back door and was immediately assaulted by the smell of stale air, but there was no assault of a garbage smell usually found in a hoard of this size. Every surface in the kitchen was stacked with tins, boxes, bag, papers, and containers, but they had been washed and orderly arranged. The victim was a hoarder, but a 'clean hoarder.' Each item had been lovingly and carefully organized according to their size and shape. There were tunnels between the piles, leading to various rooms.

"OCD and a hoarder, curious? Pictures guys." She picked her way carefully across the kitchen into the living room. It was suggested it might be a B&E that was interrupted by the victim, but the kitchen remained undisturbed, and there were no signs of forced entry. The techs snapped and clicked behind her, collecting evidence.

Dr Wilson stood in the living room doorframe and systematically surveyed the scene. She scanned from top to bottom, and then side to side. Like the kitchen, this room was stacked and stuffed; it was also very carefully organized. The only flaw to the organization was the dead body lying on the floor in front of the fireplace. Besides the dead body, someone, perhaps the burglar, had emptied several boxes and thrown some of the items about the room. Several pieces had landed on top of the body.

"Take a shot of these. It appears the victim was down before the perp starting empty the boxes ... looks staged. Let's keep going."

"The victim is an elderly female, thin and emaciated. Looks older than her stated age of seventy-eight years," Angela reported to her tape recorder. She stepped closer to the body and asked the techs to photograph it, the dried pool of blood, and the wooden bat lying next to it. She checked the body temperature and determined the time of death to be approximately ten hours ago; meaning the evening before.

"Photograph the laceration on her nose and the bruising on her right cheek. Looks like these happened recently; like someone struck her." She picked up the broken glasses lying next to the woman's body placing them in an evidence bag; the nose piece was smeared with blood.

The team turned the body, and Dr. Wilson continued her report. "Appears to be a large laceration— approximately seven inches long—on the occipital area of the skull. The occipital skull bone has sustained a fracture, and there is blood on the bricks of the hearth. Patient sustained a blow to the back of the head. Take pictures of this, please."

Dr. Wilson shifted the body a little to examine the occipital wound and spotted something 'red'. "Mike, can you turn the victim just a bit further over, there is something wedged under her."

With the body tipped on its side, the medical examiner was able to dislodge the item of interest. It was a red leather wallet, embossed with Gucci on the front.

Dr. Wilson carefully picked up the wallet and turned it over. The clasp was open, and she checked for any identification.

Speaking into her recorder, she said, "A red leather wallet was found under the victim's body. There is a driver license, three AMEX cards, a Diner's Card, a MasterCard, a VISA Infinite Privilege card and cards to Holt Renfrew and Nordstrom department stores, all in the name of Olivia Proctor. The wallet also contains twenty-five dollars in assorted bills. Please photograph these items, then place them in an evidence bag."

The ME tech was puzzled. "Why is Olivia Proctor's wallet under the victim's body? You know who she is, don't you?" Mike asked.

Dr. Wilson paused her recording. "I have no idea, is she someone of importance here in Campbell River?" Wilson lived in Temple and did not have the time or interest to follow small town gossip streams.

"You're kidding me ... aren't you?"

Dr. Wilson shrugged. "Tell me more."

"Olivia Proctor is Campbell River's socialite and influencer. She's a real hot looking babe. She is, or was, married to Andie Proctor; the owner of Proctor Automotive. If you believe social media, she has just left her millionaire husband for the hired help ... some guy named Jake Adams. A real scandal in this small town."

She shrugged again, and then with a gloved hand picked up the wooden bat found next to the body and showed it to the young man. "There is blood on the end cap of the bat, but no blood splatter to indicate the victim was struck with it. Curious?" She turned the bat over. "Jake Adams, you said?" She showed the tech the engraving. "There's writing on it: 'To Jake Adams! Super Dad!'"

"Shut the front door!" Mike gasped. "You're kidding? This is turning out to more than a boring dead body case!"

"Indeed," remarked the medical examiner, handing the bat to the other tech, Seth. "Here, place this with the other evidence." She leaned down over the victim's body. "Wait, is there something in her hand. Take a pic, Mike." She waited. "Looks like some paper."

She pried open the woman's closed grip, and with forceps she pulled the paper out. "It has writing on it. 'Rebecca Adams 369-555-6112.'"

"Rebecca Adams? Is this Adams related to Jake Adams?"

"Holy cow!" Mike exclaimed. "Rebecca and Jake Adams are married. You know about this Seth, don't you?" The other tech nodded. "The story was all over the internet last week. Rebecca Adams accused Olivia of having an affair with her husband Jake, and Miss Socialite Olivia Proctor didn't deny it. Wow what a soap opera!" Mike continued. He was enjoying the drama of an otherwise routine call.

"Enough Mike!" Dr. Wilson snapped. "Just photograph the items, bag them, and stop with the drama. The whole scene just looks wrong; like the victim's death was an accident but someone staged these other items, perhaps to point the blame at some person or persons. Hmm?"

Mike clammed up and finished his work. Seth raised his eyebrows, then whispered. "Eagle Eye has the bit in her teeth, so you'd better toe the line. She can get a bit edgy!" Having heard the whispering, Wilson turned to look at the two techs. They hurried to look busy.

"Bag the body, then take her to the morgue. I will follow-up with an autopsy later today. Hand me those items." She pointed out the bagged wooden bat, wallet, and paper. "I need to show these to Chief Pritchard." Pritchard had just arrived on the scene, and he was talking to witnesses.

Dr. Wilson had a headache starting behind her eyes. *I only took this case because they told me it was cut and dry, it is far from that. I was supposed to be starting a much needed two-week break. Guess it will have to wait.* She removed her PPE and sought out the chief.

"Chief Pritchard, can I talk with you for a couple of minutes?" She pulled him aside from the junior officers, then showed him the evidence and explained her findings. "This is a very bizarre case; it appears the victim died of blunt force trauma. She either fell backward or was pushed and struck her head on the edge of the fireplace, but here it gets odd."

She showed him the evidence bags. He turned them over in his hands. "This wallet was found under the body; Olivia Proctor's wallet?"

"Yes and this wooden bat was at the scene too." She handed it to him.

"On our initial survey my officers noticed the bat lying beside the body. But now you don't think it fits with the blunt force injury?" He ran his thumb over the name embossed on the bat.

"You're right; the injury was sustained when she struck her head. The blood on the bat seems to have been rubbed on it, after the fact, probably much later as the blood was already drying. I believe this was staged. I will need to see if there are fingerprints on it," Dr. Wilson explained.

She took the bat and handed him the last evidence bag. "And this paper was clutched in the victim's right hand; it has a Rebecca Adams' name on it. My techs tell me this Jake—she lifted the bat—and this Rebecca Adams—she pointed at the evidence bag—were married. I understand the Adams couple recently separated, and Olivia Proctor was the wedge that drove them apart. My tech told me about it; apparently he follows social media, and it is all over the net. What is with this love triangle?"

"It's complicated." Pritchard shook his head. "Do you think this a murder case or an accident?" He handed the bat back to the medical examiner.

"Well ... there are signs of old injuries, bruising on her arms, and also fresh wounds and bruises on her face, and she is very underweight and neglected. I am suspecting elder abuse that went too far. Probably an accident that someone else discovered, and then did a little rearranging before it was called in." She paused. "Who called in the incident?"

"The call came from a 'neighbour', no name was given. I can track the phone from the EMS centre and see if we can find out where the call came from."

Pritchard had some suspicions, but didn't want to express them now. "Can I hold on to these pieces of evidence for now?" He indicated the wallet and the paper. "There are some people I want to talk to about these items." Then he pointed at the bat. "I also want to take a picture of the bat." He used his cellphone to capture the image.

"No worries, I'll log them out under your name." She turned to leave. "I should have the autopsy completed later today, but I think it's obvious that the head trauma is the cause of her death, probably last night between five and ten. What we need to find out is who pushed the old lady, if it was accidentally or not, and who staged the scene to point the finger of blame at Olivia Proctor and Jake Adams."

He stood holding the bags, contemplating his next move. *Rebecca Adams, it's time to talk!* He left the junior officers to tie up loose ends, then headed over to the Adams' house.

CHAPTER SIXTY-ONE

Shit, do I open it? Rebecca looked around the living room; it looked back to order, well at least presentable. She didn't want the chief to start snooping around and suspecting anything; this could spoil her plans. Olivia's credit card was still on the computer table, and the screen was open to the vacation resort page. She would need to distract him away from the computer desk.

Does he suspect my involvement across the street? What should I do?

The knock came again.

I guess I better open it. Pull yourself together, Rebecca. She inhaled a deep breath, smoothed her hair, tightened the housecoat sash, and opened the door a crack.

"Yes, Chief Pritchard, how can I help you?" She pulled the door open. "I saw the ambulance at Miss Graham's house. Is everything okay?"

"Mrs. Adams, may I come in?"

"Yeah, sure." Rebecca reluctantly stepped back, allowing Chief Pritchard to enter the house. His sharp eyes picked up the marred walls and broken items on the mantel place; it looked like a battle had occurred there. He suspected Jake Adams had had a hand in it as well as Olivia Proctor. Now it looked like someone, probably Rebecca, had quickly tried to return it back to normal, but it still looked trashed.

"Andie wanted me to check on you, and since I was in the neighbourhood..." He stopped and gestured toward the Graham house. "I thought I would drop over. Can we sit?"

Rebecca nodded and gestured to a chair; she settled on the edge of the couch. They sat in silence until Chief Pritchard spoke.

"I spent the morning at Ethel Graham's house, but I think you know that." Rebecca nodded, so he continued. "It seems like someone killed Miss Graham; probably last night." He pulled out an evidence bag and handed it to Rebecca.

He watched her reaction.

She sat quietly holding the bag, playing it cool. She did not have to look at it, she knew it was the piece of paper she had written her cellphone number on and had given to Ethel. She could see it was wrinkled and dotted with what looked like dried blood.

"You want to know why Ethel Graham has my phone number." She looked directly at the officer; he simply raised an eyebrow. Rebecca quickly spun a story and hoped he would believe it.

"She often called me, two or three times per week, and kept telling me she was sorry for Indie's death. We both know she testified against me at the inquest into my son's death. Recently she told me she was afraid of someone, and she wanted me to come over and check on her and the house. I had given her my cellphone number ... it was a sad situation. I wish I would have checked on her yesterday, perhaps this wouldn't have happened."

She handed the bag back to Chief Pritchard.

"When was the last time you saw her?" He tucked the bag into his police vest.

"Well, I was in the hospital, but you know that." He nodded. "I have been lying low since then, so maybe two days ago. I helped her take her groceries up to the house. She was struggling with them."

"I would have thought you wouldn't help her. Considering your history and all."

"Guess I'm a nice person." She shrugged and avoided eye contact.

Pritchard sat watching her. Andie had told him about the break in at Proctor Automotive, the missing video surveillance tapes, and the vandalism of his office, but he insisted it couldn't have been Rebecca. *'I let her into the office, so why would she wreck it and steal the tapes?'* When the computer was smashed, the surveillance system had been ruined as well, so there was no way to prove his assumptions.

Should I bring Rebecca in now and pressure her with some questions? No, I'll do it later; it doesn't look like she's going anywhere. The silence stretched between them. "Well I guess I'll be leaving; just as long as you're okay, Andie has been asking after you," he said, standing up to leave.

Rebecca nodded and smiled reassuringly. She actually thought it came off kind of phony, but she needed him to leave. "Yup, I sure am. Please let Andie know I am okay."

Kevin turned towards the door and then stopped. He pulled out his cellphone; opened up the picture of the bat and held it up to her. "Does this look familiar?"

"Gee, it looks like Jake's bat. I remember it now. It has his name engraved on it; the high school baseball team did that for him, before Indie was born."

Pritchard only nodded. He struggled with his next decision, pausing before continuing. "Andie told me about the surveillance tapes and what he saw." He watched her reaction. "I would like to bring you down to the station for questioning at a later date."

Rebecca remained closed mouthed for a moment, then she said. "Is there anything else you need?"

"Not for now. If I need to talk with you further, can I get you on your cellphone?"

She nodded, reciting her number for him to write down. Rebecca stood up and guided him through the living room to the front door. His eyes scanned the room and he noted a Platinum credit card on the computer desk. It was hard to make out, but it looked like it was in Olivia Proctor's name.

"Curious?" He thought, but kept walking. He let himself out of the house.

After he left Rebecca, collapsed on the floor inside the door. She put her face in her hands and stifled a laugh. *Holy shit!! I'm sure he saw the credit card, but he didn't say anything. What about the paper I was making notes on, did he see that too?*

She pulled herself up, grabbed the items and quickly turned off the computer. *I gotta get out of here, before he comes back, asking more questions. Shouldn't he be out questioning Jake and Olivia; lord knows I left enough evidence to convict them of Ethel's death, but I still have a couple of cards up my sleeve.* She still had the audio recordings on her cellphone, both from the shop and now Ethel's message.

She shuddered and looked around, the family home felt very unsafe now. *"Am I going to be next?* " She realized she was in danger. *If Olivia will go to such lengths as to kill her old aunt, what would she being willing to do to get rid of me?*

She stood in front of her closet and was just about to start stuffing her clothes in a garbage bag; she was going to throw them out, when she paused. *I don't think I'll do this; if I leave them in the closet and then if I suddenly disappear, wouldn't it look even more suspicious?*

She hung the items back up, and rummaged around in the back, looking for something to wear. She found an old T-shirt and skirt from before Indie was born and pulled them on. The skirt was snug, but she pulled the T-shirt over top and it didn't look too bad. She left all her toiletries and personal items in the drawers. *No matter, I still had Olivia's cash, I can buy whatever I needed with this, but it would be best if I don't use the credit card here in Campbell River.*

She moved down the hallway then stopped. Standing outside the closed door, she knew there was one last thing that to be done before she left her family home for good. She flung open the spare bedroom door. She squeezed her eyes tightly shut and waited. Every other time she had stepped into this room she had been flooded with an intense wave of emotion and grief.

Huhn? She slowly opened her eyes and waited once again. *Nothing?* She blinked in surprise.

Rebecca looked around the room; the room where three years ago Indie had fallen from the dormer window, and where her life had broken apart. But instead of crushing despair, now she felt calm and peaceful ... the demons that once haunted this room and her life were gone.

She glanced around one last time. *I guess this is goodbye, Indie!* She left the house where she had lived her whole life, and stepped into the future.

CHAPTER SIXTY-TWO

Jake had just finished cleaning the kitchen and was pushing the vacuum around the main floor, when he heard the intercom system buzz. He hated doing household chores, in the past he usually left these menial tasks to Rebecca, but Olivia certainly wasn't going to chip a nail doing anything. He turned off the machine and checked the security camera screens by the kitchen door; someone was at the main gate, and the insistent buzzing continued.

What? Shit, it's the cops, and Pritchard is with them. What the fuck! Chief Pritchard stood outside the gate and had brought reinforcement; he wasn't alone. He dropped the vacuum powerhead and hollered.

"Olivia!" No answer. "Olivia!' he yelled louder. No response again.

Moments later, he heard the clatter of her pumps on the tile floor. She was once again glammed up and perfectly coiffed, but she had lines of stress under her eyes that even the best concealer couldn't hide.

"What is he doing here?" She pointed at the camera feed. She could see Pritchard pacing outside the gate and watched as he pressed the buzzer again. With him were Officer Hoffman and Deputy Sinclair.

The annoying sound throbbed in Jakes' temples, he just wanted them to go away, but that was unlikely knowing Pritchard's dogged personality. The alcohol was starting to wear off, and the withdrawal jitters were starting to return.

"I guess we'd better let them in, they aren't likely to go away." Jake blew out his breath and pressed the intercom button. "Yes, can I help you?"

"I need to speak with Mrs. Proctor. Is she in residence?" Pritchard responded.

"What?"

"Is Olivia home?" He responded professionally. He had to bite his tongue to prevent himself from saying what he actually thought.

"Why? What do you want?" Jake thought he was being coy, but he was actually coming across as smug and simple. Pritchard and the officers rolled their eyes.

"We need to speak with her about a police related incident that happened in town last evening. Can you please let us in?"

There was a long pause before the gate swung open. As the officers drove through and made their way up the front drive, Olivia was inside, unravelling.

"What the hell! What does he want? Could he know about Auntie Ethel already? What are we going to do?" She was flapping around the kitchen. "I'm not going to jail because of that evil old woman! It was an accident." Jake grabbed her arm and pulled her to him. She resisted, but he pulled her close. He needed to get her under control before she blew it and they both ended up in jail.

"Calm yourself, Olivia," Jake crooned in her ear. "Go powder your nose and touch up your makeup, and I'll deal with Pritchard. He doesn't know about the relationship between you and your aunt, the only person does is me, and I won't tell him about it. Now go. I'll put on a fresh pot of coffee, let's play nice."

She scurried off and Jake prepared for the officers. He put the vacuum away and put on the coffee. He ran his hands through his hair and took a deep breath. He needed to calm his shaky hands; it had been hours since his last drink, and the alcoholic itch was increasing as the minutes passed.

An abrupt knock sounded at the door. *Let the games begin.* He opened the door and came eye to eye with Chief Kevin Pritchard and his team.

"Mr. Adams." Chief Pritchard could barely maintain civility.

"Chief Pritchard, officers, please come in." Jake stepped aside to allow the group to enter. "Mrs. Proctor will be down in minute." He ground his teeth as the big man passed by him.

The police stepped past Jake, noting the smell of alcohol wafting off him. He still wore the apron he had donned for his 'housekeeper task,' over his wrinkled clothes. His whole person seemed stale and unkept, just like the house.

"New style, or are you and Mrs. Proctor role playing?" Deputy Sinclair grinned and pointed to the apron.

Jake flushed maroon and pulled off the offending item, he glowered at her. His headache thumped, and his tempered flared; he didn't think he could keep his shit together. He was just about to say '*screw it*' and usher the three out the door, when Olivia sashayed into the room.

"Good morning, Chief Pritchard, how is my husband? Are you taking good care of him?" Olivia smirked.

Ignoring her snide comment, he continued in a businesslike manner. "May we sit Mrs. Proctor? We have some questions about a death that occurred last night here in Campbell River."

She waved them into the sitting room. "What could that possibly have to do with me? Jake dear, can you get us some coffee?"

Jake glared at her. *She's treating me like the hired help!* He stomped into the kitchen, feeling he had been treated poorly. "Fine honey!" He growled.

"Let me help you with that Mr. Adams. I have some questions for you, while you serve the coffee of course." Officer Hoffman followed him into the kitchen. He was hoping Jake's frustration and anger would loosen his lips.

Chief Pritchard and Deputy Sinclair settled themselves on the couch; Olivia sat and preened opposite them, plucking at the lint on her cashmere sweater, and straightening the crease on her slacks. She glanced up at Pritchard and fixed her icy blue eyes on his steely blue ones. Each hoped the other one would look away first. Pritchard won ... Olivia glanced away and fiddled with her thumbnail, which looked ragged and reddened.

"Deputy Sinclair, will you continue with the questioning?" He pulled out his notepad and settled back to observe. He had briefed the two officers about the other evidence found at the scene, so both of them were aware of the wooden bat and the wallet. They all had plenty of questions.

Pritchard reached into this jacket pocket and pulled out an evidence bag; he set it on the table in front of Oliva. He didn't say anything, he just watched and got the reaction he was hoping for. Despite her best attempt to act 'the cool bitch,' she eyed the item. She quickly glanced away; avoiding eye contact.

He smiled to himself and remained silent, wanting to observe the scene as it unfolded.

"This morning," Deputy Sinclair began, "An emergency call was received saying a woman was in distress. When the EMS team arrived to 532 Riverview Place they found an elderly woman, she was deceased. She had apparently been dead for approximately ten hours."

"How horrible!" Olivia feigned surprised. "But, what does this have to do with me?"

"Do you know the owner of 532 Riverview Place? An Ethel Graham?" Deputy Sinclair reviewed her notes.

"Why do you ask? Do you think I know something about this woman's death? Do I need a lawyer?" Olivia huffed. She was afraid she might slip up, especially under the scrutinizing eyes of the chief.

"Do you need one?" Chief Pritchard broke in, raising an eyebrow.

"Of course not!" she snapped. "Go ahead and ask your questions."

"Make a note that Mrs. Proctor is declining legal counsel." Chief Pritchard commented to his junior deputy.

Olivia was worried, did they know something? Should she call her lawyer? She chewed on her nail. *Shit, I need a manicure.*

"Now back to the questions. Do you know Ethel Graham?" Deputy Sinclair waited.

Olivia paused before she answered. She had no intentions of providing details. "Yes," she finally responded.

"How do you know Miss Graham?" Sinclair asked; this was going to be a long process if she was going to ask every question repeatedly, but Olivia seemed on the edge. If she kept probing, she might be able to break her.

On the other side of the room, Olivia sat thinking. *How do I get out of this? Do I expose the truth, or should I lie? Perhaps the truth is the best, at least this time. Where is Jake? I need him here.*

"Mrs. Proctor, please answer the question. We can do it here quietly, or I can put you in the squad car and drive you downtown to complete these questions," Sinclair warned.

"That is not necessary!" Olivia spat. She took a deep, shuddering breath, and then blurted out. "Ethel Graham is my aunt!"

"Pardon?" Deputy Sinclair croaked. Pritchard sat silently observing Oliva. He already knew from Andie that Olivia and Ethel Graham were related; Andie had figured it out years ago. He had discovered cancelled cheques written to Ethel Graham from Olivia's bank account. When he had questioned her, Olivia had confessed that she was an annoying distant relative she felt obligated to assist. Andie had been surprised by her compassion, never dreaming that Olivia was actually supporting the elderly woman in exchange for spying and information.

Andie had never met the woman and now she was dead; perhaps at Olivia's hand. Pritchard wanted to watch and see how she dug herself out of this hole.

"She's my mother's aunt actually. She came to live in Campbell River when we moved here." She paused and smiled. "When my father died, I inherited her; she is very needy and demanding!" She was rambling on, trying to keep her thoughts straight.

"Okay, so we have now established that you are Ethel's great-niece. So just to be clear Mrs. Proctor, you say you 'inherited' your aunt Ethel Graham, does this mean you are her legal guardian too?"

Olivia nodded.

"Just to make it clear Mrs. Proctor, are you responsible for Ethel Graham's care, including food, clothing, and medical needs?" Olivia nodded, sighing. "And the upkeep of her home?" She nodded again.

"Where are we going with this?" Olivia was tired of all their annoying questions. "I have things to do besides answering questions about my bothersome aunt."

"The coroner feels Ms. Graham was a victim of long-term elder abuse and neglect." Deputy Sinclair paused, allowing time for the information to sink in.

"What do you mean?" Olivia was momentarily confused. She frowned at the officers. "Are you saying you suspect me of mistreating and abusing my aunt?" She started to stammer, but Deputy Sinclair interrupted.

"The coroner also feels that the victim had been struck or pushed, resulting in her striking her head, which is suspected to have caused her death."

Suddenly Olivia stood up. "I never ..." She stumbled. "I didn't ... !"

"You never did what? When did you see her last?" the deputy interjected.

"I don't know! Jake!" She yelled. "Jake, come in here!"

Jake came running into the room closely followed by Officer Hoffman. Hoffman had been asking Jake about his activities in the last twenty-four hours, and Jake was relieved to get away from all the probing. As he entered the living room, Jake spotted an evidence bag on the table; it looked like Olivia's red Gucci wallet was in it.

"What's your wallet doing in that bag? Didn't you say you'd lost it last night? Where'd they find it?" He blurted out. Realizing his error, he clammed up.

"The wallet was found in Ethel's Graham home," Deputy Sinclair stated.

"Thanks for returning it." Olivia reached to grab it, but Chief Pritchard snatched it up.

"This is evidence in a possible murder scene investigation. It will be returned after the investigation is complete." Pritchard returned it to his jacket pocket.

"What?" Olivia gasped. "It's mine!"

"The wallet was found under the victim's body in her house. Can you tell us how your wallet ended up there?"

Olivia suddenly stood up and pointed at the door. "Leave!"

"Please sit Mrs. Proctor; we have a few more questions." Deputy Sinclair instructed.

"I will not! I don't have to because this is my house." Olivia stormed to the front door. "You need to leave!"

The three officers exchanged silent looks; they rose from their seats and were escorted from the estate. Olivia may have slammed the door in their faces for now, but as they left the property, they knew that this was far from over. Olivia would surely be calling her lawyer, and the two stooges inside the fancy house would be hatching a story; their guilt was obvious!

"Let's meet back at the station this afternoon to compare notes." Pritchard wanted to talk with Andie first before he talked further with his colleagues. He wanted to let Andie know about both Rebecca and Ethel Graham.

As he drove down the driveway, Kevin noted the beautifully manicured rosebushes and smelled their heady perfume, but as perfect as it seemed, the whole place stunk of lies and deceit.

CHAPTER SIXTY-THREE

As the officers drove away from the scene, the tempest inside Proctor Estate had just started to boil.

"You idiot!" Olivia screeched. "I had it all under control until you came barging in and blabbed that I had lost my wallet last night. They found the damn thing in her house!"

The two stood nose-to-nose; he flat footed and her spiked heeled, and neither was going to back down.

"I was going to tell them that I took Auntie Ethel for groceries last week and she must have stolen it from me. You fool, now what are we going to do?"

Clenched fisted and tight jawed, Jake was itching to let fly! He reined in his anger and turned away from her; things were getting too heated, and he was worried that he wouldn't be able to control himself. He walked to the liquor cabinet and poured two stiff fingers of whiskey. He gulped the amber liquid, relishing its burn and the calming effect on his jangling nerves.

"Hoffman had me cornered in the kitchen, and he was asking odd questions about a baseball bat." Jake tried to explain. "He kept asking me if I owned a wooden bat, and did I know where it was."

"What bat?" Olivia was confused.

"All I can think of is the wooden bat the guys gave me when I got married, but that is at Rebecca's place. He kept on about it, asking if it has identifying marks on it. I told him it had my name engraved on it. What is going on?" He rubbed his eyes and poured another drink.

Olivia wasn't much help; she was picking at her nails and ignoring him.

"Something's up." He glowered at her through bleary red eyes. "I think we need to call a lawyer."

* * *

Across town at Campbell River Police Station, Pritchard and his team sat in his office reviewing the facts from the morning's investigation. On the evidence board they had written three headings: 'the victim,' 'suspects,' and 'people of interest.' Under each title were names: Ethel Graham, Olivia Proctor and Jake Adams, and under the 'people of interest' column was a question mark; who was this mystery person who placed the call and planted the evidence?

Dr. Wilson had expedited the autopsy, and Chief Pritchard and his teams now had the results. Added to the evidence board were pictures of the victim, showing new and old bruising and the injury to the back of the head. Other items include the wooden bat, Olivia Proctor's red Gucci wallet, and finally, the crumpled paper with Rebecca Adams' name written on it. The crime scene photographer had also included pictures of the victim's hoard inside the house as well as the shabby gardens and rundown exterior.

"Let's review what we have so far." Chief Pritchard pointed at Janice Sinclair.

"Some of the evidence is kind of hinky. For example, the bat; Dr Wilson says the bat was not the murder weapon. Ethel's skull was bashed in when she fell against the fireplace edge. Also, there was no blood splatter. Even stranger is the blood on the end cap of the bat, it was 'applied' after the blood was already drying. Wilson feels it was staged." She explained.

"Any prints?" Pritchard studied the pictures on the board.

"None. Whoever planted the bat did a thorough job of cleaning off their prints. Same with the wallet."

"Ah, the wallet. So how did Olivia Proctor's wallet end up under Ethel Graham's body?" Pritchard asked the pair.

"It was put there?" Sinclair suggested.

"You're absolutely right. But by whom? Who would want to go to such lengths to frame this pair?" Pritchard scanned the evidence board and picked up a dry erase pen. He wrote Rebecca Adams under the 'person of interest' list.

He turned to the officers. "The EMS recording indicates the caller was a woman, and even more interesting is that the call was placed from the victim's own phone. I spoke with the Adams woman this morning because I was suspicious of this paper." Chief Pritchard tapped the picture on the board.

"Adams told me the old woman often called her and told her she was 'afraid' of someone. When I showed her the paper, Adams said she had given her phone number to the victim as an emergency contact. She said she had written it on the paper found in Ethel's hand. Strange behaviour for someone whom the victim had once accused of murder."

Derek Hoffman looked puzzled at this comment. He had recently moved to Campbell River and was unaware of the details of the infamous murder case. "I'm not sure what you mean by that Chief, how are these two connected?" He pointed to Rebecca and Ethel's names on the board.

"Three years ago, Rebecca and Jake Adams' son died. He fell from the upstairs window of his home. It was ruled an unfortunate accident, that was until Ethel Graham came forward and accused Rebecca of murdering him," Pritchard briefly outlined.

"What?" Officer Hoffman was astonished.

"It gets better," Deputy Sinclair added. "Go on, Chief."

"Two days after the incident, Ethel Graham arrived at the police station saying she urgently needed to speak with me because she had some importance evidence on 'the boy's death.' She sat in this very room and told me she witnessed Rebecca Adams push her son from the upstairs window of their home."

"Unbelievable!" Hoffman gasped. 'What was the outcome?"

"Well," Pritchard continued. "Because it was the death of an innocent child and there was an apparent witness to the crime, we had to charge Rebecca with murder. A very messy and public trial was held, but Ethel Graham's evidence was found to be sketchy at best; it really seemed like someone coerced her into making the statement. The old gal kept changing her story, and eventually Mrs. Adams was found innocent of the crime, but in a small community like Campbell River she has been permanently sentenced to a life of misery and speculation."

"Interesting." Hoffman said. "So that's why it seems kind of suspicious that she wanted to help Ethel Graham. You'd think she would avoid her at all cost ... unless." Here Officer Hoffman paused and thought for a moment.

"Unless what, Derek?" Janice Sinclair asked.

"Well, Adams has lived across the street from the victim for years, and she has firsthand knowledge of the ongoing neglect. So maybe she takes pity on the old woman and has been trying to help; in fact, she actually gives Ethel her phone number. Maybe she is just a kind person, you folks would know her better than me?"

Both Sinclair and Pritchard nodded. Despite all the negative challenges in her life, Rebecca Adams had never been known to be an unkind person; quiet and withdrawn, but not malicious.

"The neighbourhood survey indicates that Adams has been seen helping Ethel with her groceries." Officer Hoffman stopped and looked at his notes, then at the evidence board.

"We know Adams has had recent contact with the victim, and maybe she was concerned when she hadn't heard from Ethel in a few days. So she goes to check on the old gal, and she finds her dead. By this time Rebecca was well aware of her husband's infidelity, so she decides to use this opportunity to frame not only her unfaithful husband, but his lover too. Did Rebecca know that Ethel Graham was Olivia Proctor's aunt? Besides burning her husband, perhaps she wants to avenge the old gal as well? Perhaps our quiet, unassuming Rebecca Adams has another side to her?" The officers looked at each other; nobody knew the answer to that question.

Hoffman continued. "She could have staged the scene, leaving the bat and wallet, and then placed the call, ensuring the police would find Ethel and these incriminating items. I can understand how the bat got placed at the scene, but how did Rebecca Adams get the wallet; it's kind of a loose end. Your thoughts?"

"Good theory, Hoffman, sounds like a possibility, but it does seem a bit farfetched!" Pritchard said. "So what do we do next? How do we prove this?"

A knock came at the door. It was Alice, the chief's secretary. "Sorry Chief, there is an Olivia Proctor and a Jake Adams with their lawyer in Interview Room Two. They want to talk to you about Ethel Graham's death."

"That was fast!" Pritchard exclaimed, looking at the others. "I knew Mrs. Proctor would drag her lawyer in here, proclaiming her innocence, but I didn't think it would be so soon!"

CHAPTER SIXTY-FOUR

In the interview room, Olivia sat picking at her thumbnail while Jake paced back and forth. Following the visit from the police, Jake and Olivia had decided it would be in their best interest to contact a lawyer. Olivia placed a hasty call to Raymond Duncan, the lawyer that had reviewed her pre-nup. Upon receiving their frantic call, Duncan had dropped everything and rushed to Proctor Estate. The young associate was aware of Clarence Reid's hospitalization after the Proctor woman's last visit, and he didn't want a repeat performance at the office.

Duncan had arrived promptly and entered a war zone. He spent the first hour soothing a frantic Olivia and sobering an intoxicated Jake. The air was thick with threats and accusations, each one blaming the other for 'some old lady's death.' He had put on a stiff pot of coffee and sent a rumpled Jake to the shower, while he tackled Olivia's ravings. He learned from Olivia that her elderly aunt Ethel Graham had been found dead in her house earlier that morning. According to Olivia, Chief Pritchard and his team had come to the Estate with some 'lofty accusations' and 'crazy evidence.'

Over the next two hours, Duncan slowly deciphered what had happened—or at least Olivia and Jake's version of the events—and he was able to formulate a statement for the police. Olivia had as much as admitted her guilt in the death of her aunt; granted it was accidental, but none the less she had shoved the old woman, causing her fall and deadly injury. He was disgusted by Proctor's suspected abuse of Ethel Graham, but lawyer-client confidentiality prevented him from discussing this with the appropriate agencies. As soon as this crisis was abated, he was going to quit as their legal representative ... he did not want to 'be owned' by the likes of Olivia Proctor.

When it came to the baseball bat and the wallet, he had to agree that it was suspicious. Olivia's wallet could be explained away, but the bat was another thing. Jake could only recall seeing it in the closet at home, but 'that was some time ago.'

"Perhaps that bitch of a wife of yours threw it out, and then Auntie Ethel picked it up and added it to her hoard," Olivia had suggested.

"Sure, sure that's a good possibility." Jake had eagerly agreed. He had showered and shaved and was nursing a strong black cup of coffee.

Together they had rehearsed their statements, and now they sat waiting in the interview room for the Chief and his team. Duncan really disliked this pair; they were guilty as sin! He ground his teeth as they waited to spin their semi-truths, and he decided the bill for his assistance would be very costly. Olivia could afford it!

Duncan didn't know what to think about the recent media announcement about Andie Proctor and Chief Pritchard. It definitely was a conflict, but he really hated Olivia Proctor and wanted to see her pay at minimum for her abuse and neglect of her elderly aunt, but what to do?

This horrible bitch leaves her elderly aunt to live in squalor, but then when the old woman gets to be too demanding, she conveniently gets rid of her. He watched as Olivia applied lipstick in the two-way mirror. He hated this woman, the case, and the waiting game.

Back in the office, Pritchard paused before moving the team to the interview room. He needed to talk with the team before this investigation moved forward; he was morally at odds with himself. He was determined to 'burn' Olivia and Jake, but he was afraid his personal involvement with Andie Proctor would taint the investigation. Their lawyer would spin it to their advantage, saying Pritchard was using his power to convict his lover's estranged wife of this horrible crime. He knew Olivia would use 'her pictures' against him; he needed to make this right!

"Wait a minute team, I need to discuss something with you before we go and talk with Adams and Proctor. I am going to remove myself from this investigation. I feel if I continue it would be a conflict of interest and could jeopardize the outcome."

He took a deep breath and continued. "I know you have seen the social media announcement, and I believe Mrs. Proctor and her lawyer will use my private life to get the case dismissed, stating an abuse of power. I won't let that happen and allow the case to be dismissed on a technicality. Ethel Graham deserves better than to die in squalor and neglect." Pritchard stopped and waited for their response.

Both officers sat quietly, what would happen now?

"Sinclair I'm assigning you as lead investigator, and Hoffman will assist. Be careful! Mrs. Proctor will try to twist you into believing her story." Pritchard looked at his officers. He had complete confidence in the pair; he knew they would follow this case to completion.

He returned their attention back to the case, carefully reviewing the last details. He knew he was making the lawyer and his clients wait, but having the guilty parties sit and 'stew a bit' was always a useful ploy. Sitting in a locked, sterile interview room had a tendency to soften haughty attitudes, but he wasn't sure anything would soften Olivia Proctor.

"Deputy Sinclair, it's time to go and interview your suspects. Just be aware Mrs. Proctor is a very cunning and slippery devil. Hoffman, make sure you get everything on videotape; record everything. Also make sure you read both of them their Miranda rights before you start asking any questions; let their lawyer know you are pursuing them as suspects. Try and capture her in her lies. Now ... good luck."

Chief Pritchard opened the door and ushered them out. He grabbed his coat and car keys and as his officers headed toward the interview room, he headed toward the exit. "I will be leaving the building, please contact me on my private cell number if you need me." He turned away, leaving the junior officers in the hallway.

The pair entered the interview room together; they had conferred on their game plan and had a strategy to manage the situation. They were casting their net, and they were prepared for any reactions or tactics they would meet as they reeled in this slippery fish.

"Let's go and interrogate the hell out of this bitch; let's make her pay for her actions."

"Where is Pritchard?" Olivia snarled as the duo entered the interview room. She was looking forward to confronting Chief Pritchard and forcing him to drop out of the investigation. "I want to talk with Pritchard!" Her voice was shrill and demanding. All her scheming was getting messed up.

"Settle down Mrs. Proctor. Chief Pritchard has withdrawn from the investigation, for personal reasons. I am Deputy Janice Sinclair, and this is Officer Derek Hoffman; we will be conducting this interview."

The officers sat at the conference table, across from Olivia, Jake, and Raymond Duncan; Hoffman placed a table recorder on the surface. "We will be recording and videotaping this entire session."

"What the hell!" Olivia jumped up and yelled.

"Calm down Mrs. Proctor, please sit down. You too, Mr. Adams." Duncan firmly clamped his hand down on Olivia's shoulder and whispered in her ear. "Stop with the dramatics; don't give them anything more than they already know. Deputy Sinclair said they are recording as well as taping the interview. They are watching!"

He pointed to the table and to the two-way mirror. "Just read your statement and nothing else. Remember this is what *you* wanted."

"What I wanted was to make Pritchard squirm!" Olivia hissed back. She shook the lawyer's hand off and turned to the officers. "I want to provide a statement on the things Pritchard accused me of earlier." Duncan gave her a stern look.

Hoffman pushed the record button. He stated the date, time, and names of the all the members in the room so it was official. Next, Hoffman read both Proctor and Adams their 'rights' before allowing them to begin their statements. Hoffman nodded at the lawyer. "Do your clients understand their rights?"

"Is this necessary?" Raymond Duncan interjected. "My clients are here to provide a statement. Are you considering them suspects?"

"Just covering all our bases, I don't want to leave any loose ends. Do your clients understand their rights?"

Duncan looked at them. "Yes," Olivia snapped. "Can we get on with this?" Jake just nodded.

Sinclair waved Olivia Proctor to continue with her statement. She could see the woman was becoming more agitated since her plans had fallen apart, and she wanted to give Olivia lots of rope to hang herself.

"Let it be documented on the record that Mrs. Proctor has received legal counsel, and she has decided to provide a statement, freely and without coercion." Officer Hoffman stated.

Duncan rubbed his forehead where the beginning of a headache was starting to settle in; it promised to get worse as this fiasco continued. He sat back and watched this train wreck happen. He wanted off this case as quickly as possible, before the Proctor woman could convict herself and ruin his career.

Olivia picked up her prepared statement and locked her icy blue eyes on the officers across the table.

"I want to make my statement because I am innocent of killing my aunt. Now let me begin!" She paused. Sinclair waved her on. The lawyer cringed.

"This morning Chief Kevin Pritchard, Officer Hoffman, and Deputy Sinclair arrived at my home to inform me that my aunt, Ethel Graham, had died. My aunt and I were estranged for the past several years, but recently with her decline in health, I had attempted to intervene. She refused help with personal care and homemaker services; I had spoken to her about moving her to assisted living. She refused. I was concerned that she had multiple bruises, and I suspected she was falling. I knew she was a hoarder and was concerned about her health, but she refused any help. Last week I took her for groceries, and it was after this that I noticed my wallet was missing. Not many people knew of my relationship with my aunt; it was her choice, she had issues with my mother. I was not involved in my aunt's death." She stopped and smiled smugly at the officers.

Take that! She thought to herself.

Deputy Sinclair was sitting and making notes in her notepad. She looked up and studied the Proctor woman. She knew without a doubt she was lying. The officers had already canvassed the neighbours living around Ethel Graham and each one, including the minister down the street, denied anybody ever coming to visit on a regular basis. One neighbour did recall seeing Rebecca Adams help her with her groceries, but that was about two or three days ago. No one remembered seeing Olivia Proctor's distinctive red Porsche until the night of Ethel's death, when one neighbour stated they had a seen red car, but couldn't be sure of the model.

A well-staged and uncomfortable pause passed before Sinclair finally responded. She wanted to make the suspects squirm and as she watched the pair, she could see her tact was having the appropriate effect. Proctor was nervously picking at her thumbnail, and Adams looked sweaty and shaky.

"Well," she started slowly. "Thank you for that interesting statement. Now I have a couple of questions for you, Mrs. Proctor. Let's talk about this." She set an evidence bag containing the red wallet on the interview table.

Olivia reached to grab it, but it was pulled back by Deputy Sinclair. "Can't touch. Not yours."

"What do you mean, not yours? Of course, it's mine, and I want it back!" Olivia's face was flushed, and she was becoming increasingly agitated. She pointed at the evidence bag. "I just told you I lost it last night." Realizing her mistake, she stammered. "I mean Auntie Ethel took it last week. Why can't I have it?"

Olivia turned to her lawyer and tried to change the subject. "Do something; I need my wallet and my credit cards. I need them to buy groceries, clothes ..."

Great job you idiot, you just screwed that up. Duncan cringed at his client's obvious blunder. Now he needed to prevent any further damage from occurring. He quickly interjected before the blonde idiot ruined their entire strategy.

"Mrs. Proctor, remember your wallet was found at the scene of Ethel's' death, and they can't release it now. It is evidence in an investigation." He turned to the officers. "Mrs. Proctor has made her statement. She will not be answering any further questions." He turned to Jake. "Mr. Adams, are you ready to make your own statement?" He was desperately trying to stop this slow-motion train wreck.

"I can answer her questions!" Olivia pointed at Sinclair. She felt she was losing control on the situation, and she wanted to show she could outsmart these simpletons.

"Mrs. Proctor ..." Duncan attempted to intervene, but Olivia glowered at her lawyer. He was uncomfortable with where this was going, but before he could contest the issue, Olivia ignored his concerns and blundered forward.

"Go ahead! I have nothing to hide," Olivia snarled. Duncan threw up his hands in disbelief. "Go ahead Deputy Sinclair, ask your questions."

Janice Sinclair peppered Olivia with multiple questions over the next thirty minutes, taking time to revisit her answers and highlight the inconsistencies in Olivia's statement. She continued until a red faced and flustered Olivia turned to her lawyer. "Do something!"

Duncan shrugged; his headache was starting to pulsate. He hoped this whole rotten scene would end soon. "Mrs. Proctor has completed her statement and has nothing more to add at this time." Olivia slumped back in her chair and crossed her arms, scowling darkly at all of them.

Deputy Sinclair pushed the recorder toward Jake Adams. "I believe you have a statement as well. Are you willing to provide it now?

Jake had been sitting quietly watching the contest between Olivia and Deputy Sinclair. It was very obvious that Sinclair had cleverly manipulated Olivia into admitting that she had lied. Jake was more confused and didn't know what to do; he was getting more anxious. He took a deep breath and made the most important decision of his life.

"I'm sorry Deputy Sinclair, Officer Hoffman." He nodded his head at the officers. "I have decided to withhold my statement until I confer further with my lawyer." He then sat silently waiting for Olivia to flip shit. He knew he was going to pay for his actions, but he refused to give them any more evidence; Olivia had done a good enough job already.

"Idiot!" Olivia leapt off her chair and struck Jake. "What are you doing?"

Jake's face flushed purple, but he kept his cool; he clenched his hands together in tight fists and thought about whiskey; its warm amber colour and malty flavour. It sat on the bar back at Proctor Estate and called his name.

Lawyer Duncan stood and faced the officers. "We're done here, officers. Unless you have anything more for my clients, we will be leaving."

Deputy Sinclair pushed the stop button on the recorder. "Not for now, but please make yourselves readily available for further questioning. Please don't leave town."

As Duncan hustled the two from the room, the officers overheard the conversation that followed. They heard Olivia yelling, "What kind of lawyer are you; obviously a very incompetent one! You're fired!" Then they heard Duncan respond, "Fine with me, Mrs. Proctor, as you wish. I will no longer be providing further legal counsel. As of now you need to find yourself another lawyer."

This was all followed by a stream of colourful verbal abuse and slamming doors. The two dumbfounded officers turned to each other and shook their heads in disgust. "These two idiots are priceless! Their performance has just about convicted them, now all we need to do is measure them for their orange jumpsuits."

Both officers left to further explore and finalize details of the case. Sinclair was going to ask for a warrant to check Proctor's credit card receipts and phone records, and Hoffman was going to try and track down Rebecca Adams; he had some more questions for this 'person of interest.'

As Raymond Duncan left the police station, he laughed. "Getting fired today is the best thing that has ever happened to me!" He noticed his headache was gone!

CHAPTER SIXTY-FIVE

Buzzzz ... Buzzzzz. The delivery man from EX-PRESS DELIVIERIES continued to press the intercom button, but no one was responding.

"Well shit, now what!? You order an EXPEDIATED delivery, and then no one is here to accept the delivery. Really?" He had to drive out of his way, delaying the rest of his delivery route, to ensure it was ON TIME and now the idiots had stood him up.

"Rich people!" he snorted.

He got out of the delivery vehicle, lugged out the two large boxes containing the items from the hardware store, and then dumped them on the ground in front of the Proctor Estate gates, blocking it from freely swinging open.

"If you ain't gonna answer the intercom, then have fun opening the gate."

"Have fun getting into your big old mansion." He tossed the invoice out the window, where it fluttered down onto the gravel drive. Then he hopped back into the panel van and drove off.

* * *

As Olivia and Jake fought with their lawyer, and a frustrated driver was dumping an order in front of the Proctor Estate gate, Rebecca was flying down the highway to the nearby town of Cedar Falls. She needed to add some final items to her plan, but her face was too familiar in Campbell River to allow privacy. She pulled into the shopping district, locating an esthetic shop that she had found on the internet.

Rose's Esthetics and Essentials offered the products and services she needed. She wanted a makeover and also to purchase two wigs; a 'blonde bob' and a 'redhead/copper toned fall.' She was looking 'to change things up,' she explained to the receptionist when she booked the appointment, but this was just a ruse. Her plan was to actually create a bit of chaos. She knew she couldn't mimic Olivia, their physiques were too different, but she certainly could throw some confusion into the case. People would wonder who the woman with the blonde bob was.

When she placed Olivia's Platinum VISA card on the counter, the esthetic team fell over each other to give her the best service. Each esthetician was vying for the 'big tip,' and Rebecca was more than happy to afford it, especially since Olivia was paying!

She was lovingly escorted to the private change rooms and bundled into a fluffy terry robe in preparation for her multiple treatments and therapies. She sipped a glass of champagne while she settled into the body wraps, facial treatments, and a pedi/mani. She sighed, relaxing into the facial massages; she couldn't remember the last time she had felt so pampered. She was provided with several expensive wigs to try on, and she finally selected a platinum blond bob and a sassy copper wig that flattered her green eyes. The makeup artist expertly finalized her new look. Armed with application instructions and all the treats including silk mascara, radiant blushes, mineral eyeshadows, and lush lipsticks, Rebecca strutted out into the morning sun. She had purchased a new fashionable outfit the day before, and now freshly outfitted, she donned the new platinum bob before leaving the salon. She was leaving a 'changed woman,' and she gratefully rewarded each of the eager young women with a healthy tip for their skillful attention.

"Well done, ladies. Many thanks!"

Rebecca sashayed to her little Honda and headed to her next location; 'Ed's Sporting Goods Store.' She had already ordered several items online, and just needed to pick them up. The exchange was brief, and the only thing the clerk remembered was that the blonde woman was very attractive, and she tipped well.

Lastly, Rebecca pulled into Cedar Falls Cabins and Resort to book a room. The quaint getaway was snuggled along the Campbell River, only three miles from the beginning of the Lachlan Pathway system. Here she could exercise, practice running, and also strategize her 'final escape.' She had decided to leave Magda's apartment after she went on her shopping spree. She hadn't been thinking clearly when she had arranged for the delivery to be sent to Magda's address.

"Not the best plan, Rebecca! If Olivia decides to track her credit card activities, then she will be able to trace the location of the deliveries; right to me." She mused when she recognized her error.

She requested a secluded room at the edge of the property, explaining to the clerk that she was recuperating from a 'long illness,' and she needed peace and quiet to rejuvenate. She actually needed to be able to slip unnoticed into the woods to connect with the forest pathways; here she would build her strength to complete her last race. Campbell River's Dash for Cash was only one month away; she had some work to do.

She changed from the blonde bob to the copper mane, then entered the lobby and registered the room under Elena Lipska. She used the money from Olivia's wallet to secure the room, promising to pay the remainder later that day.

Afterward, she returned to Magda's apartment in Campbell River; she needed to retrieve the clothing she had ordered. She stopped at Cascade Credit Union along the way and did another quick change, donning the blonde wig and dark sunglasses, before taking a hefty advance on Olivia's credit card. She needed more cash to pay for the cabin and other upcoming expenses. For once she was happy that Olivia was so 'flashy' with her credit cards; she had done little to protect her PIN number, which made things easy for Rebecca.

She inserted the card, typed in the number, and let the bank video camera record a well-dressed blonde woman making a large cash withdrawal.

* * *

Rebecca hummed to herself as she drove back to Campbell River. She felt in control for the first time in many years, everything was coming together with her plan. She pulled into the apartment parking lot and was confronted by landlord Invonitz. He was trimming the scraggy shrubs around the entrance, and he startled when she approached. Recognizing the platinum blonde hair, he assumed it was that 'pepper spraying bitch' and beat a hasty retreat. She smirked to herself.

She let herself into the small apartment and set herself to the task at hand. She was going to remove any personal memorabilia to take with her; the other items she would leave for Invonitz to deal with. Rebecca removed the wig and her new clothes, then donned an old pair of baggy jeans and a sweat shirt; she was stepping back into her old persona, and she hated it.

Buzz! Buzz! Someone was pressing the intercom button. She cautiously answered. "Who is it?"

"Delivery for Olivia Proctor!" The delivery man announced.

"Just a minute! I will come and meet you at the front door." Rebecca replied. She quickly donned the blonde wig and grabbed her purse. She wanted to tip the driver for his efforts.

She rushed to the front entrance and ushered the man in. He followed her to Magda's apartment, efficiently unloaded the boxes and accepted the generous tip from the blonde woman. He had often delivered to Proctor Estate and Proctor Automotive, and he was curious why there was a delivery for Olivia Proctor at this squatty little apartment. He followed social media and knew that the Proctors had separated.

"Are you Mrs. Proctor?' he asked as Rebecca signed for the delivery.

"Nope, she just asked me to pick the stuff up her for her. She is leaving on a trip to Mexico." The blonde pointed at the suitcase.

"Lucky her!" he muttered as he accepted the tip.

Rebecca secured the door and removed the wig. *The only trip she is going on is to prison!* She laughed aloud and started opening the boxes.

She removed each item, carefully transferring them from the boxes into the newly delivered suitcases. She stroked the fresh new items, taking time to relish in the moment. She finished off the day by using the delivery boxes still labeled with Olivia's name to pack Magda's remaining items.

"Invonitz can have these, Magda could care less." She sealed the last box and looked around the apartment. It looked sadder since she had removed the few personal items.

"Time to leave," she announced to the empty space.

The last thing Rebecca needed to do was call a cab to take her back to the Cedar Falls Cabins and Resort. It came with a surge of sadness as she dialed the taxi cab number; her little Honda had been her constant companion for so many years and now she needed to say goodbye. She was often seen driving around Campbell River in her dilapidated vehicle, its ruined shell symbolizing her tragic life, now this sad separation was the last break from her former life.

As the cab pulled away from the apartment she hoped the police would find her car and wonder where she had gone.

CHAPTER SIXTY-SIX

Now that Rebecca was safely tucked away in her snug little cabin, she could relax slightly. The last few days had been a furl of chaotic activity, and she needed to calm her nerves and steady herself for the next steps. She had spent the remainder of the day unpacking her suitcases, sorting and trying on her new clothes. She now wore a comfortable tracksuit, and she was testing out her new runners. On her last run she had slipped on the trail and twisted her ankle, but it was definitely improving since she had taped it. She was planning to test it out on a run this evening; she was just waiting for the light to fade so she would have some privacy.

On the table in front of her was all the evidence she had been collecting, and alongside it sat the notepad she had brought from home. She picked up each item, making a notation on the paper:

1. Jake's cellphone—videotape conversation between Jake and Olivia conspiring on my death at the hospital and at Proctor Automotives.
2. The computer disk—tampering with Dad's car.
3. The accident report- it raised suspicion that the loose lug nuts may have caused the accident.
4. My cellphone—Ethel's call that turned deadly.

Wow, what more do I need to prove these two are murderers? I guess I need to be dead too! She tapped the pen on the pad and wrote a couple of notes. She looked outside and saw that the evening sky was darkening,.

I need to put this in a more secure place. Tomorrow I will get a safe deposit box at the bank. But for now, I should be safe. She patted the gun, and put a note on the bottom of the list that said, *'Safety deposit box.'* She slid the items into an envelope and tucked them under the mattress of her bed.

She stretched in preparation for her run, and once she was warmed-up, she slipped into the cool evening air. It had rained briefly, earlier in the day, and parts of the pathway remained damp. She knew it was risky to run when the light was gradually fading, and even more so after the rain, but she needed to remain unseen for her plan to work.

Rebecca pulled the hood of her tracksuit over her head, then slipped out of her cabin. Looking around, she secured the lock before moving toward the gravel path; slowly she jogged along the connector pathway to Lachlan Pathway. Campbell River was well known for its beautiful scenery and the many walking paths that wound through the valley and river gorge. As she jogged along her chosen route, Rebecca approached the dangerous Skye Pointe Bend that overlooked Lachlan Falls. This area was known to get very slippery, especially after it had rained like it did that morning; mist off the falls plus the granite rocks made it very treacherous. This notorious 'bend' had been part of the Dash for Cash race course for many years, but it had recently been deemed too risky by race course officials, and a detour on the upper ridge was chosen as a safer alternative.

Rebecca slowed down as she approached the area; the footing was indeed unstable. She stopped to survey the scene. The edge of the cliff was craggy and uneven, gravel disturbed by her runners trickled over the lip to the waters below. She peered over the edge of the cliff, estimating the drop to be approximately fifteen to twenty feet to the churning dark waters below.

Bit of a drop there and the water will be pretty cold too. She pulled back and reflected. *You would need to be a good swimmer if you fell in because this branch of Campbell River drags you straight to the bay!*

Rebecca stepped back and looked at the overhang above, contemplating. *So this is where the race has been diverted to.* She clambered up the ledge and considered the viewpoint; from here she could clearly see the bend and the falls below.

Hmm, a perfect place for an accident to occur. She stood and considered the location for a couple of minutes; then she back tracked down the race course and ended up in the parking lot, where the race would begin. She studied the Lachlan Pathway map posted at the entrance of the lot; noted the area, and then took a shortcut to the left that brought her quickly back to the 'bend.'

"Good to remember," she puffed aloud as her made her way back to the cabin. She was stiff but pleased with her progress. Back at the cabin, she stripped out of her tracksuit and runners; unbundled the taped ankle, and settled into the bathtub. She sighed as the hot water eased her aching muscles; she leaned back and closed her eyes, replaying the run in her head.

Tomorrow I will check out the area a little more. She pulled herself out of the tub, towelled dry, and donned her pajamas, then sat on the edge of the bed. She reached under and pulled out the hidden envelope and Magda's gun. She reviewed her action plan, then added: *'lawyer.'*

I need to change my will. She yawned as she placed the papers and weapon on the bedside table. She turned off the light and fell into a restless sleep, dreaming of falling, icy water, and screaming. She awoke with a start, feverishly looking around the strange, darkened room; she flipped on the light and fumbled for the gun. Her chest was tight with fear, and her 'frightened brain' saw imaginary people in her room.

"No!" she moaned to the empty room. "You can't hurt me anymore! I won't let you!"

The cool metal of the gun soothed her anxiety, and as her alarm eased, she realized she was truly safe for the first time in years. She lay back down, but sleep eluded her. She tossed and turned as she mulled over her plans, twisting and turning within the sheets, until she was a knotted mess. Flinging them aside, Rebecca stepped out into the cool night air and studied the stars. She breathed in the pine scented air and rubbed her bare arms as the night breeze kissed her skin. Her father had taught her to read the stars and outside in the quiet of the night, she felt close to her family.

"Father... Mother ... give me your strength and guidance to complete the task that is facing me. Indie bless me with your love!" She prayed aloud as she gazed on the stars and constellations; their brilliance pressed down on her. She breathed deeply and returned to the cabin; she secured the locks on the door and checked the windows, then snuggled back under the covers. There she slept, dreaming of happier times that provided her with the forte to continue her quest.

CHAPTER SIXTY-SEVEN

"Who the hell left this pile of crap in my driveway?" Olivia had driven home, blind with fury. She couldn't believe how badly the meeting with the police had gone. Sinclair had toyed with her; tricking her and confusing her story; making her statement a mess of contradictions. Then Jake had royally botched up their plans by refusing to give his statement. The whole situation had left the pair looking stupid and unreliable. Then she had to fire that 'little prick' Raymond Duncan; he was so useless!

The couple had driven to Proctor Estate in icy silence; Olivia seething with anger, and Jake quietly mulling over his options—which simply meant which alcohol should he drink to drown out Olivia's racket—because at that point, that was all he really cared about. Now as they drove up to the property, they were confronted by a stack of cardboard boxes packed against the gate, preventing it from opening freely.

She screeched to a stop, flinging the door of her Porsche open. Stepping out, her spiked heel punctured a piece of paper that lay on the drive. She plucked it off her shoe; it was the invoice from the hardware store that the driver had cast out the window as he drove off.

"What the hell!?" She waved the paper at Jake. "Did you order all this crap?"

Jake begrudgingly unfolded his height from the petite car and made his way to Olivia. *What now?* he thought. "What stuff? I didn't order anything."

"Here!" She shoved the paper in Jake's face and stomped over to the boxes. As Jake read the list, Olivia tore the boxes open. She pulled out the items, tossing them on the drive. As she reached the bottom, she turned to Jake.

"Why would you order all this?" She pointed at the assorted items now scattered around her feet. "Gloves, Jake?"

"It says on the invoice you ordered them; on your VISA card." Jake thrust the paper in her face.

"Well, this is a mistake," Olivia said, attempting to push the boxes aside.

"Get over here and help me," she bellowed at Jake. Reluctantly he came over and cleared the path for Olivia to drive her Porsche forward.

She drove past him, leaving him standing on the outside of the gate. "Get rid of this shit!" she called out the window as she drove past him up the driveway. She had to call the VISA company and find out who was ordering this stuff on her credit card.

"You bitch!" Jake hissed as the little red car whizzed past. He trudged up the long gravel drive to the garage, where his old pickup truck was hidden from public view. Olivia had instructed him to hide it away because it was an 'embarrassment to be seen on her pristine property.' He pulled the creaky door open and revved the engine, belching black smoke into the air. He knew this would piss Olivia off, so he revved the engine several more times. He pulled out and bombed down the gravel drive, swerving and skidding in the gravel, churning it into messy groves.

"Take that Olivia!" he snorted. Jake knew that he would end up regretting his foolhardiness and spend hours fixing the mess himself, but for now it felt good to defy her!

He snatched up the items that were littered on the drive. He turned a plastic wrapped pair of overalls over in his hands. *Why did she order all this stuff, was she planning on burying someone?* He threw the items into a box. *Seriously! What was she thinking of; offing Rebecca and burying her in the woods? I thought we were going to push her to kill herself with pills or something? I better get this stuff out of here before someone sees it.*

Jake flung the boxes into the truck's cab and roared back up the driveway. He parked the truck in the garage, then pulled the doors shut.

"Now!" he said. "I'm going to have a little talk with 'the lady of the house.'" He clenched and unclenched his fists. "But first, a drink!"

CHAPTER SIXTY-EIGHT

Rebecca approached the front desk receptionist at the Cedar Falls Credit Union, the same bank where she had previously worn a blonde wig and made a large cash withdrawal at the ATM. Now she was arriving as Elena Lipska, and she had donned the copper wig, applied heavy makeup, and brought along Elena's identification. She hoped the pieces would be enough to secure her a safety deposit box. She had created a background story if things got difficult.

The young receptionist, whose name tag read Sara, cordially greeted Rebecca. "Good morning, how can I help you?"

In her best Polish accent, Rebecca replied. "Good morning, Sara. I am Elena Lipska, and I need to open a box. You call it a security box."

"Oh, you mean a safety deposit box."

"Yes, excuse my speech. A safety deposit box." Rebecca/Elena feigned embarrassment.

"No worries, I can help you set that up. I just need a couple pieces of identification, and then we can get started."

"I have a problem." Rebecca/Elena looked away in humiliation, but then continued. "I left my bad husband so fast that the only thing I have is my Polish birth certificate and my old passport from my home country. Please tell me this is enough."

"Actually it isn't." Sara looked at the old picture in the passport. It kind of looked like the woman in front of her, but the passport had been expired for over ten years. The woman had grown older and the picture was faded, but there was definitely some resemblance.

Suddenly Rebecca/Elena put her face in her hands. "Oh no! That man, he beats me, and I am terrified he will take everything from me. If he gets these papers, he will take my home and all my money; please can you help me?" She sobbed loudly, drawing attention to herself; people were starting to look her way.

Sara felt her anger rise; her ex-boyfriend had also been an abuser. She felt a kindred spirit with this poor woman, and she was drawn to help a 'sister in need.' She bent her head low, keeping an eye out for her self-righteous boss, and quietly whispered. "Dry your tears, Elena. I will help you. Like you I was abused, and I applaud your strength."

She pushed the necessary forms across the desk and assisted Rebecca/ Elena; it only took a few minutes to complete the forms. Under 'expiry date' Sara altered the date and entered a current one, then she copied the required identification and attached them to the form. If her boss scrutinized the documents, which he seldom did, she would have to suffer her error, but for now she felt empowered helping this poor woman. Sara brought out a key and together they crossed the bank to the vault, where Rebecca/Elena secured her precious documents into safety deposit box #315.

On the way out the door, Rebecca/Elena turned and embraced the young receptionist. "Many thanks!" she croaked. "You have saved my life." She fled, leaving Sara puffing with pride; she had helped another victim of abuse to start a new life! "You go, girl!" she said with a smile.

Rebecca's next stop was the lawyer's office; she had found a name in the Cedar Falls' Yellow Pages. The office was two blocks off the main street in a small Victorian style cottage; a sign was posted outside: *Hicks/Jensen Barristers, Solicitors, and Notaries*. Rebecca knocked on the door, and it was answered by a middle-aged woman, with a bushy head of red curly hair and a pleasant, infectious smile.

"Hello. Are you Rebecca? Good, come on in," she said as Rebecca nodded. "Betsy, my assistant, is off with a sick kid today, so I'm it," the woman gushed. "Where's is my head, I'm Vera Jensen, 'the lawyer.' Please come on in."

Rebecca immediately warmed to this woman as she was ushered into her office. The main wall was lined with bookshelves filled with books and reference materials, several filing cabinets crowded the other walls, and in the middle of the room was 'the belle' herself, an old mahogany desk. Rebecca ran her hand along the edge, it reminded her of the desk in her father's office at

Campbell River High School, it was worn and dented, but each scar made her seem more regal.

"She was my father's desk; he was a lawyer too. When he passed, she came to me, and she is a real beauty. I always feel so much smarter sitting behind her; like when I touch her, she passes along my dad's wisdom." Vera gestured to a chair across from the desk.

"Would you like some tea?" When Rebecca declined, Vera settled into her own chair, and rested her elbows on the desk. "So tell me your story, Rebecca. What can I do to ease your mind?"

"Well," Rebecca began. "I need a divorce, but I also fear for my life." She hadn't meant to tell the lawyer this, but the woman's warm smile and compassionate eyes set her at ease.

The lawyer leaned back, tented her hands together, and simply said. "Continue."

Over the next hour Rebecca not only continued, but she poured out her entire life story. At the end she felt emotionally drained, but in a good way, as if talking to a stranger allowed her to finally unburden all her anger, her pain, and sorrow. She flopped back in her chair and looked at Vera Jensen; the lawyer hadn't moved a muscle; she just sat quietly studying her.

"That's some story! You actually have all this evidence in a safety deposit box?"

Rebecca nodded.

"Then we have some work to do!" Vera reached down into her bottom desk drawer, and pulled out an eighteen-year-old bottle of single malt whiskey and two glasses. "Would you still like some tea, or perhaps something stronger?" She coyly smiled, offering Rebecca a glass of the amber liquid. Rebecca accepted the drink and grinned, knowing she had made an ally. She tipped it back and gasped as it burned its way down.

"Wow!" she sputtered. The lawyer laughed, then shot her own drink. "That'll kick start the engine. Now let's get down to working on getting you free of your marriage, and then let's make sure Jake and Miss Olivia spend a long time in jail." Vera hadn't felt this invigorated in years. She poured them each another drink and set to the task of saving her client.

Rebecca, slightly tipsy from the liquid refreshment, stood to leave the law office. Hours had passed, and Vera had outlined the divorce on grounds of 'adultery and mental cruelty,' and polished the wordings on the new will.

"Pretty much cut and dry; any judge would grant you a divorce. Just let me finish these papers, and then I can have Jake served at Proctor Estate. Let's meet in a couple of days to finalize it and finish changing your will."

Vera Jensen watched as Rebecca climbed into her cab. She liked this young woman and wanted to help with initiating the divorce proceedings and amending her will, but she was worried that there were evil people out there who wanted to harm Rebecca, or maybe even kill her.

"The next step is to convict those two monsters." She waved as Rebecca drove off. "I wonder what Chief Pritchard would think about all of this?"

Rebecca left the Jensen law office two days later, a new will in hand. She had adjusted her will so that in the event of her death, her portion of the monies from the sale of the Wright property would go to the local Women's Shelter and Win/Win, a local job creation centre for women. She smiled when she thought how this would help other women break free from abuse. The other thing that brought her comfort was the divorce action; Jake would be served today at Proctor Estate.

Her final stop was at the Cedar Falls Urgent Care Clinic, where she filled out a medical record using Elena's name, then waited for her turn. It wasn't long before the nurse called her into the exam room. Rebecca explained that she was experiencing increasing headaches and stomach pain, and she would like to have the doctor 'check her out.'

"Miss Lipska, what can I do to help?" The doctor listened to the patient's story and after an examination decided blood work would be required to complete the assessment. When the requisition was completed, the patient was directed to the lab.

As the lab technician turned to discard the used needle, Rebecca swiftly reached out and knocked one the vials into her lap. She quickly covered it with her hand. "Thank you for your help." She nodded at the tech and hurried from the building; the vial secured in her palm.

"Sure, fine," the tech responded to the patient's retreating back. *Hmm, didn't I collect three vials?* She searched the floor, thinking it had rolled off the counter. *Must have only drawn two. No worries, I have all I need to run the test.* She finished labelling the vials, then readied the area for the next patient.

Rebecca smiled as she stepped outside, the mid- summer warmth spreading to her heart.

Everything is falling into place. She hailed a cab to take her back to her cabin. Now she just needed to quietly fly under the radar until the last step of her plan played out.

CHAPTER SIXTY-NINE

The intercom buzzed loudly at Proctor Estate; after a long pause, a raspy male voice answered. "What?"

"I have a delivery for Jake Adams. May I come in please?"

"What's it about?"

"I need to speak with Mr. Adams personally. Are you Mr. Adams? This is important." Rick Manz, the agent from Hicks/Jensen law firm, was afraid he wouldn't get into the gated residence to serve the divorce papers. It was imperative that they be delivered today.

"Nope, I ain't Adams. Him and the woman are around somewhere. I'm the gardener; been hired to clean up the yard and tend to the indoor plants. Place is a flipping mess! Kept hearing the damn intercom buzzing, so thought I'd answer it."

"I'm sure Mr. Adams would like to see these papers I have for him. Can you please buzz me in?"

"Fine. Just let yourself into the house, I'm leaving; I think they're in the library." The gate swung open.

Manz drove up the driveway, and parked in front of the house. The gardener was packing his equipment into his vehicle when he pulled up. He waved to Manz, then drove off down the drive.

"Impressive!" Manz noted as climbed the steps to the main house. He pushed the heavy ornate wrought iron door open, and called out. "Hello! Hello! My name is Rick Manz, and I need to talk with Mr. Jake Adams."

His voice echoed in the large foyer, so Manz cautiously made his way deeper into the expansive residence. He peered around, noting that the place was in need of a good clean, and it smelled stuffy. He passed a large living room, but it was empty so he proceeded toward the back of the estate. He could hear arguing coming from somewhere deeper in the house, so he made his way toward the voices.

"Hello," he called again. This time he was confronted by a platinum blonde woman, presumably Olivia Proctor. The woman looked on edge, her clothes were wrinkled, and she had dark circles under her eyes. She certainly wasn't the Olivia Proctor he had seen on social media clips. The woman looked very anxious and kept looking over her shoulder; she rubbed at what looked like healing bruises on her forearms.

"Who are you? And what are you doing in my house?" the woman squawked. "Jake, come here! There is some strange man in here."

"Are you the new pool keeper?" Olivia eyed him suspiciously.

"No, I'm here to talk with Mr. Adams." Manz paused.

"Jake!" Olivia yelled as he wandered in the room. He looked even rougher than the woman; he was dishevelled and smelled strongly of booze. His red rimmed eyes glowered at the intruder.

"What now? Who is this person?" He barked at Olivia; she flinched away from his dark glare and moved out of his reach.

"Are you Mr. Jake Adams?" Manz asked.

"Yeah." Jake sized up the stranger. "Who wants to know?" He crossed his arms over the ill-fitting dressing gown he had found in the bedroom closet. It was one of Andie's castoffs, and it barely covered his naked body. Tugging the sash tighter, he approached the stranger

Manz pulled out the envelope containing the divorce papers, and he stepped toward Jake. "Mr. Jake Adams, you have been served." Jake snatched the offered envelope and ripped it open.

"Divorce papers! Rebecca is serving *me* with divorce papers?" He laughed out loud and thrust them at Olivia. She cautiously took the papers, and then slowly flipped through them.

"On what grounds; what is that bitch saying about us?" Jake snarled, stepping menacingly toward the agent.

"You'll need to take that up with your lawyer." Manz swallowed. He himself was a big man, but Jake towered over him. As Manz looked at Jake's brooding face, he saw danger reflected back in his eye; this man was unstable. He beat a hasty retreat; leaving both the front door and the security gate wide open.

After Manz left, Jake grabbed the papers from Olivia, then disappeared to the library in search of more alcohol; they were running dangerously low.

"Olivia!" He bellowed. Olivia flew into the library where Jake stood flushed and furious! "What?" She demanded.

"What ... what...?" he said, mimicking her whiny voice. He marched right up to her, leaning down into her face. He grabbed her by her arms and shoved her against the wall; his fingers bruising her flesh.

"Stop Jake!" she hissed, trying to break away from his hold. He was hurting her, and it frightened her. He pinned her harder to the wall, digging his fingers into her arms. "What are you gonna do about it, princess?"

She struggled harder; he only laughed and moved one hand to her tender throat. When he glared into her eyes, she saw something that really scared her ... pure, dark rage. She realized then that she had lost control of this man—and his temper. The tables had turned; now he owned her!

"Jake," she croaked. "You're hurting me!" She pulled at his fingers, trying to loosen his grip. He tightened his hold.

"Good!" He leaned into her tear-streaked face. "Listen to me! We need to get rid of Rebecca. Do you understand!?" Olivia nodded weakly, his fingers pressing firmly on her throat, making it hard to breathe.

"From now on, it is me who makes the decisions. DO YOU UNDERSTAND?" he jeered in her shocked face.

All she could do was nod. He flung her to the floor, then stomped off. Olivia lay on the floor, a weeping mess, afraid to move. She slept behind a locked door that night, nursing her bruises.

CHAPTER SEVENTY

R ebecca had been working hard and now it was only one weeks' time until the race; she felt prepared for both the mental and physical endurance required to complete this last leg of her journey. She had been exercising and running to build up her stamina and strength, and meditating to calm her anxieties. She was as ready as she could be; she just needed to see it through to completion.

She sorted through several items on the bed, packaged them together and addressed it to Olivia Proctor at her 'big old estate.' She included a letter with an ultimatum that Olivia meet with her, and also the USB stick; bait that was essential to her plan. All she needed now was Olivia to play her part in this final step!

"Please take the bait, please," she whispered aloud as the Cedar Falls postmaster stamped the parcel, and she paid extra for Xpress delivery.

"I beg your pardon, Miss?"

"Sorry, just talking to myself." Rebecca smiled as she quickly slipped from the post office. Now all she had to do was wait until the day of the race. Her plans were moving forward, but much depended on Olivia and Jake. *Don't fail me now.* She crossed her fingers and said a silent prayer—she figured she would cover all her bases.

As Rebecca mailed the parcel, she had no idea that everything was unravelling in Jake and Olivia's perfect little world. Since Rich Manz had delivered the divorce papers, things had gone from bad to worse for the pair. The simple act of serving the divorce papers had done something to Jake. He was furious and had leapt into an alcoholic abyss; now he was almost out of alcohol. He roomed the house late at night, scouring every room. He was afraid to drive to the liquor store in case he got a DUI; he didn't need more stress in his life.

By now his head was cracking open, and he felt unsteady. He just wanted a drink; no, he needed it. He beelined straight to the library and snatched the closest bottle and uncorked it. He guzzled it down, the liquid burning its way down to his empty stomach; where it churned and mixed with his anxiety. He clutched his stomach, and then suddenly vomited all over the carpet and his clothes. The mess was a mixture of blood and whiskey. He collapsed to the floor and seized; the episode lasted several minutes, before his pitching body stilled. He laid there until the following morning, where he was found by the new housekeeper, Hannah Bergen.

Hannah had been hired by Olivia following a brief phone interview, she was the only person who had applied to the newspaper ad, and as she approached the estate she found the front gate open. She drove up to the front entrance and then when no one answered the doorbell, she let herself into the manor where she tripped over a package lying inside the doorway. She tucked it under her arm and cautiously entered each room, calling out, but when no one responded, she moved deeper into the house. She entered the library and found a man lying unconscious in a pool of bloody vomit. She ran over to him, dropped the package, and vigorously shook his shoulder.

"Oh my God, are you okay?" When he didn't respond, she started screaming.

"Help! Somebody please, I need help!"

Olivia was hidden away in her locked room, afraid to be alone with Jake; she was unaware of his condition until she heard screaming. She hadn't slept well, and had actually kept the light on all night, worried that Jake would have another outburst. Hearing the screams, Olivia flung open her door and raced toward the noise; careening into a hysterical woman running out of the library.

"Help, there is a man lying unconscious in that room." Hannah pointed toward the library. "He is covered in blood. You need to call an ambulance." Olivia pushed past her and knelt next to Jake. She hesitantly touched him; his skin was cool, but he was breathing, however it sounded raspy. He didn't respond to her touch.

"Jake! Jake honey, wake up!" She shook his limp body. "Wake up, please!" Her fear of Jake and her anger was momentarily forgotten by this crisis. She turned to Hannah, then shrieked.

320

"Do something! Don't just stand there!"

A shocked Hannah stepped back out of the library; she pulled out her cellphone and dialed 911. She refused to re-enter the room, not wanting to look at the sick man and the mess on the floor. The ambulance arrived within ten minutes, and Hannah directed them to the library. They found Jake lying on his side, his eye lids fluttering, and he only groaned when they touched him.

Olivia sat holding Jake's hand, quietly and carefully watching him. The EMS team took control and as they assessed him, they recognized a serious situation, and decided to transfer him immediately to the hospital. They loaded the patient into the ambulance and directed Olivia to follow them to the hospital. She was so shocked that she could only nod in response.

As the ambulance drove away Olivia collapsed, and sat rocking herself on the tile floor. She neither moved nor spoke when Hannah approached her. "Ma'am. Mrs. Proctor." Hannah gently touched the woman's shoulder.

Olivia jumped at Hannah's touch. "Who the hell are you?" she gasped. The morning's events and her long sleepless night had left her nerves frayed.

Surprised by the verbal attack, Hannah stepped back. "I'm the new housekeeper: Hannah Bergen. You hired me to start work today." She was rethinking her decision to work here; it was not a good first impression.

Olivia pulled herself upright and straightened her dishevelled appearance. She had spent the night mulling over the events of the last twenty-four hours, and the more she fumed the more the old Olivia was coming back. She realized she had allowed Jake to bully her, and after studying the bruises on her neck and arms, she became more enraged. Jake needed to be straightened out, and perhaps this sudden admission to the hospital was what he needed. What *they* needed.

"Well, get cleaning then." She pointed at the mess; the old Olivia was back. "You can start here." She started to walk away but was blocked by Hannah.

"Clean up your own mess, you snotty bitch." Disgusted by Olivia's behaviour and this whole sickening display, Hannah turned to leave, but then stepped on the package that she had dropped when she found Jake on the floor.

"And here Mrs. Proctor, this was lying by the front door." She flung the package in Olivia's face, then started to walk away. It bounced off Oliva and skipped across the pile of vomit, smearing a streak across its front.

"By the way, I quit, and you look like shit!"

Olivia screamed. "Get out! Get out of my house!" Hannah just laughed and stepped away from the haughty woman, leaving her to deal with her own mess.

CHAPTER SEVENTY-ONE

At the hospital, the staff jumped into action. They removed Jake's soiled clothes, placing them in a bag; his new cellphone and wallet were placed in a separate bag, and they made note of his valuables on the patient chart. The items were given to Olivia when she arrived several hours later.

After Hannah Berg had abandoned her, Olivia had donned gloves and gagged her way through the clean-up. "My poor house, my poor carpet! I'll never get the stink out," she whined. She thought about calling 'the Berg woman' and begging her to come back, but Olivia didn't beg. After vigorously scrubbing the Persian carpet, the stain still did not lift, so Olivia decided to discard the rug. Getting on her hands and knees, she rolled up the rug, and then laboured it out into the garage. She would ask the gardener to remove it when he came next.

"If he comes," she sighed as she trudged toward her bedroom. Everyone seemed to be abandoning her. Once people clambered to work for Proctor Estate, now they ran from her. "How dare they do this to me ... me, Olivia Proctor!" she snorted.

She passed the library and sniffed the air. She gagged and reached to pull the door shut, and then spied the package resting on the floor. She carefully picked it up, not wanting to soil her hands. She was going to throw it in the garbage, when she spotted the return address; it had been sent from *Rebecca Adams*. She savagely ripped at the package, forgetting about soiling her hand. She broke a nail in the process; this and Rebecca's name ramped up Olivia's foul mood.

As she ripped and tore, she roared out loud. "This is your entire fault, Rebecca Adams. If you would have just died, then all of this wouldn't be happening. Dammit, I wouldn't have broken a nail!" She finished tearing the parcel wide open, its contents spilling on the floor. A bright pink tracksuit, runners, a USB stick, and a letter scattered on the floor. She pushed them around with her bare foot, and then picked up the letter. Her mouth hung open in astonishment as she read the note.

Olivia,

I suggest that you take a look at the USB stick because it contains evidence of your treachery and deceit. My father's death was not an accident nor was your aunt's. Either you meet with me or I go to the police. It's your decision.

If you want to be free of me for good, meet me at Skye Pointe Bend on the day of the Dash for Cash race.

I have registered you in the race. Wear the pink tracksuit so I can identify you. If you don't come, I will forward the evidence to Chief Pritchard.

The remainder of the note included the instructions on how to reach the designated location of the meeting.

Olivia scooped up all the offending items and was about to dump them in the trash, when she suddenly paused. She dropped the other items on the counter, except the letter. She reread the part that said: '*If you want to be free of me for good.*'

"Damn right I do!" she yelled to the empty room. She paced for a moment, silently plotting. *Alright Rebecca, let's meet. Let's see what you are up to! I am sure I can turn this to my advantage.*

Olivia decided to take the letter with her to the hospital; she wanted Jake's opinion. She stuffed all the items back in the parcel, including the tracksuit, and as she did she looked at the label. *At least you picked a classy outfit; maybe you have some taste after all.* She dumped the package on the counter with dirty dishes and discarded flyers.

She had no idea that the tracksuit had been purchased with her missing credit card. With all the chaos of the last few days, she had neglected to check her credit card statements. If she had, she would have been shocked at the purchases; ones that would later come back to haunt her.

CHAPTER SEVENTY-TWO

O livia arrived at the hospital three hours later. She had taken a long luxurious bubble bath and 'reset' herself; she even stopped by the nail salon for an emergency nail appointment. She tied a silk scarf around her neck to hide the bruises that Jake had left on her skin. Appropriately 'turned out' she arrived to visit Jake, the perfect Olivia Proctor once more; heads turned as she sashayed to the nursing desk.

She waited, and when no one immediately rushed to her assistance, she banged her hand on the counter. "I'm looking for a Mr. Jake Adams," she snapped.

An older nurse looked up from her charting. "And who might you be? Are you his wife, Rebecca Adams?" she asked.

"Are you kidding? I'm Olivia Proctor, and I need to see him!" She was aghast at the thought that someone might think she was Rebecca. "The Adams are separated. I am a close personal friend," she barked.

"I bet you are," the nurse replied. "He's in Room 861." The nurse reached to hand her an envelope. "Since you're so close, here are his personal items."

Olivia reluctantly took the envelope. "So, what's in it?"

"I don't know personal items I would guess. Room 861." She pointed down the hallway and returned to her paperwork. She had no desire to engage with this pretentious woman any further, there were other more important issues to attend to. Olivia stuffed the envelope in her purse, then tottered down the hall in her spiked heels.

She found Jake's room, four doors down the hall from the nursing station; the door was partially closed. She took a deep breath, and then pushed it open. She was shocked when she saw Jake lying on the bed; he was pale with dark circles under his eyes, and he was motionless when she entered the room. He was hooked to an intravenous; its bag and tubing snaked down to his right hand, under a bulky dressing. What shocked her most were the restraints; both his hands and feet were secured to the bed, and there was a belt across his midsection holding him in place.

"Jake, honey!" Olivia clasped her hands over her mouth and dashed to his bedside. Jake startled awake and pulled forward against the restraints. He stared at her, looking like a wild animal. "Who? Olivia?" he mumbled.

"Yes Jake, of course it's me!" She held his hand, but he pulled it way. He didn't want anyone to touch him; his skin felt like ants were crawling all over him. They had been giving him medication into his IV and it calmed the sensation, but now it was crawling back with a vengeance.

He opened his eyes and squinted against the harsh light; it hurt his eyes. Although a blur, he recognized Olivia, standing next to him. "Take these things off me," he demanded, shaking the wrist restraints.

"Do you think I should?" She reluctantly stepped forward, unsure if she should do what he had requested. She liked him under control, especially when he seemed so angry. She was starting to feel that familiar sense of uneasiness as she looked down at his restrained hand; she feared those fists.

"Yes!" Jake hissed and ground his teeth against the returning headache. Olivia jumped, but conceded to his demands and unbuckled the wrist, ankle, and body restraints. He gingerly swung to a sitting position and glowered at her. "Thanks. Now call the nurse, I need some drugs!" Olivia repeatedly pressed the call bell.

The nurse was surprised to find Jake sitting upright. "I see that your restraints have been removed. Did you do this?" She questioned Olivia; Olivia nodded. The nurse assessed Jake's symptoms and decided to administer a hefty dose of medication. As his agitation abated the nurse agreed to leave the restraints off as long as he controlled his temper. But within the hour his symptoms started to return, and Olivia shrunk back when he stomped around the room, looking for his clothes. He located a bag of soiled items in the closet; the clothes he had worn when brought to the ER.

"Why didn't you bring me any clean clothes?" Jake grumbled.

"You don't have any clean clothes, the housekeeper quit." Olivia stepped toward the door; she was afraid he was going to have another outburst; she could see his hands shaking again, and his face wore a sheen of sweat. "Your shakes are starting again. I should get the nurse."

The door suddenly opened and Dr. Grey, Jake's attending physician, entered; the nurse had called him, as she was concerned that Jake was becoming more agitated. He stood in front of the patient and concluded that Jake was still in the throngs of alcohol withdrawal, and he was in danger of serious complications if it was not kept under control.

"I wanna go home." Jake mumbled, rubbing his throbbing head. He lifted his aching head and glowered at the doctor.

"Mr. Adams, you are not going anywhere. Your blood alcohol level was extremely high when you came into the ER this morning, and this combined with your symptoms of sweating, tremors, light sensitivity, headaches, and seizures puts you at risk of future problems. You need to stay here and let us treat you. If you refuse, we will have you deemed mentally incompetent and have you detained for thirty days."

Jake muttered and continued to pace the room.

Recognizing the worsening symptoms Dr. Grey decided Jake needed further treatment. Alcohol withdrawal required aggressive medication therapy, especially with the severity of the symptoms Jake was experiencing. The doctor momentarily left the room, returned with more medication and swiftly administered it intravenously to Jake. He quickly settled, his symptoms easing. He sighed and laid back; Olivia also gave a shaky sigh of relief. She was worried about his aggressive, unpredictable behaviour.

"He needs to rest now, Mrs. Adams." Olivia didn't try to correct him. "He's suffering from severe alcohol withdrawal, and if it is not treated, he could have more seizures, and if they continue, he could die. Do you understand?"

She nodded.

"Jake needs to stay in the hospital for at least four to five more days for observation. After that I am recommending he be admitted to a rehab center for treatment of alcohol addiction. Any questions?"

She just shook her head.

"Here is my card if you need to talk, or you can also call the nursing station for updates. I suggest you leave now and let him rest." He firmly directed her to the elevator.

"Please take care of yourself as well," he said, then turned away, leaving Olivia holding his card.

* * *

Olivia sat in her red Porsche, mulling over the day's events. She shook her head, reflecting.

I'm living in some kind of crazy nightmare, some horrible TV show. She tapped her nails on the steering wheel and stared out the front window at Campbell River's main street. *I can't believe this is happening to me. Me . . . Olivia Proctor! What am I going to do?*

She realized she was still holding the doctor's business card, and as she stuffed it into her purse, she came across Rebecca's letter. She pulled it out and re-read it, one particular line playing over in her mind. *'If you want to be free of me for good Olivia.'*

She pulled out the cellphone and checked the date; the Dash for Cash was in four days. *Okay Rebecca, time to meet. Let's finish this.* She started her car and aimed it toward her home; she had several things to take care of before they met.

Olivia roared into the driveway of Proctor Estate, the tires of the Porsche spraying gravel as she braked. She was a woman on a mission; she needed to put her house in order, literally, and then she needed to get her act together. She had to be at her best for her meeting with Rebecca. She dug through the mess on the kitchen counter, searching for Hannah Berg's phone number. She swallowed her pride and placed the call.

"What do you want?" Hannah scoffed, when she discovered who the caller was. "The last time we spoke, you fired me. I guess you think you can snap your little fingers and everyone will come running. Well that isn't me. I have principles."

"Do your principles include tripling the salary and receiving a large bonus?" Olivia queried.

"How big?"

"Obscenely big!"

"Fine, I'll start tomorrow."

Begging was far beneath Olivia's self-important standards, but today it was necessary. She fully intended to fire Hannah immediately after she completed the clean-up, because nobody made Olivia Proctor beg.

She tossed Rebecca's letter on the kitchen counter beside the package. She was more interested in finding a posh spa to soothe away her stress and tension than securing this secretive bundle; she completely forgot about it until much later.

CHAPTER SEVENTY-THREE

It was now three days before 'the meeting,' and while Jake detoxed in the hospital and Rebecca prepared for race day in her quiet sparse cabin, Olivia handled her stress by checking into a five-star hotel and spa. She handed the house keys over to Hannah Berg after forking out a fortune to the reluctant housekeeper.

"Make in right again," she instructed Hannah. "For what I'm paying you, I expect nothing less."

The housekeeper smiled at her employer but inwardly thought, *No worries, you stupid cow. I should have charged you even more.*

Olivia left Hannah to start her work while she prepared to leave for the spa. She pulled open the closet and tossed some clothes in a bag; she rummaged through the pill bottles in the bathroom medicine cabinet. She pulled out a bottle labelled 'sedatives'. These were Andie's; his doctor had ordered them when he hadn't been sleeping well after his father's death. She recalled they helped him relax and she sure could use some 'relaxation' right then. They were outdated, but she thought they'd still be effective.

On the way out the door Olivia passed the library, and she had a vivid flashback of the previous day's events. For a fleeting moment the memories of Jake's prone body came flooding back. She looked down at the bare floor; the spoiled rug was gone, but not the images. She scrunched her eyes shut and moaned.

"I need to get out of this place." She slammed the door and blazed a path to the car, leaving Hannah to deal with the mess and disorder.

Hannah patiently waited until 'the lady of the house' departed, and then her real work began. Hannah's sister was a local news reporter, and she wanted a scoop on the haughty Olivia Proctor, especially since Andie Proctor's explosive media announcement. This was the only reason she decided to return after Olivia had been so rude to her. The money was a bonus, but her sister had insisted. "Find me some dirt on this nasty bitch. I could use a juicy news story."

The plan was that once Olivia left, Hannah would dig deep and clean, but in truth she would dig deep and snoop into the Proctor's private life. Hannah was sure that she could find something tasty to provide her sister. She was pleasantly surprised when she found Rebecca's package amongst the kitchen litter.

"Bonus!" she exclaimed, reading Rebecca's letter. "Wait until sis sees this." She took pictures of the items with her cellphone and forwarded them to her sister. She turned the USB stick over in hand. *I wonder what is on this baby. Hmm, I'll take it home, copy it, and return it later.* She also decided to pocket the letter.

Hannah returned the remainder of the items to the package, then placed it on top of a pile of papers on the kitchen table. She wanted Olivia to know she had seen it.

"Careless Mrs. Proctor. Very careless!" Hannah sneered.

Hannah proceeded to search the large house. *Rich people are so foolish, they assume the 'hired help' are blind or don't overhear their personal conversations. They are so, so naïve,* she mused.

She probed drawers and opened closets; trying on Olivia's clothes and sampling her expensive perfume. *Ugh, nasty!* She was repelled by the scent.

As she searched, she clicked pictures of Olivia's sexy lingerie and tasted her vintage wine. She laughed as she helped herself to Olivia's makeup drawer, pocketing unopened lipsticks and eyeshadows.

Such fun! This gig is turning out to be worthwhile; even if it did include cleaning up rich peoples' messes. She finished her spying duties for the day and pulled the door shut, the free makeup and USB stick and letter tucked neatly in her handbag.

She wanted to copy them for Gretchen; her sister hadn't had a great story since the Campbell River Baby Killer trial and this would certainly bolster her career. *Perhaps I'll make a copy for myself. Who knows when this might come in handy?* The day's work had been profitable in more ways than one.

CHAPTER SEVENTY-FOUR

While Hannah busied herself snooping and scoring at Olivia's, Olivia arrived at Fairview Mountain Spa and Resort. She wanted to put as much space as she could between herself and Proctor Estate; she was rattled by the reoccurring images. *That place, my own home, has become a haunted house!* She shuddered when she thought of Jake's sudden collapse.

Nope! She shook her head and refused to think about that scene. She dug in her purse and pulled out the sedatives she had brought from home, popping one in her mouth. *Couldn't hurt to take a few.* She popped another.

As Olivia checked into the resort she accepted the complimentary champagne, greedily tossing it back and presenting her glass for a refill. She felt relaxed and more in control then she had in some time. The cocktail of pills and alcohol was loosening her fears, but also her lips.

"Being away from all that craziness makes a big difference." She slurred and winked at the concierge as she completed her check-in. She grabbed another flute of bubbly and tottered toward the spa on wobbly legs. She booked an exotic blue seaweed wrap and Egyptian mud facial, telling the receptionist, "My doctor recommended this. He said to take of myself! Yup, it's all about me!"

Nothing else was important to her right now except herself. She even turned her cellphone off; she wanted no interruptions as she reset. She was escorted to her suite by a young bellhop that did his best to avoid her groping hands and leering advances. Olivia had a hot body, but she was a sloppy drunk. He deposited her and her luggage in the room, and then beat a hasty retreat.

That woman has more hands and arms than an octopus! He looked down at the tip she had thrust in his hand as she grabbed his butt. *But she does give a good tip.*

Now safely tucked away in her luxuriously appointed suite, she pushed off her heels, staggered to the king-sized bed, and passed out. Several hours later, she was awoken by the ringing of a phone. She startled awake and was confused by the strange room, and it took her a moment to locate the source of the ringing.

"What?" she mumbled. Her eyes felt grainy and her mouth tasted nasty.

"Mrs. Proctor, we are waiting to start your spa treatments. Are you still able to attend or should we rebook?" Olivia pulled herself upright, the room spinning around her. Steadying herself on the dresser, she responded. "I'll be there, don't cancel my treatments. I need them."

She hung up the phone and changed into a plush terry robe, dropping her rumpled clothes on the rug. Her makeup was a ruin, and her hair was a tangled mess, but she didn't care; the technicians at the spa could transform her. She pulled open her purse and popped another pill. She liked how they took the edge off things.

Olivia relaxed on the massage bed, letting the masseuse ease the knots out of her back and shoulder muscles. As her muscles unknotted, she tried to untangle her thoughts. The last week had been insane; she couldn't believe that her perfectly planned life had gone to shit!

Jake is fine for now, someone else is taking care of him for a change. She was getting very tired of dealing with his drinking and his temper. She couldn't believe how he had treated her; he'd actually left bruises on her skin! *Not anymore!*

I'll visit him after the race. Her brain was foggy. *Oops! I didn't even get a chance to tell him about Rebecca's letter and the race. After Rebecca is dealt with, then I'll explain it. He'll be proud of me! Damn that Rebecca. She needs to die.*

The masseuse worked harder on a new knot, and Olivia wiggled under the pressure. She wasn't sure if this was pleasure or pain. Her thoughts travelled back to the package that Rebecca had sent. *Where did I leave that thing? On the kitchen counter?*

She tensed up thinking about this error in judgement. She doubted the housekeeper would notice it or even care. *No need to worry, the hired help is so lame!* Olivia exhaled as she tried to ease her stress; but worry still nagged at her, causing her to tense up.

"Relax Miss, you're tightening up!" Her masseuse rubbed and kneaded.

"Ouch!" Olivia hissed. "You're hurting me!" Her temper was short since she had awoken for her drug and champagne induced nap. She pushed the woman aside, wrapped herself in her plush robe, and stomped off in search of more champagne, more 'happy pills,' and the mineral pools.

"No tip for you!" she snarled as she shoved past the masseuse, rubbing her sore muscles. She popped another pill on the way to her room.

At that very moment, Hannah and her sister Gretchen were reviewing the materials on the USB stick; they had opened a gold mine!

CHAPTER SEVENTY-FIVE

Rebecca's day was far different than Olivia's, no spas and champagne for her, she worked out her own muscle knots. She had been running along the pathway and tweaked her ankle again. She sat massaging her aching joint, once again reviewing her plans for the race in three days. She needed to complete her final plans tomorrow, so her ankle needed to be in good shape.

As she sat on the floor, she pulled her knapsack closer. She had checked and rechecked its contents for the millionth time.

Leave it Rebecca! she chided herself, then zipped the bag and pushed it aside. *You're good to go! Now go have a hot bath and relax!*

Far away from the two women in his life, Jake lay in the Campbell River Hospital and stared at the dots in the ceiling tiles. His thoughts drifted and ebbed like the medication that streamed through his veins.

"Rebecca ... Olivia ... what a mess!" he murmured.

Jake was having trouble remembering everything that happened in the last week; he just couldn't pull the memories forward no matter how hard he tried. He settled back on his pillow and drifted in and out of sleep. He hadn't felt this calm in some time, he had decided the doctor was right, he was drinking too much. He could use some time away from this whole Rebecca/Olivia thing to get his mind straight.

"Don't think I'll go back to her," he muttered as he fell asleep; he wasn't sure who 'her' was. His brain was like scrambled eggs, he couldn't disentangle his imagination from real memories; they thrashed, collided, and blended together. He finally fell asleep and dreamed of women: blonde and brunette, all yelling at him. He suddenly couldn't breathe.

He awoke thrashing and screaming, in a full-blown seizure. The staff flew in, needing to treat this episode by administering larger doses of medication. Dr. Grey was worried about Jake's condition and needed to admit him to the Intensive Care Unit; but he wanted to confer with his family first. He attempted to contact Olivia, thinking she was Jake's wife. He received no answer at home or on her cellphone.

"Does anyone know how to get a hold of his wife?" he asked. He was very frustrated with the patient and his family. People demanded instant world class health care in this small-town hospital, but the reality was Jake would probably need to be sent to Vancouver; the severity of his alcohol withdrawal related seizures required more intense intervention.

Jake suddenly seized again.

"Shit, move him out!" The team jumped into action as they prepared to transfer him to ICU, where he would be kept under heavy sedation until his condition improved or he was transferred to a larger hospital in Vancouver. No family was contacted about the transfer.

CHAPTER SEVENTY-SIX

The day before the race, Rebecca escaped to the solitude of her cabin. During this time, she gently stretched and exercised her muscles, and visualized her plan for the race course. She ran through the various twists and turns in her mind, focusing on the treacherous footing around Skye Pointe Bend. She had spent several days walking and running the course, plotting her best options for footing and timing. At 'the bend' she had peered over the edge to Lachlan Falls, marveling at the force of the waters below. From the edge it was a straight drop into icy waters.

The fall alone would kill or at best hurt you, and the temperature of the water would cause hypothermia. She looked down into the turbulent waters. *I must be aware of the footing here; the earth is slick like oil.*

As she sat on the carpet stretching her tight calf muscles, she rehearsed the course over and over in her mind. Leaning forward into a lunge, she clicked on the TV and checked the weather report. *'Cloudy and overcast with seventy-five percent chance of rain; the forecasted temperature is ten- twelve degrees Celsius.*

The river temperature would be well below that. She eased into a deep stretch.

She lay awake that night, mulling over the events of the past few months. She sighed and turned over, facing the window. The stars winked down; reminding her of the many nights she had rocked Indie in his room, staring up at the midnight sky, pondering her future. Once again, she tracked the familiar orbs. *Orion's Belt, the Big Dipper, and the North Star-Polaris; the star that guides travellers.*

"Guide me on my journey," she whispered, rolling on her back and closing her eyes. She struggled with sleep on this night; dreaming of faces past and present, dreams lost and found.

After seven long hours, Rebecca rose from her fitful sleep. She stretched, yawned, and assessed the day's weather. *Just like the weatherman said; rainy, cold, and generally miserable!* She sipped a strong coffee and gazed out the window. Two hours before the race, she performed a final series of stretches and donned her race gear; multiple layers to protect her from the elements. She set about straightening the cabin, and then with one last glance around, she exited, firmly shutting the door behind her.

She waited patiently in the drizzling rain for the cab she had arranged to take her to the race. As she climbed into the vehicle, the driver noticed her running clothes were sodden and ruined. She had been out in the rain yesterday, securing her knapsack behind a fallen tree close to Skye Pointe Bend, and her running gear hadn't completely dried; the outer layer was still mud splattered, but the inner layers were snug and dry.

The knapsack she had packed and repacked while staying at her cabin in Cedar Falls was her 'survival kit' and it was vitally important to her plan. It contained all she needed to finish this chapter of her life. She had carefully bundled all the items in plastic to protect them from the elements, and then stashed the bag underneath the tree.

"Where you heading, lady?"

"The Dash for Cash Race," Rebecca replied. She had donned a baseball cap, neck scarf, and sunglasses to disguise her features, and also to keep her warm.

"Say, it looks like you already fell in the river. Are you actually going to run in that outfit; you already look soaked?" The cabbie studied the dishevelled woman sitting behind him. He worried her soiled clothes would ruin his vehicle's seats.

"Worried I'd catch my death by cold?" she smirked. "The cold won't kill me, but my husband and his girlfriend are going to!"

The cabbie was taken aback by such a strange comment; he didn't know how to respond, so he just shook his head and clicked on the meter. *Odd people, I get all kinds.* He eased his vehicle onto the highway, making his way toward Campbell River and the Lachlan Pathway. Although it wasn't a long drive, he was concerned his passenger would skip out on the fare.

"You are gonna pay your fare?" he spoke to the rear-view mirror.

Rebecca smiled as she tossed money over the seat. "Does this take care of it?" The cabbie eyed the pile of bills, and he nodded. It was more than enough to cover the fare, plus a hefty tip.

"Just fine! Now you relax, and I'll have you there in no time." Appreciating the generous tip, the cabbie turned on the heat to warm his chilled passenger; a few minutes later he pulled into the parking lot, which was already bustling with activity.

"Good luck with the race!" he called as Rebecca exited the vehicle.

"Thanks!" she replied, but then paused to hold the door open longer. "My name is Rebecca Adams. Do you remember what I said about my husband and his girlfriend?" He nodded. "Good, now have a great day! I sure will!" she said and closed the door.

As she picked her way through the crowd many people turned to look her way; they recognized her despite her disguise. She could feel their eyes trying to bore into her soul and seed their judgement. Rebecca passed a group of women clustered around the starting line, and she heard their snide comments.

"Is that Rebecca Adams, the 'baby killer'? Is she going to join the race?" This was the same woman who had mocked Rebecca in the grocery store many weeks ago. "She'll probably drop dead!" She heard the women tittering and laughing as she walked past.

She overheard other comments from the crowd as well. "Who does she think she is? Ballsy bitch! So sad, she is going to make a fool of herself!"

She smiled to herself, and murmured softly. "Keep staring folks, the show is just beginning!"

At the registration booth, the volunteer was having trouble locating Rebecca's name on the race participant list. Rebecca could see the registration for Olivia that she herself had completed online, but her own name did not seem to be on the list. She hadn't seen Olivia in the crowd yet, but apparently she had already picked up her racing bib and completed the waiver form.

"Are you sure you are registered?" Jill Harrison, the race volunteer asked. "Mrs. Adams ... Rebecca ... you don't impress me as the running type! Are you sure you want to participate in this race?"

Rebecca was annoyed by this comment, although she appeared large and bulky, she was prepared and had practiced for the event. "Of course, I can run," she snorted. Suddenly, she recalled that she had registered under her maiden name. "Try Wright ... Rebecca Wright." She crossed her arms in annoyance, then waited as Mrs. Harrison rechecked the registration list.

"Ah, yes ... here it is. Rebecca Wright." The volunteer handed over the race bib, two safety pins, and then touched Rebecca's hand, and said, "I apologize for my comments, dear. Be careful out on the course, there are many dangers on that slippery trail."

"Thanks!" Rebecca smiled at her. She remembered that Mrs. Harrison had been one of the few people in Campbell River who had been civil to her during the trial. *You have no idea just how truly dangerous it is going to be!*

Rebecca moved away from the crowded starting line toward the back of the racing pack. From across the excited throng, Rebecca spotted Olivia's bright pink tracksuit. "Ah, the queen has arrived!" she said aloud. She looked around for Jake, but he seemed to be absent; Olivia had come alone. "Good, less interference!" She had no idea that Jake was currently housed in Campbell River's ICU department, pending transport to the larger city hospital for more aggressive interventions. No one had been able to contact her ; her cellphone was turned off and secured in a safety deposit box in Cedar Falls.

"What do you mean, less interference?" A voice came from behind her. She startled and turned around, coming face to face with Chief Kevin Pritchard.

"Chief Pritchard." Rebecca regained her composure and nodded.

"Rebecca," he responded. "Haven't seen you for a while. Andie was worried and thought you'd left town. I still need you to come to the station and talk about those videos." He studied her up and down, taking in her mud splattered clothes and racing bib. "What are you doing here?"

She gazed up at the man and caught his steely grey eyes with hers. "I'm just joining the race like everyone else here." She waved her hand at the developing crowd, and then turned away. She didn't want him to see her face; she felt fearless and powerful, it was written all over her person.

He pulled her around to face him. "I need to talk with you, and soon. Come in of your own free will or I'll have one of my officers come and get you. Where are you living right now?" One of his officers had reported seeing her little Honda outside an apartment building on the west side, but Rebecca remained unseen.

She smiled coyly and deflected his question. "Of course, I will. Perhaps tomorrow after the race." But to herself she thought. *Not likely! Got other plans, Chief!*

Across the parking lot the participants were getting loud, excited for the race to begin. The Campbell River Police department had volunteered to assist at the event, providing both security and crowd control and now he needed to get to his post. "I have to go, but don't consider disappearing again; I think you know more than you are letting on." He warned her and left to assist with the excited crowd.

CHAPTER SEVENTY-SEVEN:

The parking lot was packed with increasing numbers of racers and spectators and with the worsening weather Chief Pritchard was concerned about the course becoming increasingly hazardous. Portions of the race had been changed, but the new route had an overhang that was equally as slippery. He had images of racers sliding off the top and falling into the cascading water below.

Should I post more officers along the race course? He wondered as he walked away. He would be glad when this race was over; the whole thing just made him feel exasperated. He had more important things to deal with, but he had promised Andie to provide race course support. He put Rebecca out of his mind as he walked towards the noisy throng.

Rebecca adjusted her running attire. Under her soiled tunic, she smoothed out her neoprene suit; it was designed to protect her from the rain and cold. She hoped it would be enough! She stretched and jogged on the spot to keep warm, unaware of icy blue eyes watching her every move.

From the front of the racing pack, Olivia glowered at Rebecca. She watched as Rebecca and Chief Pritchard had words and judging by their body language, it didn't appear to be a friendly meeting. He had broken off now, and Rebecca stood alone and isolated.

When Olivia had arrived home, she was in a foul mood; her spa break had been a flop, and she felt tenser than before. She was running low on pills, having relied heavily on them the past few days. She had also come home to find the 'useless bitch of a housekeeper,' had walked out on the job, leaving the place worse than Olivia had originally left it. It looked like Hannah had been rifling through her private stuff, looking for something, but what?

Probably jewelry or cash. She had checked her jewelry box and nothing seemed to be missing, and she had no cash left in the house, having already given all that to retain Hannah's services. *Try working in this town after I'm done with you!*

As she had milled around her ruined home, she'd dug in her purse for the pill bottle; popped one in her mouth, and washed it down with a sip of Chardonnay. The mixture of wine and sedatives had dulled her otherwise cunning mind, but she didn't care, it just made things easier. She had come to understand why Jake drank.

She hadn't thought about the package from Rebecca until she was getting ready for the race. She had pulled out the tracksuit and runners, but she couldn't find the USB stick or letter. She doubted that Hannah would have found it, much less taken it.

"Why would she want those?" she scoffed. *Must have stuffed it my other handbag.* She assumed wrong and her carelessness might have cost her everything.

She had donned the bright pink tracksuit and running shoes and headed to Lachlan Pathway, and now she found herself shivering in the rain. She hadn't thought to bring an umbrella, so she was cold, wet, and very annoyed. She was getting edgy again, so she dug in the tracksuit pocket for the bottle. She dry- swallowed a couple of pills, hoping no one would notice, but as she looked around she realized that no one was paying attention to her at all.

Since Andie and Kevin's announcement on social media, the town folk had been snubbing her. She had noticed the tittering and long sideways looks today when she arrived at the race. Her usual tribe of Campbell River house-wives had turned their backs on her, and they had actually moved away when she approached. Even when she had entered Charlotte's Confectionaries that morning for her favourite early morning coffee beverage, the usually doting server had ignored her, and made her wait.

It's your fault! She scowled across at Rebecca again. She popped another pill and seethed, making no attempt this time to hide her actions. *When does this silly race begin? I'm freezing. I need to get this 'so called evidence' from Rebecca, and then get on with my life. Then I suppose I should visit Jake.* She sighed. She had no idea Jake was being rushed by ambulance to Vancouver General Hospital; he was in grave condition.

Now cold and miserable, Olivia pushed through the crowd and made her way to the front; along the way she bumped into Gretchen Berg, the reporter for the local Campbell River Gazette. Gretchen had enrolled in the race immediately after she read the letter her sister had found at Proctor Estate. Gretchen smirked as Olivia shoved past; she recalled she was working on a boring report about the influx of garden moths when Hannah had crashed through the door to her office.

"Look what I have for you!" her excited sister had exclaimed. Hannah had discovered an interesting package on Olivia's kitchen counter and when she snooped inside, she couldn't believe her luck. She found a letter from Rebecca Adams and was shocked by its contents. *I know someone who would like to see this.* She snapped several pictures on her cellphone and immediately rushed over to meet with Gretchen.

"Sis, this is just the scoop I'm looking for. I need to be at that race to see what goes down. If Olivia Proctor does follow through with this 'invitation,' I might be able to catch wind of what this is about!" Gretchen had hugged Hannah tight. "What do you think is on this stick?" Gretchen had plugged it into her computer, and the two sisters had gasped in shock as they watched Jake and Oliva plotting Fred Wright's murder.

Gretchen whooped. "Bingo Hannah, it's the next big story I've been waiting for!"

Gretchen knew a delicious exposé when she saw one, and this one was exceptionally tasty. Gretchen loved gossip, and in the past she had extensively covered the Campbell River Baby Killer story. She had been instrumental in vilifying Rebecca. *This would be the perfect follow-up, especially with the treasures Hannah has provided.*

She had immediately contacted the race to sign-up as a late registrant.

CHAPTER SEVENTY-EIGHT

N ow Gretchen stood near Olivia in the rain, keeping close to her prize. *I'm not going to let this one get away!* she thought as she shivered in the damp.

Olivia wanted to be first off the start line so that everyone would notice her. She doubted she could win this race, but she could certainly start it out with a flourish. She strutted over to the official race starter and hissed in his ear. "Get this damn race started, John!"

John Terrance jumped when he realized it was Olivia Proctor, the sponsor's wife.

"Well, Mrs. Proctor!" He gulped. "Certainly, we can start right now!" He looked at his watch, it was almost time to begin the race anyway; a few minutes earlier wouldn't make any difference. The crowd was getting antsy; the rain and wind were making them cold and bitter.

He lifted his megaphone and boomed to the crowd. "Racers! Please join me at the start line!" His amplified voice echoed, jangling Olivia's taut nerves. She smacked him on the arm, making him fumble with the megaphone.

"Idiot! You just about deafened me!" she spat. "For God's sake, get on with it!"

Terrance cringed and motioned the racers to the line. He lifted the starter pistol.

"Let the race begin!" When the starter pistol fired, the mass of racers moved forward in a throng, Olivia leading the pack.

They surged along, soon leaving Olivia to struggle near the back. She looked around to spot Rebecca but could not see her. "You'd better not have copped out on me!" She huffed and puffed. She toiled along, her legs already feeling wobbly; she seldom participated in organized exercise, preferring to get her activity in bed. The sedatives had their affect as well; she felt sluggish and stumbled slightly. Gretchen Berg had been keeping pace with Olivia, and she caught her arm to steady her.

"Thanks!" Olivia mumbled, looking up at her. "Oh, it's you, the town gossip monger! Push off!" she hissed. Gretchen backed off, but she continued to follow at a convenient distance. She wasn't going to miss a moment of this drama as it unfolded.

Across the parking lot, Rebecca hung back and watched. As expected, Olivia was causing a scene and she wanted no part of it; her part of the drama was yet to come. As the crowd moved forward, she watched for the best time to make her move. As the parking lot emptied, Rebecca veered off to the left, taking an alternate route along Lachlan Pathway toward Skye Pointe Bend. As she made her way north, she spotted Gretchen Berg hanging near Olivia, and as much as she despised the woman, she welcomed her attendance at today's race.

"Go for it, Gretchen," she laughed. "I think this will be your next big story!"

As Rebecca raced away from the body of runners, Sam Miller, an off-duty EMT and volunteer for today's race, noticed Rebecca and called out. He recognized her; he had attended to her emergency when she had overdosed this past summer. "Where are you going ma'am, the race is that way!"

Rebecca disappeared around the corner, out of sight of the volunteer, ignoring his re-directions.

He scowled. "Damn cheater!"

Rebecca ignored Sam Miller's calls as she ran deeper into the woods. She had a goal and she needed to follow through with her plans, but she had heard his comments. She struggled along the winding trail and laughed to herself. *I'm not interested in winning this race, there is another bigger prize awaiting me up ahead.*

She picked up her pace, she needed to get to Skye Pointe Bend and set her final plans in motion. She slipped and slid her way along the alternate route, the footing was getting worse as the rain continued. She was worried that they may close the race as the trail worsened. She turned the final curve, and there it was at last ... the 'bend.'

She looked up at the overhang, where the racers should soon be entering. *Did I arrive in time to set my plan in action?* She studied the area; no racers were yet to be seen. *I need to get the backpack that I stored here last night.*

The wind from the ongoing storm had littered the area with forest debris; leaves and broken branches were strewn about. *I stored it here, where is it? Did someone find the bag and remove it?* She dug through the ruined trees and shrubs, then at last located it. It was hidden by fallen branches from the rainstorm. *Is everything inside it okay?* She dug through the bag's contents. *Everything is damp, but at least it's still intact.* She sighed in relief. *Good to go, now time to set my plan in action!* She set the pack down on a log, and she rehearsed her plan; she ran it over in her mind, searching for any potential holes. The only flaw she could see in her plan was Olivia.

Will you actually finish the race? If you don't come past me ... my plans will be ruined. I know you started the race, but it is very wet and slippery and you will get messy. Are you willing to endure a bit more to finish this game?

From her vantage point, Rebecca could secretly observe the racers as they entered the overhang. Forty-five minutes had passed, and most of the serious racers had already gone by her hiding place.

As she waited for Olivia, she set out the items from her backpack; gloves, Magda's revolver, a vial of her blood, and Jake's cellphone. She carefully donned the gloves and loaded the revolver with three bullets, and then wiped the gun of her fingerprints. It had started to rain steadier making it harder to see the racers, but Olivia's bright pink tracksuit would make her easier to spot. She anxiously paced as she waited for the runners to arrive. *Come on Olivia, time to play your part!*

CHAPTER SEVENTY-NINE

Through the misty rain, Rebecca at last spied Olivia's bright pink track-suit, rounding the corner. She was part of the slower runners that included Gretchen.

This is good; it could work to my advantage. She hesitated for just a moment, closed her eyes, and said a silent prayer. Then gathering all her strength, she took a leap of faith. *It's now or never!*

Rebecca clambered out from under her hiding place to confront Olivia. She stood boldly in the middle of the slippery path as Olivia rounded the bend. Olivia reeled back in surprise, sliding on the slick surface. The blonde woman, once her best friend now her enemy, stood directly in front of her.

"What are you ... doing ...you crazy bitch ..." Olivia was mud covered; her breath coming in hitches. She leaned against a tree clutching her side; it ached from the running. She wasn't used to this physical exertion. "So where's ... this so called evidence?"

Rebecca stood firmly obstructing her exit, watching for activity behind Olivia. There were no other runners in sight yet, including Gretchen; she needed to wait until someone arrived to witness the event.

"What am I doing, you ask?" Rebecca laughed and smiled smugly. "I am here to help you. Don't look so surprised, I know that both you and Jake want to kill me to get the money from my parent's estate. But if I have to die Olivia, we do it my way!"

Soiled, wet, and cold, Olivia had had enough of Rebecca's crap, she just wanted to go home and get in a warm bath. Her 'happy pills' were wearing off, she was feeling irritated, and now Rebecca was making her raw nerves feel worse. Olivia tried to push past her, but she was roughly shoved back.

"Back off bitch!" she spat, but Rebecca didn't budge. She continued to block her way; both women were precariously close to the cliff edge. "You're not going anywhere until we finish this!" Rebecca held her ground; she had the upper hand now. She held up Jake's missing cellphone, and then pushed the play button on the video. Jake and Olivia could be clearly heard plotting Rebecca's death. Olivia's mouth hung open in shock; Rebecca just smiled, enjoying Olivia's discomfort.

"Give me that!" Olivia lunged at Rebecca, slipping in the mud. Rebecca just stepped back, and laughed. "You want it, go get it!" Rebecca tossed the phone over the embankment, where it got hung up in the shrubs below Skye Pointe Bend.

Olivia gasped. "What are you doing? Was that the evidence?" Olivia was confused; Rebecca's game wasn't making any sense to her. She stood shivering in the rain, wondering what the hell was going on. Rebecca was running the show, and Olivia didn't like being out of control. She stomped toward Rebecca, but stopped short when Rebecca pulled out a gun.

"Oh my God! You're going to kill me!" Olivia gasped and shrank away in fear. In the distance, Rebecca could see another runner slowly approaching. It looked like Gretchen Berg. *At last, this couldn't have worked out better!*

She smiled at Olivia, and winked. As Olivia stood stock still, Rebecca started screaming.

"Olivia please no ... no don't shoot me! Please you can have Jake ... you can everything, just let me live!" Her shrill cries echoed off the steep mountain walls. She aimed the gun in the direction of the falls below, and then fired it three times. The gunfire loudly reverberated, making Olivia cringe back.

Olivia stammered. "What are you doing?"

"Setting you up, Olivia. Oh yes, I am going to die, and you will be charged for my murder. Everything is falling in place." She pulled out the vial she'd smuggled out of the lab last week; it was time for it to play its part.

"Didn't see this coming, eh Olivia? Stupid naive Rebecca, too dumb to know what was going on right in front of her face! I was taught by the best ... my best friend that is." She pulled out the vial's stopper and sprayed it on Olivia's clothes and face, then dribbled the remainder down the front of her own clothes. She stuffed the empty vial into the pocket of her jacket.

Olivia gasped in shocked. She was struck speechless by the bloody assault, and when Rebecca pointed the gun at her, she raised her hands in defense and whispered.

"Don't, please don't! Please don't shoot me, please!" Tears smeared Olivia's makeup and spilled down her face, mixing with Rebecca's blood. Olivia was convinced that she was going to die and was stunned when Rebecca tossed her the gun.

"What the hell are you doing?" Olivia was confused. She fumbled the gun, almost dropping it, then gaining control pointed it at Rebecca, and with shaking hands pulled the trigger. "CLICK."

The cartridge was empty!

Rebecca laughed at Olivia. "Do you think I am that stupid ... really?"

Out of the corner of her eye, Rebecca saw Gretchen Berg rounding the bend. The reporter had heard a woman screaming, followed by gunshots, and true to her inquisitive nature, she had wanted to know what was happening. She peered around the corner and blundered into a deadly scenario; Olivia was holding a revolver on Rebecca; both women were covered in blood.

Seeing that Gretchen was close enough to witness the scene, Rebecca played her last card, and screamed loudly, "Olivia, you shot me! Why?" She then lunged forward and slumped against her; raking her nails along Olivia's neck; tearing at her pink tracksuit. A shocked Gretchen put her hand to her mouth, stifling a scream; she was watching a murder scene unfold.

Rebecca struggled and momentarily clung to Olivia. "Why, Olivia ... why?" Her voice was weak, but loud enough to carry to Gretchen. From her hiding spot Gretchen witnessed the ongoing struggle.

"Olivia, stop! Please don't push me! AHHH!" Olivia reached to grab her back, then screaked, "You can't do this to me!"

Rebecca paused, looked Olivia in the face, and winked; then purposefully fell back over the cliff edge to the ledge below. As Rebecca fell away, she laughed. "Oh, but I did!"

Gretchen watched as Rebecca's lifeless body tumbled from Skye Pointe Bend, plunging into the water below. She didn't see her enter the river below, but she heard the splash.

CHAPTER EIGHTY

Gretchen screamed as she backed away from the scene. Olivia turned in slow motion to stare at the other woman; Olivia hadn't seen Gretchen until now. With hands shaking, she raised the revolver, pointed it at Gretchen and pulled the trigger. Gretchen grabbed her stomach, expecting to feel pain and see a gaping hole, but there was nothing: the pistol was empty. She watched in shock as the crazed Proctor woman repeatedly pulled the trigger. It clicked and clicked.

They stared at each other over the barrel of the gun.

Olivia was muttering to herself. "I didn't do it; I didn't do it!" She dropped the gun and started rubbing her hands. "So much blood, so much blood!" She rocked back and forth; it brought back memories of her father's death.

Realizing she was unharmed, Gretchen turned and ran, slipping and sliding down the pathway. She wanted to be as far away from the scene as possible. Her mind was numb; she had just witnessed a cold blooded murder.

As Gretchen ran, she screamed." Help! Help me, please! Olivia Proctor has just murdered Rebecca Adams!" She ran like her life depended on it.

Alerted by gunshots and the sounds of screams, Officer Derek Hoffman ran toward the sound. He was one of the officers providing support, and he careened into a frantic Gretchen Berg as she rounded a bend on the pathway. She yowled and pulled back.

"Murder!" she gasped. "I saw a murder! Oh my God. Olivia ... Rebecca." She pointed back down the pathway. Officer Hoffman grabbed the woman and spoke firmly. "Go down to the finish line and find Chief Pritchard. You know who he is?" Gretchen stared wide-eyed, but nodded.

"Go find him and stay there! I am going to radio for help." Gretchen fled to safety. Officer Hoffman watched the woman slip and slide her way down the path, and once she was safe, he made his way toward Skye Pointe Bend. He clicked on his radio.

"Gunshots fired at Skye Pointe Bend. Officer assistance required. Proceed with extreme caution."

He pulled his pistol from its holster, concerned about what he was going to find. He had heard three gunshots; most revolvers held six bullets, which meant that there were three rounds unaccounted for.

This could be deadly. He silently crept forward. He rounded the final curve to find Olivia Proctor sitting on the ground, rubbing her hands, and murmuring. "So much blood, so much blood!" Her pink tracksuit was splattered with blood and torn at the collar; Hoffman noticed bleeding scratch marks on her neck. On the ground lay the revolver, the smoking gun!

As he stepped forward the gravel crunched under his foot, startling Olivia. She snatched up the revolver and pointed it at Hoffman.

"Stay away!" she screamed. "I didn't do it. She jumped! She killed herself." Her hands were shaking and Hoffman was terrified she might accidentally discharge the gun; he was in very close range and this could be lethal.

He lifted his service revolver and directed it at Olivia.

"Put the gun down. Drop the gun, Mrs. Proctor! Drop it, or I will be forced to shoot." He was looking into the eyes of a crazed woman. Her pupils were large and wild looking. Olivia dangerously waved the gun at him, and he prayed that he wouldn't have to shoot her.

Olivia suddenly blinked; she was looking down the barrel of a gun; she couldn't believe an officer was pointing a gun at *her*!

"What?!" She gazed around. She stared down at her blood splattered hands and realized that she was still holding Rebecca's gun. She dropped it to the ground, shrieking. "I am innocent. I didn't hurt her, the lunatic threatened me with that gun, and then she jumped off the cliff edge. She is crazy! Why are looking at me this way?"

Hoffman leapt toward the revolver, kicking it out of Olivia's reach. At this point Deputy Janice Sinclair and Officer Alex Hiscox had arrived on the scene, having been alerted by Hoffman's radio. Onlookers were starting to gather, including runners still completing the race, volunteers, and spectators. In the middle of the chaos sat a dazed Olivia Proctor, who had again slumped to the ground, rocking and mumbling. "I didn't do it! I didn't do it!"

Chief Pritchard also came running up the pathway, alerted by the radio call as well as by a breathless Gretchen Berg. She had arrived at the finish line, gasping out the news.

"I saw her. I saw Olivia Proctor with the gun in her hand and that poor woman, Rebecca Adams, covered in blood. Olivia shot her, and then pushed her off the cliff as she begged for her life! Olivia Proctor is a murderer!"

CHAPTER EIGHTY-ONE

Leaping into action, Pritchard delivered Gretchen into the arms of John Terrance, the race marshal, and ordered him to care for the distressed woman until EMS arrived. Terrance bundled the shocked woman in his jacket and drew her toward one of the warming tents. He offered the distraught woman a warm drink and seated her under one of the heaters.

Gretchen readily accepted the beverage savouring its warmth. She pulled out her cellphone; dialed the newspaper's main phone number, and sputtered at the Gazette's receptionist.

"Send Ray, the videographer, to the Dash for Cash race. I just witnessed Olivia Proctor shoot Rebecca Adams. I need someone here to capture all this on film. And have someone bring my makeup; I need to look my best!" The shock was quickly dissipating.

Chief Pritchard had grabbed Sam Miller, the race paramedic and together they headed up the pathway. They arrived at the chaotic scene where the officers were trying to get everything under control. Deputy Sinclair had secluded Olivia from the crowd, and the others were working to push the onlookers back.

When Gretchen Berg named Olivia as the 'possible shooter' Pritchard knew this situation had become very complicated. He had already excused himself from the Graham investigation, and now this new crime scene involving his lovers' estranged wife had landed him right in the middle of the hornet's nest ... again!

This Rebecca/Olivia conflict keeps getting more complicated. He had never been involved in such a snarled web of deceits and lies. Pritchard approached Deputy Sinclair, and he pulled her aside. "I am going to have you and Officer Hoffman lead this investigation again; I think you know why." Sinclair nodded.

"You two seem to have it under control. I'll send Officer Manning to help with crowd control."

He radioed for the other officer to lend assistance at the crime scene, and then turned to leave. "I'm going to return to the main parking lot to manage the press; it is certain to turn into a media frenzy. Gretchen Berg, the reporter from the Gazette, was the primary witness, so I'm going to take her with me to get her statement before she spews it to the network."

As Officer Manning arrived Chief Pritchard announced, "Deputy Sinclair, I want you to remove Mrs. Proctor from the immediate scene; EMS can assess her for injuries, and then we can move forward with the next process. The rest of you follow Officer Hoffman's lead, finish gathering evidence, and continue to push the crowds back. We need to keep this drama under control!"

He turned to leave, regretting he couldn't bring justice to this situation, but it was a hotbed of conflict. He nodded at Sinclair, then moved off down the slippery pathway.

Sinclair donned gloves, knelt down next to Olivia, and gently shook her. "Mrs. Proctor, can you hear me? I need you to come with me." Olivia looked up with dazed eyes, and she whispered, "Oh, are you a police officer? Rebecca is dead, she is dead." She giggled. "I didn't do it; she killed herself!" Sinclair pulled her up and handed her over to Sam Miller.

Sam looked her over and assessed that the blood spatter was not a result of any injuries to Olivia. The only marks on her were four scratches on the right side of her neck, which appeared to be from fingernails. He flashed a light into Olivia's eyes and found her pupils large and dilated. He reported his findings back to Sinclair and the other officers.

"She doesn't appear to be hurt, except for some scratches to her neck, but boy is she stoned! Her pupils are the size of dinner plates."

Sinclair nodded and pulled the other officers to the side. "We need to read the Miranda rights to her and then get her out of here. She has evidence all over her person, and we need to get that tracksuit off her. Miller believes she is impaired, so we need to be extra careful. Did we bring the video equipment?" Officer Hoffman shocked his head. "No, but I'll tape the arrest on my work cellphone, including the reading of her rights."

As Hoffman documented, Officer Sinclair read Olivia her rights. "Olivia Proctor you are under arrested for the suspected murder of Rebecca Adams ..."

Suddenly something triggered in Olivia's drugged fuelled haze, and she went berserk. As the arresting officer attempted to read Olivia her rights, everyone witnessed Olivia flail, kick, and scream.

"No! No, she did it to herself! No!" The once passive Olivia now howled and shrieked as the Campbell River officers handcuffed her and marched her down the slippery Lachlan Pathway to the waiting squad car.

As Olivia was hauled away many of the onlookers documented the arrest on their cellphones, it soon would be posted to the internet for all to witness. She provided a fantastic show and social media would be buzzing tonight! The media had been alerted and eagerly waited to report the unfolding story.

Chief Pritchard could hear Olivia screaming in protest as she was dragged away. He blocked her out and turned his attention to the scene developing in the parking lot. He hastened over to where Gretchen Berg's media team was assembling. He beckoned Gretchen over. "Ms. Berg, I understand you are a primary witness for a possible murder?" She eagerly nodded as she smoothed her hair and applied fresh lipstick.

"Do you want to provide a witness statement?"

"Absolutely, I saw that crazy woman shoot Rebecca Adams, and then push her off 'the bend'. Of course, I want to make a witness statement; I want her to pay!"

"I'm afraid if you want to provide an official statement," he waved his hand at the camera crew, "You will not be able to 'go live' with your show, or your eyewitness report may be tainted. We need to get your statement first, or the courts may throw it out. You do want Proctor to pay for her crime?"

"Well shit!" Gretchen spat; her hope for an exclusive scoop had just been dashed. "Ray! We got a problem!" she bellowed. She knew Pritchard was right, but dammit she needed, no wanted this news story. As she stomped toward her team, she reassessed the situation and plotted her next strategy. If she couldn't be the lead reporter, she certainly could be the brave 'heroine' who risked her life to stop this horrific crime. Her bravery was going to save the scoop.

Pritchard lifted his radio. "Alert the Search and Rescue team, we have an incident at Skye Pointe Bend, along Lachlan Pathway. Someone has gone over the edge into the falls."

He thought about the dark waters below 'the bend'. "No rush, it won't be a rescue, just a retrieval effort." He sighed, and then turned away. *No one could have survived that fall and the icy waters below.*

CHAPTER EIGHTY-TWO

What a weekend! Chief Pritchard had returned to the office after a very long couple of days. His eyes burned and his head ached from the overwhelming strain of the crisis that had happened at Skye Pointe Bend. What had started as a boisterous annual race had turned into a screaming shit show. The evidence was mounting, and the eye witness accounts were still coming in. There hadn't been such a spectacular event since the Adams' murder trial three years ago, and now once again Rebecca Adams was involved in a murder, but this time it was her own.

He had mobilized his entire team to assist with this disaster and each member of the team had eagerly participated. They wanted justice for Rebecca Adams, whose ruthless murder was witnessed by Campbell River's latest superstar Gretchen Berg. Berg had become an overnight celebrity when it was reported that she 'had come across the horrific scene and risked her own life to try and stop this senseless murder.'

Pritchard had personally taken her witness account and believed it to be truthful—that was up until the point where she had apparently endangered her own person to save Rebecca. Gretchen would 'die' for a scoop, just not literally. Her story had been shared with the multi-media syndicated networks, and now every news media outlet had descended on Campbell River. The place was pure chaos.

The tables have certainly turned for Olivia Proctor and Rebecca Adams. He thought about the two women; one was cooling her heels in jail, and the other's body was still not found. He shook his head; both women's lives were ruined. With her death, however, Rebecca had been escalated from 'baby killer' to a 'tragic victim.'

Maybe there is justice in this mayhem after all. Jake Adams was in Vancouver General Hospital being watched closely by security, and Olivia was seething in the Campbell River Jail.

These two will be spending a lot more time in cuffs and behind bars; they'd better get used to it.

He picked up the Campbell River Gazette and read the morning's headlines:

From Social Pariah to Unfortunate Victim

A quiet tap on his closed door interrupted his deliberations. "Yes?" he snapped.

"Sorry boss." His administrative assistant Alice Wilson stuck her head in the door. "This just arrived this morning." She held out a large manila envelope. "And this letter was dropped off by a Phyllis Arthurs, a nurse from the Campbell River Hospital. It appears Alex Hiscox had received it during a domestic dispute investigation, but it must have slipped behind the seats in the patrol car. Deputy Manning found it last week and asked me to give to you, but I got it mixed up with the outgoing mail. The mailman discovered it this morning, and he dropped it off with the other item. Sorry boss."

Alice placed the envelopes on his desk and scurried from his office, quietly closing the door. She knew how he hated to be disturbed; especially when his door was closed. *But this seemed very important, especially after the recent events.* She thought as quickly exited.

"Thanks Alice." He picked up the larger of the two envelopes.

It was addressed:

Kevin Pritchard, Chief of Police. Campbell River Police Station. IMPORTANT.

But this didn't catch his eye as much as the sender's name: Rebecca Adams.

He looked at the post date; it was before the race. Rebecca had disappeared off his radar for at least a month until she unexpectedly reappeared at Dash for Cash, and now she was dead. Andie had been worried about Rebecca and urged him to look out for her, but instead of being protective, he had been rude and impatient. He regretted it now. *Little did I know the drama that would unfold and its deadly outcome.*

You could have come to me, but I guess I closed that door in your face. Now it seems the deceased woman had sent him this package instead. *Now you're reaching out to me from the grave, and this time I won't push you away.* He tore open the envelope, its contents spilling out on his desk; a handwritten letter from Rebecca, a DVD similar to ones used in Andie's surveillance system, and a safety deposit key.

What is this all about? He picked up his phone and called his assistant. "Is Hoffman on duty today? He is. Tell him to come and see me." As he waited for his junior officer to arrive, he pulled open the other letter. It was from a Magda Bodrug; he had no idea who this person was, but it was addressed to him personally.

He read the shaky handwriting.

To Chief Pritchard,

I am an old woman who needs to bare my soul to someone I believe is a good man and can help. I overheard two people talking out in the hospital hallway. They said they want to kill Rebecca Adams. She needs your help. These evil people are her husband and that tramp, Olivia Proctor. I taped their conversation on a phone, please listen to it. Rebecca has the phone. Please help her.

It was signed: *Magda Bodrug.*

"Who is this woman? And where is this phone?" He spoke aloud as Officer Hoffman entered.

"What's up, boss? Alice told me you wanted to see me."

"You best sit down for this one." Pritchard gestured to the chair opposite. "Things are about to get wilder than they already are!"

CHAPTER EIGHTY-THREE

"Checking out?" the elderly desk clerk asked the young woman standing across from him. She nodded, and adjusted her sunglasses. "I hope you are feeling better. It was a terrible fall you took last week, that pathway can be very slippery when it is raining."

The clerk had been returning from taking out the garbage when he found her on the pathway, struggling to walk. She was soaked to the bone and had multiple bruises and bleeding scratches on her face. When he had found her, she explained that she had been out running and misjudged her footing. He had assisted her to her cabin where she had retreated to nurse her wounds; she had refused medical attention. He had left her in peace; in the hotel business he had learned to respect people's privacy, but he had worried about her until she had reappeared, still battered but not broken.

"Yes, thank you once again for coming to my rescue. I can't believe I slipped! How clumsy of me."

The pretty copper haired woman smiled as she pushed the key across the desk. She paid in cash and refused a receipt. "No need."

Her smile was very sincere, and she reached to press his hand. "Thank you once more for your help and discretion. You are very kind."

Now as she limped across the lobby, he was relieved she was okay; under the healing bruises he recognized an attractive young woman. He watched as the cab driver loaded her luggage and assisted her into the back seat. As the cab drove away, the clerk said a silent prayer for her; then went about his duties.

Across town at the Campbell River Bus Depot, the same young woman boarded the intercity bus leaving Campbell River for Vancouver. The driver witnessed her limp, and he gave her a hand as she stepped up the stairs.

"Many thanks. Is the bus leaving on time?"

"Yup. Right on schedule," the bus driver replied. He looked at her as he took her ticket.

"I know you." He thought he recognized her under her dark glasses.

"You must be mistaken, sir. No one knows me in this small town, I'm just passing through." She cocked her head, smiling at him.

The bus driver pulled the door shut, and then took his seat behind the wheel. He looked up into the rear-view mirror momentarily studying the young woman seated four rows behind him. She did look familiar, but it couldn't be the missing woman, or could it? He shrugged his shoulders; he had a schedule to keep.

He shook his head, and then called out. "Leaving Campbell River, next stop ..." His words were drowned out by the roar of the bus as it chugged out of the station.

The woman in row four smiled in anticipation.

CPSIA information can be obtained
at www.ICGtesting.com
Printed in the USA
BVHW031552271121
622656BV00001B/1

9 781039 122765